THE PAINTER OF FLORENCE

GEOFFREY HARGRAVE

THE PAINTER OF FLORENCE

✠

NEW
PRESTON
HILL

One braccio = two feet.
One league = about three miles, maybe more.

Copyright ©2014 Geoffrey Hargrave
All rights reserved.

Published by New Preston Hill
newprestonhill.com
ISBN 978-0-9904237-0-6

NEW
PRESTON
HILL

Part One

LA PROCESSIONE

Drifting smoke from billowing clouds of incense filtered the slanting, early-morning sunlight into misty shards. The walls of every house were freshly painted in festive colors, or hung with woven cloth and tapestry. And the people of the city, reveling in the motive glory, lined the route and hung from their windows and balconies waving, cheering the uniformed clergy – alb and chasuble – acolytes swinging smoking censers in unbroken rhythm.

Statues floated aloft, high above their heads, swathed in curtained baldachins and balanced on swaying poles five, ten *braccia* high; the Apostles, the Virgin, and the Lord Jesus himself, slowly rolling from deep blue shadow into golden sunlight and back. And last, with morbid finality, floated those twin tokens of fear and hope, Saint Roch and Saint Sebastian, the plague saints, their dual presence sufficient to keep that fearful pestilence at bay – for today at least.

The twisting train stretched far behind the massive crucifix carried high in the van. After the clergy had slowly passed came the children, pristine and angelic in white linen, singing praises in their agonizingly perfect harmonies – the *Pueri Hebraeorum* – '*Hosanna in Excelsis.*' Next marched the mendicant monks in sackcloth and ashes, hoods pulled low over shaven heads, carrying their saints grimly before them – from Santa Maria Novella and Santa Croce, Santo Spirito and Santa Maria del Carmine.

After the monks came the laity, four deep, robes, hoods and symbols colored for their Guilds and Confraternities; and last the penitents, backs bared, whipping themselves with symbolically silken ropes, timed perfectly to their swaying gait.

Once they had passed, oxen yoked in pairs with curved horns gilded and painted, their huge heads swinging from side to side in a sparkling golden rhythm, towed decorated carts – festive floats both entertaining and edifying that towered high above the street.

The image of death was all about – performers emerging from their graves swaddled in funeral shrouds, as souls to be saved on the day of resurrection – our Lord crucified with two criminals as a Roman centurion is converted – a castle, sacked by a militant horde, its inhabitants put brutally to the sword – a battle at sea between galleys rigged and crewed, Turk against Christian. All these pageants were performed, with perhaps more relish than skill, on floats, single, double, triple, built so high they threatened to topple at every bump – cheered on lustily from below.

In between these moving *memento mori* rolled the assurances of salvation, as if mitigating the world's suffering by the glory that was to come – angel choirs, with wings feathered and bejeweled, hung from wires, seeming to float over the onlookers – a baby, a live baby, gilded and giggling as the Christ child, both subject and object of his attendant angels – the Lord, received into heaven, hauled aloft by two burly workmen concealed in the scenery – the last supper, Apostles arranged in mute horror around their gloriously doomed Messiah.

And in the last of the floats the historical pageants were reenacted – lives of the saints with miracle and martyr – great victories of the Florentine state – knights in armor dueling in chivalrous combat – each one an inspiring and uplifting struggle of the mortal realm.

Finally, after the last float was long past, came the carts loaded high with dung, pulled by scavengers the length of the route – with sanction of the Holy Church – collecting the droppings of the host of animals. A fitting earthly resolution to the transcendent magnificence that had preceded.

By the glory of man, to the glory of God.

Il Duomo

Two figures trotted through empty streets, the clatter of their wooden clogs echoing off the narrow rows of houses. The younger figure was in the lead, her heavy damask cloak billowing behind in rippling emerald folds. She seemed to float effortlessly as a shimmering green cloud over the morning grey stones. Laboring behind her was an older woman of more portly build, wearing an equally green cloak but perspiring profusely as she struggled to keep pace with her charge. It seemed it had been this way for almost the entire eighteen years of Virginia's young life: she running ahead and her nurse Maria rushing to keep up.

The city was closed; barred and locked. Even the harlots who regularly plied their trade in the *Mercato Vecchio* were absent. *Abundance* herself, the only human figure they had so far seen, regarded the uncommon emptiness of the market with stony glare from her sunlit viewpoint high above it. The two women ran on, past darkened shops and shuttered houses – all would be at the Cathedral for the service.

Late, they had already missed the procession – Virginia's fault. She had missed her father representing his guild in silken robes, missed the floats and animals and performers, both the divine and the profane. She had missed the dancing and the singing, the meaning and the metaphor, but could not, under any circumstances, miss the service. Everyone would be there; to stand in their ordained spots, listen to the Florentine sermon and the Latin liturgy, to see and be seen – and receive a modicum of unction for their trouble.

Principally, Virginia wanted to be seen, and to see those who would see her. She had gone to a deal of trouble in choosing her clothes for that very purpose. Her chemise was a spotless white linen lawn, and as it spilled delicately over the bodice at her breast her flawless white skin could be seen glowing warmly through its translucence. Her gown, fashioned from rich voided silk velvet in a subtle shade of coral was tightly laced at the side, the bodice outlined in matching satin ribbon. A similar band of silk, embroidered with gold thread and small pearls, cinched her narrow waist, securing a small girdle book in a soft leather binding that hung in her lap. It was an illuminated vellum book of hours that had belonged to her dear mother. Her sleeves, pinned and tied to her gown at the top of the arms, had also been her mother's. Over a base of dark green, almost black velvet lay heavy embroidery in gold thread, and, slashed from shoulder to wrist, they allowed the soft white chemise to billow down the length of each sleeve in a neat row of fluffy clouds. Her hair, long and pale red, was braided and twisted with coral ribbon, constrained in the back by a delicate snood, punctuated with tiny pearls. Small strands of hair tumbled casually to either side of her face, softly framing her unreserved beauty. A simple string of coral beads circled her neck, and coral earrings swung busily from her ears as she hurried as fast as her clumsy clogs would allow towards the Cathedral.

Before they even drew close to the *Misericordia* the crowds began, in sharp contrast to the emptiness of the rest of the city. Maria now led the way as their pace slowed, pushing an opening in the throng like Moses parting the Red Sea, Virginia flowing regally in her wake. Most people knew who Virginia was, or at least knew what level of society she occupied, so deferentially made an opening to let the two women pass. They skirted the oddly shaped Baptistery – a Roman temple went the story, although, far from an expert, Virginia did not consider it a very Roman-looking building – and climbed the steps of the Cathedral. Virginia gazed upward at the broken façade towering over her and idly wondered why they had never bothered to finish it. It was mounted with statues and decorative stonework to a little over half its height but the top was still the bare, rough material of the underlying structure. It was as if unforeseen events had conspired against the builders and they had collectively shrugged, declaring it good enough, and moved on to other projects. To Virginia it seemed that public works just happened, the politics and intrigue that most often accompanied such apparently effortless creation was foreign to her world. That was her father's purview.

The interior of the Cathedral was almost as crowded as the streets outside, although these people were not the *ciompi*, the common folk. These people were the merchants, the artisans and craftspeople, the aristocracy – or what was left of it – and all their collective servants and retainers, along with various visiting dignitaries from all across the Roman Empire and beyond. They were there enthusiastically to enjoy the fruits of the city that stood at the center of the world, the sole rival for Rome in beauty and magnificence; a magnificence most conspicuously on display in the riot of color and fabric and jewelry that sprawled across the gleaming new marble floor of Santa Maria del Fiore. The creative output of a myriad of interconnected guildsmen was laid out for all to see and marvel at; spinners and weavers and dyers, tailors and embroiderers, goldsmiths and jewelers, shoemakers and belt makers, all had contributed their style and skill. The cost of dressing this congregation had been staggering, a visual and tactile testament to the success and superiority of Florence above all cities.

Following Maria as she threaded her way deftly through the press, Virginia nodded greetings to various young women of her acquaintance, and a few others whose acquaintance she would like to make, but she angled her eyes downward demurely if she caught sight of a man looking in her direction. Virginia was deeply aware of her position as her father's daughter. At all times she was a representative of her family and must deport herself accordingly. Her father had dressed her in his finest wares, and she was a walking ambassadress for the family honor and the family business.

Part way down the nave she slipped her feet from the clogs that had served to protect her from the dirt of the streets, revealing delicate little slippers that perfectly matched her dress in color and style. She handed the clogs to Maria who always seemed to have room under her cloak for such things, and stepped gracefully into her position beneath the gleaming white dome that soared high over her head. All the great families of Florence had their positions in the Cathedral, hers was to the left of the altar in front of the New Sacristy, near the position occupied by the Medici, but several rows back from them, as befit their station. She had only ever known Medici rule, but her father would tell her stories of bad times in the past when the Medici had been banished, when monkish insanity and worldly incompetence had almost destroyed the Republic. After all that she had been told, she considered it safer to be close to them.

Maria looked uncomfortable and Virginia asked after her problem. "Should have gone before we left home," muttered Maria.

"Well go quickly, the choir will start soon," replied Virginia, who loved the sweet harmonies of the choristers, singing directly at her from their massive stone pulpit. Maria hurried off. There was a spot in the south transept where calls of nature could be answered, men on one side and women on the other for modesty's sake. With a hoist of the skirt a lady could relieve herself in a minute, and none be any the wiser.

While Maria was thus occupied and Virginia was sure nobody was watching, she gazed about her at Santa Maria del Fiore. She was enchanted by the Cathedral, despite the austerity of the building, its interior consisting mostly of whitewashed walls and stone pillars, not painted frescoes like the parish churches. The size and scale of the place was astonishing to her, especially the dome floating way above her head, its white void colorfully illuminated by the stained glass windows at its base.

Virginia was lost in rapture when suddenly her attention was drawn to an unusual sight. Scaffolding had been erected to one side of the sacristy, she imagined for some purpose of maintenance, and had not been removed before the service. What was even more surprising was the sight of two figures climbing the scaffolding. They negotiated the climb nimbly as if they were practiced at such things, and stood upon the platform at a little above head height, putting them about level with Virginia's beloved choir. She was outraged. How dare these two men place themselves above the level of the finest citizens of the Republic, and on a level with those whose sweet song was surely the dominion solely of Our Lord?

Maria returned and Virginia asked her who these two brazen devils could be, to insult the church, the choir and the Lord himself so. "That's Luca, he is the newest painter to the finest citizens, or aspires to be, and the young scruffy one with him is his assistant. Luca's a buffoon." She added the last comment by way of explanation for his sacrilegious behavior.

Maria was right; the second figure was young, maybe no more than fifteen or sixteen years, and most definitely scruffy, and on such a day! Virginia tried to remember the words of Cosimo about clothes and an honorable man, but failed at the attempt as her mind began to wander. The other man – the buffoon – was, however, very well appointed, as would suit an artist of his position and aspirations. He was dressed head to foot in black. Black *farsetto* – the heavily padded and constructed doublet that defined his chest – and a matching tunic with full sleeves, both in a detailed brocade; tight black woolen hose; slim, pointed black shoes decorated with black beads; and long black curling hair that fell to his shoulders. The somber tone was only relieved by the shocking whiteness of his linen shirt that billowed and thrust from every slash and seam and cuff, as if offended that its indulgent luxury should be so meanly constrained.

Virgina's unspoken opinion was that he did not appear in the slightest bit buffoonish, despite his behavior. She also noticed that in keeping with his stylish dress his attitude was of one who belonged in this elevated position; one who felt at home towering over his fellow citizens; one to whom such an honor should be paid. At least that was how it seemed to Virginia, who had become intrigued despite her best efforts, while at the same time outraged, and yet again fascinated by this handsome and arrogant young man.

The cantor of the choir had come down firmly on the side of outrage and was in no mood to permit such an insult. He had his acolytes chase the interlopers from their perch and they disappeared laughing, back into the crowd. Virginia, in the midst of her own outrage at the wicked behavior of this painter and his messy accomplice, had felt something else, a movement inside, a feeling she had never felt before. She pushed such thoughts to the back of her mind as her father appeared smiling, weaving his way through the congregation. She raised her hand and greeted him deferentially.

"Did you see us in the parade?" asked her father.

"Yes Papa, you were magnificent!"

Maria shook her head and turned her eyes to heaven at the casual lie, and in the Cathedral on a feast day too. She muttered a prayer for Virginia's immortal soul as her fingers worked their way along the paternoster beads that hung from her sleeve.

COTIGNOLA

Two figures rode across a bleak landscape. It was cold. Steely grey sky, dark grey rocks; the entire world was drawn in shades of grey, with two silhouettes moving slowly along the skyline. Luca rehearsed in his mind how he had come to be so cold in such a cold place so far from home. His landlord, guardian and friend Bernardo had received a commission for Luca's services from a convent near Cotignola, and Luca was to travel there to receive it, along with an advance payment for materials. So, much against his better judgment, here rode Luca on a rented horse, along with his young assistant Carlo on a borrowed mule, through dangerous country, in the mountains, in the late winter cold.

They had waited as long as possible, at least for the unseasonably frigid rains to stop, and had finally set out for the several days' ride to Cotignola.

"I cannot feel my feet," complained Carlo.

"You do not paint with your feet. Anyway, we will be there soon. The town is the other side of these hills."

"We are too close to the Spaniards. We could die out here and nobody would know, raped by a Spaniard." Carlo spat to emphasize his dislike of Spaniards.

"You are too ugly for a Spaniard, and in any case, I am reliably informed that they are several days north of here, at Ferrara. I will sign the commission and receive the money for materials and we can leave."

"Why did they not choose a painter from Bologna? Isn't this place just a day's ride from Bologna?"

"Because they wanted the magnificent brushwork of Luca the Painter of Florence not Luca the Painter of Bologna. You asked all this before we left."

Carlo was not to be dissuaded, "Why do *I* have to be here?"

"This is part of your training. Being a painter is not all about fame, money and beautiful women in fine dresses."

"So far it has been about none of those things."

"You are beginning to vex me..." Luca's voice trailed off as they both caught sight of the ominous pall of smoke slowly obscuring the sky from just beyond the horizon.

They left the narrow, boulder-strewn road and urged their mounts upwards, to the top of an outcrop of rock giving a vista the length of the valley. The sight that met their eyes was a sobering one that obliterated all thought of cold feet and minor discomfort. The town of Cotignola, a small fortified settlement at a crossroads commanding the center of the valley, was the source of the smoke. Numerous fires seemed to be burning in and around the city, and the area about the main gate seethed with activity. They both squinted against the oppressive light of the solidly white sky, trying to make out what was happening. Then it became clear, the seething was the movement of thousands of men, soldiers, foreign soldiers, in and out of the city, carrying objects and dragging people.

The farm houses and villas around the city were all engulfed in flame, and once in a while the loudest scream of one of the victims echoed up to their vantage point; the flash and clash of weapons piercing the still, cold air. The town was being sacked, pillaged. Anyone who stood in the way would be killed, women would be raped, and everything movable would be loaded into carts and wagons, and stolen. The army surged and crashed like waves against the town, in one brief moment destroying the health and wealth of its inhabitants – none would be spared – all they were, and all they might be, taken in a moment by a godless, ravening horde.

Luca and Carlo crossed themselves reflexively and muttered short prayers for the suffering they beheld, then grimly turned their mounts around and headed silently back towards Florence – a silence broken only by Carlo through clenched teeth, "I hate Spaniards."

It was a long, cold ride home.

✠

Luca, The Painter of Florence, lived with an apothecary at the sign of the Lion. Theirs was a complex relationship that had been forged many years before in love, misery and death. Bernardo the apothecary had been a fellow guild member and close friend of Luca's father. Luca had just begun his apprenticeship as a painter when the plague had visited the city. It had come one night, and with its bony hand had touched houses, seemingly at random, throughout every quarter of the city. An angel of death, it had been invisible and merciless, and had killed with no apparent plan or reason.

Plague had taken Luca's older brother and sister; then a few months later his father and mother. He had been the only one to survive from his entire family, and from time to time, usually when it was quiet and the memories of his childhood flooded back, he would feel guilt at being the last. Yet at the same time he would give thanks to the Lord for saving him. Since he must have been saved for a purpose – so ran his thoughts – he had pledged himself, from that moment on, to create paintings for the glory of God; and had done passably well at his occupation, so far as his twenty-five years on this earth would allow.

Immune to the plague, Luca had nursed his father during the height of the pestilence, once the swollen buboes had fully formed. He had not wanted to commit his beloved father to the tender mercies of one of the many *lazzaretti* that would spring up during an outbreak.

On his deathbed his father had prevailed upon close friend Bernardo to take Luca into his home and treat him as a son, making sure Luca's apprenticeship was completed and he was matriculated as a full guild member. Bernardo had more than taken the dying man at his word, and had spared no love and attention guiding Luca in his chosen profession. Since the painters were represented by the same guild as the apothecaries, Bernardo was quite able to smooth Luca's path through the difficult process of guild acceptance, and in his turn Luca forever considered himself in Bernardo's debt.

The latter owned a large house with several shops built into the ground floor level. One, the largest, was his apothecary's shop, the others he rented to various other shopkeepers for additional income.

Despite the large capacity of the house it always seemed overrun. This was mostly due to the eight healthy children he and his wife had brought into this world – five boys and three girls – his large and florid wife Clara herself, who took up enough space for two, and the five servants who helped her run the household.

Clara was a delightful woman and had been the perfect surrogate for Luca's natural mother. She did, however, have some unusual preoccupations outside her housekeeping duties. She loved to play the lottery. Bernardo was very lenient in that respect, believing it more to everyone's advantage to have a happy wife than to have the few coins she spent a week on her gambling. Once in a while she would win, and would buy something special for the household and throw a big feast for the entire extended family.

Another pastime she particularly enjoyed was attending auctions. Every few weeks the auctioneers would collect merchandise – objects left at pawnbrokers, households of the deceased or the merely bankrupt, and property that various citizens had need to sell in a hurry – attracting buyers and lookers from around the city. Clara loved to bid. Whether or not she needed a bolt of cloth or a new *cassone* or a particular book, she would not be able to stop herself getting caught up in the excitement of bidding, especially if it was a bargain. So the house was eclectically scattered with the fruits of her auction forays, displayed for all to see, and adding yet further to the overcrowding.

Again, Bernardo had no qualms about his wife's purchases, she always bought items of value at a decent price, and thus that value was stored until he needed to sell something. So far, thank the Lord, that need had not yet come.

By way of relaxation, and a brief but worthwhile respite from the hectic atmosphere of the house and its contents, Luca and Bernardo would withdraw to the latter's study to play Tric Trac and talk. The Tric Trac board was a beautiful set that Luca had designed as a gift for Bernardo the year he had matriculated. The outside of the box was parquetry in two shades of wood, and could do double duty as a chessboard. Unclasped and opened, the inside formed the two trays of a Tric Trac board. The individual triangles of the board were darker wood on a lighter wood ground, the game pieces and dice fashioned from ivory and ebony. They took to the game with relish, absorbed in it as an antidote to the world – a world that was growing progressively more unstable and dangerous. But, inevitably, the talk turned to the events of the day, to politics, to the church and to war.

"You know you nearly sent me to my death," observed Luca drily, "one day earlier..." He paused for effect.

"I am so sorry, but how was I to know that the Emperor's army was on the move, they have been camped at Ferrara these several months now."

"Worry not on my behalf," said Luca with a grim smile, "they were otherwise occupied."

"What of Bologna and Ravenna?" asked Bernardo, eager for any news of the approaching army.

"We heard from some travellers on our return journey that the army avoided Bologna."

"Too hard a prize to win I dare say."

"And Ravenna is not worth the trip since the French sacked the town the first time we lived through this purgatory."

"Those were hard times indeed. You were what – nine or ten when we got the Medici back at the point of a foreigner's sword?"

Luca nodded silently.

Bernardo was reminded of something he had meant to speak with Luca about. "You know you really should think twice before playing such games before the Medici, they can be gracious patrons and fearsome enemies," began Bernardo, referring to Luca's performance on the scaffolding in the Cathedral.

"The Medici, all I hear is talk of the Medici, but who are they?

Two bastards, one a moor, with a dissolute Cardinal as their minder," declared the Painter.

"Luca!"

"You know it to be true."

"And the Pope, he is Medici too."

"He is busy with matters of state, and selling Rome's dispensation by the pound."

"You talk like a Lutheran."

"Nonsense! You know my father was a follower of Brother Girolamo." Bernardo nodded in agreement. He too had followed Savanorola's fiery sermons as a much younger man, and still his sympathies lay with the *Piagnoni* – as the followers of Savanarola were yet known. "All I am saying," continued Luca, "is that the Medici, the Pope included, are leading us to our destruction. God will not save us if we do not save ourselves." He was becoming fired up with righteous anger now. "And did they not force themselves back upon us bringing a Spanish army and the plague with them?"

This was true as far as it went. The Medici, with the help of the Pope, had thrown out the Republican government, and the plague seemed to have returned with them, at least in the popular imagination. Luca blamed the death of his parents on the plague, and the plague on the Medici.

"Having a Medici Pope is always good for Florence though," countered Bernardo.

"And yet here we are with another Spanish army a few days from here, ready to march on Florence as soon as the weather improves or the whim strikes them, simply because the Medici Pope has decided to join forces against the Emperor – he who commands the strongest army in the world."

"They would not dare attack us, we are too powerful and they would starve to death besieging us," scoffed Bernardo.

"But how is it good for Florence if all the farms and villages and towns for days around are stripped bare, and smoking ruins?" Luca was remembering the fearsome sight of the sack of Cotignola. "Even if they lose we do not win." There was silence, confirming his bleak outlook.

"Your turn," said Bernardo quietly.

TAROCCHI

Vincenzo di Piero de' Cavalcanti was a successful silk merchant –
a setaiuolo – and prominent member of the Silk Guild, the *Arte di
Por Santa Maria*. He imported and exported silk fabric, had fields
of his own mulberry trees hanging with silk cocoons and, once they
were gathered, workshops full of girls unwrapping and winding
their delicate threads. Moreover, once the labors of the worms had
been harvested, he employed spinners, weavers and dyers to
produce fine, finished, silk fabric. He was the quintessence of a
successful Florentine businessman, restrained yet proud in manners
and dress, and relentless in his pursuit of commerce.

His buying and selling trips had taken him all over the world,
but more recently, since the death of his wife, he tended not to
travel beyond Venice to the north and Rome to the south. He really
did not need to travel much further, since Florence made the finest
silks available anywhere, for any price. Where once they had
imported fine silk fabric from the Levant, now, by means of the
same trading galleys of Venice, they produced and exported better
silks back to Damascus, Istanbul and Baghdad. The irony of
Florentine silks dressing the very Turk that was waging unceasing
jihad against them was not lost, but being able to use
Mohammedan gold for the glory of Christ's church was a
worthwhile compromise for all concerned.

It was a necessity of life as much as was providing for the

defense of Christendom with its ever-fluctuating borders.

Vincenzo Cavalcanti managed his minor silk empire from the study in his house a few streets away from the Guild *palazzo*, the old *Palazzo de' Lamberti*, in perhaps the most cramped area of the city. Despite the constant spread of new construction both within and without the walls, many of the silk workers still lived and earned their pay a short walk from the *Vicolo della Seta* – Silk Alley – which ran alongside the old church of Santa Maria that had given the guild its name.

Vincenzo's house was large and old. His grandfather had purchased it almost a hundred years before, and had it reconstructed to meet the needs of the family. It was based on a row of existing houses to which had been added a modernized façade unifying the row into one edifice, the rooms inside rearranged into a single residence.

Vincenzo had planned to build a new *palazzo* for his family as he had become more successful, and had purchased a plot on the far side of the Arno for the purpose, but the death of his wife and infant son had dampened his enthusiasm, and he continued to live in the old family home with his daughter.

His work was interrupted this day by a visitor. Beppo Bagnolo was a small nervous man for whom the slightest problem became magnified into a calamity – it had occurred to Vincenzo that if Beppo ever ran into a genuine calamity he might die of apoplexy on the spot. Beppo's function in life was to inspect silk for the Guild. As a requirement for continued membership all guildsmen were required to submit to regular inspections of their materials and equipment, from mulberry tree to loom and from worm to finished cloth, and Beppo was one of the Guild's inspectors – diligent yet diffident. He was also active in Guild affairs and worked as an *ad hoc* social director for some of their meetings.

Vincenzo was bemused, he was not due for inspection for another few weeks and the expression of mild annoyance on his face conveyed his displeasure.

"Vincenzo, I am here for your opinion on something I plan to present to the Guild," began Beppo nervously.

"And my viewpoint will be of use to you?"

"Yes, Vincenzo if you have the time."

Vincenzo put down his pen and turned from his desk to face the little man, who seemed more agitated than usual, bouncing as he was from foot to foot awaiting a reply.

"Do continue." Vincenzo waved his hand dramatically.

"Yes, well, it seems *Signor* Niccolò is in the city on a task from the Pope himself..."

"Niccolò? I know twenty Niccolòs, twenty times twenty even – whom exactly do you mean?"

"I mean to say *Signor* Machiavelli, he is in the city..."

"Well he lives not a half day's ride south of here. Should it be a surprise that he comes into town once in a while?"

Beppo was becoming more and more agitated as Vincenzo toyed with him for his own amusement.

"I mean to say that *Signor* Niccolò Machiavelli has been charged by none other than the Pope himself to accomplish an inspection of our defenses. The walls of the city are in a state of disrepair and he is to report on ways to improve the strength of those walls, and thereby the safety of the citizens."

"I am positive he will do a fine job. His friend Guicciardini is the Pope's man in the field, so I am sure *Messer* Niccolò is more than qualified to secure our walls. Thank you so much for telling me this most excellent news, I feel safer already."

"That was not my point," squeaked Beppo, exasperated. "His qualifications are without doubt. What I mean to say..."

"You continually mean to say and yet whatever it is still remains unsaid."

"I mean..." Beppo took a deep breath, "that since Niccolò is here and the Guicciardini you mentioned is a member of the *Por Santa Maria*, he, *Signor* Niccolò, could be prevailed upon to join us for an evening with the Guild; and could be further prevailed upon to give us any intelligence he has on the conduct of the war and how it might affect our business." He gasped for air.

Vincenzo stopped making sport of Beppo for a moment and slowly removed his glasses, thinking about the suggestion. "Beppo, you have outdone yourself!" he decided, and Beppo sighed with relief. "This is an excellent idea. Perhaps we can have *Signor* Niccolò

to dine with the Guild and play some games and drink some wine –
yes, and loosen his tongue to our advantage." Vincenzo smiled
conspiratorially. "Tarocchi!" he declared, "we will play Tarocchi."

So invitations were sent out and preparations were made. A
grand feast was designed in honor of *Messer* Niccolò, and the guest
of honor personally conveyed his pleasure at accepting the Silk
Guild's most generous hospitality. In all honesty, a good courtier
will always go out of his way to graciously accept the hospitality of
the rich and powerful, and Niccolò Machiavelli was a very good
courtier.

This was in spite of his recent problems involving the return of
the Medici from banishment, not the least of which was his own
de facto banishment. In addition, Niccolò was currently somewhat
impecunious due to this banishment and consequent lack of work,
so a free supper and the chance to win some money at cards from
a group of extremely rich men was not an opportunity to be
overlooked.

The *palazzo* of the Silk Guild was a magnificent building, at
least inside, arguably the most sumptuous of the guild *palazzi*. On
the outside though it was surprisingly hard to see, squeezed into
the conjunction of three very narrow streets behind the *Mercato
Nuovo*. As the *Palazzo Lamberti* it had been the home of an old
and well respected Florentine family, so was the perfect location
for the *Por Santa Maria* – central in their traditional neighborhood
and sumptuous as beseemed the richest guild in Florence.

The *palazzo* housed meeting rooms and offices of the Guild,
richly appointed by the best of the guildsmen's skill, along with
paintings, frescoes and ornamentation of gold and silver donated
by many respectful – and wealthy – members. Additionally, the
Guild officers lived at the *palazzo* during their tenure, so it was also
fitted with both kitchen and latrine for their use, with cooks and
servants to tend their needs, along with a magnificent dining room
for formal occasions.

The meal was well thought out. Beppo was an excellent social
director despite any of his other shortcomings, and he had arranged
for meat, poultry and vegetables to be supplied from some of the
guildsmen's own farms, along with several barrels of wine from

Vincenzo's personal vineyard in nearby Fiesole – a smooth red, yet quite potent. As master of protocol he had lined up the leading members of the Guild to greet the honored guest, who arrived, diplomatically, a few minutes after the appointed hour.

As the Pope's envoy, Niccolò Machiavelli had been provided with a guest room at the *Palazzo della Signoria*, the city hall of Florence, pending completion of his inspection of the condition of the city walls, and this evening he had walked the relatively short distance between the two locations. Accompanying him was Luigi, the brother of his friend Guicciardini, currently serving as *Gonfaloniere* – the mayor of Florence – so they were also accompanied by four men-at-arms from the Militia. The center of the city was not particularly dangerous in the evening to a gentleman armed with the customary short sword beneath his cloak, but political feelings had been running high of late, and prudence dictated an armed escort.

The 'men of silk' knew *Messer* Machiavelli both by name and by reputation. His name was a byword for Republican Florence. He had labored with Soderini, in vain as it had turned out, to create a Republic that would be immune to the Princes, to the Emperor, to the Pope; immune especially to the Medici. The fact that he had failed was by no means an indictment of his skill and commitment. A Spanish army was an eventuality that not even the most experienced courtier could contend with.

As far as his reputation was concerned, he had gained some measure of fame by successfully negotiating the Lucchesan Problem back in 'twenty. A spendthrift from the neighboring town of Lucca had owed a large amount of money to a significant number of Florentine businessmen and had gambled away much of what he had left. This spendthrift had then come into a large inheritance but it had been settled upon his children to avoid becoming forfeit to his creditors, or simply being gambled away. Niccolò, at the behest of the *Signoria*, had lobbied the government of Lucca to release those funds, and move the Florentine businessmen to the head of the line of creditors, ahead of the gamblers, as the businessmen's debts had been accumulated in honest trade rather than through games of chance. The positive outcome of the negotiations had established Machiavelli as the hero of the Florentine businessman, and had saved many of the Silk Guild's members from significant losses, even bankruptcy. He was indeed a most honored guest.

"So what are we playing?" asked Niccolò cheerfully, "Cricca?" The meal, long, full and delicious, was over and it was time for games.

"We thought..." Beppo shot a swift glanced at Vincenzo, "Tarocchi?" It was a question.

"Splendid!" exclaimed Niccolò, and Beppo sighed in relief. "Partners, or are we playing solo?"

Vincenzo was quick to answer. "With your permission Niccolò, I thought I might be your partner."

"Splendid!" Niccolò declared anew, smiling broadly. "Then I am sure we shall win handily. Five soldi a point?" He spread a deck of cards out smoothly in a neat semi circle with a practiced hand. Several eyebrows were raised around the room as everyone watched the guest of honor; and Luigi laughed quietly. "I have a lot of time on my hands lately, and a game of cards with the townsfolk helps to pass it amusingly," was Niccolò's explanation for his dexterity.

"Five soldi a point, as you wish *Signore*," answered Beppo deferentially.

And with that they all sat down to play. Twenty four middle-aged men dressed formally in red, grey and brown in twelve pairs switching from table to table at the end of each game.

Niccolò and Vincenzo were the decisive winners of the evening, and in the spirit of hospitality Vincenzo refused to take his share of the winnings, giving it all to Niccolò. As he did so he asked the question that the whole evening had been building up to, and the reason for all the food, wine and games.

"*Signor* Niccolò, may I ask you, for myself and for my brothers in the Guild, a question that has become very important to us and to Florence herself?"

"Certainly," replied Niccolò, smiling that devilish smile he was so well known for, "how could I refuse such an excellent and gracious partner? What is your question?"

"*Signore*, we are well aware that the Emperor has his army at

Milan and we hear they are spread out all the way to Ferrara. The Emperor appears to be intent on waging war on the Pope. He sues for peace and yet continues to wage war. Spanish soldiers have been seen arriving from Naples, and lancers from Germany to swell the number of foreign soldiers in Italy. Venice has still not fully recovered from the last war twenty years ago, and we can ill afford to suffer a foreign army rampaging through the *contado* like a swarm of locusts killing everything in their path."

"Very true," observed Niccolò, his black eyes flashing in the candlelight, "and your question?"

"As you are well known to be a confidant of *Signor* Luigi's brother who is in the field with the Pope's forces, and you are a party to intimate knowledge of the day to day situation..." Niccolò nodded in agreement with Vincenzo's assessment, "what will become of us – of Florence? What is the conduct of the war so far and what will the outcome be? It is difficult for us to do business and pay our taxes when there is such uncertainty in the world."

The notorious Niccolò Machiavelli began to speak and the room fell silent, hanging on his every word. "Gentlemen, first, thank you so much for a wonderfully pleasant evening among such charming and erudite men. This excess of pleasure is sadly unusual for me in these dark days. Now to the point: it is true, Luigi's brother Antonio is a close friend and I have much information which I am happy to pass along, but to keep it comprehensible let me do it this way." He again spread out a deck of cards face up across the table with the speed of long practice, and began pulling cards from the deck as he spoke.

"The Emperor." He placed the 'Emperor' trump card face up at the top of the table. "Our modern day Caesar. Here he sits in Vienna or Ghent or Valladolid – who may know where he is at any given moment? He is the master and protector of Christendom. By marriage, inheritance, conquest and gold he now owns most of the old and the new worlds. Castile and Aragon, Naples, the Netherlands, Austria, the German states, as well as Hispaniola and the New World territories, he owns it all, and can draw on that enormous wealth and power at any time; truly an Empire on which the sun never sets.

"The Pope." He placed the 'Pope' trump card at the bottom of the table. "And here *he* sits in Rome, the spiritual leader of Christendom, surrounded by his cardinals and courtiers, men whose sole job it is to agree with him." There was stifled laughter around the room.

"His problem is that he has the ambition of Julius but the political acumen of Leo. Pope Julius, as you know, was overly ambitious, acting much like a prince in his efforts to acquire land, but he had the skill to win wars and conquer territory. Leo, in his way, had the understanding to leave the politics to others, merely selling indulgences to raise money, and reading Plato with his inner circle. Clement, our Medici Pope, has neither the skill of the one nor the understanding of the other. He thinks he can out politic and out fight the Emperor of the world at a bargain price. In his infallible wisdom he has even dismissed the mercenary forces that were protecting Rome just to save a few florins, because his advisors believe that the Emperor would not dare to attack Rome herself – the Emperor, of course, being the nominal protector of Rome and the church." He shook his head.

"Now who lies between these two giants?" Niccolò pulled out the 'King of Swords' and laid it below the 'Emperor.' "The *Constable de Bourbon*. French of birth but an Italian from Mantua on his mother's side, and made an enemy of both by a vicious old French woman with plans of marriage." More laughter as Niccolò referred so irreverently to the French King's mother who had confiscated the Constable's estates upon the death of his wife in an effort to force him to marry her.

"The *Constable de Bourbon*, as he is known, is neither a constable nor a Bourbon, yet he is one of the most accomplished field commanders of the modern era. With good troops this man is unbeatable. Dressed in white and in full amour he will personally lead his troops in battle, and is invariably first into the breach.

"Fortunately… well, not for Milan which has fallen and has been claimed by the Constable as his own, but at least for the rest of us, he has terrible troops." Niccolò placed the 'Knave of Staves' below and to the right of the 'King of Swords.' "The *Landsknechts* – the foot lancers from the German principalities – they are good fighters but are owed months of back pay by the Emperor who is disinclined to pay them. He believes they should take their pay from Italy by sacking our cities and raping our women – and in some cases our men. This puts the Constable in a difficult position as the lancers could easily sack a small city, satisfy themselves and go home. He has to convince them that their payment is imminent and that there is more to be gained by following him than by doing anything else.

"And on the other side of the Constable's camp are the Spaniards." Niccolò laid the 'Knave of Swords' to the left of the 'Knave of Staves.' "These are veterans from the Emperor's previous campaigns – soldiers returning from the New World, troops that have sacked Italy before and have sent the French running from the field. Hard, unforgiving men they are.

"Now the Spanish hate the Germans because they believe them to be Lutheran barbarians dressed in ludicrous uniforms – which, more or less, they are." Nodding and grim smiles of understanding came from around the room. "The Germans hate the Spaniards because they hate everyone, and they think the Spaniards are getting paid before them because the Emperor favors Spain over Germany. Bourbon spends much of his time just keeping the two groups apart as they fight amongst themselves whenever they are not fighting an enemy."

Niccolò placed the 'Tower' trump card – an image of a tower struck by lightning – beneath the group of cards. "This bizarre confraternity took Milan without much of a fight and lived there like a parasite for months eating and raping as they saw fit, with the Constable wrestling to control them.

"That is what Caesar has brought to the field, a truly frightful plague that leaves death and devastation in its wake.

"The Pope's army is commanded by Francesco Maria della Rovere, the Duke of Urbino." He placed the 'Fool' trump card at the Pope's end of the table.

"Niccolò, I was under the impression that Antonio Guicciardini, *Signor* Luigi's brother, was the Pope's General," interrupted Vincenzo.

"Ah yes, Antonio is the Lieutenant General; that is, he

represents the Pope. However the commander of the army is the Duke. It is a very difficult situation because Antonio can recommend and report to the Pope, but has no power in the field, and the Pope trusts the Duke to act in his best interest. Why a Medici Pope would trust a della Rovere who is in the pay of the Venetians, and who has a personal grudge against the Medici, I do not know, but trust him he does, probably in another effort to save money. Undoubtedly he has chosen to forget the Duke of Urbino's involvement in the Pazzi Conspiracy.

"Unfortunately, since the Venetians control the Duke, his primary objective is to keep Caesar's army away from Venice. The Duke is also, without doubt, the most timid and incompetent yet preening and arrogant general ever to take the field. His army is strong and well fed, and ready to fight, yet he refused to attack Milan until after the Imperial troops had left, and refused to help any of the cities on their route through the mountains. He saw fit only to follow them at a safe distance. A coward, and as you can see from the card, a fool.

"So who will save us?" It was a rhetorical question, and Niccolò pulled the 'Force' trump from the deck – an image of a man wrestling with a lion – placing it between the two opposing camps in the center of the table. "A brave man, a bold man, a master swordsman, horseman and ladies' man. And a Medici, a son of Florence to boot – *Giovanni delle Bande Nere* – Giovanni the *condottiere* with his 'Black Bands.' They are a disciplined and skilled group of mercenaries who are pledged to follow their leader wherever he may lead.

He is the only one who dares raise his voice in the Duke's staff meetings against the policy of inaction, advocating an immediate attack on Milan. In the end he attacks Milan alone with just a thousand of his men and, with any support, would have driven Caesar's sick and dissolute army from the field. This is the only man that Bourbon and his men fear, the only general who wields authority. He could save us."

The group looked nervously from one to the other in the half-light of flickering candles.

"But," continued Niccolò, with a dramatic flourish, "he is no more. Dead. Hit by a random ball from a falconet and dead from fever after losing his leg." His sparkling black eyes surveyed the room, seeing the disquiet on the faces of the assembly as he flipped the card over so only its richly patterned reverse showed on the table. "And as if that were not bad enough, Caesar's army has just received reinforcements from Porto Santo Stephano, despite the best efforts of Andrea Doria. Hardened fighters, Spanish and German, seasoned from fighting the French on the Spanish borders."

"So who *will* save us?" Vincenzo put into words the question in the minds of all.

Niccolò smiled his characteristic, knowing smile and dropped the 'Wheel of Fortune' trump into the middle of the table. "On the one hand a merciless foreign army of cutthroats and brigands is carving its way across our fair land, leaving a trail of burning destruction and death in its wake." He looked at the crowd gathered around him in the circle of candlelight. "On the other hand, this army has also spent a brutal winter crossing the mountains in rain and snow. They are half dead from lack of food and decimated by disease. They have enough strength to sack a few small towns on their way, but they could never take Florence." The group sighed in relief. "Our walls are strong and our forces well motivated. *Orsanmichele* is full of grain and we have allies outside the walls who would ride to our defense. Caesar's rag-tag army would not survive a siege and would melt away when confronted. They will almost certainly avoid Florentine territory entirely."

"But wait." Niccolò smiled his devilish smile again, "who is this?" He dropped the 'Hanging Man' trump card onto the table next to the Pope. "A man hanged by his feet holding bags of money. This man is a traitor. The biggest danger from the Emperor's army of death is already within Rome. There are many inside her walls, indeed from inside the Pope's inner circle, that would see him humiliated. He has made many enemies with his politicking, double-dealing and vacillation. Cardinal Colonna, through his family and their faction, just recently betrayed and attacked Rome with a handful of soldiers, and the Pope was forced to hide in the *Castello*. Even his own General, as a della Rovere, has reason to see him brought down. If the Constable and his crew can survive a march to Rome then Rome will fall. Rome will fall to the most vicious and cruel army since the Visigoths."

"You really believe the Roman Emperor would attack Rome?" asked a new voice, in astonishment, from outside the circle of light. Machiavelli narrowed his eyes, peering into the darkness, and his answer was grim.

"The Pope has sued for peace many times and the Emperor has agreed to terms, and yet the Imperial army continues to march on Rome. The commander of the *Landsknechts* carries a silken rope, which he tells his troops he will use to hang the Pope.

"You have to understand, these Lutherans are crazed with a blood lust. They blame all the ills of the world on a series of corrupt Popes, and plan to set it straight by spilling blood." So saying, he dropped the 'World' trump down next to the Pope. "And we all know how bloodthirsty and evil the Spanish can be."

He added the 'Death' card to the row next to the Pope. "As long as the Emperor can harness the fury of the Lutherans and the evil of the Spanish to bring a renegade Pope to heel, then his demonic army will be in Italy; and as long as the Pope trusts in incompetents and traitors he is doomed – one way or another."

IL CUGINO

"But father..."

"No arguments!" barked Vincenzo.

He was having problems with his daughter. Niccolò's relatively good news about the war had inspired him to continue with his plans, and they were inevitably creating friction between himself and his daughter. In fury Virginia flounced out the door and headed for her bedroom. "She will do as she is told," muttered Vincenzo to himself.

Virginia slammed the door shut behind her and dropped onto her bed sobbing wet tears of despair. Maria slipped into the bedroom and sat down beside her.

"Gina, what's the matter?" *Gina* was her pet name for Virginia and its use could soften her saddest and angriest moods, reminding them both of happier times.

"Go away!" shouted Virginia.

"Come here Gina and tell me all about it." Virginia could not say no to those arms that had held her since she was a baby, that had hugged away all her childhood pains and furies, even, finally, the death of her poor mother. So slowly and with much crying and anger, Virginia explained what her father had done.

When Virginia had been a little girl the house had been a busy, bustling place. Her father's *major domo* had run the household, smoothly and with a firm hand directing its many servants. This allowed Virginia's mother to spend much of her days with her daughter. She had taught her to read and write, to pray and keep track of the Holy hours and Holy days, to play the virginals, standing on a small stool so she could reach the keys, and to sew and make lace – 'Nun's work' as her father had jokingly called it.

But the most fun young Virginia had was going upstairs to the kitchen and helping the cook. The kitchen was the highest room in the house, opening out onto the roof with its panoramic view of the city. There was always a fire burning up there even in hot weather, and the huge room was infused with the rich incense of wood smoke, soft clouds escaping the confines of the massive fireplace and permeating the room as a fragrant fog.

The kitchen was in a constant state of activity, with upwards of thirty mouths to feed on a daily basis – family and servants, and workers in the silk business, which had taken over the lowest floor of the *palazzo* as a storehouse and sales room. Into this bustle young Virginia would insert herself and demand to be given a task, plucking a fowl or cutting vegetables maybe, and her sweet, youthful charm was such that none could refuse her.

In those years, three generations of the family had lived together in the *palazzo*, each with their own rooms. Virginia, her mother and her father, who had taken over the silk business from his father, lived in a suite of rooms on the east side. Her unmarried uncle Giovanni had a room on the west side, and her paternal grandparents had retired to the back of the house where it was quieter – although her grandparents, of whom she had very little memory but of two elderly people, spent much of their time at their villa in Fiesole.

When Virginia was about six years old, her mother had fallen pregnant again. The betting in the household, which even, scandalously, included her father, had been for a girl, based on how her mother was carrying. Virginia herself had been secretly hoping for a brother. She imagined herself dressing and playing with the little boy as if he were an oversized doll, her fertile imagination already planning games they could play together.

Her mother, growing larger by the day, had been wishing the whole business should be over. It was a hot summer, and as her confinement approached Antonia would spend her days waddling uncomfortably from her bedroom, down the stairs to the courtyard to sit in the cool shade by the fountain. Then, after a half hour of the fountain's musical tinkling, she would waddle back upstairs to her room to relieve herself in the close stool; an uncomfortable routine.

To everyone's surprise, and Virginia's delight, the child had been a boy; an heir to the family and a vision of the future. Yet, ironically, the happy day of her little brother's birth had marked the beginning of the end of young Virginia's idyllic life. At first both Antonia and son had seemed healthy, and Virginia had marveled at the miniature perfection of the tiny boy wrapped tight in his swaddling bands. But, as the autumn wore on and the weather grew wetter, Antonia had fallen ill with a fever – *influenza di febbre* the doctor had called it, signifying that he had no idea what it was nor how to cure it, and that it might just be some malign predestination of the stars.

The cook, to the contrary, had been a fountainhead of folk wisdom and had applied compresses and poultices with a grim enthusiasm, relieving, to an extent, the discomfort of the fever, which had now passed on to the infant boy. Yet it had all been to no avail. The mother had died a few days after her son, sobbing for her child's life as much as for her own. Both the present and the future of the family gone in one frightful moment – a mother, a wife, a son and an heir.

Many others in the city had suffered and died that winter from the fever, but that meant little to young Virginia who had just seen her family rent asunder, her dear Mother torn from her and her baby brother gone as if his existence had been but a sweet dream. She had cried for what seemed like months in the arms of her nurse, who could do little to comfort her. Her father had been entirely inconsolable.

At that time the family had begun to fall apart. Uncle Giovanni had married a well-to-do woman from Siena and moved to that city, and Vincenzo's parents, mournful at the loss of their grandson and growing more infirm as the years wore on, had moved out of the city for good, to spend their last days in their country villa.

The house had become quiet now; servants dismissed, and sections of the building closed off. The ground floor of the *palazzo* had still housed the silk business, but try as he might, Vincenzo could muster less and less interest in business when he had no heir – no future.

There had occurred a brighter moment a few years later when Virginia's father, sufficiently recovered from his wife's death, had planned a new marriage. His wife-to-be had proved a charming and intelligent woman, and, most of all, a potentially fecund vessel for a male heir. Even young Virginia had been won over by the charm of the new woman – her name had disappeared into the mists of Virginia's childhood – but in keeping with the cruelty of fate, the plague had come that year.

The plague had carried off her stepmother-to-be along with her grandparents, and had even reached out its bony hand to Siena, dispatching her Uncle Giovanni. Ever since that time, her dreams had been haunted by a glimpse she had caught of the Plague Doctor as he entered the house, while she was being hurriedly removed elsewhere to avoid the pestilence. The Plague Doctor, with his enormous foreboding shape, draped in creaking oilcloth, was the stuff of her nightmares still.

Now Virginia, the trials of her childhood sadly remembered, lay again in her nurse's arms explaining what her father had told her and why she was so unhappy.

It seemed that in a familial masterstroke Vincenzo had negotiated with his late brother Giovanni's wife to come and live with them in Florence, so that Giovanni's son, Virginia's cousin, could be groomed to take over the family silk business. Vincenzo would provide rooms in the *palazzo* and a living for his sister-in law, and in return would adopt Giulio, the cousin, as his own son – and more importantly his heir.

This bothered Virginia more in the telling than in the fact, as she loved her Sienese family and would enjoy having them living in the house, making it more like the house of her childhood. But her father's abrupt manner hurt her deeply. Indeed, she had even entertained girlish notions of inheriting the business and running it herself.

She had articulated these ideas to her father, citing Isabella d'Este and other powerful women, of whom she had some limited knowledge. He had pointed out that d'Este was nobility and part of a dynasty, not a member of a guild, and that there were no women business owners in the Silk Guild. And unlike Isabella d'Este, no retinue could buffer Virginia from the everyday roughness of trade. He had finished with the cryptic comment, "Florence is not Mantua – nor Ferrara."

But this was not the worse part of the news her father had imparted so casually. She was to be married. And not to a Florentine, but to a Venetian! An associate of her father's, who owned a wholesale silk business based in the German Market of Venice, had a son who was to inherit the family firm and was now in need of a wife. Virginia was to be that wife. Married. Married and dressed in Florentine silks simply to be a walking display of Florentine craftsmanship. Married and sent packing to a foreign city full of odd people. A place full of foreigners with strange customs, and days of difficult travel away from her beloved father. And worse, to be treated as chattel by that same beloved father. She sobbed for the loss of her innocence, and her unknown fate, while Maria attempted for a second time to console the inconsolable.

✠

"So how are his legs, this cousin of yours?" asked Ginevra.

"I have never seen fit to look at his legs, at least not to judge their quality. Although I can verify that he has legs," replied Virginia with a touch of sarcasm.

"Well I like to judge a man by the shape of his legs," continued Ginevra enthusiastically, "I like a well formed thigh and shapely calf, and the latest style of tight hose and short tunic fortunately leaves very little to the imagination." The girls giggled as Ginevra raised her eyebrows provocatively.

"He is only a boy, maybe ten or eleven years," observed Virginia dismissively, "not yet a worthy object for your discerning eye."

"And not an opportunity of marriage for you then?" asked

Ginevra.

"Hardly. My father needs *him* more that he needs me," sighed Virginia, "so I am to be packed off to Venice to be wed to an old man I have never met."

"But think of the dresses!" exclaimed Theresa, floating back into the conversation from her reverie.

"I thought he was thirty-five or so," said Ginevra, ignoring the interruption.

"Yes, old."

"Hardly old my dear." Ginevra smiled conspiratorially. She was a year or two the senior of Virginia and had aspirations. "I have seen many a fine pair of legs on a man of forty."

"Yes, and a fine purse to go with them," Virginia replied acidly.

"There is nothing wrong with wealth as you yourself know – she who dresses in silks and finery," Ginevra shot back.

"And the linens!" They both stopped and turned towards Theresa. She looked back at them, "What?"

"You seem to be in a world of your own," said Virginia.

"I was just thinking – of all the beautiful dresses, and cloaks and hats and fine, fine hose, and beautiful shoes. The all of them embroidered and bejeweled." Theresa's eyes twinkled brighter than the brightest jewel at the thought of all those beautiful clothes.

"I have pretty dresses."

"But new and more. You would be the toast of the town!" Theresa had obviously been giving this a lot of thought. "And we two could visit with you and wear some of those beautiful clothes. What a fine group we all should be!"

"She has a good point," Ginevra chimed in.

"Oh no, not you too," sighed Virginia.

"That could be your counter offer," continued Ginevra undaunted, "your father is a businessman and a man who values his peace, so make him a businesslike offer. You can force him to spend a fortune on your dowry in return for your meek acceptance of his marriage plan. What can he possibly be doing with all that money he makes anyway, certainly not spending it on the house." She waved her hand around airily.

"He is planning a new and lavish *palazzo* in *Oltrarno* for his new family, that's what he plans to do with all his money," observed Virginia.

"Then if he wants to build his new and fine *palazzo* he must pay you handsomely to go away gently, and keep you well outfitted in Florentine silks in your new location. That will give you your financial independence whatever happens to your new husband." Ginevra drove home her point and its thinly veiled *memento mori* with a thrust of her delicate bejeweled finger. "You will wear your wealth on your back."

"Rather than earning my wealth on my back?" asked Virginia blandly, and they dissolved in giggles.

"*Oltrarno?*" asked Theresa in horror, just catching the drift of the conversation, "You will be leaving Santa Maria Novella?"

"Theresa, haven't you been listening? I will be leaving Florence entirely, not just moving to another quarter! Leaving Florence and going to stupid Venice to marry a stupid man whom I care not for in the slightest! Santa Maria Novella indeed!"

"Oh."

Il Pittore

"Luca, Luca... where are you?" Bernardo was hurrying as best he could through the crowded house looking for his wayward ward, the Painter. "I have a commission for you." Maybe that will get his attention, he thought. He was wrong.

Luca was out. He had been feeling itchy ever since they had, just recently, closed the last bathhouse in Florence. He had really enjoyed immersing himself in the hot water and letting all the cares of the world steam away. He had tried bathing at home but the exertion required was so enormous that he had given up in disgust. The hot water at the bathhouse was so effortless. They, meaning the Eight, had shuttered the bathhouses against fear of the plague which some claimed could be spread in the hot and steamy atmosphere. Luca was dubious. He had bathed regularly for years and had never had so much as a runny nose.

His opinion was that some hypocritical churchmen had developed a moral indignation over the idea of naked men bathing together, and the putative acts they indulged in; and that the Medici, or their creatures, had curried favor by closing the baths down. Although Luca had to admit there were some assignations between men and their paramours, both female and male, and that some business was transacted under cover of the steam, nevertheless, the bathhouse was hardly a bawdy house any more than was a tavern or an inn.

Yet there it was: the war came, the plague came and the baths were closed. It was all the fault of the Medici.

As a consolation for the loss of his bath, Luca treated himself to a shave twice a week at a barber a few streets from Bernardo's. It was a poor substitute, but the razor sharp steel scraping the fragrant foam from his skin left him feeling clean and crisp, his face smooth and light.

It was, thus, a clean and crisp Luca that emerged from beneath the awning of the barber's shop into the light, bright morning. He adjusted the fall of his soft, oversized black velvet hat, and fluffed the sleeves and neck of his flawlessly white linen shirt, artfully arranging the puffs of white fabric that emerged from the slashes in his jet black brocade sleeves. He buckled his cloak loosely at the neck and swung it stylishly over one shoulder, the more to reveal the contrasting layers of cloth beneath, flipped the hem of his tunic so it hung just so, and strode off down the street – his feet, covered in soft black kid, carefully avoiding those steaming mounds of manure that had not yet been scavenged.

It was at this moment that Bernardo rounded the corner in his quest to find the errant Luca. Bernardo, in his position of apothecary to many wealthy and influential families, was also, from time to time, in a position to steer commissions in Luca's direction. In point of fact, Luca did a brisk trade in portable Madonnas, Evangelists and similar small paintings of personal devotion. But a painter's reputation is established and secured by the large and visible commissions he completes, not from any number of small images that can only be seen in bedrooms and *studioli*. Bernardo had obtained a commission, two in fact, joined in the bestowing, that would go a long way toward consolidating Luca's reputation.

"Perfect!" cried Bernardo as he caught sight of Luca.

"I would not dare to contradict your estimation," joked Luca, "but, may I ask, perfect for what exactly?"

"Why to do a little business of course."

"Do you mistake me for a tavern girl?" They both laughed.

"No, I mean your kind of business," Bernardo assured him. "I have obtained a commission for you to paint a Madonna for the chapel of the *Innocenti*. They have the frame already made and you are to paint a panel to fit."

"Bernardo!" exclaimed Luca, "you have outdone yourself."

"Don't thank me yet, there is a condition."

"There is always a condition – the Lord said to Adam: 'Here is life, but there is a condition...'"

"You must take Eve as a companion?"

"I was thinking more of forbidden fruit, but aye, there is truth to that too." Luca smiled.

Chatting amiably, they walked slowly back to Bernardo's house, and he explained the details of the commission.

✠

Later that afternoon, for moral support, Luca worshipped the Lord at the *Santissima Annunziata*, lighting a candle for his mother and father, and, on his way out, spending a few minutes looking at the frescoes by his former master in the small cloister where they display the wax sculptures. He stopped at the top of the steps as he exited the church, enjoying the long view down the *via dei Servi* to the *Duomo*.

Then, walking to the center of the square and turning to the left, he worshipped the perfect symmetry of Brunelleschi. He paused there in the middle of the square gazing at the low, long loggia, the elegance of the spacing, the perfect curve of the arches punctuated by the glazed terra cotta roundels of Della Robbia.

As an apprentice of art the façade of *Lo Spedale degli Innocenti* had been an object of study and wonder for him. Four generations had passed since the laying of the first stone and still the shapes were clean and modern, as if Brunelleschi had personally drawn inspiration from the past and projected it onto the future – a monument, as much as the dome of the *Duomo*, to Florentine style and intellect.

Now he, Luca, was to decorate the interior of this magnificent building. This was a seminal moment in his career.

As he walked across the square towards the loggia he experienced anew that singular visual effect. From a distance the building looks low and relatively simple – no towers, no multiple stories growing shorter as they grow higher, just a simple, small, perfect structure. It is only as you approach the steps to the loggia that the enormous size of the building becomes apparent. The architect had planned the building to present itself as elegantly as possible while concealing its size within its simplicity.

Behind him, across the square from the *Innocenti*, a new façade was going up that exactly mirrored the one by Brunelleschi. It was mostly complete, still partially obscured with scaffolding; the shouted calls of the workmen echoing around the square.

Luca slowly mounted the steps to the loggia. He was to meet the donor of the commission here beneath its smooth arches; under which arches the unwanted babies of the city could be assured of a living, an education – a life. *Lo Spedale degli Innocenti* was a foundling hospital built and run by the Silk Guild. There was a basin outside the main entrance where babies, undesired for various reasons, could be deposited. The children were nursed, raised and educated; the boys trained in professions suited to their intelligence, the girls taught to sew, cook and keep house, and provided with a modest dowry. In fact, Luca's assistant Carlo had been placed with him by the *Innocenti*. Luca stood there gazing upward at the arches.

"Beautiful, is it not?" The voice was deep and assured. Although phrased as a question it was delivered as a statement.

"This was the beginning of the modern era," replied Luca squinting against the glare of the afternoon sun as it slanted across the square.

"Indeed it was," concurred his interlocutor, stepping to one side, out of the light.

Luca beheld an expensively yet understatedly dressed citizen of the Republic. His graying hair cropped short in the neo-Roman style, topped with a dark red pillbox hat. His *lucco* – the long tunic worn by all of Florence's gentlemen – was of a deep red silk velvet, trimmed with marten fur at the neck and cuffs. His cloak of soft brown lightweight wool was lined in matching silk brocade, then gathered high at the shoulder and held with a gold and ruby clasp. This Luca took in with a single glance – by his clothes, a well-educated, wealthy and well-connected gentleman stood before him.

"My name is Vincenzo," continued the gentleman, "and you must be the painter, Luca." Luca removed his hat and bowed dramatically with a practiced flourish. The older man smiled and with a terse, "Follow me," walked through the portico into the hospital; Luca followed at a respectful distance. They passed first into the men's cloister and Vincenzo stood for a moment watching the young children play. He beckoned for Luca to join him.

"So who was your master?"

"Master Andrea, Andrea del Migliore."

"The tailor's son?"

"The same. I was placed with him when he returned from France."

"Is his wife truly as abhorrent as is said?"

"I believe he used her as a model for the harpies on the Macci Madonna."

The two laughed together. Since the beginning of time, complaining about women has always been a successful way for two men to get to know each other.

Vincenzo turned again to watch the children playing. Luca noticed several games he remembered from his own childhood: tops, hoops, odds and evens, tipcat, and his personal favorite span counter.

"Look at all the healthy boys," exclaimed Vincenzo, "why was I not blessed with a son?" Luca kept silent, assuming correctly that the question was rhetorical. Vincenzo looked quizzically at Luca and continued, "Twenty years and still not a son – I believe I grow too old."

It occurred to Luca that, in his experience, wealthy men loved to talk about themselves and their problems as if they were the most important things in the world. He endeavored to look thoughtfully interested, more as a business decision than from any true empathy.

A moment of silence for Vincenzo's lack of male issue was observed, then suddenly he laughed, breaking it. "I am sorry, I should not burden you with my personal problems, although every time I visit this place I am struck by that same thought. And, in a manner of speaking, my lack of a son affects our business today." Luca breathed a sigh of relief – back to business.

"In what respect?" he asked.

"You know I would like you to paint a Virgin for the chapel?" asked Vincenzo, Luca nodded his assent. "Then you know that I could have summoned any number of painters here to do so." Luca nodded again, somewhat less enthusiastically. "Well, I thought that you might be the perfect painter, matching skill with – how shall I put this – a desire for advancement. I know you will not let me down in the quality of your work, and I trust you will fulfill the other part of the commission with equal endeavor." Luca wished most heartily that the man would get to the point.

Vincenzo launched into what seemed like another digression: "As you know from my previous words, I was not blessed with a son of my own. However, I will be adopting my late brother's son as my own and my heir; consumed, as my brother was, by the plague." They both crossed themselves at the mention of the one killer they feared worse than war.

"This leaves my daughter as my only child, and my single opportunity to make a successful marriage. It happens that I have arranged just such a marriage with the son of a business associate in Venice which will help cement our relationship, and I need a representation of my daughter, a portrait, to send to her betrothed. It should be seen as a gift from a future father-in-law, so should depict my daughter as demure and virginal, yet at the same time remind the groom of her comeliness and beauty." Vincenzo raised his eyebrows and looked at Luca. "And who better to complete this task than a painter of Virgins?"

"Indeed," was all that Luca could think of replying.

"And one more thing, it must be completed within three weeks."

"Impossible!" declared Luca, adding, "the varnish alone will take that long to dry."

"Then you should perhaps begin immediately. It only need be small, not more than a *braccio* in height, with width in proportion. Once you have the exact size I will have a simple frame made in time for its completion."

"What about the drying time?"

"It can be packaged in such a way that it can dry on the journey. Young man, I have shipped innumerable bales of the most fragile silk from one end of the world to the other, a single small painting hardly seems to create an insuperable problem. The question is, do you want the commission or not?"

"Yes, *Signore*, I do want the commission, but I am pledged only to paint devotional images."

"Yet surely *Il Beato Angelico* painted portraits on occasion."

"Fra Angelico painted portraits of Dominican monks, yes, not betrothed girls," exclaimed Luca, exasperated.

"Look at it this way, I need a portrait, and you need to paint a larger Madonna for a renowned patron. Think of it as a means to an end. By painting the small portrait of my daughter you will be inspiring devotion in a larger audience, and your audience will only grow from here."

"I have an idea that may make the portrait work," conceded Luca slowly.

"Perfect!" exclaimed Vincenzo, "let me show you where the Madonna will hang."

They continued their walk through the cloister, the staff and older children nodding to Vincenzo deferentially as the two passed – he acknowledging them with a friendly wave. By and by they arrived at the chapel, which was situated directly behind the men's cloister. It was fairly dark inside, lit only by the small high windows and a single candle on the altar. The two knelt at the end of the nave briefly, crossing themselves and each muttering a short prayer. Luca walked slowly towards the altar, his eyes becoming accustomed to the gloom. He had never ventured this far into the *Innocenti* and had only heard tell of the magnificent altarpiece. There it was, suspended above and behind the altar, as yet invisible, obscured by its curtain of blue brocade.

"May I?" Luca turned to ask Vincenzo as he approached. Without an answer Vincenzo walked to the side of the altar and tugged on a cord; the curtain swung aside and the glory spilled out.

The flame of the single candle was reflected a thousand times from the bright, gilded cornice frame that held the central painting with its row of story-telling *predella* images arranged along the bottom, and lit up the faces of the two men as they gazed upon it.

"Magnificent, is it not?" asked Vincenzo. It was the Adoration of the Magi visualized in a busy modern landscape.

"I had never laid eyes on it before today, only heard of it," replied Luca, allowing himself time to take in the detail, the complexity, "and truly it is beautiful." He leaned close to examine the brushwork. "Do you know how hard it is to get that smooth a texture with tempera? Incredible. And look how the cloak of the Virgin creates a diamond of blue that draws the eye to the red of her dress and the Christ child." He stepped back. "See how the colors work? The rhythm of blue and red with the splashes of yellow that frame the Madonna."

"Never have I heard such an artist's appreciation of Master Domenico's work, it gives me a different perspective," observed Vincenzo.

"You knew him?"

"I was just a boy. My father was involved from time to time in the affairs of the *Innocenti*," recalled Vincenzo, "but I do remember Master Michelangelo visiting to collect the monthly payments."

"Buonarroti?" asked Luca in astonishment.

"Indeed! He was no more than a boy himself, an apprentice of the Ghirlandaio studio."

"I wonder if his hand is anywhere in this panel," said Luca as he returned to examining the altarpiece.

It was at that moment Luca stepped backward with a sharp intake of breath, his eyes fixed on the complex image.

"What? What is it?" asked Vincenzo.

"There," Luca pointed with a trembling finger, "I have seen this before, in my dreams, in my nightmares, this same image. The women running, screaming, dying, the walls of the city, the monuments of another time. Soldiers killing, raping."

"Where?" asked Vincenzo studying the image. And then he saw it. A little over half way up on the left side, almost lost in the complexity, was the image of death Luca had seen. It was a depiction of the Murder of the Innocents – that frantic killing of all the newborns in Bethlehem by Herod, in his desire to destroy the Christ. It was the same event that had given its name to the hospital.

"Perhaps the dangerous times we live in have affected you,"

mused Vincenzo.

"I did witness from afar the destruction of Cotignola, but no, that is not it. I have had dreams recently of this exact image, like a foretelling of the future. And here it is."

The two men stood there in silence, bathed in the glow from the altar and its grim prophecy.

L'Incontro

Monsters were coming. Demons were climbing up out of the mist, climbing the walls, howling dreadful cries from their evil, feral mouths – slashing and cutting, killing everyone in their path.

Luca awoke in a sweat. The dreams were still with him and had developed new and fearsome subtleties. Perhaps it really was the memory of the recent sack of Cotignola, still fresh in his mind, perhaps it was the image of murder in the *Innocenti* altarpiece, but he was unconvinced. The nightmares were so specific and they did not look like Cotignola.

He shrugged it off and struggled out of bed, still tired. He pulled off the soft, crumpled white shirt and wiped his naked body down with it, then balled it up and threw it into the corner.

The room was one large single space for both working and living – Luca was not yet successful enough for more – with four tall windows that gave onto a small balcony. Opposite the windows was a platform not quite a *braccio* high that carried the huge bed. To the right of the bed was the door; to the left was the workspace. It was a very simple arrangement, but despite the large size of the room and the relative lack of furniture it still managed to be a mess. The servants had long since refused to enter the room, complaining about the stink of turpentine, although they were never too shy to ask for some when they needed a remedy for lice, or stomach problems, or what have you. Every week Luca would collect his linens for the laundry and the rest of his housekeeping was his own affair – hence the mess.

He splashed water on his face from a majolica bowl and ran wet fingers through his hair. Today was the day he was to meet Vincenzo's daughter – the subject of the importunate portrait – so he spent extra time making sure he looked his best. Luca lifted the heavy lid of a *cassone*, a massive painted chest that he had himself decorated, and selected his clothes for the day. He first pulled on his most expensive clean white shirt, the one with lace at the collar and cuffs, then, on his lower half, his tightest black hose. Over that went a blue silk *farsetto* and a black tunic that dropped just below the upper thigh, topped with a blue cloak lined with black fur. As a final touch he kneaded a little perfumed oil into his dark curls and set his large soft hat at just the right angle.

He had learned many years ago that the clothes create the man. If you dress a certain way you become that man in the eyes of the discerning public. He thus spent a good deal of money he did not quite yet have on his clothes. This required, as it did for many a well-to-do Florentine citizen, juggling expenses on a weekly basis to maintain solvency – along with frequent trips to the pawn broker, the trading of one debt to pay another, and plenty of credit. This was not considered an inherently bad thing; living beyond your immediate means was a very Florentine custom, provided you showed up looking your best and accomplished the task at hand with *pennacchio*. He pulled on a pair of high, soft black leather boots and walked down the narrow stairs to the street.

Luca travelled by sedan chair to Vincenzo's residence due to the early spring rain, and bade the men wait under cover of the portico while he conducted his business. Once inside he mounted the wide stone steps, and was shown into a large room on the *piano nobile*. It overlooked the busy street through huge windows fitted with window seats let into the thick walls. One end of the tastefully and expensively decorated room was dominated by a fireplace, a fire burning to ward off the damp chill in the air, the other end by two large doorways leading to other parts of the *palazzo*. Set between the doors stood a massive sideboard displaying a sparkling set of silver dishes and serving trays.

The effect was dramatic yet old fashioned. The style looked like something from the days of Cosimo, only the paintings on the long wall facing the windows hinted at a more modern aesthetic. They were four in number, large and horizontal, each hung over a similarly sized *cassone* and depicting the four seasons. Luca did not have a chance to examine them closely to determine the hand that created them as he was plunged immediately into the business of the hour.

The woman who had brought him upstairs and guided him in was a short, rotund figure, with a vaguely foreign aspect to her face, introduced as Maria. She then began the introduction of the three attractive young women who thinly inhabited this large salon. The three were all impeccably dressed in floods of silk and waves of taffeta, but with white linen aprons demurely covering their dresses, appropriate to the location and time of day. There was Ginevra, Theresa, and the subject of the proposed portrait, Virginia. Luca nodded, charmingly formal, and swept the soft, oversized hat from his head. Dress the man, be the man. He was the Painter, he had arrived.

"Look at the cut of his calves!" whispered Ginevra admiringly.

"Be quiet!" hissed Virginia.

"I merely point out..."

"Shhhh!"

Virginia stood and greeted her visitor, noticing that Ginevra was essentially right; he was a very attractive man. And then, before she could speak further she realized she had seen this handsome man before. He was the jackanapes that had made such a spectacle of himself at the Cathedral, climbing the scaffold with the scruffy boy. She was thus determined to dislike him and be aloof no matter how attractive he was. It was her pious duty to treat him with as little pleasantry as possible, and just get the picture done and him out of her house.

"*Signorina* Virginia, your father did not begin to adequately describe your beauty. It will be a personal pleasure to have the honor of immortalizing that beauty in paint. I simply hope I have the skill to render such transcendent comeliness," was Luca's opening gambit. And Virginia had to admit, despite her best efforts, that he did have a charming turn of phrase. A turn of phrase she was not about to be charmed by – she was determined.

"You are too kind," she began offhandedly, "so where do I sit for this portrait, and what should I wear?" Straight to business she went.

"You look perfect just where you are!" exclaimed Luca. "The light gently caresses your exquisite face in just the right way to bring out all your natural beauty."

"He is very good!" whispered Ginevra standing beside Virginia. Virginia turned her head and glared.

"And your sense of style is impeccable," added Luca, "I would simply ask that you remove the apron."

"If he is as good a painter..." Ginevra was cut off.

"Excuse me for a moment," Virginia said to Luca, and promptly turned to Ginevra. "This man is a buffoon and I will hear nothing good about him," she said, low enough that Luca could not hear. He assumed they were talking about what an attractive man he was, he received that kind of attention a lot from women of all ages and social levels.

"He is the man," continued Virginia, "who climbed the scaffold at the *Duomo* last week and made an exhibition of himself."

"Oh!" exclaimed Ginevra in a low voice, "I remember that. He did look very fine standing up there."

"You have no respect!"

"I respect a fine looking man. Look, his tunic is just the right length to show off his thighs when he turns. See how the light gently caresses..."

"You are too much!"

Virginia despaired of trying to convince Ginevra to her point of view, and returned to Luca with a snort in her friend's direction. Quickly composing herself she continued, "Again, sir, you are too kind," smiling wanly.

"Allow me!" exclaimed Ginevra, fiddling with the ties of Virginia's white linen apron.

"You painted a Madonna for my father as a gift for my mother. It was a very pretty thing," Theresa suddenly blurted out. All heads turned in her direction and she blushed slightly. "It was a very pretty thing," she repeated, a little bemused.

"Where does she come up with this chatter?" asked Ginevra of nobody in particular.

"Thank you *Signorina* Theresa, I am merely a conduit of the Almighty. A poor and humble man sent to do his bidding. I am glad my meager efforts gave pleasure." And he bowed again in her direction, his eyes fixed on hers, appearing considerably less poor and humble than he had just professed. He noted in passing that she was the prettiest of the three, but her predominantly vacant expression did not enhance her overall attractiveness. Theresa stifled an admiring giggle.

Luca produced paper and chalk from a leather portfolio he carried beneath one arm and drew an ornate chair up close to Virginia. He had her sit opposite him and gazed deep into her eyes, examining her face and hair. She had never before been the subject of a painter and felt deeply uncomfortable being peered at like a prize cow at an auction.

"Please *Signore*."

"Luca. Please call me Luca."

"*Signor* Luca..."

"Just Luca," he smiled a disarming smile.

"As you wish, but must you sit so close and examine me so – intimately?" she asked plaintively.

"I merely need to get your likeness on paper as accurately as possible. I assure you that examining you is an unfortunate requirement of the process," he smiled again that charming smile and she sighed her acceptance of the terms. He proceeded to sketch.

The other two, Ginevra and Theresa, watched from across the room, pleased to be a part of the excitement, but, at least on Ginevra's part, just a little envious of the attention being paid to her friend. Theresa was too ingenuous to feel such a negative emotion, she was just happy and sad depending on the moment. Right now she was happy for her friend, but sad that her friend would be moving to Venice, but happy that she would be able to visit and wear pretty clothes.

Virginia sat perfectly still, divorced a little from reality – frozen, as the world continued around her. She could see her friends out of the corner of her eye watching and talking, the fire over the

Painter's shoulder crackling and spitting as it consumed a green log, and reflecting its golden light like a halo from his dark curls. She watched his hands moving rhythmically as he created something from nothing, a likeness from a blank sheet of paper and a sharpened piece of red chalk. He had changed somehow from the jackanapes of the *Duomo* and the practiced, charming businessman of the last few minutes, and now he was at work. His face took on a concentrated frown but also a calmness and clarity. No longer was he affecting a pose as this or that, he was simply what he was, a painter.

Virginia was finally able to see him, understand him, admire him. He was not just a handsome fool, he had a gift, a gift from God, and she was the focus of this gift. It had been against her better judgment, but she was just beginning to admit that her judgment may have been flawed, or at least prejudiced. Now she was heartily glad she had allowed this man to become, albeit temporarily, a part of her life. The scratch of the chalk on the paper and the rustle of linen and lace as his hand moved swiftly across the drawing were spellbinding as she sat there immobile, the passage of time condensed inside their own little world.

And then it was over. Luca spun the paper around and showed her. There she was in monochrome hues of russet and cream. The likeness was excellent, yet it did not quite comport with her own vision of herself in her looking glass. There was something around the eyes, a thoughtfulness, and a little devilishness about the curve of the mouth. This was more than a likeness; it was a portrait. This man had looked into her very soul, by the Grace of God, and put her thoughts and feelings down on paper.

She looked up from the paper to the Painter who had made the image and their eyes met. He smiled, not in a flattering, simpering way, but in a straightforward friendly way. It was as if their minds had met for the first time.

"That's..." she stuttered, clearing her throat, a little parched, "that's perfect. You made me look..." She thought about it, trying not to appear too conceited, "You made me look beautiful."

"No, I drew you as you are. You *are* beautiful." Was he flattering again, was the moment over? He looked serious. But then he was gone; walking out, bowing to the young women, making his apologies, through the door and down the stairs. She watched him, rooted to the spot, feeling hopeless; feeling as if something really important had happened and somehow she had missed it.

"Maybe *I* need a portrait," murmured Ginevra as she peered out of the window to try to catch a last sight of Luca. She turned around looking for a reply and caught sight of the look on Virginia's face, understanding immediately. "Oh my! You like him!"

"Don't be ridiculous," replied Virginia unconvincingly.

"Well, I suppose you could do a lot worse, he is very talented and your father could connect him with all the right people. These days good painters make a lot of money."

"Don't be ridiculous!" repeated Virginia louder for more effect, her voice breaking slightly, "I am engaged to another man." And she shook her head for emphasis. But she still felt a little empty inside.

"You looked very pretty in the picture," said Theresa, smiling.

La Fiera

The fair was in town!

It was New Year's Day in Florence – the twenty-fifth of March 1527 – and following hard on the heels of the Feast of the Annunciation came the fair.

Temporary shops, made of wood and painted canvas, were erected for their temporary tenants. Merchants from all over the city, all over the *contado* and all over the world came to Florence to show and sell. Along with this embarrassment of riches travelled all manner of entertainment: singers and musicians playing and singing the popular songs both secular and devotional; mountebanks selling their obscure and intriguing cures; actors with their plays, poets their sonnets and intellects their discourses; and, bringing up the rear, fortune tellers and gypsies, and other minor heretics.

Normally, such a variety of the barely lawful, and in some instances, blatantly lawless would not be permitted within the city walls – at least not without a permit and suitable taxation – but during the fair rules were relaxed, taxes were overlooked and a marvelous time was had by all. The Eight continued to have the fair patrolled by the Militia to prevent direct theft and assault, but lesser commissions such as small heresies, and excesses of dress and behavior could be allowed to pass unpunished.

Virginia loved the fair. She and Ginevra pushed, laughing,

through the milling, morning crowd, their clogs beating a high-pitched tattoo on the straw-strewn stones, for all the world like two exotic, shimmering butterflies flitting from one beautiful flower to the next in sparkling shafts of sunlight.

They dwelt in perhaps the most well supplied city of the world, yet the fair would bring still further wonders to fascinate them – for a while, at any rate. Lifting their dresses with one hand and holding tight to their purses with the other, they trotted rapidly from stall to stall, trying on jewelry, hats, scarves, shoes – smelling perfumes, soaps, creams and pomades, all promising to further enhance their beauty – touching and stroking lengths of fabric, and talking knowledgeably about them, as both their fathers were in the business. Finally, and perhaps the most enjoyable part of all, there was the food – sweet and savory, fried, boiled, baked and battered, and more often than not dredged with sugar – delicious!

Virginia loved the fair. As she was, on any normal day, in excess of the sumptuary laws, during the fair she enjoyed the freedom to indulge her flamboyant side, the laws being suspended. This was no small thing as she had been fined three times for sumptuary transgressions during the previous year, although had managed to argue her way out of one of them by confusing the enforcement officer. Little grey men, she characterized them, lurking in doorways waiting to punish their betters for dressing well; either from envy or a misplaced excess of religious zeal. During the fair Virginia twinkled and sparkled even more than usual.

The *via dei Servi* runs straight from the *Annunziata* to the *Duomo*. In fact if you fired a shot from the steps of *Santissima Annunziata* aimed directly down the length of the *via dei Servi* you would hit the back of the *Duomo* a second or two later. It is that straight. And during the week of the fair this long, narrow street, home to some of the wealthiest families of Florence, was turned over to the stalls, barrows, benches and stages of itinerant merchants and performers.

Among those merchants were Luca and Bernardo, who shared a stall at the fair as they shared a house and a shop. This year, as part of his apprenticeship, it had been Carlo's job to paint the decorative canvas *facciata* that framed the opening. He had designed a motif of columns entwined with ivy and surmounted by winged *putti* at each end, connected by a scroll with a lion's head in the center, entirely realized in a monochrome scheme to resemble carved marble. All who saw it confirmed that he had outdone himself and he was justifiably proud as they tacked the painted canvas to the wooden structure.

The street was a hive of activity as merchandise was loaded into booths and all manner of temporary stages were set up for the performers. Handcarts and barrows were maneuvered into position and the various dray horses, mules and oxen were led into temporary stables in the side streets and some of the small meadows that lay behind the new and elegant façades.

Luca and Bernardo had barely finished organizing the display of goods at their booth when the fair was officially opened. All the stallholders stood proudly before their merchandise as a small but glittering parade walked the length of the street blessing the fair and all its participants. The Bishop of Florence performed the blessing, attended by acolytes with holy water and incense. Silvio Passerini, the Cardinal-Bishop of Cortona followed with his wards, the two young Medici, Ippolito and Alessandro – 'Two bastards, one a moor, and a dissolute Cardinal as their minder,' as Luca had described the group, not entirely inaccurately – attended by the best and brightest of Florence.

"They are trying to convince us all that they care a whit for Florence rather than just their own well-appointed hides," muttered Luca to Bernardo as the Cardinal and his charges passed them. Bernardo dug his elbow into Luca's ribs as they both bowed deferentially. And then the throng descended upon the fair.

✠

A *cutpurse* is a thief who employs a very sharp knife with one hand to slice open an unsuspecting individual's purse, and with the other hand catches the money as it tumbles out. The fair was a perfect place for the cutpurse to work, and despite the best efforts of the Eight to keep it crime free, work he did.

The cutpurse who targeted the two butterflies was part of a team; one man to jostle the target, the cutpurse himself and a third man to assist their escape over a nearby wall and through a small meadow that lay beyond. The butterflies had just finished trying on jewelry and were moving on to the next stall when the thieves struck. The 'jostler' moved between the two young women and separated them, bumping Virginia with his elbow. She stumbled slightly falling against the cutpurse. He complained loudly at the inconvenience, keeping her attention focussed on his face while his hands relieved her of her money. He took off swiftly down the crowded street – a little too swiftly – Virginia suddenly realized she had been robbed and shrieked at the top of her lungs. The chase was on, bystanders joining in along with the Militia, the butterflies bringing up the rear; the whole train weaving in and out of the throng.

Luca heard the hue and cry and stepped out of the stall to see what was happening. Just at that moment the cutpurse popped out of a group of fairgoers on the escape route towards his accomplice. Luca took the scene in quickly, and stepping forward extended his leg. The cutpurse tripped, sprawling face down in the street and Luca, drawing his dagger, swiftly put his knee in the criminal's back, the knife to his throat.

The pursuers caught up, breathing heavily, and there was much enthusiastic cheering and backslapping as they hauled the thief away. Virginia especially was surprised and pleased to find *her* painter was her savior – or at the very least the savior of her money. She thanked him profusely and he, as ever, was charmingly indifferent.

The conversation turned inevitably to the immediate portrait, which Luca produced from the back of his stall with a dramatic flourish. He had brought it to the fair to be picked up by Vincenzo's servant, but was happy and proud to display it to the subject herself. It was small, about a *braccio* in height, and took the form of a devotional Madonna, but instead of the Virgin Mary, there was Virginia looking back at herself with the same charming quirks of character that Luca had caught in the original sketch.

It was as if her soul had been captured in this small wooden panel. Others would simply see it as a picture of a pretty girl, but for her it was her heart laid bare. She had the same emotional response she had experienced after seeing the sketch – this man she hardly knew had seen inside her. She flushed and smiled weakly, waving her hand in front of her face as a fan. "Does the weather not grow warmer?" she temporized, her voice catching a little in her throat.

"Is it not to your liking?" asked Luca, rather bemused at her response.

"No not at all," she replied confusingly. Luca frowned. "No, no, I mean it is very much to my liking. It just seems..." she leaned forward conspiratorially and whispered, "so very... intimate." She almost hissed the last word.

Luca was taken aback. This was not, in his limited experience, the usual reaction to a portrait. He had not painted many portraits, but the few he had done were of a very pragmatic nature – a likeness created for money, devoid of much of the personal involvement and rapture that a painting of a religious image could invoke.

"That is very pretty," opined Ginevra leaning over Virginia's shoulder, "you captured her perfectly Painter, well done," she added by way of an offhand compliment. "Now let us be on our way, there is much to see." This was directed at Virginia. "You need a new purse."

"Sorry for being so late." Theresa appeared from the press of fairgoers looking a little pink, and perspiring slightly. "Oh, good day Painter," she added politely.

"Are we going?" asked Ginevra.

"I would speak a little with the Painter," replied Virginia.

"As you wish," decided Ginevra, "come Theresa." And with that she was off, Theresa following in her wake, waving goodbye, their several servants trotting obediently behind.

Luca turned back to Virginia, "Intimate? You used the same expression whilst I was drawing you. I assure you that I meant no presumption, the intent was merely to render you most faithfully on the panel."

"No *Signore*, you did indeed faithfully render me – my image that is – and I am very pleased. It just seems that you captured something more, like a small window into my very soul." She could not believe she was using such language with anyone, least of all this man.

"I claim no particular insight nor skill beyond my God-given talent to paint a likeness, but many paintings posses something more than the superficial, more meaning than that ordinarily apparent; a story beneath and beyond that of the obvious." He paused momentarily as a thought struck him. "If you are interested, and if it would please you, I could take you to see some works by well known painters, and articulate their meaning."

"I should like that very much," declared Virginia enthusiastically, despite the innocently forward nature of Luca's offer.

They both realized that Luca was holding her hand. Suddenly the moment was past as one became two again, and their hands self-consciously separated. "Since the fair is so dangerous this year perhaps I can escort you as far as the *piazza*?" asked Luca, swiftly recovering his composure.

"I should be pleased to accept your offer *Signore*," she replied smiling.

"Back in an hour," shouted Luca to Bernardo, the unwilling witness to the entire foregoing.

"Be careful!" shouted Bernardo in return, "in more ways than one," he muttered to himself, shaking his head as Luca and Virginia strolled off into the fair, Maria in mute pursuit.

The fair opened up to the two as it never had before, as if simply their being together made everything more pleasurable. The jewelry shone more brightly, the songs sounded more sweet, and the food – the food was ambrosia as they took small bites from twists of oiled paper gripped tight in sugary fingers. They listened to bad poetry and it did not matter, watched a repetitive morality play and it seemed like the most subtle performance ever. Their mere presence in each other's lives made everything better, lighter, brighter.

Luca kept Virginia entertained by explaining how this street, even as recently as fifty years ago, had been mostly meadows, where the fair had originally been held, and only as the city had become more populous had the Servites who owned it leased the land for building. His knowledge of the city was considerable, but she could have listened to him talk forever about anything, no matter how mundane.

This, thought Virginia, this was what she had been looking for, a man she could enjoy being with and who enjoyed being with her, a man who made her feel special. The fair disappeared into the background and her world was reduced to just the two of them.

Their meanderings brought them, in due course, to a fortuneteller. The crowd ebbed and flowed around his booth, swirling in multiple eddies while he sat there immobile, a dark rock in a colorful river of people.

He was a foreign-looking gentleman of middle age, a faint, enigmatic smile playing about full lips beneath a heavy moustache, and sporting a black turban mounted with a large ruby. He certainly looked the part of the mystical exotic – dress the man, be the man. Virginia stopped, momentarily entranced by the Other. Luca motioned to her to continue. "Do you not desire to know what the future holds?" she asked.

"I am happy to be part of God's plan, but to aspire to supernatural knowledge of that plan is surely blasphemy," he replied matter of factly. She looked at him quizzically, seeing him now in a different light, not expecting such a pious reaction to a simple fortuneteller.

"But is he not simply using the talents that God gave him to glimpse the possibilities the future may hold?" was her cunning retort. Luca had no ready answer so obediently allowed himself to be dragged before the exotic fellow in the black turban.

"Welcome," said the soothsayer.

"What may you tell us of the future?" asked Virginia directly, placing a coin on the table.

"*Signorina*, I am a palmist, show me your hands and I will tell you what I see. If the future is written in your hands I will see it, by the grace of God."

"Are you not a Moor?" asked Luca, surprised at this foreigner's invocation of the Lord, "you dress like one."

"No *Signore*, I dress for my business as you no doubt dress for yours. People expect an exotic from *outremer* as their teller of fortunes, hence the turban." He indicated his headgear with a wave of his hand. "But I am a Christian, baptized and raised. Although none has, thus far, demanded to know the nature of my religious faith before availing themselves of my services," he finished tartly.

"My apologies for any impertinence on my part," said Luca, "I meant no disrespect. Although I must still wonder whereby you came to be reading palms in a travelling fair."

"My services alone have been paid for, my history will cost further," replied the palmist without hesitation.

"Now, I believe that palm reading is gibberish, but a history – now *that* is something I would gladly pay for," declared Luca, enthusiastically throwing several coins onto the palmist's table.

"As you wish *Signore*," obliged the fortuneteller, with an enigmatic smile, and promptly began his story.

"My name is Timothy and I was born in a small village in Ardeal north of the Danube, I believe you know it as Transylvania. The people of my village were *Aromani* – Eastern Christians although our lands were ruled by the Turk – and we lived the life of our ancestors. Reading palms is a common skill amongst the *Aromani* and I received that knowledge from my father. Then one day when I was twelve years old the slavers came. We were not well armed and they rode out of the forest with such overwhelming speed and brutality – there was nothing we could do to stop them. They needed women as servants and concubines, and boys to be trained as soldiers to swell the ranks of the Grand Turk's Janissaries.

"They killed most of the men including my father and loaded the rest of us, women and children, into wagons for the long trip to Ragusa. We arrived at the slave market half dead, in fact several of the girls had already died along the journey, and we were put up for sale. This is where the good Lord in His wisdom saved me. Amongst the buyers at the market were two Italian merchants who were acquiring slave girls to work as servants in the Venetian households, and they purchased most of the girls from my village. As they passed me I offered to read their palms. I told them things that surprised and intrigued them so they purchased me too, as a novelty. I was thus saved from fighting in the Turk's army and, more likely than not, dying on Rhodes with a hundred thousand others – sacrificed for a speck of rock and Turkish pride. In Venice I was sold to a merchant as his servant and was well treated. I would give palm readings to his guests at parties and eventually, after more than twenty years service, when he was close to death, he granted me my freedom. And here I am many years later, living by my wits and by the Grace of God."

"Now *that* was an excellent history!" exclaimed Luca, clapping Timothy on the shoulder.

"You can see why I reacted so, when you called me a Moor," continued the fortuneteller.

"Of course Timothy, I completely understand."

"But what about my future?" asked Virginia, apparently unmoved by the harrowing tale. Timothy smiled his enigmatic smile and took Virginia's pale, delicate hands in his, dark and lined. "Well, what do you see?" asked Virginia excitedly after a few moments. Thereupon the fortuneteller began his second story.

"You have seen much sorrow in your young life," he began.

"Who has not?" muttered Luca.

"And yet you carry no bitterness in your soul. In fact you have a lightness of spirit I rarely see in these troubled times. I would say it is from ignorance of life, but your suffering has made you painfully aware of the grief this world can bring. But here is what I see: you want something you should not have but will have anyway at a terrible cost; you need something you do not understand and will lose before you realize it is gone; and you will travel many days across difficult country to find something you want – only to lose it."

Virginia looked blank. "That is a dreadful fortune!" she exclaimed angrily, "you make me sound like a fool and a wanton, and I assure you *Signore* I am neither."

"I am sorry you are disappointed, but I report only what I see. I have been performing this service for many years and I shall not lie. What you describe as foolishness and wantonness could equally be considered part and parcel of the mutability of life." The fortuneteller warmed to his theme. "Young lady, we know not what God has planned for us. In His wisdom He has permitted me a brief glimpse past future's dark curtain – which most thoroughly obscures even the most proximate occurrence – on the chance that it might thereby offer you some benefit should you choose to heed it."

"You presume much Fortuneteller," said Virginia, chastened yet still defiant, flushing slightly.

"*Signorina*, again I am sorry," he sighed, "if my reading displeases you sufficiently then by all means you may keep your money and I wish you well."

"No no!" exclaimed Luca, "you gave an honest reading and deserve to be paid for it. May you have a profitable week."

The fortuneteller nodded his head in acknowledgment and the ruby in his black turban twinkled in the morning sun, like a glowing red flame in the enveloping darkness.

The palm reading had seriously discomfited Virginia, and the fair had thus lost a good deal of its lustre. Luca did his best to cheer her, but her mood had been overcome by a melancholy. A melancholy whose depth seemed beyond her years to bear.

La Pittura o La Calunnia

The bells had rung Vespers three hours previously and it was pitch dark in the narrow alleyway. Virginia had bribed a servant to let her out the side entrance which opened onto a lane giving shared access to the stables behind the row of *palazzi*. She slipped her clogs on, and walked as stealthily as she could to the front of the house where the street was weakly illuminated by the lantern over the massive studded front door – locked and barred for the night. As promised the sedan was there, the two porters waiting patiently for her arrival, and as she crept out of the alley into the light they removed their hats politely.

"If you would care to step into the sedan *Signorina* we will carry you to your destination," began one of the porters.

"And where would that be?" asked Virginia nervously.

"Unfortunately that must remain hidden, *Signorina*. You understand."

She did not, but Luca had insisted that the destination must remain secret. Nevertheless, she had hoped she might tease that intelligence from the porters – to no avail. Obviously they were part of this conspiracy. She reluctantly stepped into the sedan as one of the porters held the door open, firmly closing it behind her. She comforted herself with the fact that the sedan was liveried, the porters wearing the colors of their employer, as the two gripped tight to the handles and they all lurched off into the night.

The curtains were drawn and secured so she could not see out. She tugged at the corner of one of them and peered through the small gap, yet did not recognize the houses they were passing. They seemed to travel for an eternity, the heavy boots of the porters beating rhythmically on the empty streets, the sound echoing off the dark, shuttered houses.

Virginia was just beginning to convince herself she had been kidnapped when the rhythm slowed and the swaying was brought to a halt as the porters grounded the sedan. The door popped open and the masters of her fate helped her out onto the street. She looked around; they were in another dimly lit wide alley or rather, narrow street alongside a large *palazzo*. The building looked newer and much larger than her home; perhaps one of those massive new homes the very rich were building on large plots across the Arno, where her father was planning his new dwelling, although she did not recall crossing the river during her obscure journey. The simple fact was that she had no idea where she had been taken, except that they had not passed beyond the city walls, of that alone she was sure.

Taking her clogs, the porters indicated she should walk down a short flight of steps set into the street at a right angle to the *palazzo* and she obliged, nervously descending into the pitch-blackness of a low archway cut into the massive rusticated stone. As she reached the bottom of the steps, her eyes growing accustomed to the gloom, she made out the shiny brass studs of a small but heavy door and she tapped nervously on it with her exquisitely gloved knuckles. Surprisingly the door immediately swung inward, and a warm inviting glow spilled out into the chill spring night.

She was bundled quickly inside with the nervous air of a deep conspiracy. A servant, dressed in a black cloak that obscured the uniform of his master, and wearing a black mask across his eyes, disguising his identity, held aloft a multi-armed *chaundelabre*. He put a finger to his lips as she began to ask a question, planned as the first of many. She obliged and the servant led the way, Virginia, her cloak rustling in the silence of the night house, hurrying in his wake to remain within the safe glow of the candles as the darkness closed relentlessly behind her.

They traversed a vast cellar made of heavy vaulted stone, as gleaming eyes stared back at them from the darkness – Virginia squeaked as a cat, braver than the rest, ran across her path and disappeared once more into the gloom. They passed storage areas full of huge pottery containers, shelves stacked with all manner of goods, and workshops with tools and benches, coming finally to a wide stone staircase leading upward.

The masked servant, his candles flickering from the speed of his progress, swept up the staircase, Virginia rustling in his train, and down a long corridor, past the shapes of sleeping servants to left and right, curled on *palliasses* laid on the bare floor.

They were now in a large entrance hall that reached up two floors into the building, the dancing candlelight playing off the rich carvings and gilt artifacts, seen only in their obscurity as the two whisked past, then consigned to the darkness. Virginia recognized the inside of two massive front doors as they turned again and mounted a much larger and more ornate staircase, upward towards the *piano nobile*.

She was quite out of breath when they reached the top and turned towards the salon, yet still had to suppress a squeal of relief and excitement as she caught sight of Luca waiting at the end of the hallway with another masked servant and another *chaundelabre*.

As she approached him, Virginia made a conscious effort to appear indifferent to her bizarre journey, but her flushed cheeks and gleaming eyes betrayed her. "I hope your trip was not too disconcerting," began Luca in a conciliatory tone.

"Not at all," replied Virginia dishonestly, "although it was extremely unorthodox." This latter part was certainly true.

"We had our reasons, but we are almost there," declared Luca triumphantly as their small group progressed through the grand salon. Virginia wished she could have had longer to look at all the beautiful things, sparkling in the flames of multiple candles, displayed all about the room – a room whose extent seemed boundless, the candlelight insufficient to plumb its depths. They floated along together, the four of them, a small moving pool of warm, scintillating light throwing massive, luxurious shadows.

They reached a doorway at the far end of the salon, and passing through it they were suddenly in a completely different environment. The scale was reduced and intimate and the *chaundelabres* could easily illuminate the entire room. It was a *studiolo*, a small, private study filled with books and all manner of unusual objects stacked and piled onto shelves built into all four walls in one seamless, wooden marquetry. There was just space enough for the four of them, the two servants standing like a pair of statues at the back of the small room holding their *chaundelabres* high to illuminate the object of the evening's endeavors.

Virginia's heart was beating hard after all the excitement and exertion of being whisked across Florence in the dead of night, and then smuggled like a thief into the *palazzo* of a very rich yet painstakingly anonymous man. The whole affair had taken on a clandestine air, which made it even more thrilling, and there at the centre of the conspiracy was Luca, smiling conspiratorially.

He extended his hand, guiding Virginia's gaze. The object he indicated was a painting. It was small, for a work so filled with figures and apparently so central to the conspiracy, maybe a *braccio* in height and one and a half in width, and painted in extremely fine detail. Virginia stared at it in the warm flickering light. It looked familiar, having a classical perspective and layout, yet there was something extremely odd about the collection of figures, and she was confused as to exactly what they were doing. She looked back to Luca, bemused. He smiled again and began:

"So here we are at the invitation of the master of the house to view a painting that has remained hidden since it was painted some thirty years ago and will probably remain hidden another thirty or more, until all involved have passed on. Although it is merely an illustration of a classical painting, yet it has a deeper meaning that makes it dangerous to all those who would view it. Let us peel away the layers of meaning like an onion to reveal the true story beneath."

His eyes gleamed as he spoke and Virginia listened in rapt attention. His whole manner had changed again, as it had when he had sketched her portrait. He was no longer the foppish artist concerned only with appearances, he had become dynamic, focused – fascinating. "First, what do you see?"

"Ummm…" replied Virginia gazing at the picture, and against her will her mind fluttered, butterfly-like, back to the moment he had invited her on this nocturnal adventure. It had been shortly after the fortuneteller's ambiguous reading, and she had been in a darker mood, unusually quiet. Luca had suggested the trip to view this secret painting mainly, she surmised, to cheer her, but he had done better than that, he had made her love him.

She stared at his beautiful face, immersed. He was staring back and she realized he was still expecting a reply. "Ummm… I see it is very pretty and finely painted, the girl on the left has a beautiful figure and the other women are wearing pretty dresses."

"Indeed," agreed Luca, "the composition is appealing and the characters are well drawn and wonderfully colored. Do you see a story?"

"Well, those beautiful women are dragging that poor man across the floor. And that man on the throne has the ears of a donkey. Oh!" She had suddenly recalled a story from school, "I remember this, it is from a classical painting, but I forget the name."

"That is right, it is a classical story of calumny, an allegory of lies and treachery played out by the characters in the scene." Thereupon, to Virginia's delight, he began to tell the story in the painting, pointing to the characters one by one.

"Here is the King, Midas perhaps, with the ears of an ass bestowed upon him by the mighty Apollo himself as punishment for his lack of prudence, but worn here with pride as he sits upon his throne in mortal judgment. Huge ears indeed, the better to hear the whispering of his two advisors: Ignorance and Suspicion. They are prettily poisoning his mind against the truth. There is Envy, a shabby and wasted hermit, angrily leading this group before King Midas, reaching out his bony hand almost to the head of the King. The beautiful woman he leads forward is Slander. She carries a flaming torch as a symbol of all the lies she has spread and the destruction they have wrought. Meanwhile Treachery and Deceit, pretty girls both, are dressing her up, secure in their knowledge that beauty and fine clothes will help to sell her wicked lies to the credulous King. Slander is dragging the object of her calumny by the hair to be judged. He is dressed as was our Lord at Calvary, his feet crossed for crucifixion and his hands raised in supplication to the Heavens for a relief that will never come in this world. To the left of this group stands the solitary figure of Repentance; old and sad, and always too late, she draws her cloak around herself with crooked hands. She casts a mournful glance at Truth, naked in her honesty, needing no pretty clothes nor fawning attendants, her finger pointed to heaven to indicate whence her power comes."

Luca paused to observe the effect of his words. To hear the painting explained in such poetical terms had moved Virginia's heart and she glowed, her eyes sparkling in the candlelight. He continued: "Now let us look at the background. Do you see the statues in the niches? What does that bring to mind?"

"*Orsanmichele!*" exclaimed Virginia.

"And what are the subjects of those statues?" she leaned close to the painting and carefully examined the small details.

"Well this one is Judith and Holofernes, and this one looks like it could be David or perhaps some hero of antiquity."

"So where do you think the loggia is located?" Virginia did not wish to appear dull in front of Luca so thought intently about the question.

"Florence!" she almost shouted it.

"Yes, and that is what makes this painting subversive. It is by the master Sandro Di Botticelli and was probably the last painting he made. In it he has concealed his belief and his loyalty, along with the story of the downfall of the monk Girolamo Savonarola." Virginia could not hide her surprise and gasped slightly.

"But my Father said…"

"I know," continued Luca, "you have been told that Brother Girolamo was insane and a heretic and an evil man who threatened Florence, the Medici, the Pope and the very Mother Church herself; but your Father is wrong, he was none of those things. That malicious slander is the work of the Medici and their supporters in Florence and Rome.

"And that slander is what this image depicts – how Brother Girolamo was, like our Messiah, dragged by his enemies before the foolish and easily manipulated, and sentenced to death for a heresy that he did not commit.

"He simply wanted to do the same work that Martin Luther is doing in the north; to reform the church to be, once again, God's house on earth, not the plaything of corrupt and venal men. After the French banished the Medici from Florence he almost single-handedly recreated the Florentine Republic and brought her closer to God. Unfortunately he made the error of crossing swords with that monstrous evil, the Spaniard Borgia who was Pope during that time."

Virginia had heard the stories of the Borgia family, of their betrayals, their murders and their dissolute lifestyle that had finally claimed their own lives. "*Piagnoni* they call us because we complain and protest at the depravity we see all around us. So to avoid what could be a dangerous confrontation we conduct ourselves almost as a secret society, pledged to keep alive the memory and teachings of Brother Girolamo, yet never threatening the power of the Medici and their creatures, the *Signoria*."

As she returned home in the sedan Virginia burned with a love that rivaled the light that had just illuminated the object of that love. She determined he should be hers. She gave no thought to cost.

L'AMORE

A seed is planted, the smallest kernel of life, its essence covert in a sullen, dead shell; yet slowly, inexorably it grows. Something appears where, seemingly, there was nothing. Nourished by that cool, damp envelope of the earth and the life-giving light of the sun above, it transforms from a tiny green spiral of potential into a full-grown plant. It drives its roots deeper and wider into the alimental soil until the plant and the earth are of one piece; continuing to grow until the emptiness is now completely occupied with roots and greenery.

Such is love: adamantly and mercilessly filling the void; concerned not with the good of the host but with the imperative to life. But just as life has its measure, love's days also are numbered.

After their secret nocturnal visit Luca continued about his business. True to his word, once the portrait had been delivered, Vincenzo bestowed upon Luca the commission for the *Innocenti* Madonna, even introducing him to several new clients in the following weeks. Nevertheless, the seed had been planted and was growing within him. He found himself thinking back fondly to that night in the *studiolo*, the smell of her hair and the glow of her skin as they stood side by side in the small, candlelit room; the delicate tilt of her chin and the lively twinkling of her eyes as she looked up at him with an aspect of – what was it, admiration, favor?

It was love. Virginia already knew this – the seed was yet grown within her to a small and burgeoning plant. Indeed, her desire for the Painter was an open secret amongst her close friends, and Ginevra especially was enjoying herself planning ways for the putative lovers to be together. "You are like Abelard and Eloïse! It is so enchanting," she waxed.

"Did they not geld him and lock her away in a nunnery?" asked Virginia nervously, "I would rather this amour not end in tragedy."

"I meant in the fancy not in the outcome," Ginevra explained with an airy wave of her hand, and continued with barely a breath, "He, a man of skill and learning, urbane... erudite. She – that is you – an intelligent and beautiful young woman, the thrall of this powerful man."

"Hardly his thrall; although I am most certainly in love," she sighed, and the girls giggled at this novel and exciting turn of events.

"So are you no longer to go to Venice?" asked Theresa, still confused at the true import of the recent developments.

"Therein lies the problem," murmured Virginia as she considered the options: to stay and defy her father causing untold family convulsions and who knows what retribution, or to accede to her father's will, and leave the man she loved for a loveless marriage in a foreign city.

"A problem we must face with audacity," affirmed Ginevra with a flourish.

"That is simple in the speaking," replied Virginia, unconvinced.

Ideas were proposed and discarded; schemes made and unmade. Finally, after much discussion, it came down to one course of action with one mission, to confirm whether the Painter loved Virginia as she believed she loved him, and, as a corollary, to coalesce that love through action. The latter would, of course, depend on Virginia's powers of seduction. The scheme went as follows: Ginevra was to contact Luca and request a visit from him in order to estimate the cost of frescoing her bedchamber. Upon his arrival Virginia was already to be in the bedchamber and the two would be left alone for Virginia to test his love, Ginevra and Theresa standing guard outside to guarantee their privacy.

The plan sounded easy enough, but involved distracting Maria so she would not be there to chaperone the pair, and arranging a time when Ginevra's family and servants would not be able to confound the schedule.

In the outcome, the scheme was harder to accomplish than the girls had anticipated. To begin with, Virginia could not convince Maria to stay at home. Ginevra's house was a spacious *palazzo* near the *Ponte Vecchio*, and, as such, was but a short walk from Virginia's home, yet Maria insisted that the way could be dangerous despite the mid-afternoon hour chosen by the girls.

Finally, not wishing to draw too much attention to herself, Virginia relented and the two set off in usual fashion – Virginia leading the way and Maria scurrying to keep up. Upon their arrival, Ginevra was barely able to control her surprise at seeing Maria, which comprised various looks and hand gestures behind Maria's back.

But in an impressive performance of nimble thinking Virginia was able to send Maria back out into the city on an errand to her tailor that would be good for a few hours. The two scuttled upstairs to where Theresa was keeping watch down the street.

"He is coming, he is coming!" she cried meeting them at the top of the stairs, and they all promptly changed direction in a flounce of billowing fabric, and hurried towards the back of the house.

Ginevra's room was on the far side of the courtyard on the main floor, one floor up from the street, and the three conspirators trotted around the loggia that overlooked the courtyard. Servants and household staff watched with bemusement as they whisked past.

Ginevra's father was currently in another city on a business trip, and her mother was visiting friends, so the back of the house should have been fairly quiet. But just as they reached the door to Ginevra's room her twin brothers, Giovanni and Giuseppe, appeared from the far corner of the loggia, yelling and thrashing at each other with sticks.

"What on earth are you doing?" demanded Ginevra sternly, but in the absence of their parents her authority was limited, "I said…"

"We are playing war," yelled back one of the two, as what now seemed to be a mock sword fight continued past the three girls, catching them up in its fury as the two boys used their sister as protection from each other's blows.

"Well play it elsewhere!" bellowed Ginevra swatting at them ineffectually with her open hand.

"He is coming!" repeated Theresa superfluously.

"Who is coming?" asked Giovanni instantly intrigued. His sister shot an angry glance at Theresa.

"None of your mind," replied Ginevra gathering up the boys in her ample sleeves and pushing them on their way.

"Ginni has a gentleman caller," sneered Giuseppe, and the two burst into laughter.

"He is a painter, he is not a *gentleman caller*," Ginevra insisted.

"Oh a painter. Can we meet him?"

"Is he going to paint something now?" The two boys had suddenly stopped playing at *condottieri* and were now interested in painting.

"No, no, no!" shouted Ginevra, "now go away!"

Reluctantly the two boys reverted to their roles as swordsmen and fought their way back towards the front of the house.

"Hurry," whispered Theresa urgently.

"Why are you whispering?" asked Virginia, and Theresa looked at her blankly. Ginevra threw open the door to her room and pushed Virginia and Theresa inside.

"Get her ready," she hissed at Theresa and, skirts rustling, she rushed back to meet Luca.

He was being shown in through the front door as she arrived at the top of the stairs, and she waved at him from above with forced indifference as he whisked the soft velvet hat from his head and bowed low. "Thank you for coming at such short notice," began Ginevra, doing her best to disguise the fact that she was out of breath.

"My pleasure *Signorina*, I could not say no to a friend of *Signorina* Virginia," he replied, and started up the stairs. His progress was interrupted briefly by the warring *condottieri* as they fought their way down the stairs and around him. They stopped once they realized who he must be, and with the characteristic bluntness of children Giovanni asked, "Is this the Painter?"

"Yes, and his name is *Signor* Luca," admonished their sister. The two boys promptly stood to attention, their wooden swords held vertically in front of them, and bowed their heads stiffly.

"Good day *Signor* Luca," they said in unison. And suddenly they were gone again. A yelling, swirling mass of war, swords clattering, down the stairs they went.

"I am so sorry about my brothers' behavior," began Ginevra.

"Not at all," replied Luca, carefully readjusting the fall of his cloak, "I was a boy once."

She led the way through the house, and as they approached her room she peered discretely to left and right to make sure there was nothing untoward, but the loggia was empty and the door to her room was closed.

The next part of the girls' scheme was still rather poorly imagined. Ginevra was obliged to get Luca inside her bedroom with Virginia but without it seeming like an ambush – more like a propitious accident. She gave up on the idea of shoving him through the door and closing it swiftly behind him, and instead threw open the door and invited him through with a wave of her delicate hand.

Unfortunately, the throwing open of the door coincided with Theresa's attempt to exit the bedroom. Theresa squeaked loudly and fell backwards onto the floor in a rustling mound of yellow silk taffeta. Luca stepped back in surprise and trod on the exquisitely shod foot of Ginevra, who cursed under her breath. Luca lost his balance and he and Ginevra collapsed in a heap on a conveniently placed bench.

The clever scheme was rapidly degenerating into a farce. Through all this chaos came Virginia, stepping carefully around the prone Theresa who was flopping about on the floor like a landed fish, struggling to get up. She glided through the door just as Luca sprang, as if he had been stung, from Ginevra's lap, where he had fallen. He attempted to adjust his clothing and bow to Virginia at the same time, and she stifled a giggle at his discomfiture.

"*Signorina* Virginia," exclaimed Luca in surprise.

"My favorite painter," she exclaimed in return. "I notice you have been getting to know my friend Ginevra," she added, and Ginevra made a face.

"Indeed. In fact I am here to see her bedchamber. That is…" he paused and rephrased in order to avoid any ambiguity, "I am here to advise on the decoration of her bedchamber." He stepped across the threshold and reached a hand down to Theresa who had achieved a sitting position and was about to attempt to stand.

"Luca," Virginia spoke softly and urgently, "I would like a word." And with that the two disappeared inside the room and the door closed behind them. Winded, Theresa dropped down onto the bench beside Ginevra and sighed.

"Well that went well," she commented brightly. Ginevra glared at her. But, for better or worse the scheme had worked. It was now up to Virginia.

Il Paradosso

"What are you, a lunatic?!" Bernardo was shouting now, and he rarely raised his voice, even to his sometimes-wayward brood. "She is the daughter of one of the most powerful merchants in the city and he would happily have you banished for interfering with his daughter!"

"I would hardly call it interfering," replied Luca nervously.

"Did you not deflower this wench?"

"No, no I did nothing of the kind!" and then more thoughtfully, "and she is not a wench."

"Whatever she is or is not, did you not tell me she shut you in her bedroom and seduced you?"

"Not exactly."

"Then what did happen – exactly?"

"She expressed her undying love for me."

"And you just stood there like a rock?"

"Well no, I told her that I had a great respect for her."

"So you told her you love her too? By the Evangelist, you are a such a fool!"

"No I just said 'great respect,' I am sure of it."

"But no doubt *she* thinks you said I love you too." Bernardo arched his eyebrows in a question to which they both already knew the answer.

"He told me he loves me too!" exclaimed Virginia to her friends, both of whom sighed in unison.

"So our scheme was a success!" cried Ginevra, "But what else did he say – and do?" she added knowingly.

"He embraced me as a lover, but did not suggest anything improper," she sighed, almost disappointed.

"But do we not need him to do something improper?" asked Theresa, confused.

"It is not improper between lovers," corrected Ginevra brusquely, "but she is right, do we not need him to actually become your lover – in fact?"

"We must give him the right opportunity," declared Virginia, "a half an hour in the bedroom of another girl, with two people listening outside, hardly favored passion." She smiled a wicked smile. "We arranged to meet again soon, in the same way we did when he showed me that painting; so we will have an entire night to spend together."

"You agreed to spend the night with her?" Bernardo was quieter now, which was worse, in a way, than his shouting. "Why do you not just throw yourself from the *Campanile*?"

"Well, that would be a blasphemy," mumbled Luca trying to change the subject; a subject he wished he had not raised.

"You know what I mean. If her father discovers what you are doing he will finish you, one way or another."

"I was only planning to show her another painting like I did last time."

"Last time!" Bernardo was yelling again, "You spent the night with her?!"

"I took her to see the Calumny, that is all."

"But her father is part of the Medici government!" Bernardo was yelling louder, "If he believes you to be a *Piagnone* as well as the seducer of his daughter then he will have you put to the *strappado* at great length – then killed!"

"But my father must never know," insisted Virginia. "If he becomes aware of our scheme and Luca's love for me then he will put a stop to it. He must be presented with our love as an accomplished fact so that he has no option but to agree."

"Indeed," replied Ginevra, "you must establish your love and, if necessary, elope to Siena and be married. Once that is done your father will have no choice but to comply with your desires."

"Siena?" asked Theresa, "will we not be going to Venice with all those pretty dresses?"

The other two looked at her in astonishment.

"No of course not! For what do you think we were scheming these past days?"

✠

Later, that evening, Virginia's father was returning from the Silk Guild *palazzo* to his home when he was approached by a cloaked and hooded figure that emerged abruptly from the shadows of an alley. Vincenzo, startled, took a step back, his hand moving to the hilt of his sword. The figure, a good head shorter then he, put up a single finger for silence, and beckoned Vincenzo to follow into the alley. The whole performance was very theatrical rather than threatening, so Vincenzo determined to follow the diminutive figure into the shadows. The figure, which he was now convinced was a woman, turned and made off into the alley with a rustle of fabric and a waft of perfume, Vincenzo following.

Once in the safe darkness, the woman beckoned him closer, as if to whisper in his ear. He bent forward and listened to her furtive communication. "Married!" he exclaimed after a few seconds and the woman hissed at him for silence. She whispered for a few more seconds, but with a clang of weapons and armor a band of Militia carrying lanterns marched by the alley, and a splash of light illuminated their covert conversation. The woman squeaked in surprise and ran out of the alley, and was gone. As she departed, Vincenzo could not help but admire the flounce of yellow silk taffeta that burst momentarily from her dark wool cloak.

Il Carcere

"Wake up Luca!" The shrill sound of a woman's voice pierced Luca's dread world of appalling dreams like the point of a pike. He struggled to sit up in the large bed and shake off the mist of a monstrous sleep that still enveloped him. "What on earth is the problem Aunt Clara?" he asked wearily. It was early; the church at the end of the street was just ringing Prime.

"Bernardo sent a messenger, you must get dressed right away."

"A messenger?" he asked, confused, "Where is Bernardo?"

"He entreats for you at the *Signoria*. Quickly!" Clara was bustling around, gathering clothes for Luca to speed his progress.

"This early? What compels him to entreat for me?"

"You have been accused of some misdeed, he was not more informative than that. Now hurry!"

Luca clambered out of bed and quickly dressed, still trying to focus his mind. What misdeed had been ascribed to him, what falsehood perpetrated against him? He finished dressing and sprinted downstairs to the parlor. The house was in turmoil, children and servants scurrying hither and thither in what seemed like blind panic. Bernardo bounded in from the street, taking the stairs two at a time. "Are you ready to leave? We must leave soon!" he exclaimed immediately without removing his cloak. He was panting. He had apparently run all the way from the *Signoria*.

"Leave? What do you mean?"

"The Eight have issued a warrant for your arrest."

"On what grounds?" asked Luca, shocked.

"Your credit has been withdrawn, you are a debtor."

"That is impossible. I am owed much more than I owe."

"Yes but your creditors want money and those in debt to you will not pay."

"But how can this happen?" Luca was right to be surprised, the Florentine economy ran almost exclusively on credit, one debt being used to pay off another. He had never heard of credit being arbitrarily withdrawn.

"Somebody very powerful – and I think we can imagine who that must be – has set wheels in motion to deny you the very stuff of life: the credit you need to exist in Florence."

"Who do you mean?" asked Luca, still foggy from sleep.

"Vincenzo Cavalcanti of course! He is understandably incensed that you despoiled his virgin daughter, and now seeks revenge!"

The household froze in mid scurry, children and servants staring at Luca with wide-eyed surprise. "I did not despoil, deflower or in any way sully *Signorina* Cavalcanti," exclaimed Luca to the room. The room looked back aghast and he felt the need for reinforcement. "Honestly!" he added. "Tell them Bernardo," he finished, almost desperate.

"No, he says he did nothing and I believe him. But the truth of your relationship with the girl is moot. It is hard to argue your case from prison."

"Prison!" it was Luca's turn to be aghast. "How can they lock me in prison? How can I pay my debts if I cannot work."

"Luca, you still do not comprehend. It is not about justice it is about revenge. Nobody cares about your half dozen florins of debt. Vincenzo Cavalcanti wants you to suffer and to be kept away from his daughter. He has, no doubt, secretly guaranteed your debts. You could be in prison until the next amnesty. Six months maybe, a year perhaps – even longer."

"We have to leave now!" exclaimed Luca, finally grasping the deep troubles that had befallen him.

"I warned him," sighed Bernardo as Luca ran back upstairs to gather a few valuables with which to make his escape.

Escape was not to be Luca's fate however. He ran from the house just as the Militia rounded the end of the street, and with a shout they were off, the hunters and the hunted – hounds and hare. Dodging in and out of a street-full of people and animals, hurdling a carefully laid out stall of vegetables, and bouncing nimbly off the side of a wagon, Luca was making ground on his pursuers, as the onlookers shouted their encouragement and made bets on the outcome of the chase.

Luca's intimate knowledge of the lanes and alleys of the neighborhood gave him an advantage over the Militia as he jumped, rolled and sprinted through the early morning bustle. But, just as Luca thought he had beaten his pursuers, a handcart carrying bundles of hay tipped over directly in front of him, sending the bundles breaking and spilling across the street. He tried his utmost to dodge but was almost immediately engulfed, and in seconds they were upon him. He sat in a pile of hay, multiple swords already drawn and pointed at his throat. There was nothing for it but to be led meekly away, his hands in chains.

They brought him first to the *Podestá*, a formidable building that gave the appearance of an ancient fortress dropped into the midst of modern Florence, and served as the center for security within the city. As should be expected of an ancient fortress it was cold and damp, and Luca enjoyed a miserable morning sitting in a cold, damp stone cell contemplating his fate and what he might have done to avoid it.

That afternoon he was brought to the *Palazzo della Signoria* – the heart of government and the location of the courts. His guards dragged him from a dank holding cell in the basement through seemingly endless stone corridors until he emerged into a magnificently frescoed courtroom, where, behind a long judge's bench, sat the Eight. They were eight stern men in hooded robes charged with the preservation of order in the Republic. After the reading of the charges – a long-winded version of what Bernardo had told him – and after taking into account the petitions on his behalf, they summarily condemned him to prison until his case could be argued at some point in the future. Luca, confused and scared and wishing he had eaten breakfast, was taken to prison.

LE STINCHE

The prison guards brought Luca from the *Signoria* back to the *Podestá* for a few minutes to complete some paperwork, and then off to prison. The three buildings are within a few minutes of each other, but the way passed through the most populous area of Florence. The shame of being dragged through the streets in chains was mortifying to Luca, even though the guards were fairly nonchalant about their task and chatted amiably with him. He was able to hide his manacled hands in his cloak, and endeavored to look as if were out for a stroll, but still the shame beat down on him, hot as the afternoon sun.

The prison of *Le Stinche* was an ancient building like the *Podestá* but the differences between them far outweighed their similarities. The *Podestá* was a dramatic crenellated and decorated fortress; *Le Stinche*, to the contrary, was composed simply of four blank walls reaching twenty to thirty *braccia* in height.

The effect was sobering. As you approached, it was as if you were leaving the warm and inviting world of Florence – a world of windows and doorways and balconies – and entering a dark, forbidding tower. *Isola delle Stinche*. Luca, approaching from the west, had plenty of time to appreciate the seeming featurelessness of the gloomy walls as his captors led him around the building to the entrance. They passed a small tabernacle let into the corner of the building where the pious could leave offerings to the Almighty on behalf of the unfortunate inmates, and turned to follow *via Ghibellina* along a second featureless wall.

At last a feature presented itself. Set into this long north wall was an entrance, but an entrance like none he had seen. It was wide enough for three to pass, but so low that everyone who passed through it was forced to bend, as if in supplication to the power of justice.

Justice was very much in Luca's mind as they led him to this horrible building, or rather, injustice; the injustice of incarcerating someone for a perceived slight that had not even occurred; the injustice of a wealthy and powerful man abusing his position to lock up an innocent; the injustice of putting away a hardworking Florentine into a world of enforced inactivity. His mind wandered down such tortuous alleyways as the three walked beside the oppressive walls of *Le Stinche*.

"Don't worry son," reassured one of his guards, "you're going to love it here. It's like a home away from home." Presumably he had read the horror on Luca's face, or perhaps he spoke the same words to every new inmate out of the goodness of his heart, to cheer the gloomy and the persecuted.

The three passed, stooping, through the portal and continued up a set of stone steps, the treads worn low by hundreds of years of passage. The place smelled of old, damp stone, and hopelessness. At the top of the steps was a small room, and the guards sat Luca down on a narrow bench as the door to the street slammed shut with the sound of bolts being driven home. The room was fairly dark, the only light coming from another smaller room for the guards, and a tiny window set high in the wall. Slowly he began to make out his surroundings; a dirty rug on the floor and a Madonna hanging on the wall. They were stone walls like the rest of the place, dressed and fitted by ancient hands. Strangely enough, Luca could appreciate the history and architecture, dismal as it was, through his interest in the story of Florence. He just wished he could be there visiting rather then as an inmate.

One of the guards beckoned to Luca and brought him out of his melancholy for a moment. Luca walked to an archway in the wall between the two rooms, divided by a wooden plank set up as a counter. The guard on his side of the counter asked questions and Luca, on his, answered them.

"Name?"

"Do you not know my name?"

"Name?" repeated the guard, with one eyebrow arched.

"Luca Painter of Florence."

"You are here as a debtor. Your accuser has provided for your basic care. Do you wish to pay more for better accommodations?"

"I have no money to pay," muttered Luca sadly.

"Vagabond," spoke the guard aloud as he wrote.

"No, no, I am a painter. I have possessions, just no money right now."

"We will leave that section blank then. If you decide to improve your accommodations you may do so with a payment of five soldi."

And that was that. Luca was led through the door at the far end of the room into the prison proper.

The first thing that struck him was the smell. It was similar to the everyday smells of the street but concentrated and intense. The tangy, sharp smells of urine and sweat, and the deep, warm, fetid odor of feces were the overwhelming notes. He stood a moment, allowing his nose to become accustomed to the stench; then he was propelled forward by a firm yet friendly shove along with a comment from the smiling guard, "You get used to the stink."

Luca walked out from under a stairway that led to an upper level into a roomy, straw-covered courtyard, open to the sky. Despite being open, the height of the walls was so great that nothing of the surrounding city could be seen. The effect was of standing, trapped, at the bottom of a well, with only the heavens above visible, and no hope of being rescued.

As he walked into the courtyard he heard a noise, something like a whooping or cheering. "Your fellow prisoners are greeting you," claimed the guard as Luca saw faces crowding at the bars of the several rooms that let off the courtyard. He noticed a woman's face and shape at one of the doors and asked the guard, "There are women here too?"

"Oh yes, but they have their own cell over there." The guard indicated the room on the far side of the courtyard where Luca had seen the female face. "But most of them will do a little business on the side." He flashed a gap-toothed smile. "So let me know if you need anything, we'll take care of you," he said with a wink. It took Luca a moment to gather exactly what the guard was implying, then he mumbled a confused thank you. "Don't worry, plenty of time for that kind of thing." The guard winked again.

He led Luca towards a cell to their right and opened the heavily barred door with a large key. The inmates at the doorway stepped back deferentially, and the guard invited Luca to enter. As he stepped inside the stench grew worse. Luca could swear it was burning the hairs of his nose. "You'll get used to that," a voice came from the gloom. Presumably Luca had betrayed his horror at the hideous smell.

He walked into the center of the room and looked around. The entrance through which he had passed opened to the courtyard and was blocked with floor to ceiling bars, a doorway in the center. The room ran about twenty *braccia* in length to the end wall where one small window looked out onto a blank interior wall, and struggled to illuminate the scene. The cell was about ten *braccia* across, and wide beds, or more exactly sleeping benches, ran down both sides, their heads to the wall. Under the window he could see the worn wooden seats of a communal latrine – the source of the smell no doubt.

There were several figures milling about in the gloom and others laying in their beds despite the hour, two to a bed. The walls, unadorned except for a solitary crucifix, were stone, long ago painted with streaked and dirty lime wash. The floor was formed of plain stone flags. He imagined it must be freezing cold in the winter and unbearably hot in the summer.

"My you're a handsome one," exclaimed one of the inmates, approaching Luca.

"*Signore?*" asked Luca.

"Welcome to *Le Stinche*, do not concern yourself with the smell," continued the inmate, "my name is Daniele Bongiorno." He bowed low. "It is always a good day when I am around," he smiled, referring to his welcoming surname, and a cackle of sarcastic laughter burst out from the room. "Even in this den of lions," continued Daniele, which was accompanied by further and louder jeers and boos. "And your name is?"

"Luca."

"Luca, pleased to meet you *Signore*. You are very well dressed, may I ask what is your business when you are not gracing us, humble prisoners all, with your presence, that is?"

"I am a painter – Luca the Painter of Florence."

"Perfect!" exclaimed Daniele, "You can elevate the tone by frescoing these walls." He indicated the dirty lime wash, scratched, as Luca now noticed, with many crude drawings. "Perhaps a cycle of the life of Christ," continued Daniele, warming to his theme, "or perhaps a scene of a famous battle to inspire us in our mutual love of Florence." Sarcastic cheers echoed around the room.

"Then I will send for my colors immediately and we can all work together to improve the appearance of this dormitory," declared Luca, joining in the collective irony.

"Bravo!" exclaimed Daniele, "your spirits will return sooner than you think. This is not such a bad place once you get used to the heinous smell – truly an abomination. Let me show you around your new accommodations." He led the way as Luca obediently followed, indicating and calling out points of interest as they went. "That is the latrine. Use it quickly and early and close the lid immediately afterwards," he admonished. "The newer visitors get to sleep next to the latrine and slowly earn a bed closer to the door. But I have a space next to me which I offer to you, as one gentleman to another."

"That is very kind," gasped Luca, still not reconciled to the reek.

"These are your cellmates." He waved at the haphazard group of about fifteen men scattered around the room. "We only have one murderer at the moment, and he merely murdered his wife, so he is not to be considered a violent fellow." A man in the back of the group waved his hand. "Tell me Luca, are you a married man?"

"No *Signore*, but I am, perforce, here in your company because of a woman," sighed Luca.

"Well know that, although painful, your troubles are only temporary, not having taken this woman as your wife. On the other hand, those of us married men must deal with all the troubles women inflict upon us 'til called by our Maker. All that is save the Prince who makes his own world."

After a brief pause Daniele continued, "As you can see your neighbors are a motley group of thieves, debtors and ruffians. The truly bad men are kept upstairs and we have little contact with them." Luca was relieved. "Finally, we have three meals a day, a barber once a week, a bath once a month, and can spend two hours a day in the courtyard, during which time we may pursue the salvation of our immortal souls in the chapel – a poor thing, but charming in its humility."

Luca, still numb from the morning's proceedings, was slowly absorbing all this new and foreign information. He cast a glance at his interlocutor. Daniele was a handsome man of about fifty years with a wild and unruly shock of silver hair. His clothing, although crumpled and a little greasy, was not inexpensive, but looked as if it had spent a lot of time in prison with its owner. "*Signore*, how long have you been incarcerated?" asked Luca trying to assess the length of his own incarceration by approximation.

"Call me Dani. But to your question, I have been here these twelve years."

"Twelve years!" Luca's voice rose an octave as he imagined being locked away for more than a decade.

"Luca, my friend," Daniele presumed, "I love this place – once you get used to the hideous odor of course. I am a poet, for my sins, and as such I need to have the time and concentration to write. Living here takes away all the distractions of the dreary quotidian so I may devote myself to my writing. My wife, Gemma, my own precious jewel, brings me writing supplies and carries away my finished poems to sell. For a few soldi I may have a night alone with my wife, but I am not forced to live with her. I can live here instead, amongst this collection of intellectual giants." He waved expansively to jeers and yells. "It is a success on all fronts!" he exclaimed with finality.

Luca shook his head. It was his determination to escape these walls as soon as possible, one way or another, Daniele's impassioned speech extolling the virtues of prison life notwithstanding.

As night fell the prisoners finished their meal, which consisted of some kind of meat, boiled in a thick broth, served from a large cooking pot into individual bowls, along with plenty of bread to mop up the remains. This hearty and nourishing food was brought to the prison by a group of local friars who were charged to do so by the prison management, so it was clear that Luca was not destined to starve. The prisoners prepared for bed by the light of a single candle and Luca settled down to sleep next to Daniele whose bed, as promised, was next to the bars, furthest from the latrine. Luca was exhausted. The stress of the day's events and his pitiful position had taken their toll and he soon fell into a deep sleep despite the periodic rustle of insects and vermin, and the snoring of his neighbors.

Sometime during the night Luca was awoken by an unusual feeling below his waist. In his dull and sleepy state it took him a few moments to realize what was happening. A hand, not his own, was fondling his nethers. With a shout of anger Luca leapt from the bed, stubbing his toe on the bedpost. "What unnatural thing are you proposing *Signore*?" he asked redundantly, hopping on one foot as he massaged the other.

"I am sorry Luca, I thought I was touching my own member, not yours, please pardon me," assured Daniele. "Although," he added, "your body does not appear to have repudiated my attentions," indicating the bulge beneath Luca's white shirt that glowed in the dim light from the courtyard.

"Keep your hands to yourself *Signore!*" said Luca firmly and slipped back into bed, his pillow placed between himself and the wandering hands of Daniele. The inmates could be heard laughing gently in the background. Luca was sure he had heard that excuse before, but could not place it.

That was the dramatic end of Luca's first day in prison. The next day he moved his sleeping arrangements to a free space closer to the latrine. The stench was preferable to the unnatural attentions of Dani, although the latter continued to deny any such thing had occurred, and he and Luca remained friendly, as needs must when two are confined so close.

La Grazia

Luca's first and startling experience of the seamed side of life within *Le Stinche* inured him to any potential future offenses by his cellmates, and he settled down to an uneasy but livable existence.

He slept a lot for the first day or two, a malaise of the spirit having settled upon him that rendered him almost immobile. On the third day Bernardo appeared with both good and bad news. The good news was that Luca's belongings had not been seized and that Bernardo had been successful in gathering funds by pawning and selling many of Luca's valuables. "We will soon have you out of here and you can make your peace with *Messer* Vincenzo," assured Bernardo confidently. The bad news was that Bernardo had not been able to achieve an audience with Vincenzo with a view to interceding on Luca's behalf. In fact he had been rebuffed at every turn. Bernardo hugged his ward and departed, leaving Luca to return to his bed and sulk.

The next day Luca was summoned to the office of the *Soprastante*, the Superintendent of the prison, a person Luca had never met but whom the inmates referred to as *Il Grasso* due to his impressive bulk. *Il Grasso* was standing behind his desk when Luca was shown in, and looked surprisingly deferential for a man who held the power of incarceration, if not actually life and death, over Luca. The reason for his attitude was soon apparent. From behind the door stepped a familiar figure, resplendently subdued in a crimson *lucco*.

"*Signor* Cavalcanti would like to speak with you privately," explained *Il Grasso*, before excusing himself, and sliding slowly but gracefully from behind his desk and out the door, which closed behind him. While the *Soprastante* was making his lengthy exit Vincenzo did not look at Luca, rather fixing his eyes on a small and poorly painted Madonna on the wall over Luca's head.

"So," began Vincenzo, "I am sorry it has come to this. When first we met I thought you an impressive young man; an opinion reinforced by your painting of my daughter's portrait."

"Thank you *Signore*," said Luca. Vincenzo held up his hand for silence. He had obviously rehearsed this speech in his mind and did not want to be interrupted in the midst of his thoughts.

"But your becoming the object of my daughter's affections was not a consummation I had anticipated. In the normal course of events you would not be completely unwelcome as a suitor, however, in this instance I have particular plans for Virginia that do not include you. So here we are. You are incarcerated in this rather unpleasant place and I hold the key."

"I did not deflower your daughter!" blurted Luca at the thought of release.

"I understand Painter, I have spoken with my daughter. I am neither an evil nor an unreasonable man.

"You know," continued Vincenzo after a moment, veering off at a tangent in his usual fashion, "it is all rather ironic. A relative of mine was incarcerated in this very prison a hundred years ago. The irony goes further than that; he was incarcerated because he was anti-Medici. Funny, no? Yes, I am aware you are a member of the *Piagnoni*, but I am not punishing you for your anti-Medici views. Far from it – I understand. As a distant member of an old patrician family I realize how you might consider the Medici poisonous to the Republic. You may well be proven right. I am not looking forward to the next few years with much hope in that direction.

"But back to the problem at hand," declared Vincenzo, his historical reverie at an abrupt end. Luca was relieved the old man had swerved back to the topic of his freedom and began listening again. "Do you love my daughter?"

"*Signore*, I have nothing but the utmost respect for your daughter and she is a beautiful..." Luca trailed off as Vincenzo held up his hand again.

"Answer the question. Do you love her?"

Luca considered the question for a moment or two. He realized, of course, that upon his answer rested any chance he might have at freedom. This was not an answer to be rushed and he was still unsure which answer was the correct one from Vincenzo's viewpoint. He took a chance. "No *Signore*, I do not. My attentions were as those of a brother, who might help his younger sister with her education, especially in areas where she had shown an interest." He held his breath.

"Perfect," said Vincenzo, and Luca breathed again, "that is the problem of *you* solved. You will not be a rival for the hand of my daughter."

"No *Signore*," said a relieved Luca.

"But," Vincenzo had not finished, "that does not solve the problem of my daughter."

"*Signore?*"

"She is determined to have you, do you not see? As long as you are in Florence she will pursue you, and at the very least will do her utmost to block my plans for her marriage to the Venetian. If I send her to Venice she will be nothing but trouble, both to me and to her husband. No, this cannot stand, it is not acceptable." Vincenzo was thinking. "You must be gone, removed, departed from her heart."

"But not in here?" Luca was almost desperate now.

"No not here, she would visit you and pine over you, and ultimately you will be released. No, she would just wait for you. You must repudiate her; throw her over and disavow your love and leave the city. Preferably in the opposite direction to Venice.

"So I have a proposition." Luca held his breath once more, as Vincenzo outlined his idea, "You will leave today. Slip out of the *Porta Romana* this very night and ride directly to Siena. There you will travel with the Post to Rome. I will give you letters of introduction to several Cardinals I know and you will establish yourself as a painter in Rome. There is much work to be done there and you will be a glorious part of it. The painters of Florence are much in demand." Luca breathed a sigh of relief, but Vincenzo had not finished. "Or you could remain here, in prison, for as long as my money and influence last and I will simply tell Virginia that you have gone to Rome. It is your decision."

"But *Signore*, is the Emperor's army not headed Romewards?"

"As I said Luca you may remain here in prison – in *Le Stinche*."

"I will go!"

And that was the end of the negotiation.

Luca wrote a letter at Vincenzo's direction informing Virginia that he did not love her. He was provided with a horse and a heavily armed four-man bodyguard, partly to protect him during his journey and partly to enforce the terms of the agreement. He bid goodbye to Bernardo and his family after explaining what had happened. There was much crying and hugging on both sides. He loaded up his saddlebags with valuables and the money Bernardo had been able to raise, and, armed with a long sword and a short dagger, rode with his company south across the Arno.

Through the quiet streets they rode, past dark houses, blank convent walls and neatly pruned orchards to the *Porta Romana*. The gate was locked for the night and guarded, but the power of Vincenzo Cavalcanti preceded them and they were allowed to pass unmolested. Luca looked back as they rode south through the dark countryside. His last view of the city of his birth was its familiar jagged shape lit by the full moon, silhouetted against the starry night sky.

IL VIAGGIO

The five men travelled through the night as fast as was safe for the horses, past quiet villages and olive groves, stopping for a couple of hours rest at Poggibonsi in the early morning before pressing on to Siena. The bodyguard acted as one man and, despite Luca's occasional efforts to engage them in conversation, did not speak except for the most basic of communication, presumably on the orders of *Messer* Vincenzo. Upon arrival at Siena they brought Luca to an inn where all five took one room. They had food brought up and did not leave the room for the rest of the day and night, one member of the bodyguard staying awake at all times, by turn, to guard Luca, to whom it seemed the walls of his prison had extended all the way to Siena.

The city of Siena is constructed on top of a hill and the streets descend the hill to the central *piazza* where most outdoor activity takes place. Early the next morning Luca was conveyed to this *piazza*, which he noticed, as they traversed it leading their horses, resembled nothing more than half a giant brick pie divided into slices. He was in the process of trying to count the number of slices when he was brought out of his contemplation by his silent brotherhood of a bodyguard. They had stopped in front of the *Palazzo Publico*, the Sienese equivalent of the Florentine *Signoria*, a dramatic crenellated brick building with a huge clock tower. As he looked around the *piazza*, Luca observed that the Sienese seemed very proud of their bricks, and unlike the Florentines took every opportunity to display them, to great effect.

He realized why they had stopped, as parked before the *Palazzo* was a covered wagon bearing the Papal arms boldly on its side. Four horses caparisoned with the Papal colors – steaming in the cool morning darkness – were in the process of being hitched to the wagon. This was the Post.

Collected around the Post wagon, which was being loaded with sacks and boxes carried from the *Palazzo*, was a small group of travellers prepared for the journey to Rome. The majority of the ten or so people were pilgrims – a group of friars on mules, their tonsures gleaming in the faint rays of the early morning sun as it broke the horizon, and two nuns riding crosswise on their palfreys, such that they needed a servant to lead them, being unable to control their mounts from that unusual position. Along with the pilgrims were two merchants leading additional horses piled with merchandise. To this varied group Luca added his presence, his bodyguard still watching him carefully, while they awaited the Post's departure.

After a few minutes the horses were hitched to the wagon and the guards rode up in formation. They were a spectacular group of men, six in number, dressed in the colors of the Pope. Swiss mercenaries they were, to whom the Pope had seen fit to trust his body and his possessions these last twenty years, rather than his native Italians – perhaps from fear of plot or betrayal since the mortal horror of the Borgias. The guards were armed variously with crossbow and arquebus in addition to their swords, and the two leading horsemen carried long pikes bearing standards, vertically attached to their saddles. They must be travelling through some dangerous country, and Luca drew comfort at the sight of these particolored mercenaries.

The bells of the clock tower struck Prime, accompanied by all the churches and bell towers of Siena, and off rumbled the Post with its convoy in train. Luca joined the end and waved a relieved farewell to his personal bodyguard, who stood motionless in the *piazza* watching his departure.

The group wound their way through the streets of the town,

the pealing of a hundred bells echoing off the brick, townsfolk watching from their doorways as they would a parade, and children and dogs running happily alongside them as they began the long journey to Rome.

After a day's ride through fields of mulberry trees that made Luca think back fondly to his time with Virginia, they spent the night in the village of Buonconvento whose entire existence seemed to be predicated on the traffic of pilgrims and merchants to Rome. The night in the inn passed uneventfully except that the merchant with whom Luca shared a bed snored loudly enough to wake him up at regular intervals. Thus a tired and aching Luca took the saddle again at daybreak for the ride to their next port of call, Radicofani.

The country had grown barren and rocky with barely a tree to be seen on the hills as the convoy climbed slowly and tortuously upward. As they approached their destination the road became steeper and rockier, the Post wagon bouncing over the stony roadway and the horses picking their way carefully. They rounded a rocky outcrop and the castle of Radicofani appeared before them, glowering in the distance. It was a magnificent if terrifying sight. The ancient fortress was built at the peak of a barren conical mountain and dominated the road for half a day in either direction. The garrison was heavily manned to protect the route to the Tuscan *contado* from the south and as a visible symbol of Tuscan power to all who might behold it.

The convoy stayed at an inn among the small collection of houses at the foot of the castle rock whose gloomy eminence dominated the town from all angles. This time Luca slept in the stable with his horse, preferring an undisturbed night in the warm straw to tossing and turning with the snoring merchant. He had attempted to strike up conversations with several members of his party but most had terminated in shrugs and blank looks. He had prayed with the friars on occasion, but otherwise he travelled alone.

Next day they began the long twisting route down the mountain, and a wilder or more barren place could not be imagined. It would have been a perfect place for thieves and brigands except for the lack of any cover for their approach, so empty of human occupation was it. Indeed, wild and inhospitable was the country such that it could be mistaken for the mouth of hell itself, sulphurous, desolate and bleak; like a scene from antiquity destroyed by the fire of the gods. The way was tough going for the horses as they strove to hold back on the long descent, the teamsters pulling hard on the brakes to keep the wagon from running away. The mules, however, had no problems stepping nimbly between the stones, and conveyed their charges with more safety than style. Slowly the road evened out as they approached the custom post at Ponte Centino, the point at which they would officially quit Florentine territory for Rome.

Along the route they had occasionally passed travellers moving in the opposite direction but their numbers had increased as the convoy approached the border. They were frequently assailed with shouts of, "Turn back!" from what were seemingly fugitives leaving Rome. Luca rode ahead to the guard at the front of the group and asked him why they were being warned to retreat.

"The Emperor sends his army against us and these weaklings are running before the city gates are closed to them," was the soldier's stern reply, rendered more so by his German accent.

"Is there a chance the Emperor will overrun Rome?" asked Luca nervously.

"None at all. Rome is well defended and well provisioned. The Emperor's army is a group of half-starved ruffians." Luca was cheered a little, although his trip was mandatory, war or no war.

They arrived at the border station at Ponte Centino amidst a scene of chaos. A long line of travellers in wagons and carts, on horses, mules and on foot were waiting to pass to the Tuscan side of the border, all intent on fleeing the war, and the Florentine officials, try as they might, could not keep up with the throng. People were shouting and crying; so much so that Luca momentarily rethought his decision to head to Rome. It was only the mental image of *Le Stinche* that kept him from turning on his heel and riding directly back to the safety of Florence.

The passage to the Roman side of the border for the several members of the convoy was fairly simple, albeit expensive. In order to pass one had to submit to a search and multiple questions from a uniformed customs official. At length it was Luca's turn.

"What's in there?" asked the official gruffly, poking Luca's bulging saddlebags with a stick. Luca had seen him make frequent use the stick in lieu of bothering to open the luggage of other members of his party.

"My clothes and personal belongings," answered Luca.

"That doesn't feel much like clothes," observed the official as his stick struck something hard.

"I have some small paintings."

"Show me your hands." Luca held out his hands. "You are a painter," declared the official knowledgeably, as if he had unmasked a master criminal, "let me see them."

Luca had brought three small paintings as examples of his work to show in Rome. "Pretty," admired the official, "you know there is a tax on paintings being imported into Rome from Florence?"

"No *Signore*, but I need these to show off my skill, not to sell."

"There are plenty of painters already in Rome," insisted the official unpleasantly, "I should really confiscate these on the spot."

"*Signore....*" Luca was about to remonstrate for the return of his paintings when the official made him an offer.

"I will confiscate this one and let you pass with the others, since I like your face and you look like an honest man."

Luca found himself in the aggravating position of thanking the customs official for taking his property in return for permitting him to continue his journey. He grudgingly relinquished the painting and repacked his bags, silently furious. As the convoy continued on its way one of the merchants could be heard muttering: "They let the thieves out of prison and give them a uniform and put them on the border to pillage honest travellers..." Luca nodded his agreement as they crossed a wide bridge over a rushing stream into Roman territory, past the long line of fugitives patiently waiting for their chance to cross into Tuscany. It was not an auspicious arrival.

The line of fugitives was strung out along the road half way to Acquapendente, a sad collection of folk with all the goods they could carry on their backs or in their carts. Luca was beginning to worry again about the shrewdness of his trip to Rome during such turbulent times; a worry that was shared by several of his companions. However, their attention was directed back to the exigencies of the journey by their repeated partial fording of the *Paglia,* as the road was frequently inundated and hard to follow. The going was slow and muddy as their mounts picked their way carefully through the rocks and swirling waters at the edge of the swift flow, swollen by the heavy spring rains.

The *Paglia* was a bourn that would not make up its mind between river and stream, and could be treacherous in its indecision. The travellers drew rein at the last and longest ford that would take them clear across the river, and put them again on the dry road to Rome. They gazed across the river at the opposite bank. The muddy water was in full spring flood and the crossing was not to be easy. The commander of the guard stood up in his stirrups and addressed the group: "This crossing will be taxing. We will do our best to help you, but if you have no stomach for it you should return to Ponte Centino. The water will be considerably lower in a few days."

The travellers murmured amongst themselves, debating the wisdom of the crossing, and one of the merchants promptly turned his horses and trotted back down the trail cursing under his breath. The rest, either from religious conviction or pressing need, steeled themselves for the crossing.

The wagon led the way, paying out a rope secured on the near bank to a suitably sized tree. The weight of the wagon and the strength of the horses grimly resisted the muddy surge of the flooded river as it spurted between the spokes of the wheels and splashed up onto the canvas cover. Once or twice one of the horses would miss its footing, eliciting gasps from the onlookers, but each time the horse would recover and continue to drag the heavy vehicle onward until it gained the safety of the farther bank. Once ashore the teamster tightly secured his end of the rope to a tree on that side, leaving a taught line as a guide to those who would follow.

A prayer was said, led by the monks, and the crossing began. Four of the Swiss Guards went first, demonstrating how to use the rope to stay on course and not allow their mounts to stray from the middle of the ford despite the downstream pressure. As good fortune would have it the ford was wide and fast, but not terribly deep at the center of the way, so even those mounted on mules were yet able to cross without being overwhelmed – wet but safe. The two nuns had sent their servants on before them in the wagon and tethered their palfreys to the mount of the Swiss Guard who preceded them, in order to make the crossing. Luca brought up the rear, riding behind one of the nuns who lifted her feet from the footrest of her sidesaddle in an effort to keep them dry.

The crossing proceeded, slowly. Luca could feel his horse struggling to find a foothold in the gravel with each step, as he gripped tight to the rope with one hand and held the reins in the other. He pushed his feet forward in the stirrups and lay back, gripping the saddle tightly between his thighs in an effort not to be unseated. The nun ahead of him was having similar problems, but due to the crosswise nature of her saddle, every time the horse stumbled she swayed back and forth precariously. Luca began to have concern for her safety. She was not very old, barely more than a novitiate and this was probably to be her first pilgrimage. Her skill on horseback demonstrated equal inexperience as she rocked in her saddle, clutching desperately at the tethered line. Her flawlessly beautiful face was marred with fear, framed tightly in black and white.

Luca was about mid-way into the crossing when the inevitable happened. The nun swayed backward a little too far as her horse stumbled slightly and she was left suspended from the rope, her feet dangling into the rushing waters below. The rope passed under her armpits and she swung back and forth screaming in mortal dread, doing her utmost to keep her head above the rope. The horse, tethered to the next in line, stumbled onward leaving its rider floating over the torrent, the waters dragging at her feet.

There were only a few seconds to spare before the rushing water would pluck her from the line, weighed down by her sodden habit, and carry her downstream, whelmed by the flood to end up who knew where. Luca urged his mount forward, and leaning as low as he dare, plucked the flailing girl from her fate just as her grip gave way. With one massive effort he righted himself and draped the dripping, screaming nun across the pommel of his saddle.

The soldiers lit a fire on the Romeward side of the river to aid in the drying of the travellers and their clothing, and they camped there for an hour or two. Once she was recovered in spirit and in dress, the young nun led Luca aside. "My name is Emma. Thanks to you *Signore* for your rescue. I was surely dead without your timely intervention," she said.

"Sister Emma, I can claim no credit for what any man would do. I can only thank God that I was there when you needed me. And you should address me as Luca."

"When I took Holy Orders I foreswore all earthly things. But Luca, I am from a wealthy family and there was one thing from my secular life that I simply could not give up." She produced a small gold object hanging on a gold chain – a walnut in fact, covered in flawless gold leaf – in the palm of her hand. "It was a gift from my Mother at the time of my first Blessed Sacrament. She died not long after."

"I am sorry to hear that Sister."

"No Luca, you do not understand. For sentimental reasons alone did I not give this up as I had promised I would; and I faced death by water. You were there to save me, by the Grace of God. You should have this."

Before Luca could refuse, Emma opened a hidden clasp on the walnut shell and separated the two halves. Within were two miniature scenes linked together by a hinge. In the lower half were depicted Adam and Eve in the Garden of Eden, each tiny figure and all the foliage perfectly carved, painted and gilded, and arranged within the hollow of the shell as if it were a diminutive stage with its tiny actors and scenery. In the top half the serpent slithered, wrapped around a tree, awaiting his opportunity. "Sister, I could not take this," protested Luca, but Emma held up her hand.

"This is the perfection of Eden at that moment before the Devil worked his evil. Take it and let it be a token of that perfect love."

With that she pressed the small shell into his hand and smiled a sad, beautiful, forlorn smile. The renouncing of this world and her place in it was accomplished. Luca held the last remnant of Emma's temporality in his hand as she gave herself, at last, to God.

✠

In the aftermath of their harrowing river crossing there was muttering anew amongst the travellers about the future of Rome and the wisdom of a trip there across such dangerous country. This muttering continued all the way to the waterfalls outside Acquapendente, but the delightful vision of the sparkling waters through the trees in the late afternoon sun cheered the group, and Luca even made sketches as they rode slowly by.

It was raining the morning they left Bolsena. After descending from the hills to the marshy, aguish town of San Lorenzo, they had ridden a quarter of the way around the circular lake, myriad tiny flying creatures determined to make a meal of them all the way. Eating and sleeping at Bolsena they had begun their journey again early.

The convoy rode silently through the grey, rainy countryside, wrapped in dripping wet cloaks in an attempt to stay dry against the relentless storm; the Nuns' servants making slow going as they trudged through the thickening mud.

The rain was finally mitigated as they entered a huge and ancient forest. It was, though, as if they had been relieved of one problem only to acquire another. The forest was dark and full of mystery; those of a superstitious nature could imagine it the habitat of all sorts of fabulous creatures. The moss encrusted trees were massive and towered high above the road, forming an unbroken green canopy which only permitted the most infrequent splash of light from the steely sky above. The soldiers seemed uncomfortable. They did not travel at night for this very reason, the way was dark and provided too many places of concealment for brigands and thieves.

The travellers pulled tighter together in the green half-light, following close in the wake of the mail wagon as the two soldiers at the rear dropped back. Two of the guards rode ahead so they were almost out of sight and would periodically ride into the forest only to appear a few moments later making signals back to their compatriots. Luca's hand rested on his sword as they continued through the obscure and interminable dripping vegetation.

It was inescapable, but when it came it still startled and frightened the travellers. A shot rang out; an arquebus fired by one of the rear guard as, with a blood-curdling yell, a throng of figures ran from the shadows of the misty forest and descended on the convoy.

Their tactics were well practiced as they quickly blocked both advance and retreat, so there was no hope in galloping away. There was a brief exchange of crossbow and arquebus fire and then it was to be hand-to-hand. The nuns fell from their horses and crawled under the wagon as the men prepared to fight. The two Swiss Guards riding way out front cantered back to the fray their swords swinging in glistening arcs in the half darkness as they smashed into the gang of attackers, slashing and cutting about them until they were dragged from their horses and butchered.

The remaining soldiers, the teamsters and the travellers gathered around the wagon as the attackers formed a ring about them. The manner of their attack had slowed now that they had their prey surrounded, and Luca, his sword extended before him, had a chance to observe his enemy, so close he could smell their putrid stench. He recognized, beneath the filth of many months of rough living, the extravagant uniforms of German *Landsknechts* – sewn from prodigious lengths of expensive fabric that were now muddied and bloodied beyond repair. Here he was, face to face with the very soldiers that formed the infernal blackness of his dreams, the very soldiers that he had witnessed raping the town of Cotignola, the very soldiers that were at this moment bearing down on Rome like some Biblical plague of vermin, implacable as it was inevitable. They all stood there for a moment, facing each other – feral faces of monsters from a child's nightmare brought to life.

For all their wild and demonic appearance, their approach had been very professional. Half the force carried long pikes with which they now menaced the travellers, the other half used arquebus and crossbow, alternating through the group.

"If you wish to live throw down your weapons and give us your food, money and baggage," shouted a voice in heavily accented Italian. "If you refuse you will be killed, if you do as we say you will be spared."

There was a brief moment when Luca thought – really believed – he was going to walk away with his life without having to fight for it. He knew his fellow travellers were thinking the same thing as he – give them what they want and we may live. But the decision was not theirs to make.

"You are threatening the mail of his Holiness Pope Clement. This is illegal, and blasphemy against the Holy See. You will stand down and permit us to pass!" shouted one of the Swiss Guards stepping forward to face the *Landsknechts*. There was a second of silence and then the Germans burst out laughing as the import of the Guard's speech became clear to them. Evidently they were unimpressed by the invocation of the Pope's name.

The German who had spoken, that was standing opposite the Swiss Guard, shouted, "Pope!" and spat on the ground. Then thrust his pike into the Guard's neck. That was when Luca knew he would have to fight and probably die in this primal forest at the hands of these foreigners.

The travellers presented their swords and steeled themselves for the battle. Then, just as quickly as it began it was past. The Germans had suddenly lost interest in the Papal Mail. From both directions came the thunder of galloping hooves. Cavalry, carrying lances and swords, burst into the throng of Germans, slashing, stabbing and trampling. The German line broke and those remaining alive ran for the forest, a detachment of cavalry pursuing them intently.

Luca and his companions crawled from under the wagon where they had taken refuge, and took stock of their rescuers. They were irregular troops – they wore no distinguishing uniform – but they all rode black horses and wore black silk armbands. The Black Bands. This was a remnant of Giovanni de' Medici's mercenary force that had been fighting the Imperial army for months, harrying them on their march to Rome.

The leader of the cavalry dismounted and bowed low to the travellers. "*Capitano* Ercole of the Black Bands at your disposal *Signore e Signori.*" Luca and his fellows thanked the good *Capitano* for his timely arrival. He was dressed as most of his group, in a combination of metal and leather armor – metal on his shins, thighs and forearms along with a metal breastplate, leather leggings and jerkin and a splash of white shirt puffing from the various openings.

"These are Germans from Caesar's pestilential army that marches on Rome," he waved his hand at the dead that littered the ground, and the screams of the dying that periodically emanated from the forest. "They are a week or two behind you, coming this way, following the *via Cassia*. This is either a foraging party or deserters, it matters not which. We will kill them all wherever we find them and leave their corpses for the crows." The friars and the merchant nodded enthusiastically, but the nuns crossed themselves, no doubt saying prayers for eternal souls.

"Excuse me sisters for my bluntness," continued Ercole, "but this is war. Our leader has been killed in battle and now we roam the *contado* avenging his death wherever we may find the opportunity. Nevertheless, the Lord Himself knows that not even a hundred thousand dead Germans or Spaniards would begin to expiate the death of his Lordship Giovanni." The Black Bands stopped for a moment of silence at the mention of their dead leader's name.

The remaining Swiss Guards lifted their fallen comrades into the wagon for the remainder of the trip to Rome, so that they might receive a Christian burial. The merchant had received a deep cut to his shoulder in deflecting a lance thrust, which was bandaged. The Black Bands had taken no casualties, so fast and effective had their attack been. One of their group had twisted his ankle while dumping the corpses at the side of the road, which had occasioned much laughter from his fellows. After an hour or so the Papal Mail was underway again. Ercole provided an escort to bring them into sight of the Holy City then rode off with the rest of his cavalry in search of more Imperial troops to kill.

The remainder of the journey was uneventful. In fact Luca could not recall it, so exciting and frightful was the ambush in the forest. The one thing he remembered thinking was that he had never seen a friar in habit and tonsure wielding a sword before. He had a new found respect for the priesthood.

LA MISSIVA

"He is gone!" shouted Vincenzo to his weeping, wayward daughter. "Away! Away from here, never to return! Ever! Gone! Not a fare-thee-well!" He waved his hand vigorously at the window to indicate definitive departure. "Let this be an end to all this nonsense about the Painter." Virginia flinched as her father wagged his finger in her face. "Here is his sworn statement that he does not love you and prefers to be anywhere than with you." Vincenzo brandished a sheet of paper in his other hand as his words cut deep into Virginia's heart. Her father dismissed her and she rushed from his presence as if he had the plague.

She seemed to be making a habit of it lately, as once again she threw herself on her bed sobbing uncontrollably. Maria was nowhere to be seen and Virginia redoubled her crying, crying because she had lost her true love, and crying more because she was alone in her misery. Whereupon, like a ghostly apparition, Maria floated mistily into Virginia's field of view. "Maria!" she wailed, the single name of her nurse sufficient to compass all her ills, then fell back on the bed sobbing anew. She wanted to ask where her nurse had been, but could not draw breath for long enough.

"Easy my sweet Gina, do not cry," she comforted.

"But my love is gone and does not love me," gurgled Virginia.

"Perhaps, but maybe there is something you do not know."

"He wrote a letter saying he never loved me," continued Virginia, wailing louder, ignoring Maria's pregnant comment.

She took Virginia's face in her hands and spoke directly to her, "There is somebody you must meet. Somebody who has a message for you, a message from your painter, Luca." Virginia's mouth fell open.

Maria had initially disapproved of Virginia's tryst with the Painter, but after Vincenzo's heavy-handed treatment of the affair she had come down on poor Virginia's side. And in doing so she had become the accidental conduit of the Painter's communication – a second communication, and more intimate than the one Virginia's father had pressed him into writing. At Maria's behest a red-eyed but more optimistic Virginia donned her cloak, and the two slipped out into the late afternoon crowds.

For the first time since Virginia was a child Maria took the lead as they worked their way northward, away from the bustle of the city center into quieter streets, mostly residential, surrounded by gardens and orchards – out near the San Gallo gate. After consulting a scrap of paper Maria rapped on the door of a small house in a row of small houses. The door opened to reveal a middle-aged woman in a spotless apron, her hair pulled back under a white scarf. "Maria?" asked the woman.

"Yes, and this is Virginia." Maria indicated the puffy-eyed girl next to her who nodded politely.

"Come in, come in," invited the middle-aged woman and the two followed her upstairs into a small but equally spotless parlor. They all sat in X-shaped chairs and stared at each other.

"Would you care for some wine?" asked the woman after a moment.

"You invited us here?" replied Virginia, eager to hear any news.

"Yes my dear, I am sorry, let me get right to it," said the woman smiling suddenly. "My name is Gemma. My husband Daniele is incarcerated in prison, and was a cellmate of your friend Luca, the Painter." Virginia gasped. Gemma continued, "Despite his incarceration, my husband is a poet and by way of plying his trade I visit him once a week to bring him commissions and supplies, and to collect the finished poems." Virginia and Maria looked quizzically at each other at this uncommon arrangement. "Before your painter was released from prison he penned a letter to you and entrusted to my husband its delivery."

"I received a letter from him through my father," said Virginia sadly.

"But this letter is different. It tells a different story," Gemma blushed slightly, "I have to admit to reading it. Wait there." And with that she rushed from the room, reappearing a moment later, a folded piece of paper in hand. Virginia flinched slightly as she recalled the image of her father brandishing a similar article. "Here, take it."

Virginia took the proffered document and turned it over in her hand, scared to open it. She stared at it, fascinated by its soft creamy color and firm, dry texture. Slowly she opened it and gazed at the neat black handwriting, a tangible memory of her beloved painter. As she read the letter her heart began to flutter and she could not quite catch her breath.

✠

"And then I fainted – dead away. They had to revive me or I would have expired on the spot, I swear it!" exclaimed Virginia breathlessly.

"This is so enchanting!" Ginevra was more animated than either of her friends had seen her before, "Your father drives away the man of your dreams who pretends he never loved you, but he secretly writes you a love letter to let you know his true feelings. The Painter writes the letter not your father – well, the second letter not the first. Oh you know what I mean," she finished, exasperated.

"But what to do now?" asked Virginia, who had been giving this very problem much thought of late.

"You must go to Rome of course!" insisted Ginevra immediately.

"But is there not a war to the south?" asked Theresa nervously.

"Not in Rome surely," declared Ginevra with the unassailable conviction of the truly ignorant, "the Pope has the safest house in the world! None would dare attack him."

"Yes, but I know not where the Painter is living. How would I find him?"

"He is a Painter of Florence. Rome is the city of painters and the best are those of Florence. It could only take a few days to track him down."

"Then I must go," said Virginia, her voice tremulous. It was a statement but it sounded like a question. She was understandably anxious about travelling alone to a foreign city.

"I can secure you transport to Siena with one of my father's teamsters," assured Ginevra, "he owes me a favor," she added obliquely with no further explanation. "From there you can ride with the Post to Rome. Bring plenty of money and you can stay somewhere safe until you find your painter."

She made it sound so simple. Simply travel half way around the world. Simply find a single person in a city of fifty thousand. Simply stay somewhere safe. Yet Virginia was intrigued. Moreover, she had become obsessed with this Painter and would indeed risk her life to find him again.

In the midst of her excitement she vaguely recalled the words of the palmist at the fair. It was something about wanting what she could not have and travelling a long way only to lose it – something similar to that anyway. She shook off the nagging feeling that had come over her – that of stepping into the abyss – and once more became caught up in the moment.

"Rome," asked Theresa, "are we not to go to Venice?"

BENVENUTO A ROMA

By the time he passed through the *Porta del Popolo*, Luca was saddle sore and physically exhausted. The difficult and almost deadly ride to Rome had taken its toll on both his health and his humor. He traversed the wide *piazza* and entered the long, narrow *via Lata* that cut through the city deep into the heart of Rome. He had never travelled to Rome before and was immediately struck by the odd mix of modern building and the ruins of antiquity. Buildings were tightly packed together in the modern style then suddenly there were open spaces of rubble, columns and broken, overgrown walls. The modern world was slowly robbing the grave of the ancient, as the two worlds continued to exist, uneasily, side by side – the one growing stronger as the other grew weaker, gradually fading away.

Luca had been recommended to an inn behind the *Palazzo San Marco* at the end of the *via Lata*, and had no problem obtaining a room there, and a stall and feed for his horse. He paid extra to have his own room, having had enough of sharing and the attendant sleepless nights. The good burghers of Rome had not yet seen fit to ban the bathhouses, no doubt in order to more conveniently pursue their unnatural lusts. Luca's only lust was for a much-needed bath, and after a long soak in hot water, followed by a shave from a very voluble barber, he retired to his rented bed and slept.

The barber had, rather sanguinely Luca thought, explained the current political situation in Rome while expertly shaving the scruffy beard of Luca's trip. The barber seemed to know, for example, that the Emperor's army was coming to Rome to exact vengeance on the Pope for all his purported sins, real and imagined, and that they would probably prevail against the poor defenses of Rome and sack the city. Luca could not help but ask the barber what his plan was for the arrival of the besiegers, to which he had replied that he had arranged a place for himself and his family to take shelter in a nearby *palazzo* in return for assisting in its defense. Apparently he had undertaken the same arrangement when the Colonna clan had sacked the city the previous year and had hopes for the same resolution this time. Luca prayed that he should be proven right.

By next morning Luca had put thoughts of the Imperial army behind him; he had more pressing needs. His first task after breakfast was to look for work. As one of his inducements to depart Florence, Vincenzo had given Luca a letter of introduction to the Archbishop of Florence, currently resident at Rome. Cardinal Niccolò Ridolfi was barely a year older than Luca, at twenty-six, but had been a cardinal since the tender age of sixteen. He owed this swift and spectacular advancement to his being the grandson of Lorenzo de Medici, *Il Magnifico*, and the attentions of a pair of Medici Popes keen to promote their kin to positions of influence.

The Cardinal's *palazzo* was nearby, and after donning the best clothes he had brought with him, Luca walked there, through the narrow streets at the heart of Christendom. Surprisingly, the streets were not as busy as Luca had expected them to be. Most of the shops remained closed and bolted, and only the market stalls tucked into archways and loggias were open, but with few people to buy.

The Cardinal's *palazzo*, to the contrary, was a hive of activity, with men and supplies, and horses and carts coming and going. The household was preparing for siege. Luca's heart fell at the sight. He realized that he had come to Rome just in time to die at the hands of the Emperor's army, and that the attack on the road to Rome was merely a precursor to the chaos that was to come. He wondered if Vincenzo had sent him here to die. He liked to think not, but ultimately it did not matter. What was intended was of man, what was to transpire was of God.

He mounted the steps of the *palazzo* and asked for the Cardinal's secretary. He was directed to an office at the top of a wide staircase decorated with a series of magnificent statues, ancient and modern, the walls adorned with beautifully executed frescos. Luca remarked to himself that these poor churchmen certainly knew how to live well.

The Cardinal's secretary was hard to see in his *studiolo*, almost buried, as he was, in papers. The distress of preparing the Cardinal's household to withstand a siege, and the threat of the siege itself, seemed to be taking their toll on the small man. Luca approached him and displayed the letter of introduction. "*Signore*, I beg pardon for this interruption but I am newly arrived in Rome and..." Luca did not get a chance to finish his opening remarks as he was interrupted by the secretary.

"And you wish an audience with Cardinal Niccolò of course. Yes, you have a letter of introduction from some man of importance and seek the Cardinal's patronage." The secretary looked over the top of his reading glasses with arched eyebrows, challenging Luca to deny the validity of his words.

"Yes, *Signore*."

"May I ask you where you are arrived from?" continued the secretary seemingly at a tangent.

"Florence."

"Well, I know not how Florence views the Emperor's army but here in Rome we take it very seriously. A ravenous pack of wolves is snapping at our heels, and we have not the time for itinerant sculptors, poets, goldsmiths..." he waved his hand.

"Painter," affirmed Luca.

"Painters. Indeed." Luca nodded his understanding and turned to leave. "Wait," the secretary called out in a moment of weakness, "go and see this man, and tell him I sent you. He is a fellow Florentine, a goldsmith, and will prove a useful ally during our current problems. Once the situation with the Emperor is sorted out you can have your audience with the Cardinal." Luca thanked the small man profusely, taking the scrap of paper from his hand and bowing deeply. "Just be careful," shouted the secretary down the stairs at Luca's departing back, "this man is... mercurial. Do not anger him, he can be dangerous." He shouted the last few words and shook his head at the impetuousness of youth as he returned to his mountain of paper.

Luca headed west towards the river. The address he had been given was behind the *Banchi*, in the Florentine section of Rome; a wealthy half moon shaped area tucked into a bend in the Tiber like a juicy slice of orange. The area was bisected by the long and wide *Strada Giulia*, a new street full of expensive modern houses, but the side streets were the narrow ways of the old city, hardly more than lanes and alleys, and poorly signposted. Luca twisted his way through the neighborhood feeling more lost by the minute.

Suddenly, from an otherwise anonymous door in a dirty wall, two figures tumbled out onto the street directly in front of Luca. They leapt to their feet and drew swords, dancing around each other brandishing their blades and cursing. More men exited the doorway – which turned out to lead to a dark tavern – and stood around the two swordsmen, better to observe the altercation.

"Prepare to die Spanish scum!" yelled the larger of the two men.

"Death to all Florentines!" yelled the other in a heavy Spanish accent and they set to with passion, whirling around each other slashing and parrying.

The Spaniard seemed to be getting the better of the fight, scoring a hit on the large man's chest, cutting his doublet to reveal a chainmail vest, but the larger man fought back hard, opening a deep wound in the Spaniard's arm. He pressed his attack on the wounded Spaniard who backed up until he was against the wall of the alley desperately fending off the rain of blows. At that moment the half dozen observers of the duel drew their swords and advanced on the large man. He stayed his attack on the wounded Spaniard and backed away holding the group at bay as two of them moved to the sides to flank him. Soon he would be surrounded and as good as dead.

"Will no Florentine help me?" he cried out, more in anger than in fear. "Will nobody help me teach these Spaniards what it means to insult Florence?"

"I will!" Luca heard himself cry out, unable to watch a fellow countryman murdered before his very eyes by a band of drunken foreigners. So saying he promptly drew his own blade and slashed the sword arm of one of the Spaniards. The man cried out and backed away from the fight. Luca pushed through the group and stood side by side with the large man.

The Spanish group was down to five, but their swordsmanship was good and they finally managed to flank the two Florentines. Back to back the two fought the circle of Spaniards without taking or inflicting wounds. They were lucky that the way was narrow which favored the defenders, and that the Spaniards were becoming progressively less enthusiastic about being spitted on a Florentine sword in this filthy alley.

"May I ask your name *Signore*?" asked the large man over his shoulder, slashing and parrying, "I would consider it a favor to know the name of the man who is willing to die by my side for the honor of Florence."

"My name is Luca, but I am hardly by your side, nor does dying feature in my plans for the day," returned Luca over his shoulder.

"Well met *Signore*," the large man laughed as heartily as his exertions would allow.

"And your name *Signore*?" asked Luca.

"Benvenuto," replied the large man.

"Then you must be the one I seek, as I cannot imagine there is another Florentine in Rome named Benvenuto."

"Nor in Florence neither I would warrant," exclaimed Benvenuto heartily, thrusting at a Spaniard.

At that moment a group of young men appeared at the end of the alley, friends of Benvenuto by their cheerful calls. Swords were drawn, and the Spaniards, outnumbered, fled. The battle was done in a moment.

"I hate Spaniards," muttered Benvenuto, examining himself for wounds and finding only his wounded doublet.

"Do you always wear mail?" asked Luca surprised.

"These are dangerous times my friend," declared Benvenuto, stroking his beard. "But much thanks to you for your assistance," he continued, and bowed deeply, "Benvenuto Cellini at your service. Come let me buy you a drink."

LA MARCHESA

Virginia reluctantly led her horse across the giant brick pie of a *piazza* towards the *Palazzo Publico*, the clatter of metal shoes echoing off the buildings in the early morning quiet. It seemed to her, in the sobering chill, that Ginevra had enjoyed all the excitement but that she, Virginia, had suffered all the discomfort of this romantic adventure. She was already beginning to regret her rash decision to pursue the Painter to Rome.

It was not as if her love for him had become diminished, far from it, she burned inside from her unrequited ardor. However, the idea of a journey to Rome, alone, in the middle of a war was perhaps overreaching. Surely a correspondence could have been initiated and plans made for a meeting at some indeterminate date. Yet here she was, an hour before dawn, shivering in her riding cloak, leading her horse across the same *piazza* that Luca had crossed barely a week before. It was too late to go back. She had made her decision for better or worse – or had it made for her.

As she approached the Post wagon, being loaded under the flickering lanterns of the *Palazzo*, a commotion broke out at the far side of the *piazza*. A group of twenty soldiers cantered across the closely packed bricks and lined up in pairs next to the Post. Almost immediately a wagon pulled by four perfectly matched white horses followed them and lined up in train.

Virginia squinted at the new arrivals in the half dark. The

soldiers were all similarly dressed in red and black livery, their
horses caparisoned and barded in the same scheme. The men were
heavily armed and well-trained professionals, although Virginia did
not recognize the coat of arms emblazoned on the side of the
wagon.

The commander of the soldiers jumped from his horse and
consulted with the Swiss Guards and they beckoned to Virginia,
the sole traveller taking the road to Rome.

"*Signorina*, you will ride behind the Mantuans and we will
follow you. The roads are dangerous and this will ensure your safety
– as much as is possible." Virginia nodded in agreement and swung
up into the saddle with a practiced flourish. She had been riding
since she was a little girl and had become an accomplished
horsewoman.

So it was the Gonzaga coat of arms on the side of the wagon.
Virginia wondered why an armed guard of Mantuan soldiers was
in Siena, and what, or who was hidden by the rich curtains of the
wagon. They were a long way from home.

The train set off through the early morning town, hooves
dashing glittering sparks from the dark stones. As the sun rose over
orchards full with mulberry trees Virginia was beset with a deep
melancholy. The sight of those serried ranks brought back
memories; both of her father's silken fruit, and of a different love
story gone terribly awry in far off Babylon.

She wished for nothing more than to return home to her father
and her nurse and her bed, and not be shivering out here on
horseback, heading inevitably toward a war, in pursuit of the
chimera of love. Virginia was all but determined upon return –
galloping back to Florence without a stop – when she was brought
out of her sad musing by the appearance of a hand at the rear
curtain of the wagon she followed. It was a woman's hand, nails
trimmed and polished, with rings that twinkled in the warm eastern
light. The hand was followed by a glimpse of eyes and then the
curtain dropped back into place. Virginia was intrigued, but as
nothing further happened she returned to her thoughts of home.

Some moments later one of the soldiers dropped back in line
and rode up next to Virginia. "*Signorina*," he began politely,

"Madama would have you ride with her."

"Madama?" asked Virginia, puzzled.

"Our mistress travels alone and desires some female companionship for the journey." The soldier's reply did not answer the question.

"Very well," agreed Virginia, "at the next stop." The soldier nodded and rode back in line to report.

They stopped to water the horses at a tiny village a few hours later, and Virginia dismounted and approached the Gonzaga wagon. It was not draped in a hooped canvas cover like the post wagon; rather it had a flat-topped canopy with a fringe of fabric and side curtains for the comfort and privacy of the traveller within. As Virginia came close, the soldier who had spoken with her appeared before her. "Let me take your horse," and so saying he took the reins from Virginia and tied them to the wagon, then proceeded to open a door and fold out a hidden set of steps. With the soldier's assisting hand she climbed inside and sat down on an extremely soft and comfortable bench.

"Now let me ask; what kind of foolishness would bring a pretty girl like yourself out onto the open road in wartime?"

The question was unexpected and stung just a little. Adapting to the lack of light inside the wagon, Virginia's eyes took in the spectacle of her inquisitor. Virginia was not surprised this woman travelled with twenty armed men. Her dress was of brown silk velvet embroidered across its entirety with an interlocking design worked in gold thread. Her shoes matched the dress and were sewn with jewels – real jewels Virginia supposed, not colored glass. But the part of her ensemble that most impressed was the necklace. It was composed of three perfectly matched strands of pearls mounted in gold with a single, huge ruby at the throat; set off perfectly by matching pearl and ruby drop earrings.

"*Signora*," began Virginia carefully, aware that this woman was wealthy and influential and not to be trifled with, "I am travelling to Rome on a matter of great urgency and would not attempt such a journey under normal circumstances."

"A man?" asked the woman arching a cynical yet perfectly plucked eyebrow. Another unexpected question. She studied the woman's face. She must be in her fifties Virginia decided, but a beautiful woman. Her face was roundish in shape yet still showed a dimple in her chin; her eyes were soft, brown and large, and her lips bowed prettily, and twitched easily into a smile. The woman was smiling now as the question hung there between them.

"Yes a man. A painter named Luca."

"A painter, of course," she gazed off into the past. "I loved a painter once," she reminisced, "the incomparable Raffaello. He was such a magnificent man. Always had a string of beauties following him." She laughed briefly, then: "Dead now of course."

"Raffaello da Urbino?" asked Virginia, stunned. "You knew him?"

"Certainly," replied the woman, "I knew all the good ones." Then suddenly back in the present, "Oh, you know not who I am."

"No *Signora*, it pains me to admit that I do not," answered Virginia, confused.

"Isabella is my name. I was born in Ferrara but married the Marchese of Mantua..."

"Oh!" squeaked Virginia, suddenly realizing in whose wagon she was riding, "you are Isabella d'Este!"

"The same," smiled Isabella prettily.

"Your Eminence, I did not realize."

"Silly girl, I am not a Cardinal – although, the Lord be willing, my son is soon to be one," she mused. "You must address me as Madama. It suits my station as matriarch." There was that easy smile again.

"Madama, it is an honor to be invited to travel with you."

"Nonsense child, it is you who does me honor; by entertaining an old lady on a long and tedious journey."

"I will do my utmost to entertain, Madama."

"So, your name?"

"Virginia."

"*Beata Virgo?*" asked Isabella, smiling.

"Sadly an all too earthly Virginia, and despite my best efforts full of sin." Virginia bowed her head demurely.

"And what drives your pursuit of this painter, Luca?"

"We were in love and my father had him banished to Rome. Upon his departure he wrote me a letter stating his true love for me, and I resolved to follow him."

"Was he not acceptable to your father?"

"My father is a *setaiuolo* and considers himself an important merchant in Florence. His desire is for me to be wed to a business associate of his in Venice, an older man I have never met."

"If this is an example of his wares then he is right to consider himself important," opined Isabella, gently fingering the fabric of Virginia's dress.

"Nevertheless, I prefer the company of the man I love to the love of the man my father prefers."

"Well said child. Although, you know, a woman need not be circumscribed by her husband's failings, nor those of her father for that matter. A strong woman, as you have shown yourself to be, can mark the pale of her own world."

Virginia was not exactly sure what Madama meant but was too timid to ask her, not to say unwilling to appear dull-witted to a woman whose intellect was the toast of Italy. Madama continued: "*My* marriage was arranged by my father who only saw the world in dynastic terms. I was betrothed at the age of six but by the time I came to marry him that husband had passed on," she laughed grimly, "but that did not deter Papa, I married the dead man's brother and became the Marchesa of Mantua. Francesco was not a handsome man but he was strong and we loved each other well enough." She looked up at Virginia. "So perhaps you would find what will complete you in this dynastic marriage of your father's. Perhaps Venice is in your future."

"I had almost determined to return to Florence when Madama invited me to join her."

"So now I am at fault for dragging you to Rome against your will," laughed Isabella.

"No Madama, surely not, I was merely suffering a moment of doubt. Did our Lord not have his moment of doubt?"

"*Deus meus, Deus meus, ut quid dereliquisti me?*" replied Madama arching an eyebrow questioningly, and Virginia nodded. "I like to think that Our Lord was quoting the Psalm of David to draw a parallel with the events of his Passion," mused Madama, and Virginia looked confused.

"But never mind that. How do you know that your painter will not despoil you and reject you, leaving you in Rome to fend for yourself?"

"If it were asked by any other I would take offense at the question, Madama, but I choose to believe you have my best interests in your heart. Luca had opportunities several to avail himself of my body and did not. Although, before you ask, his eyes betrayed his desire."

"*Nam nemo quisquam illorum scito ad te venit,*

　Quin ita paret sese, abs te ut, blanditiis suis,

　Quam minimo precio suam voluptatem expleat," quoted Isabella.

"Is that Terence?" asked Virginia unsure in her Latin.

"Yes it is child, I am glad that Florence is not neglecting the education of its young women. But can you translate?"

"It says something about 'no man comes to you but to have his way with you through flattery' does it not?"

"Something very much like that. Perhaps it is too captious, but your current predicament brought it to mind," she smiled.

"I think I prefer: *Nemini plura ego acerba credo esse ex amore homini umquam oblata. Quam mihi: heu me infelicitem!*"

"So you do know your Latin!" exclaimed Isabella delightedly. "Any Greek?"

"No Greek Madama, I had no aptitude with that language," admitted Virginia, sad for a moment that she had not paid better attention in class. "Although," she added, keen to please, "I do play the virginals."

"Splendid," exclaimed Isabella, "and I the lute. We must play together in Rome. I am staying at the *palazzo* of Cardinal Colonna, you must join me there."

"I could not impose Madama."

"Nonsense child, it will be one of the few places of safety in Rome when the Constable gets there. I will not abandon you to the vicissitudes of war. You will stay with me and we will find your painter," Isabella declared finally. She had found an interesting project to occupy her time in Rome.

✠

The days passed as the heavily armed train rolled slowly across the bleak landscape. Isabella had adopted Virginia as her travelling companion, and insisted they share a room at each of their stops. They read to each other, played cards and talked through the long tedium of slow travel.

"So Madama, why are you going to Rome in the middle of the war, why not stay home in Mantua or Ferrara?"

"I have been resident in Rome, off and on, for a few years now – I do love Rome so! But recently I had an argument with my son. He is headstrong like all young men, and he feels the need to separate himself from his mother. I ruled Mantua as his regent until he was old enough to take charge, so now he wishes to make his own decisions and spurns his mother's counsel, the impudent whelp – I was ruling the state while he was barely out of swaddling bands. So be it. I taught him well and he has managed to put himself on the winning side of this war so far," replied Madama, with more than a hint of admiration showing through her annoyance.

"But why now with the Emperor intent on besieging Rome?"

"I suppose I can tell you, since secrecy is no longer an issue. I have been busy on an undertaking for the Pope. You know I was an envoy to King Louis many years ago?" Virginia nodded, "Well, so many of my family are involved in this outrageous war that the Pope saw fit to charge me with a secret assignment – a meeting with the Constable de Bourbon in an attempt to stop the fighting and to stop the march on Rome.

"I met with Lannoy..." Virginia looked confused. "He is the Viceroy of Naples." Virginia still looked confused. "My dear, you really should pay more attention to the affairs of the world. Naples was won back from France by the Spanish so now belongs to Spain and they employ a viceroy to run the state. Since the Emperor is also King of Spain then Lannoy works for the Emperor." Isabella arched her eyebrow questioningly and Virginia nodded her understanding.

"Renzo di Ceri defeated Lannoy a month ago when he marched

on Rome from Naples, and the Pope promptly disbanded Renzo's army. My son told him not to." She shook her head in disbelief. "Anyway," she dragged her thoughts back to the present, "Lannoy was the Emperor's envoy to the army, and I spoke for the Pope. It was not a success." She furrowed her brow. "The Constable was charming enough, but his army is a frightful thing to behold. They live to destroy, like an infestation, as if they were spawned by the Devil himself." Madama shuddered at the remembrance. "The Constable smiled and dissembled, and asked for two hundred and forty thousand ducats to leave Rome alone." She laughed at the impertinence. "Lannoy and I were not empowered to vouchsafe such a prodigious sum; so we left. We felt lucky to have escaped that hideous crew with our lives, and wasted no time in getting clear of them to Siena. The army is on the march and will be in Rome in a few days."

Madama paused a moment in thought. "They will take Rome. I have seen many armies, and never have I laid eyes on such a monstrosity before. I swear that the Constable himself is afeard of them, and controls them as you would a huge and dangerous creature: by gentle goading from behind and dangling the possibility of reward under their noses. That reward is Rome and its riches."

The two women sat in silence for a few minutes as the idea that she was heading towards a city that was to be occupied by the most dangerous army that the experienced and sophisticated Isabella d'Este had ever laid eyes on gradually sank into Virginia's love-addled mind.

Isabella noticed the look of horror spreading across the girl's face. "Do not fear child, my house will be safe and it is well provisioned and guarded for a long siege. We will find your painter and wait them out. My son, a different one of course, is commander of the Italian cavalry that rides with the Constable's army. This has caused me no end of trouble, I can tell you. Many of the Cardinals are angry that two of my sons support the Emperor while I am petitioning the Pope for a Cardinal's hat for my third son, Ercole, despite the fact that my son-in-law commands the Pope's troops." Isabella rolled her eyes. "Whether they blame me or not, the Pope needs my money so Ercole will get his hat, you can be sure of that."

Virginia's eyes were starting to glaze over at Madama's seemingly endless commentary on the political situation, as much as she enjoyed it, so she gently steered her away from politics: "So you knew Leonardo?"

"Oh yes, he was an odd one, always thinking up clever ideas and making little machines. He drew a sketch of me for a painting he never finished; in fact he never completed a single painting that I remember. My stupid husband gave the sketch away when he fell in love with the Borgia *puttana* – that Spanish whore – and spent all his time rutting on her like an old goat."

"Lucrezia Borgia?"

"That was the woman; a born slut. I could tell she would be trouble from the first day I set eyes on her. She played all those whore games – pretending to be your friend while she was rubbing her body against every man at court. And she my brother's wife too!" Isabella waved her hand in anger. "I really hated her for all her games. Well, it was over for her and my husband once he caught the French disease. Although, between you and me, I think he caught it from her. Either way they are both dead now so no matter. I can light a candle and say a prayer and the world whirls onward."

La Battaglia

"Now pay attention everyone," said Benvenuto, "here is the Tiber." He drew a sinuous line in the dirt with the tip of his sword. "Most of Rome is on the right side of the Tiber," he drew a curved line that formed a letter D with the Tiber to indicate the wall, "except for the *Borgo* which extends like an enlarged male member to the top left." The men laughed as he drew the bulge of the wall that extended to the left of the Tiber. "Appropriately shaped I venture, since with all those Cardinals living in the shadow of St Peter's the working women do more business in the *Borgo* than in the rest of the city in its entirety." More laughter. "And half way down is *Trans Tiberim* as the Ancients called it, or as we call it *Trastavere*."

Luca had noticed that Benvenuto loved to brag and show off his knowledge and skill, mingled with much cursing, drinking and womanizing. It had taken a concerted effort from Luca to keep up with the big man in the last few days. Despite their similar ages, Benvenuto seemed to have a good deal more energy to go with his greater bulk.

"So here, like a soft round breast, is *Trastavere*." He drew a small rounded shape that came to a point like a nipple to the left of the Tiber. "Now, were I in charge of the defense of Rome I would blow these bridges here and here," he indicated two of the four bridges across the Tiber, "and leave the *Ponte Sant'Angelo* and the *Ponte Sisto*, but would put a charge of powder under the center arch of each bridge. Obviously Caesar's forces will show up on the left bank of the Tiber, so if we hold the *Ponte Milvio* on the *via Flaminia* just outside the city then they will not be able to cross the river and thus will not be able to get into the city."

"Why not?" asked one of the men.

"Because they will be forced to put all their forces against the *Borgo* or *Trastavere* or both, especially where the wall is low near the *Camposanto*. These can be defended, and the cannon from the *castello* will have free range against the enemy without having to fire on the city proper. And even if they overcome the defense, the defenders can fall back across the river and blow the bridges behind them, leaving the enemy trapped on the far bank and under the guns of the *castello*." The men all nodded. It seemed like a workable idea.

"Unfortunately, the Pope and his captain, Renzo, have left the bridges intact and have not evacuated the *Borgo* nor *Trastavere*, so there is a very good chance that the enemy will prevail and take Rome. But that is why we are here. We are employed to protect the *palazzo* of my dear friend and patron Alessandro del Bene." Benvenuto indicated the beautiful, modern building behind them, the façade newly frescoed for all its four stories. "Some of you helped a few months back during our recent difficulties with the Colonna and their mercenaries; but heed my words gentlemen this will be much worse." He surveyed the grim looks on the ring of faces surrounding him. "But *Messer* Alessandro is well supplied with food and drink and we will be able to withstand a month's siege within his walls; and he is paying us all for our time."

"Hurrah!" yelled the men in unison, and on Benvenuto's command dispersed into the *palazzo*, taking their places for its defense.

"Luca!" shouted Benvenuto, "You will stay by my side. Your sword work has much to recommend it and we will have plenty to talk about as fellow artists when we are not fighting." To Luca it seemed this big fool was actually looking forward to being besieged by Spaniards and Germans – the very spawn of Satan himself. Benvenuto enjoyed fighting as much as he enjoyed his goldsmithing, and he was surprisingly good at both. As a gift to cement their new friendship he had given Luca a vest of chainmail, which he now wore under a leather jerkin. Luca was dressed for battle with heavy leather boots and leather gloves, his sword on his left side, dagger on his right, his long curls tied back with a velvet ribbon.

"Can you shoot?" asked Benvenuto.

"I had a fowling piece and would shoot doves for our supper back in Florence," answered Luca tentatively.

"Excellent!" exclaimed Benvenuto in his big voice, "Alessandro has several arquebuses which will give us much sport shooting at our enemies. They are the new style with the rotating lock, much safer to use, and more accurate."

"Excellent indeed," replied Luca with a distinct lack of enthusiasm as he followed the big man into the *palazzo* to examine Alessandro's collection of firearms.

"You look good," observed Benvenuto slapping Luca on the shoulder, "ready for a fight. Mars would be proud."

✠

It was about the eighth hour and the cannon had been thundering rhythmically from the *Castel Sant'Angelo* for almost four hours, shaking the very earth beneath their feet with every shot. To the north and west of the *palazzo* they could see the balls of flame belching from the guns, lighting up the sky with each blast; and further west smaller flashes from the defenders on the wall as they fired down at the attackers. There were fires burning along the Leonine walls reflecting eerily in the black Tiber. All in all it was a scene from hell; a harbinger of the hell to come.

Luca was safe in the *palazzo* – the shutters were bolted tight and the doors barred. The men had opened loopholes in the shutters and had set up positions on the roof to cover the open courtyard in front of the *palazzo* on one side, and the *Strada Giulia* on the other, with arquebus and crossbow. They had several flagons of turpentine up there to pour, flaming, onto the heads of their attackers, enough to light up the whole street if necessary. They were ready, although at this point the defenders at the walls were holding their own.

Luca was standing on the roof looking out at the distant fiery conflict when he felt a hand on his shoulder. "Luca," said Benvenuto, "Alessandro wants to go to the wall and see the battle."

"Is he demented?"

"I tried to dissuade him," laughed Benvenuto, "but he cried like a little girl."

"We are safe here, what happens if we get caught on the street?"

"They have only been fighting a few hours, by daybreak the cannon will be able to get the range and decimate the enemy. It is unlikely they will break through tonight. My only concern is Alessandro's getting hit by a stray shot." Benvenuto shrugged and Luca rolled his eyes in astonishment. The old man wanted to go and see the fighting – lunatic.

"Let us go – and stay close," admonished Benvenuto and the three men set off carrying their loaded arquebuses, plus spare powder and shot. Benvenuto set a fast pace through the dark and silent city but after about twenty minutes Alessandro, who was older and weaker than the two young men, was begging to rest.

Instead of the quicker route along the *Strada Giulia* they cut over to the river and ran along its bank so they could see the fire of battle across the Tiber. They stopped for a few minutes at the Sant'Angelo Bridge as a panting Alessandro wiped his sweating brow with his soft hat, bald pate shining red in the firelight.

They were about to start off again when a young man carrying an arquebus ran up to them out of the shadows. "Benvenuto, is it you?" came the shout.

"Cecchino," cried Benvenuto sheathing his sword, "I almost cut you there my friend."

"Excuse my arrival but I have been running after you from the *palazzo*."

"What is the problem?"

"I have a message for Luca," Luca looked around surprised that anyone in Rome would know him sufficiently well to send him a message. Cecchino turned to Luca, "A messenger arrived at *Messer* Alessandro's from the *Palazzo Colonna* – along with an agreeable young lady."

"I know nobody there," interrupted Luca, confused.

"Apparently you do," replied Cecchino with a knowing smile, "the Marchesa of Mantua is in residence at the *Palazzo Colonna* and the agreeable young lady is staying with her. She is a Florentine, by the name of Virginia."

"Virginia?" asked Luca, incredulous, "by the Evangelist, why is she in Rome?"

"On your account Luca, it would seem," laughed Cecchino.

Benvenuto doubled over, roaring with laughter. "You sly dog," he spluttered, "not content with the local crows, you have them brought here from Florence for your pleasure?"

"No, no, she is not a working girl. She is the reason I am here. Her father was the one who had me banished. He sent me thence that I should be apart from her. She ought to be home safe in Florence."

"Well she must have followed you here, love struck. Enamored of your pretty face and soft curls no doubt," mocked Benvenuto. Luca sat down on the parapet of the bridge next to Alessandro, stunned.

"It was decided that she should meet you at the obelisk by the *Camposanto* behind St Peter's," declared Cecchino more seriously, "she is taking the *Strada Giulia* to get here; she cannot be far behind. She is heading in the same direction you are, and will await you there."

"In the middle of this?" asked Luca horrified, "What is she thinking, how could they let her leave?" Cecchino shrugged. Benvenuto was still laughing heartily. "And what is this 'obelisk'?" asked Luca. Benvenuto answered the question in his vaguely irritating, instructional manner: "It is a tall column of stone that was at the center of the ancient circus that provided the building material for St. Peter's. It is just to the south of the new church. It is hard to miss," he explained, still laughing.

Alessandro looked over at Luca and smiled a warm smile. "She must love you very much to travel this far in the midst of a war to find you. You are a lucky man Luca to have such a woman. You should never forget this. Go and find her and take her to safety."

"We have no time for love making now," declared Benvenuto in his best baritone, finally shaking off the laughter and composing himself, "let us find the battle and return to the *palazzo* before any misfortune befalls *Messer* Alessandro. Luca can fetch his girl back with us." Whereupon the three, accompanied by Cecchino, walked swiftly over the bridge towards the fire and the screaming.

About half way along the city wall, on the south side of the *Borgo* near the *Camposanto*, was a set of steps beside the *Porta Torrione* that led up to the parapet. They took the steps two at a time and within a few seconds they were on top of the wall. This was the lowest spot in the entire wall surrounding Rome, and was why both Benvenuto and the attackers had chosen it as the likely spot for an assault.

The situation on the wall was worse than they had imagined. Dead and wounded defenders lay all about and the attackers had the range of the wall, with shot and crossbow bolts flying close overhead. The four instinctively ducked and crouched in a group behind the parapet. The defenders were shooting down at the base of the walls as fast as they could load, and the blast of the cannonade from the *Castel Sant'Angelo* behind them roared repeatedly overhead.

"This is worse than I foresaw," shouted Benvenuto over the din.

"Oh Dear Lord we are going to die," cried Alessandro, suddenly realizing the predicament in which he had placed himself by his own unwholesome curiosity. "We must leave right away, I insist, I order it."

"Stay calm Sandro," declared Benvenuto sternly, "we are armed and we are at the very core of history. Should we not make our mark? Should we not take arms and blast the enemy with our shot and our invective? Let us be men and brave for the few moments it takes to discharge our weapons and loose our curses; and to give what little assistance we may to these noble soldiers, hard pressed by their foe!"

Luca had to admit to himself that whatever Benvenuto's failings, making a stirring speech was not one of them. As the roar and fire of battle screamed and burst around them, they primed their weapons and took positions between the battlements, resting their arquebuses on the stone parapet. At that moment the sun appeared over the hills before them, illuminating the valley below the walls and lighting up the bones of the new St. Peter's behind them – the new church rising slowly from the ruins of the old. Luca was frozen.

Surely, if he had not had the arquebus to hold he would have fallen in a dead faint. There below him, stretching down to the river and up to the base of the nearby hills, was a thick fog slightly above the height of a man covering the entire field of battle. It had the immediate effect of obscuring the enemy from sight of the defenders while lighting up those on the walls against the bright morning sky, advantaging the attackers.

Moreover, the artillery firing over the walls from the *Castel Sant'Angelo* could not see their targets and were firing blind, not knowing whether they were hitting their opponents or merely wasting their shot in the open fields.

But it was none of these unfortunate eventualities that had sapped Luca's spirit so. What had struck him was the similarity between the scene before him and the nightmare he had been suffering for the past six months. That incubus of death that had ridden him for so long was now laid out before him as a waking dream.

Suddenly, with much yelling and blowing of horns, ladders were flung upward out of the fog, crashing against the walls, ladders immediately mounted by an enemy hungry for victory. Luca watched horrified as the monsters climbed up out of the mist, scaling the walls like so much creeping vermin. He could look down now, straight into those goblin faces, filthy and disheveled; figures with hands raised brandishing swords and pikes as they mounted the walls, barely a couple of arms lengths away.

"Luca!" Benvenuto was shouting at him and it roused him from this horrible reverie. "Help here!" He had hold of one of the scaling ladders that had landed near their position and needed help pushing it back. Luca ran over to assist and between the two of them the ladder was dislodged, tipping its occupants screaming back into the mist. "Let us discharge our weapons and leave, the tide of battle seems to be running against us," yelled Benvenuto.

They resumed their positions behind the parapet and took aim.

"Look, there!" cried Benvenuto pointing. Luca followed his finger and saw a figure mounting one of the scaling ladders at a bend in the wall, some twenty *braccia* distant. Unlike his wild and bestial comrades he was dressed in pristine shining silver armor, and sported a white cloak that billowed about him as he climbed out of the fog. "It is the Constable himself! Kill the commander and the troops will run," insisted Benvenuto.

Alessandro promptly took a shot, but his hands were shaking so violently that his aim was wide. Cecchino hit another attacker who dropped mortally wounded from the ladder. Benvenuto took his time, and had lined up the perfect shot when one of the attackers, having scaled the wall, appeared before them on the parapet swinging his sword over his head. Benvenuto turned his weapon quickly to the side and shot the man in the chest, point blank, saving all their lives.

It was Luca's turn and he aimed at the body of the man in silver as he climbed. The man's visor was open and his eyes turned to Luca for a long second, fixing him with a wild glare, then they were gone as he turned to yell at his army to follow him. Luca pulled the trigger and the arquebus discharged in a hot flash of burning powder. Before his vision had cleared from the explosion Benvenuto was already shouting, "A hit, a hit!" Luca squinted through his watering eyes as the silver monster fell, limp, back into the mist. "A hit!" and Benvenuto was clapping him on the back.

The four men ran along the wall towards the steps as the tide had now reversed, turning back to favor the defenders, the enemy commander mortally wounded. Gouts of flame burst upwards from the walls as the Pope's ragged army, redoubling their efforts, poured burning oil onto the Imperial troops. With Alessandro in the lead, the four ran down the steps back to ground level. As they gathered their wits Benvenuto shouted again, "You hit him Luca, you killed the Constable, you have won the battle for us. But we must get ourselves back across the river to assure *Messer* Alessandro's safety." To which comment Alessandro nodded vigorously.

"I must find Virginia," declared Luca.

"Indeed, follow me. I will guide you there and we can bring her back with us."

Benvenuto took the lead and the four picked their way through the *Camposanto* – the German Graveyard – that lay just inside the *Porta Torrione*, between the wall and the obelisk. They emerged into the small square where that massive towering finger of stone pointed to the heavens, and paused a moment on the steps at its base.

"Here is the obelisk. Your lady is tardy; I pray she comes anon. But do not wait too long in case the enemy breaks through. You know the way back to the *palazzo*. May God be with you my friend," said Benvenuto clasping Luca in a bear-like hug. And with that they were gone, back to the bridge and safety.

And that was the last time Luca saw Benvenuto Cellini.

Il Palazzo

Virginia looked nervously at the *Palazzo Colonna* as she and Madama alighted from the wagon. She noticed that it was not built in the same way as the Florentine houses. In Florence the builders employed a reinforced ground level with massive doors in the center of a blank wall, or perhaps shops that were not connected to the *palazzo* behind. In either case the house was isolated from the street by the simple expedient of barring the front door. In contrast, many of the Roman houses had a ground level that more interacted with the street, making them potentially much less secure in times of trouble, which, Virginia knew even in her brief experience, could be very dangerous and destructive. Madama saw the shadow of concern flicker across Virginia's face as she looked up at the beautiful building. "They build them differently here child. They are not used to having to shut themselves up for weeks on end to avoid the mob. But fear not, I have made ample arrangements for our safety."

They walked through the archway over the central door while the servants and soldiers drove the cart and horses behind the courtyard to the stables. Virginia had never seen such an astonishing place. Every inch was covered with a painting, fresco or tapestry, with many statues embellishing the stairway. It was even more spectacular than the house in Florence where Luca had brought her that fateful night weeks ago. They took their seats in the huge salon overlooking the street, and Isabella spoke again, "My brother Alfonso is Duke of Ferrara, and since he was dispossessed and excommunicated by Pope Julius he has had a dislike of Popes in general. As he did a few years back he is fighting now against this Pope. It worked well for him last time so he marches with the Constable's forces." Servants brought wine in Venetian glass goblets for the two ladies, and Isabella sipped her wine for a few moments before continuing.

"My son Ferrante – he is no older than you my dear – has been a page to the Emperor these last few years, so he has been entrusted with command of the cavalry in the Constable's army," Isabella explained. "So young – I hope he takes care," she added with a mother's concern.

"Since I have been in contact with him from the beginning of this expedition he assures me that this house will be spared. The Constable is also pledged to protect the house of the Colonna as they are fierce enemies of the Pope. The upshot is that there are several reasons why we will be safe here, and although the house does not appear as formidable as your Florentine houses it will be made secure."

Virginia was fascinated by Madama's complex tale. It pleased her to hear Madama boil the confusing events unfolding around them down to her familial obligations – otherwise keeping everything straight in this complicated world was quite a chore. "Where is *Signor* Colonna, is he here too?" she asked.

"Old Pompeo?" laughed Isabella, "Truly he is no more than a year or two older than me but I always think of him that way – his Cardinal's robes make him look so old. He is resident at the Papal Chancellery as part and parcel of whatever it is that he does here in Rome," she waved her hand airily. "Now that reminds me, he is negotiating with the Pope for Ercole's hat." Virginia looked blank. "I am buying my son a Cardinalship because the Pope needs money," Madama explained again simply, with raised eyebrows. "Try to keep up my dear."

"Of course, I remember," answered Virginia, chastened.

"I must send word to him that I am arrived and ready to trade." She sipped her wine thoughtfully. "And we must find your peripatetic painter," she finished decisively.

✠

Two days had passed and nothing had happened. Madama had showed Virginia around the *palazzo*: the artwork, ancient and modern, the extensive gardens and the ruins of the ancient baths. She had explained to Virginia how this house had been a favorite of both Dante and Petrarch, and told her of the history of the house, how it had fallen out of and back into the hands of the Colonna family. It was all very interesting but Virginia had made no progress in finding Luca.

How hard could it be to find a Florentine painter in Rome? Well the answer seemed to be that you could throw a rock in any direction and hit a Florentine painter. To be sure, Madama had made no progress either in obtaining the Cardinal's hat for Ercole, but the Pope was getting desperate, as a messenger had brought news from the Constable that he was drawing near to Rome. The same messenger also brought news from Ferrante to his mother. She was to stay put in the *Palazzo Colonna* and he would come to her as soon as they had taken the city.

Finally news came that the Pope would make Ercole a Cardinal for forty thousand ducats. That was an impossible sum in Virginia's mind, but Madama just tossed it off with that airy hand wave and signed a sheet of paper authorizing her banker to bestow the funds upon the Pope. "He is a month too late you know," said Isabella to Virginia.

"Madama?"

"The Pope. He is too late in raising an army. He had three thousand defenders, good troops, Swiss mercenaries plus a regiment of the Black Bands, but he let them go and cried poor. With that group defending Rome the Constable would never be able to take the walls. But now he will have a few thousand shopkeepers and tradesmen up against lancers and swordsmen. The end is clear."

"But we will be safe here?"

"Of course child, do not fuss."

Isabella seemed to enjoy telling everything to Virginia. Since

Virginia was no relation to her, and of no social standing in her world, Madama did not have to mind her opinions and worry about politics. And furthermore Virginia seemed to remind her a little of herself as a young woman. Intelligent and headstrong.

"Oh yes I forgot to mention, my men found your painter."

"Madama!" squeaked Virginia.

"Yes, he is rooming with a Florentine goldsmith behind the *Banchi*. I have arranged an escort to take you there tomorrow."

"Thank you Madama!" gushed Virginia, and Madama smiled and waved her hand.

✠

The bombardment from the *castello* woke Virginia at about the fifth hour. The war had arrived and she still had not found Luca. She dressed and ran to the guard post at the front door. After persistent questioning she discovered that the man who knew where Luca was living would come on duty in about an hour, but she prevailed upon the guards to wake him right away so he could take her to Luca as quickly as possible. About twenty minutes later a bleary eyed guard dressed in Madama's livery appeared at the guard post.

"We must go now to find Luca," she insisted.

"Yes *Signorina*, but we must also return as quickly as possible, the enemy is attacking," he replied, redundantly, as the *palazzo* shook from the cannonade.

The guards opened the smaller door set into the huge front door and Virginia and her guard slipped out into the darkness of early morning. They trotted through the quiet streets, the sky lit up by the flashes from the *castello*. It took about half an hour but soon they were at Benvenuto's house and the guard rapped loudly on the door. There was no reply, but after several attempts a window opened high in the wall. "What do you want?" came a voice from above.

"We seek *Signor* Benvenuto Cellini the goldsmith," shouted the guard.

"He is not here," was the reply.

"Do you know where he is?" asked Virginia desperately.

"Yes *Signorina*, he is guarding the *palazzo* of Alessandro del Bene."

"I know where that is *Signorina*," said the guard and they set off again, shouting their thanks to the helpful neighbor.

A few minutes later they arrived at Alessandro's beautiful, painted *palazzo* and pounded on that giant studded wooden door, and another head popped out of another upstairs window. "What do you want?"

"We are looking for Luca the Painter of Florence. He is a friend of *Signor* Benvenuto Cellini the goldsmith."

"You just missed him," came the reply.

"Dear Lord, where could he have gone in the middle of the night in the middle of a war?" hissed Virginia becoming angry. "Where did he go?" she shouted up to the disembodied head emerging from the window.

"Benvenuto and Luca went with *Signor* Alessandro to the battle. The master wanted to see the fighting," then, "wait there."

A few moments later the door opened and Cecchino stepped out. "I think I know where he went," he said, "you should wait here while I find him."

"Absolutely not!" declared Virginia firmly, "I will go with you to find him."

"No *Signorina*," replied Cecchino equally firmly, "if you will not stay then we must arrange a location for you to meet him. You will go to the location and when I find Luca I will tell him to seek you there." Virginia gave it a moment's thought then agreed.

"But where shall we meet?" she asked, "I know nothing of Rome."

"By the obelisk," suggested the guard, "it is easily found from any part of the city being next to the new church in the *Borgo*."

It was agreed and they set off. Cecchino ran ahead and disappeared quickly into the darkness. Virginia could not keep up the pace, but she and the guard made decent time along the *Strada Giulia* and across the Sant'Angelo Bridge into the *Borgo*. A few minutes later she was walking through the ruins of St. Peter's staring up at the massive stone blocks towering into the glowing pre-dawn sky. "Where is this obelisk?" she asked, and Madama's guard led her outside the church. They picked their way carefully through the piles of stone and rubble of the building site towards the towering pillar. She sat down on the steps around its base and waited. She was a lot closer to the fighting than she would have liked, and the noise was fearsome, but as far as she was concerned there was a heavy wall between her and the enemy, so she felt safe enough to wait for Luca.

The sun had risen and lit up the top of the obelisk and was beginning to spill into the Cemetery behind it, and they were still waiting. The guard was starting to become nervous. "Wait here *Signorina*, I shall find out how goes the battle on the wall. I shall be back in less than half an hour," he said and with that was gone. He did not return.

Virginia was starting to lose faith. This whole trip had been a qualified catastrophe. Ginevra's hope had come to nothing, and now Virginia must suffer the consequences of the bad planning and poorer execution. She was not even sure she could find her way back to either Alessandro's house or the *Palazzo Colonna*. She was marooned in the midst of this battle in the midst of this half-built church, with no hope of ever getting home again.

She began to cry. Tears of sadness that she would never see her dear father again; tears of dismay that Luca was gone and she had not had a chance to love him; and tears of anger that she had been so silly as to think a girl could achieve a plan as optimistic as the one she had embarked upon.

She wandered, wailing disconsolately, back into the church and knelt before the tomb of St. Peter in the deep shadows thrown by the early morning light; and prayed. She prayed for her father, she prayed for Luca and she prayed for herself – her knees aching on the hard uneven stone floor.

Hot, salt tears ran down her face and dripped, one following the other, into the dust of the ages.

LA RIUNIONE

Luca sat at the base of the obelisk for a few minutes, catching his breath. It was surprisingly calm there. Certainly the roar of cannon and arquebus and the screams of anger and agony still rent the air, but they were up there – up in the sky above his head. Down in the shadows cast by the morning sun, at the base of the towering column of stone, by the silence of the graveyard, he became more of a detached observer. Nevertheless, he reloaded his weapon.

Virginia had still not appeared and he feared for her safety in this city at war, so he determined to scout the area, working his way through the remnants of St. Peter's. To the north of the obelisk stood the four huge piers of the new church, bracketed together by tenuous masonry archways, suspended high in the air.

This, along with the midden of broken stone and the dust of demolition, was all the construction that had been accomplished on the new church in the past sixty years. The last remnants of the old St. Peter's – the basilica of Constantine – were to his right, lit up by the morning light. He walked beneath the half finished archway of the new church and down broken steps to the space where the altar would stand, and which the dome would one day cover, as yet still open to the rain and the pigeons.

The tomb of St. Peter was the only piece of the old church to have survived the wanton destruction of careless Popes, and was protected by a large marble tabernacle decorated with pillars, centered under the open arches. The massive stonework cast deep shadows inside the ruined church as Luca's eyes slowly grew accustomed to the gloom. Then, as sudden as it was unexpected, one piercing beam from the ever-moving sun, focused through an angle of the arch, pointed a dusty, glowing finger from heaven down to the center of the church.

There she was; a kneeling figure in a blue velvet cloak, the hood pulled up high over her head, praying at the tomb of St. Peter. As he approached she looked up, her pale face glowing, luminous in the misty light reflected from the white dusty floor, more beautiful than any Madonna he had ever painted, the blue fabric pulled close around her head. They stared at each other in disbelief for just a moment, then she jumped to her feet as he ran across the stony floor sweeping her into his arms. They kissed. A magical kiss under a heavenly light in the midst of this ruinous church. For that brief moment the world, the war and all their worries were gone. The heavy stone encircling them dampened the clash of arms, still so close by, and they were transported. "You came for me," was all she said.

Their embrace lasted forever, or so it seemed. But, sadly, the roar of battle and the footfalls of running soldiers broke into their tiny world. Virginia took Luca's hand and led him behind the tomb, away from the fighting, and in amongst the tumble of stone blocks, stored for some supposed rebuilding that never came. There, in a spot hidden from all but the most observant, she threw her blue cloak down to cover the marble dust, and motioned Luca to do likewise. Then she drew him down to lay beside her – alone together at last in a city busy with war.

They embraced and whispered to each other – small things, the gentle, sensual talk of love and tenderness. He caressed her. His hands – the hands of a painter – strong yet delicate, defined and described her face, her body. His touch set her senses aflame, something so long wished for consummated at last.

Virginia whispered to him. Encouragement. His tender ministrations seemed unsure – diffident almost. They spoke of love, love eternal, a love that would outlive them both. She was ready, at last, to become a woman at the hands of this wonderful, adoring man. And for it to happen here, in Rome in the middle of a war – a struggle of the ages – made the entire incredible experience so intense, so immediate. She cried out as the cannon roared above their heads.

They lay in each other's arms, exhausted. A thought crossed Luca's mind as he remembered a moment from his journey – a moment of eternal love. From around his neck he pulled the gold chain with the small gold walnut shell that Sister Emma had given him. He opened the shell and showed Virginia the tiny scene inside. She was delighted, and slipped it over her head after kissing Luca passionately in thanks.

Returning slowly from the mists of love, Luca began to realize the mortal danger they still were in. "Come quickly, I have a safe place for us to stay." He spoke urgently, and gathering their belongings they walked as swiftly as they could through the rubble the length of the church, from under the new St. Peter's and through the remnants of the old, coming out at last onto the *piazza*. There were people running back and forth, crying out. Citizens and soldiers shouting, "They are in the city, we are lost."

They had left it too late. Luca, holding Virginia by the hand ran across the *piazza* hoping to get to the Sant'Angelo Bridge but stopped short as he caught sight of soldiers – Spanish soldiers – bursting like a flood through the *Porta Torrione* to his right. They were laying about them with their swords, screaming *"España, España!"* – cutting down anyone they could reach. He promptly turned about and dragged Virginia back into the church, searching for a way to avoid the butchery as their exit to the bridge had been cut off.

They emerged again on the South side of the new church, back at the obelisk, as Luca looked for a place to hide. The two stopped once more, aghast at the sight of Spanish soldiers running through the graveyard towards them. Luca kissed Virginia one last time and primed his arquebus. He pushed her back against the base of the obelisk and said, "I love you." She mouthed the same words back to him as he promptly turned and aimed at the nearest soldier, maybe forty *braccia* away and brought him down with a well-placed shot. There was no time to reload, they would be on him in a minute or less. He drew his sword with his right hand, the dagger with his left and stood at the base of the obelisk to await his fate. The thought briefly crossed his mind that this massive standing stone had been witness to the death of Saint Peter, and now was to be witness to his own.

The Spanish soldiers were half way through the graveyard now and coming right towards him. Then a miraculous thing happened. To commands barked in German by their officer, a company of Swiss Guards appeared from behind the obelisk and marching swiftly through the square took their position between him and the enemy. The officer turned and shouted to Luca in a heavy accent, "Stay behind us!" Luca sheathed his weapons and ran up the steps to Virginia, holding her in his arms as the remnants of the defenders from the walls rallied around the Swiss and prepared to fight. The Swiss lined up shoulder to shoulder, maybe forty men, and another forty behind them, the polished tips of their long pikes held high in the air, sparkling silver in the early sun as it crept further over the wall. The gunners knelt in front, leveling their weapons.

The Spanish stopped their rapid advance, now moving slowly through the graveyard, warily, like a pack of wolves advancing on a wounded but still dangerous animal. The first to fire were the Spanish. Several arquebuses and pistols were discharged and two Swiss fell, their fellows closing the ranks to keep the phalanx tight. The Roman defenders – some mercenaries, a few Black Bands, but mostly Roman citizens pressed into service – grouped themselves behind and to the sides of the Swiss, maybe a hundred or two, swords drawn, ready to face the unbridled ferocity of their bedraggled and half-starved enemy. Ready to die.

The Spanish were moving again as more of their army poured through the open gates behind them and into the city. The graveyard was now full of Spanish *Rodeleros*, swords in their right hands and bucklers – small round shields – clutched in their left. On a shouted command the Swiss gunners fired as one, the rattle of shot on breastplates and the Spaniards falling dead demonstrating the accuracy of their fire. They reloaded as their fellows dropped their pikes down to the ready – pointed forward at shoulder height. The command came again and the gunners fired their arquebuses, and another rank of Spanish fell. There was nowhere to go for the Spanish; stand and die, retreat or charge the phalanx of steel tipped pikes, each one ten *braccia* long. They charged. The gunners fell back behind the pikemen who dropped their pikes down to waist height, held in both hands. At the last second the Swiss officer shouted a command and the pikemen lunged forward at a run meeting the Spaniards in a crashing clash of steel and flesh. Another command and the pikemen fell back, leaving a squirming mass of dead and wounded in front of them, blood dripping from the razor sharp points of the row of pikes. The Italians had an appropriate term for pike warfare – they called it *Bad War*.

The Swiss arquebusiers, kneeling to either side of the pikemen, on command fired again, downing another row of Spaniards as they tried to clamber over and around the bodies now starting to fill the graveyard. The Spanish swordsmen pulled back again, but behind them Spanish crossbowmen and arquebusiers standing on the wall of the graveyard took aim at the Swiss Guard.

Luca saw what was about to happen and turned as fast as he could. Grabbing Virginia and lifting her off her feet he held her tight, and pushed her up against the obelisk, protecting her with his body. The Spanish fired, shot and crossbow bolts slicing through the air, and around and through the pikemen, decimating their ranks, tearing chips of marble from the obelisk all around the lovers – they felt the wind of their passing, invisible hands plucking at their hair and garments, but by the Grace of God nothing struck them.

With the Swiss in disarray the Spanish attacked again and began to make headway, slicing at the wood of the pikes with their swords and pushing the long weapons upwards to strike at the men behind. The gunners fell back behind the obelisk to reload and the remnants of Renzo di Ceri's ragged Roman defenders joined the mêlée, desperate to push the tide of attackers back, to no avail.

Another command came from the officer, grimly holding his arm, the elbow smashed by a Spanish ball, and the remaining pikemen fell back in good order around the obelisk, backing towards the half built basilica. Luca took Virginia by the hand and ran up the steps into St. Peter's, hiding her behind a fallen pillar next to the tomb. He drew his sword and dagger, as the pikemen retreated under the skeletal arch of the new church, and he deployed with the other defenders to protect the Swiss flank. The remaining pikemen filled the archway of what was intended one day to be the south transept, and stood once again against the encroaching horde. The horde backed away, recently made aware of the bloody damage disciplined pikemen can inflict.

Other Spaniards, tiring of hacking up the bodies of the wounded in their blind fury, started to flank the pikemen. They slunk in through the eastern arch, crawling over the tumbled stone and wood like feral dogs. Then with a yell they flung themselves on the Romans.

Expertly parrying blows with their bucklers as they stabbed underneath with swords, the *Rodeleros* cut through the line of defenders. Luca slashed and blocked, using the two blades to deflect the blows of the Spanish as best he could. He was struck in the face by a buckler and hot blood gushed from his nose as he scrambled sideways to avoid the inevitable sword. The Spaniard leaned forward to thrust and hit Luca a glancing blow to the chest. The tip of the blade cut through his leather jerkin and skidded across the mail shirt underneath, slicing a long furrow in his chest but not piercing his body. Losing his footing the Spaniard struggled to stay upright and Luca drove his dagger deep into the Spaniard's side just under the arm, twisting it as they fell.

In a moment he was back up on his feet, his white shirt stained black with blood as they fought in and out of the random blocks of stone, slashes of light sparkling in the dazzling clouds of dust kicked up by their scuffling feet. The sounds of gunfire were gone now, all that filled the air were the grunts and yells of the fighters and the screams of the wounded as the battle raged hand to hand around the tomb of St. Peter.

At length there was a respite in the flow of the battle. The remnants of the Swiss and the Romans backed up against the tomb for one last stand, their chests heaving from their exertions, their wounds bleeding, dripping and blending into a single pool of blood at their feet. They stood there, maybe twenty men left of well over two hundred. The Spaniards poised around them, steeling themselves to one last attack, knowing that they would win, but not wanting to lose their own lives in the winning.

Into the middle of this scene rode a horseman. He was mounted on a huge chestnut stallion, lightly barded in turquoise leather. He wore a large brown felt hat resplendent with a huge turquoise plume, and a gleaming silver breastplate chased in a classical design. He shouted as he reined in his horse. He screamed at the men in Castilian and they fell in around him. Luca, his back to the tomb with the last few men of St. Peter's, prepared to die.

The man on the chestnut horse and his soldiers stared at the wounded and exhausted defenders for a few seconds that seemed like minutes, then the man urged his horse forward into a pool of sunlight and began in Florentine – perfect yet tinged with his Castilian accent, "If you throw down your weapons now you will be spared but you will become the personal property of Don Cristobal de Guadix. You will hand over to my men all your valuables and become their prisoners. If you refuse you will die."

The last of the Swiss Guards presented their swords and walked towards the man on the chestnut horse. They died in a hail of gunfire. As the echoes faded, he spoke again, "The rest of you have ten seconds to decide." There was silence. Don Cristobal walked his horse up to Luca standing in the center, his shirt torn and stained, his weapons hanging at his side.

The Don drew a pistol from his belt and pointed it at Luca's head. Their eyes met. Don Cristobal's eyes were black, black voids; his hair was black and his neatly clipped beard and moustache were black; his olive skin was leathery from a long mercenary life spent fighting other people's wars. What you could see of his mouth was twisted into a sneer. "Five seconds."

All of a sudden Virginia burst screaming from her hiding place and threw herself in front of Luca in an attempt to protect him. Don Cristobal's horse shied away from the woman, almost depositing him onto the dusty floor. He reined in the horse and pointed his pistol angrily at the back of Virginia's head as she clung to Luca. He pulled the trigger. Nothing. The pistol did not fire. He looked surprised and then laughed – a mocking, jeering laugh – and the whole group of Spaniards laughed with him.

Virginia turned her face up to Don Cristobal, tears running down her cheeks, and she looked hopelessly into those empty pitiless black eyes. He beckoned to her and she walked over to him, standing – such a small blue figure – beneath the huge brown horse.

With a single movement he reached down and hoist her up, throwing her across his saddle. Thereupon, with a shout of instruction to his men, he cantered away, Virginia's ineffectual screams growing fainter until they were gone.

Part Two

CAPO PASSERO

The caravel had been underway for three days, bouncing along in the coastal currents, its two triangular sails full with the strong westerly wind. Luca was sick. If truth be told, he had been sick since the beginning of the voyage, but had actually vomited only once. He had spent the rest of the time clutching a heaving stomach in manacled hands. He had barely slept and when his eyes had mercifully closed he had been beset once more by dreams of monsters – this time with the added misery of Virginia crying out of the fog to be rescued.

He stood up and walked on unsteady feet the length of the hold to the hatchway. It was sealed by a latticework hatch cover, and Luca pushed his head up high enough to squint through the crisscross strips of wood. He could not see much; sailors moving about the deck adjusting one of the billowing sails, some blue sky and salt spray. He sat down in his place once again, amongst his companions, the thirty or so hungry, thirsty and disconsolate souls that filled the hold.

The days after he had been captured were still a blur, and during the enforced idleness of the voyage he had rehearsed those events in his head. Seeing the woman he loved stolen from him just as he had been reunited with her had incensed him. His first impulse had been to kill as many Spaniards as he could before being hacked to death himself – to leave this life in a blaze of righteous fury –

but his mind was changed by the thought of rescue. If he were to die here, now, at the hands of these feral creatures from the mist, who would remain to rescue Virginia from the arrogant Spaniard – Don Cristobal as he styled himself? So, much against his every impulse, he had thrown down his sword and dagger alongside the last of the Roman defenders, and reluctantly given himself up to his captors.

Against the word of Don Cristobal, the Spaniards had summarily executed those captives whose wounds they considered too grave, and marched the rest in single file, at sword's point, through those streets Luca had so recently roamed in freedom. They had crossed the Sant'Angelo Bridge from the *Borgo* into Rome, and the sight that had greeted them was a scene from a Flemish painting of the Inferno: fires raged, dead and wounded lay all about, and the Spanish and the Germans, finally let loose, were running hither and thither stealing, killing and raping in some sort of collective, insane blood lust.

The prisoners had been locked in a large storeroom in a house somewhere in the city, and from time to time new captives added to their group. After a day or two the Spaniards had interviewed all the captives. The ones with valuables in the city had been tortured to hand them over and the ones from wealthy families who could be ransomed had been taken away. The rest, including Luca, had been manacled and led through the hellish, burning streets down to the Tiber, and onto the caravel.

That had been the last Luca had seen of Rome: full of death, her wealth plundered, all aflame, evening-dark at midday from the somber pall of black smoke masking the blue sky.

Luca had seen Don Cristobal one more time as he had been dragged before him, thrown to the ground and questioned to establish his usefulness. He had asked after Virginia and received a cuff about the head for his trouble. "As are you, she is my property," the Don had declared, "she comes with me to Guadix." And that was it.

As they were being loaded onto the boat he had heard something that sounded like, "Dragut is at *Capo Passero*," but since he did not recognize either name he gave it no further mind. All things considered, Luca felt lucky to have escaped the death and destruction of Rome without much more than a few cuts and a broken nose. He was still having trouble breathing properly, but he acknowledged it could have been much worse. It was to become much worse.

✠

Luca was not sure where they were being taken. He had assumed that they would be brought to the Don's estate in Spain – Castile, Aragon, wherever it was he called home – but he had noticed, by the position of the sun during his daily observations through the hatch, that they were travelling roughly southward. After a few days of bouncing queasily on the open sea they put into port with much shouting and bumping and activity on deck, and suddenly the hatch was thrown open.

The prisoners were linked together on a long chain, and led across the deck of the caravel and down a plank onto the small wooden dock that jutted out from the beach. Luca looked around him, squinting in the bright sun. The deep blue sky was matched only by the azure sea – dazzling yellow sunlight reflecting blindingly off yellow rocks.

As they filed down the dock and up the rocky hillside pathway they passed a half dozen small galleys pulled up on the beach, crews hard at work on them. In addition he could see another ten or more galleys and some cargo ships anchored in the harbor. They were short fast galleys and heavily armed; *galliots* he had heard them called. They were most commonly used for raiding and fighting, but that was not the most alarming observation. Except for the crew of the caravel that had transported them there, all the other crews and workmen – swarthy, bearded, turbaned men who glared at them as they passed – were Turks.

At the top of the rise Luca was able to look back on the harbor – a semi-circle of golden rock enclosing a blue bay, a small beach, the dock and then the vast expanse of the sea to the distant horizon. From this vantage point he was able to ascertain that they were on an island separated from the mainland by a narrow channel – or vice versa. He stumbled a little as his attention was thus diverted and received a slap from one of the crew as he struggled to regain his footing. They walked away from the harbor, heads bowed, single file, strung out on the chain, along an arid, rock-strewn pathway across a flat, empty plain scattered with scrubby bushes.

After a few minutes Luca beheld the destination of their march. Rising out of the otherwise featureless plain, built from the same yellow rock and equally featureless, was a square, low tower – a small fortress. After toiling laboriously along the path in the hot sun they finally arrived at the base of the fortress. Up close Luca could see the evidence of a battle – pockmarks in the stone and sections of broken, smoke-blackened wall.

The path led behind the blank, square edifice, past a large open grave full of bodies, which a pair of Turks was in the process of filling with lime and dirt, and up a stone ramp to a short wooden drawbridge that gave access to the fortress. Across the drawbridge, beneath an archway, the row of dispirited prisoners was handed over to glowering Turks; money changed hands and their Italian crew nervously departed.

The dungeon of the fortress was a gloomy and vile-smelling place, the relentless darkness relieved by just one small barred window, being the only source of both light and air. Their hands were manacled still, but they were relieved of the chain and stumbled into the dark room with the help of a few swipes from a Turkish rod. Luca realized that they were not the only inhabitants of the dungeon. Tripping over a few feet as he crept through the darkness, inspiring curses that tracked his progress, he found an empty space against a wall and sat down.

Luca's world had finally and completely fallen apart, and he was at a loss as to what to do. His only recourse was to pray to God for help. He was mumbling in Latin under his breath when he noticed the prisoner sitting to his right was mumbling the same prayer along with him. Luca looked at the man. He was coal black and the weak light gleamed from his ebony skin. He was, however, dressed like a gentleman not like a native African. Luca finished the prayer and addressed his neighbor, "*Signore*, may I ask how you come to be here in this state of misery?"

The man smiled and replied in Florentine, his deep voice tinged with a Portuguese accent, "Well you may my friend. I was travelling to Rome and our ship was beset by pirates. Many were killed, and the rest, the ones you see sitting here, were taken as slaves."

"So is that what we are to be, slaves?" asked Luca, finally accepting the awful truth.

"Were you not captured by pirates?"

"No, we were sold into this hell by brothers of our own faith."

The black man shook his head in dismay.

"But let me introduce myself," continued Luca after a moment's pause, "my name is Luca, the Painter of Florence."

"Pleased to meet you *Signor* Luca, although I would that it were under more auspicious circumstances. I am Dom Henrique, Bishop of Utica and Vicar apostolic of the Kongo. My father is King of Kongo Nation," answered the black man.

"Oh," was all that Luca could think of saying, followed, after a moment to collect his wits, with, "Forgive me My Lord, I had not taken you for a churchman. I was not aware of a blackamoor as Christian bishop."

"I do believe I am the first," laughed the Bishop in his booming voice, "although, if I return not to my people, I fear, as all men are tempted to do, they may stray from the path of our Lord."

"Where is Utica?" asked Luca, now intrigued.

"It is a city of the Ancients, proximal to Tunis in the Maghreb."

"I would imagine that there are not many Ancients requiring divine unction."

"Indeed. It is more or less a ceremonial title, since Tunis is currently the possession of the Mohammedans. But we shall soon see. I would venture that Tunis is our destination once the Turks have collected enough of us."

"To be sold?"

"Aye. There is a slave market there which is the nearest from here."

"And where exactly is here?"

"We are at *Capo Passero*," declared Henrique knowledgeably; Luca looked blank, he had not travelled far afield from his native

Florence, except to the surrounding cities for work. "It is an island that forms the southernmost extent of Sicily – the closest point to the Maghreb." Henrique continued with his geography lesson, "The nearest port from here is probably Tripoli which is due south of us, but that is occupied by the Christian army of the Emperor, his toehold in the Islamic nation. So the nearest slave market is Tunis which is a day or two further up the coast, about due west of us."

"How do you know such things?" asked Luca, impressed.

"On our voyage Romewards I studied much the science of navigation. The Captain, may God receive his soul, had many good maps, and great knowledge to go with them."

Henrique warmed to his subject now, glad to have encountered someone with whom he could have an intelligent conversation. "The pirate captain of this small fleet, do you know him?"

"I met nobody here except a few sailors, in passing."

"His name is Dragut. He sails under the flag of Barbarossa." This latter was a name Luca was familiar with: Barbarossa – Red Beard – the seemingly immortal pirate and Pasha of Algiers who was the scourge of Christian shipping from Cyprus to Gibraltar. Luca grimaced at the thought of being in the hands of such cutthroats. "With his small group of galleys he has captured untold numbers of much larger vessels and sells the valuables, and the people, for profit."

Although it helped Luca's mood to have someone with whom he could share his suffering, he could not shake the beginnings of a deep melancholy whose waves of doom washed over him, threatening to engulf his normally sanguine nature. This was the second time he had been locked up in almost as many weeks, and he was exhausted by his recent misadventures. He slept as if he were dead for the rest of that day and through the night, curled on the hard stone floor, oblivious to the endless murmur of the captives and the rustle of vermin. He was awoken the next morning by Henrique offering him a dirty cup of weak vinegary wine and a handful of bread to mop up the dregs.

"This is our meal for the day, I trust you would not want to miss it," he said, his kindly face creasing in a rueful smile.

"Indeed I should not," affirmed Luca, choking down the meager rations. "I have not eaten in many days."

And so it went for a week, as further captives were added to their crowded, reeking quarters. Luca tried to count heads, but gave up an accurate count after reaching forty, approximating the number of inhabitants at over one hundred. Just when it seemed that the dungeon could fit no more, the barred door was thrown open and the Turks began leading their captives out – once more onto the scrubby plain before the fortress.

They lined the prisoners up in four groups of about thirty and roped the members of each group together. Luca evaluated the chance of escape at none. For one thing they were on a barren, rocky island off the coast of a barren and rocky Sicily, so there was nowhere to run. And, by the look of the Turks, they would have no hesitation in summarily ending the life of anyone foolish enough to disobey their every instruction.

As if to punctuate Luca's thoughts, one prisoner, driven mad by the days of captivity, broke free from his captors and ran with a stumbling gait across the island, away from the fortress and towards the azure sea that lay all about. There was much shouting and gesticulation by the Turks at the running man, but his run was ended as quickly as it began by a single shot from a well-aimed crossbow.

He stumbled and fell face down onto the dusty plain, never to rise again. There was a grim silence among the captives as the Turks walked up and down the lines yelling in their barbarian tongue, and slapping the prisoners at random, as if daring them to attempt the same escape while reaffirming the outcome of such an attempt. With a resigned finality the lines of prisoners moved off in single file, a pair of Turkish jailers between each line.

Back to the beach they marched, and out onto the narrow wooden pier they were led. Since Luca's arrival two square-rigged roundships had tied up to the pier – fat cargo ships pitching and rolling slightly in the swell – onto which the captives were loaded. Once more Luca was locked in the hold of a bouncing ship that reeked of brine and pitch. He could feel his stomach rising up to his throat, although he had precious little left within to expel. There they sat, side by side, hands still manacled, the Bishop of Utica and the Painter of Florence – risen so high yet fallen so low, but with so much farther left to fall.

Full with misery the two roundships pushed off and swung out around the headland of *Capo Passero*, their sails set for the slave market of Tunis. Escorting them was a pair of the sharp, narrow galleys, to protect the precious human cargo within.

Il Cavaliere

Sir Richard Weston stood on the battlements of the *San Pietro* fortress of Tripoli and gazed out across the jumbled cubes of the walled Moorish town towards the vast and endless expanse of desert stretching seamlessly to the horizon, broken only by the slow silhouette of a camel caravan.

He shivered involuntarily, drawing his black cloak, emblazoned with the narrow, forked white cross of St. John, tightly about him. It was by no means cold, quite the contrary, but the boundlessness of this heathen country filled him with an unaccustomed dread. Seeing this dusty yellow sea of nothing, this void of a country, home of the Berber and the Mameluke and a hundred and one nameless, ever-shifting Moorish tribes, made him even less optimistic about garrisoning the place than previously he had been.

He turned to his companion and spoke, "Guillaume, this is truly the gateway to hell – hot and dry and with death all about us." His hand swung around him indicating the unforgiving desert to one side of the fortress and the deep and treacherous blue sea to the other. "If we are forced to hold this castle, like a carbuncle on the rump of Mohammed, it will be a dark day for the Order. We will become a target for every Bey and Sultan from Algiers to Antioch, to say nothing of the Grand Turk himself and his filthy infestation of pirates. If any one of them gets a mind to wage war then here we should be – an easy and obvious focus for their religious fervor."

He paused, "And to what end?"

The two stood a while in mute agreement and Sir Richard once more took up his theme. "At least at Rhodes we had a well-defended harbor and outlying islands, and a supportive citizenry. Here we have just one large fortress which can be blockaded easily by sea and besieged conveniently by land. And do you see the glances we receive from the inhabitants of this hell-mouth? The sight of the Holy Cross seems to make them even more eager to fight against us for their own devilish heresy. We would simultaneously be besieged from without and betrayed from within."

"*Oui*," came the taciturn response.

"Is that all you have to say?" asked Sir Richard, surprised.

"You complain enough for ten men," replied his companion in heavily accented English, "*my* complaints would hardly be worth the speaking."

Sir Richard Weston looked at Sir Guillaume d'Aubusson and laughed – two knights standing on the battlements of a heathen fortress, silhouetted against the encroaching emptiness as their Crusader forebears had been over four hundred years earlier at Jerusalem – eternal symbols of the God of Peace set against the casual savagery of the *Ummah*. They were the last Crusaders, standing upright, alone, against the endless horizontality of the Empire of Mohammed.

Yes it was a hard and unvarying place, Tripoli, and yet it was, by the Emperor's edict and generosity, to be theirs. Strange this Caesar who takes away in the very act of giving; whose gifts, so freely given, always bear the burden of such a heavy price.

The Knights needed a base of operations since they had been so ignominiously ejected from their home on Rhodes, and who else but the Holy Roman Emperor, the modern incarnation of the Caesars of ancient Rome, to give it to them. The island of Malta was to be their new port. But no Malta without Tripoli, that was the mandate.

Malta, the fortress island, was to be handed over at the cost of a falcon – an inexpensive annual symbol of their fealty to this great Lord of worlds both old and new. Inexpensive true, yet it was a symbol that rankled – for, notwithstanding their current lack of a home, the Knights of St. John were proudly independent, devout both in their Christianity and in their allegiance to the Order, despite, or perhaps because of their multi-national composition. The King of England might be fighting the King of France on the field of battle, yet within the Order the two languages worked in cooperation, side by side, all conflicts of their home countries set aside for the benefit of the Holy Religion, united in their campaign against the Turk.

Still, beggars cannot be choosers, and they needed their own port from which to fight the predations of the Turkish corsairs – violent and relentless pirates who preyed on Christian merchant ships, carrying off their cargo and selling their Christian crews as slaves to the mercy of Moslem masters.

Richard and Guillaume – of the English language and the French language respectively – were here in Tripoli to assess the amount of work needed to bring the defenses up to the level expected by the Order. At the moment the fortress was garrisoned by a mixed group of Imperial mercenaries commanded by a Spanish general who made no bones about being glad to be leaving. The fortifications had been improved under the present commander – the walls thickened to withstand modern cannon, and towers added at strategic points along the walls to provide flanking fire at any potential attacker. Still, the location was many days from Christian civilization and relief from a siege – and the memory of Rhodes was fresh in the minds of the two Knights as they surveyed the fortress.

Just a few years earlier the Order had been safe on Rhodes within an impregnable walled citadel many times stronger than this one. Yet, for the need of just a few companies of men and a dozen galleys, they had been beaten and ousted by the Grand Turk, Suleiman the Law Giver.

They had begged for help throughout Europe to maintain their base for the protection of Christian shipping, yet had received none. The Princes of Europe were content to fight amongst themselves for pieces of each other's lands to be given as prizes to their favorites, while the Turk was rattling the gates of Vienna, and the Knights of St. John were driven from their home of over two hundred years.

The world was changing. The entire order of things was in a state of flux, and this had hardened the Knights against reliance on any Prince, for ultimately only the Lord God could be trusted. Yet here they were to be, at the whim of the Emperor, guarding the forsaken outposts of his far-flung empire. And for what purpose? It was simply so that the Emperor could brag he owned a piece of the Maghreb – that long stretch of North African coastline from Gibraltar to Alexandria, home of the Moors and the nomadic Arab tribes. People who, to a man, were prepared to wage *jihad* against the Christians until they were gone from their land.

"I trust Malta will provide us a more defensible position," mused Sir Richard as the two Knights exited the gates of *San Pietro* onto a long and wide stone pier that jutted out into the harbor.

"The way the Emperor gives land I would not expect it to be so," replied his companion as they walked with their retinue toward the ships.

The Knights had each brought the galley they commanded with them from Nizza. Magnificent craft they were, newly refitted after the damage they had received in the flight from Rhodes. Each one was a hundred and forty feet long and twenty feet wide, and was powered by two huge lateen sails, plus seventy-two oars a side. Sitting low in the water, they were built for speed and overwhelming firepower, carrying a complement of fifty men-at-arms in addition to the sailors and oarsmen.

The bristling forest of oars dipped into the glassy sea as one and rose again, dripping water sparkling in the sun. The rhythm was repeated mechanically as the two galleys rowed steadily out of Tripoli in the still morning air, their forward motion just enough to stir the red pennants of St. John, white-crossed and trimmed with gold, that flew from their masts. They were glad to be leaving this dusty and unwelcoming outpost of Christendom, both captains and crews – trimming the sails to pick up the least draft that could speed their progress. Splendid and deadly, the long sleek black hulls rounded the breakwater and slid gracefully towards the horizon, north to their next port of call – Malta.

LE SCHIAVI

The city of Tunis was a bustling free port where land and sea met in a mercenary extravagance of trade and luxury. From out of the surrounding desert came caravans, bringing from all directions every imaginable cargo – spices, silks, slaves, ivory, gold and silver. And from the sea came the merchantmen and the galleys, some looking to buy, some to sell. The center of the town was thus one huge *souk*; twisting, narrow, interlocking streets full of stalls and shops, markets and street traders, all shouting their wares to every passerby. And in the midst of this cacophony of commerce was a small island of peace – the enforced quiet of the slave market.

It was a square and fairly large space, open to the sky in the middle of the jumble of tiny streets, and was surrounded by a covered colonnade. In the whitewashed archways formed by the colonnade the slaves were chained, to be inspected by buyers from far and wide much as they would inspect livestock. Then, at the end of the week, the slaves would be brought to a raised stone platform in the middle of the square, singly or in groups, to be auctioned.

The two roundships carrying Luca and his cohort of misery arrived at Tunis about five days after departing *Capo Passero*. It had been a hard journey for the captives in the holds of the rolling ships. At first the square-riggers had moved swiftly south west towards the Maghreb, their large expanse of canvas filled by a favorable wind, but once they reached the North African coastline the winds had shifted against them and they had been forced to tack back and forth along the coast to make any headway – slow going indeed. The queasy captives had been hungry and thirsty for the entire journey, receiving just a subsistence ration of dry bread and watery wine.

The city of Tunis was set back a good way from the sea, so the slave ships were forced to tie up just inside the harbor mouth along an ancient causeway that connected the port with the city. From there to march their cargoes, chained again in groups, into the heart of the city.

Luca, Henrique and the other bedraggled prisoners struggled from the ships onto the causeway and formed up in lines as quickly as possible, to avoid a stroke of the rod from their turbaned masters. They had lost some members of their company along the way – on Luca's ship one man had been driven mad from thirst, or simply from horror at a situation to which he could not reconcile himself, and had started drinking the sea water that puddled at the bottom of the hold. The other had merely passed away, seemingly from weariness and melancholy. Both had been hurled unceremoniously into the sea.

Luca, despite his own weariness and melancholy, could not help but gaze around him in astonishment at this foreign city. The sun shone high from a clear blue sky, glaring off the bone white buildings of distant Tunis – the *kasbah*, the walled citadel within the city, rising up on a mound in its midst. And in the far distance the misty blue mountains joined seamlessly with the sky. All about them were rolling hills, planted with thick groves of lofty palms and prickly pear, that swept unbroken to the deep blue gulf.

The slaves began their slow march – maybe two leagues – under the blazing sun, down the long causeway alongside a brackish, beetle-green lagoon. The chains on their wrists clanked as they swung with every step, the Turks shouting and bullying them to move faster in their harsh, vulgar tongue.

Ships of all kinds were jammed shoulder to shoulder against the dock while bales and barrels and boxes were loaded on and off by a veritable army of porters, and transported to and from the city by a constant traffic of cart and wagon. Yet nobody remarked the train of dispirited and disheveled slaves as they passed silently behind this hive of activity. They finally reached the end of the causeway and, passing through a heavily guarded archway in a high stone wall, disappeared into the city of Tunis.

Luca had never beheld a city such as this. It was as if every house had been built without care for its neighbor, so the street was forced to wind in and out of walls and doorways set at odd angles, painted balconies and archways filling the space overhead, so that it seemed you were navigating a brightly adorned, whitewashed cavern.

The Moorish inhabitants stepped aside, glaring sullenly as the line of slaves marched by. Walking alternately into one of the pools of harsh sunlight that broke through the jumble of architecture, and then back into the perpetual half-light of the *souk*, they marched on – through narrow, winding passageways and out into small market squares, up interminable low steps and past endless shops, their wares displayed under brightly striped canvas awnings. Finally, exhausted, they passed under the low arch into the slave market, and were led along the colonnade to be chained by the ankle to stone pillars.

Luca was glad to have the manacles removed from his hands, the chafing of two weeks had worn the skin from parts of his wrists, and he rubbed his wounds in relief. He was also glad to have a trough of water before him and plenty of bread to fill his aching stomach. This was, ironically, the best place he had been since the fall of Rome and the downfall of Luca. When life becomes too unremittingly hostile a man must adjust his priorities. And the simple provision of food and drink in an environment that was well lighted and warm, rather than a dark hole that was alternately bone-chillingly cold and swelteringly hot, made Luca strangely happy, even lightheaded. They had arrived – the fear and agony of the uncertain journey was past. Doubtless, tomorrow would bring more fear and uncertainty, yet for now they were safe and fed and warm – alive. Thank God.

Luca and the Bishop said prayers of thanks in which the majority of the slaves joined – quietly, so as not to incur the wrath of their Mohammedan captors, but with relief for having so far been spared that certain death which each one of them had surely expected at any moment. Luca enjoyed the familiar Latin prayers he had been saying since he was a small child. Now, of course, he knew their meaning, having studied Latin for several years at school, but he delighted in the comfortable act of repeating them, as it connected him somehow to a warmer, better time. He was comforted.

As the day progressed more slaves were led in and shackled by the ankles as Luca and his companions had been, filling the three sides of the market square with humanity. For the first time since Rome he was able to take stock of his fellow captives. The few he recognized from Rome were dressed mostly as tradesmen and laborers – not wealthy enough to have hidden money, nor important enough to be ransomed – mostly younger men like himself, but a few in their thirties and forties; strong men mostly. Then there were the surviving crew and passengers of the ship Henrique had been aboard – sailors and a few older men who looked like merchants. Finally, the new arrivals were villagers, fishermen perhaps, probably taken in the kind of coastal raids that had depopulated many of the smaller islands, and made the fast galleys of the pirates such a fearsome sight.

The entire group appeared extremely disheveled after days or, in some cases, weeks in captivity. Luca's nose was healing – he could breathe through it now at least. But he was still covered in the blood of the battle – both his and his opponents' – turned dark brown and crusted now. His soft linen shirt was torn and jagged where he had ripped away pieces to staunch his bleeding nose, and the remnants of his leather jerkin was sliced across the chest from the Spaniard's sword thrust – the chainmail vest that had saved his life long since taken.

His face was a mess, and it was probably a good thing for his vanity that there was no mirror to be had. His nose was still swollen and two weeks' growth of blood-caked beard darkened his jowls. His hair no longer fell in soft and shiny black curls, but hung in lank, greasy strings.

Luca reached back and retied the ribbon, pulling the oily mess of hair from his face. Despite his ragged appearance he was still a striking man, just a little the worse for wear. This, as ever, was to be both a blessing and a curse.

They spent a night in this place, guarded by fierce Berber tribesmen dressed in their colorful robes, each one carrying a long, curved sword slung from the hip, hanging on a belt fashioned from twisted and tasselled cord. The slaves curled up to sleep as much as they could on the straw bedding, like so many oxen awaiting the auction.

Early the next morning a man in a lustrous blue turban arrived with a train of attendants. He seemed to be the manager of the slave market, as he examined each of the slaves carefully. Then, upon his barked command, his attendants began shouting at the slaves to strip, urging them on with painful strokes from the long rods the Moslems favored. Once they were all naked their clothes were removed and they were each provided with a pair of harsh linen trousers as their sole garment – this was how they were to be presented to their potential buyers.

About mid-morning the buyers entered the square and proceeded to walk from archway to archway along the colonnade staring at the slaves who stood or sat, glumly enduring this further insult to what little was left of their dignity. Periodically one of the buyers would see a slave he liked the look of, and would have the attendant poke and prod him to perform jumps and springs, then they would check the man's teeth as a gauge of his health. This performance went on until midday when they were once again fed.

Luca asked his new friend where they were likely to be sent to work. As far as Henrique knew there were quarries and building projects, work in the fields, and work on the docks and in warehouses. The best outcome they could hope for was to be purchased as a household servant by a wealthy man, but that was rare. By far the worst kind of toil was rowing in the galleys. All the Moslem galleys used slave labor as a more or less disposable source of power and, as often as not, once a man was consigned to the rowing benches he did not return.

Standing there, chained to a Carthaginian column, waiting to be sold to the highest bidder – to Heaven only knew what fate –

Luca was reminded, with an overwhelming rush of melancholy, of the story of Timothy the Fortuneteller at the fair, and how far away from this place was Florence, his beloved home. And how nothing is sure in this world.

In the early afternoon the buyers filed in and stood around the stage. Luca had fondly hoped that he might see a European face in the crowd – someone who might buy him and take him away from this place – but he was disappointed. The crowd was entirely made up of Moors and Turks, and the occasional coal black Nubian. Some were obviously local farmers or business owners in their simple attire, others were more expensively dressed, some quite sumptuously, who were presumably agents and merchants planning to transport their purchases on to some other destination.

First upon the stage were some of the older men in twos and threes, sold off quickly to the farmers as cheap field hands. Then the younger men were up, and the bidding started to get more intense. Finally it was Luca's turn to step onto the stage. The bidding started and he looked down into the sea of faces with a sad disinterest, he had begun to doubt that he would ever see home again.

Then he saw her. She was small and surrounded by tall servants, so he had not observed her arrival, but now she stood directly in front of the stage staring up at him, smiling behind a thin veil. The bidding moved steadily higher as the auctioneer extolled Luca's virtues, making him lift his arms and turn around to display his strong, young body. The woman's smile grew broader and she tapped the servant at her side, who bid on her behalf. Luca was bemused, but smiled back at the woman, not wishing to end up lifting rocks, or worse, rowing in a galley.

There now broke out a contest between the woman, or rather her servant – as Moorish women were not permitted to bid at auction against men – and a big ugly-looking Turk dressed in fine silks. Of the two, Luca preferred the look of the woman, so he smiled at her and tried to look as appealing as possible in his messy state, wearing a pair of somebody else's trousers. The auctioneer was enjoying the struggle between the two bidders and, as auctioneers love to do, was playing one off against the other, to the great amusement of the crowd, until finally the ugly Turk threw up his hands in defeat and Luca was sold. He returned to the colonnade to await collection by his new owner, thinking that perhaps life as a slave in this woman's household might be bearable after all.

He sat down once he was chained to the pillar and waited for Henrique to return.

"How did you fare?" he asked as the large black man sat down next to him.

"Nobody wanted me," answered Henrique glumly.

"Why on earth not?" asked Luca, wondering why a man of his strong physique did not sell.

"They have separate auctions for my people," came the dispirited answer. "All the buyers here were looking for white men so I was not purchased."

"What does that mean?"

"The galleys I imagine."

They sat in silence for a while.

"What was your fate?" asked Henrique presently.

"Rather odd indeed," replied Luca, "I was bought by a woman, by her servant actually, but she seemed to want me."

Henrique laughed, "Well you are a fine looking young man, perhaps she needs a… companion."

"Surely not." Luca was scandalized, yet intrigued. "Probably just needs a household servant – I hope."

"You are a good man Luca. I pray for your sake that is the outcome."

After the auction was finished the slaves were divided up into groups for their various purchasers, and as the money changed hands the slaves were led away. Eventually, Luca was unshackled from the pillar he shared with Henrique, and they quickly said their farewells as he was prodded towards the entrance.

There waiting for him was the woman – his new owner – and her four servants. He bowed to her in his urbane, deferential style, and that seemed to please her. He was close enough now to make out her features.

She wore a veil, as did all the Moorish women, but the fashion was for the veil to be transparent – following the letter of *Shari'ah* rather than its intent. She looked to be forty or forty-five, small of stature, not unattractive, with smooth olive skin and heavy lines of kohl defining her already large eyes. Luca concluded that being a slave to this woman might not be such a bad outcome for this terrible journey.

Two of the servants held him, one under each arm, concerned perhaps that he might attempt an escape, and started after their mistress. They had gone but a few paces when all Luca's hopes for a comfortable bondage were dashed. A man appeared, blocking their path, and he promptly began yelling at the diminutive woman. She, not cowed by his anger, yelled right back. There ensued an angry altercation, as the servants stepped nervously away from the arguing couple.

After a few minutes of this furious exchange the final outcome was firmly decided by the man. He established the supremacy of his side of the argument by slapping the woman hard across the face. She immediately burst into tears. The man shouted at the servants who led her away, sobbing, and then he turned on Luca. He screamed at Luca in his incomprehensible language, and dragged him roughly back to the market by his hair.

The man threw him to the ground, and apparently demanded of the auctioneer that his money should be returned. This the auctioneer reluctantly did, and Luca was led back to his pillar in the market.

"What happened?" asked Henrique, in surprise at seeing his departed friend returned.

"The lady's husband was not happy," muttered Luca. Henrique burst into a big booming laugh at the absurdity of the situation in the midst of all their suffering.

"I am not surprised!" he exclaimed. "So, it seems you are left with us," he added with a sigh. Luca sat down again, once more resigned to his fate with little hope for the future.

It was approaching evening and the Moors took time again to pray. Luca had remarked that these Mohammedans seemed to pray every few hours. They made the most devout monk of Christendom look quite casual by comparison. He wondered to himself how they ever managed to accomplish anything with such a rigorous devotional schedule.

While he was musing on the nature of *Muselmán* worship there came a commotion to disturb the relative quiet of the market. A noisy group of Turks had arrived and were in deep conversation with the auctioneer. Luca could easily tell the difference between the Moors and the Turks. The former wore loose robes and softly wrapped headscarves, the latter wore outlandish trousers, short-sleeved embroidered jackets and large, tight turbans.

From his vantage point by the pillar Luca watched the discussion and saw money change hands. It seemed that the profit from the slave auction was being divided with much pointing and hand waving. After business was concluded to the satisfaction of all, the auctioneer gesticulated in Luca's direction, and the Turks walked purposefully towards him.

The lead Turk was better dressed than the others and sported perhaps the largest, reddest and most ridiculously oversized turban Luca had yet seen, and Luca was a man of Florence, perhaps the world capital of outrageous headgear. He called to Henrique and asked if he recognized the lead figure.

"By the Saints," exclaimed Henrique, "that is Dragut."

"The pirate who sold us?"

"The very same."

"He does not look happy," observed Luca, and it was true the pirate looked peevish, presumably over the non-sale of two of his best slaves.

The two were surrounded by the Turks and one of Dragut's lieutenants took the lead, having Luca and Henrique walk and jump, just as they had been forced to do for the buyers. The lieutenant then harangued the auctioneer.

"Do you know what he is saying?" asked Luca quietly.

"I think he is explaining why you were not sold. Apparently you were bought by the wife of one of the local chieftains, so he was obliged to refund the money. Now the Turk is shouting at him for selling you to a woman in the first place, and he is defending himself. Now he is explaining that the crowd did not want a black man, but he can hold me until next week for the next auction."

"How many languages do you speak?" asked Luca in astonishment.

"I have come to understand many things," smiled Henrique without elaboration.

The negotiations ended with the auctioneer handing over some more money – doubtless a levy for having been a fool – and the Turkish lieutenant shaking his head about leaving Henrique until the following week. It seemed the Turks had other plans. He barked an order at his crew and the two slaves were unhitched from the pillar and shackled together.

"Not good news," muttered Henrique to his friend, "they are taking us to the galleys to replace a pair of rowers."

Luca's journey was growing progressively worse.

Dragut

The merchant galley was running. The red cross of Genoa crackled at her masthead. Sailors were scurrying back and forth trimming the sails to put to use the meanest gust, and the rowers were pulling as if their lives depended on it, which they most likely did. Less than half a league behind came the sleek *galliots* of Dragut, flying the green flag of Barbarossa. Their sails were furled and their men armed, ready to board the merchantman, the rowers straining at the oars under the rods of their overseers. The ships, the Christian and the Moslem, seemed evenly matched in the speed of the chase, which, although frantic, was taking place at a leisurely six knots.

The wind picked up, suddenly filling the sails of the Genoese ship to cheers from the sailors, and the merchantman began to pull ahead. But their good fortune was short-lived. From beyond a headland jutting from the rocky coast appeared two more corsair galleys rowing fast to intercept. Two sailors leaned hard on the steering oars and the Genoese galley began to turn towards the rapidly closing gap between their pursuers and the ambush ahead. The captain screamed his orders over the crash of waves and the snapping of the sails, and the rowers redoubled their efforts – but it was to no avail.

The four pirate ships blocked the merchantman's escape to front and to rear and the captain ordered the rowers to cease their efforts. There was a moment of calm as the ships rocked in the swell, the four corsairs at the four points of the compass their bow guns loaded and pointing at the Genoese. With one command Dragut could destroy the Italian galley in an instant and burn it to the waterline. They waited. Then came the call, "Stand down – surrender and your lives will be spared."

The Genoese sailors looked to their captain, but there really was no choice. He yelled back, "We surrender."

This was typical of the work of the corsair galleys – hiding along the coast waiting for merchant vessels and catching them in an ambush. The better sailors would steer more out to sea away from the pirate-infested coast, but that had its own dangers. Wrecks were not uncommon without a coastal bay to shelter in, and a storm might come out of nowhere, turning the smooth azure sea into a heaving grey creature that could eat the largest and most powerful galley in one bite.

Luca bent over the oar retching from the exertion, gasping for breath after the chase. The overseers walked up and down the benches throwing buckets of seawater over the slaves' steaming backs.

The slaves were set in pairs on the benches, two men to an oar, and Luca was seated on the hull side of a bench near the stern of the galley on the starboard side. The more experienced rowers sat on the inside so they could guide the movement of the oar, their companion on the hull side simply lending brute strength to the stroke. The accommodations were tight and uncomfortable, as the galley was no more than six *braccia* wide. And between the rows of benches, down the ship's centerline, ran a deck wide enough for the overseers to pass.

To Luca's left was a large square opening in the hull through which the oar passed on its way to a pivoting oarlock, set on an outrigger about a *braccio* outside the body of the ship. Above the deck that passed between the rowers was a wider deck that ran from stem to stern – connecting the gun deck at the prow with the command deck at the stern – from which the sailors could adjust the rigging and sail. Finally, over the outriggers was a pair of narrow walkways, one on either side, the length of the galley, mounted with several medium caliber swivel guns.

Crushing boredom in great discomfort under a baking sun, drenched by the cold sea, followed by moments of physically exhausting panic – then the melancholy of having helped the Turk capture another Christian vessel. This was Luca's life on board the galley of Dragut the corsair.

The *galliots* sailed in groups of four, running with the currents along the rocky Sicilian coast, and could swiftly box in and board a passing cargo ship, usually without much of a fight. To save the rowers energy for the chase, the sailors would use the single huge triangular sail while hunting, changing to oar power for a final burst of speed and maneuverability. Once a capture had been made, one of the galleys would break off and escort the prize back to *Capo Passero*, then rejoin the hunt.

Luca fell again into a deep despondency. So this was to be his fate: to live, slave and ultimately die in the unwilling service of the sworn enemies of Christendom – to labor, chained to a bench in his own filth, his naked back baked raw by the sun, until Divine Providence, or more probably his own death, should end his servitude. Contributing to the downward spiral of his overwhelming sadness was his almost unceasing rehearsal of the interlocking conspiracies of fortune that had brought him to this desperate pass. The events of his recent history were filled to overflowing with *if only*.

The command came to rest oars and, as one, the rowers pushed down, raising their oars from the water and securing them under the hook attached to the bench in front. The sailors took over, unfurling the sail, and the galley came about, once more in search of prey.

His head bent over the oar before him, Luca was in the midst of another voyage to the depths of his despair, when through his dark reverie he heard the familiar tones of his native tongue. Having become used to the barked commands and rhythmic chants in Turkish, and only whispered communications between the rowers, he looked up, surprised to hear the Florentine language being spoken out loud.

One of the sailors was walking up and down the benches asking for someone who could translate Latin into Italian. Heads were being shaken at every bench as the sailor worked his way aft. Henrique, who was chained to a bench a couple of rows aft of Luca's position, looked back at him and nodded. He and Luca had conversed in Latin from time to time while incarcerated, so as to avoid being overheard, and now he was urging Luca to take up the Turk's request – presumably to get him off the rowing bench and improve his spirits.

Luca's mind was in conflict. He dearly wished to get away from the oar if only for a day or two, but to help the Turks in their quest against Christ was surely a blasphemy. He dipped his head as the sailor passed him by. Upon reaching the last bench at the stern of the galley the sailor turned and looked into the eyes of the rowers facing him. He declared in poor Italian, "If someone does not translate for my captain then we will kill ten of you at random and the rest of you will have to row harder. I know one of you can read both Latin and Italian. So speak now or see your fellow Christians die."

There was silence, as the rowers looked nervously one to the other. "Very well!" shouted the sailor, and with a motion of his hands the overseers began to unchain rowers. Now there was no choice, the decision had been made for him. Luca reluctantly stood up. "*Signore*, I can translate for you." The sailor clapped his hands, and within a minute they were leading Luca up the narrow steps to the command deck, the rowers once more shackled to their benches.

Luca was brought before Dragut, the latter still wearing his enormous turban. He was to be found staring out to sea with a distracted look in his eyes. The sailor pushed Luca to his knees and they both awaited Dragut's attention. After a moment the corsair turned and looked down at the dirty and disheveled figure before him and grimaced. He shouted something in Turkish to the sailor who nodded and scampered off.

"If you are to be my assistant you should be dressed accordingly," he explained to Luca in heavily accented Italian. The sailor returned with a bucket of seawater and some clothing. With the sailor's help Luca cleaned himself as best he could and dressed. After his efforts he looked the image of a Turkish sailor, from the tightly tied turban on his head to the poorly embroidered sandals on his feet. His arms were bare, a sleeveless waistcoat worn over a linen shirt, the short sleeves rolled up to the shoulders. His legs were partially covered by short baggy breeches tied off at the knees, a sash worn as a belt.

"There!" exclaimed Dragut in a satisfied tone, "now you are dressed as becomes the secretary of a captain."

In the blink of an eye Luca had been transformed from the rowing bench – from the sweaty machine of humanity that powered the ship, laboring still a few *braccia* beneath his feet – into some kind of personal secretary to a Mohammedan pirate. His mind was still wrestling with the capricious nature of fate when the pirate launched into another speech.

"I had a Christian assistant but he recently... departed." He did not specify whether this assistant had departed Dragut's service merely, or had departed this world entirely. The only clue was the dismissive wave of his hand. "I find many of you Christian slaves to be very well educated, certainly more so than my sailors." He laughed heartily at his own poor joke.

"Do you know who I am?" asked Dragut, changing the subject.

"I believe you to be the pirate Captain Dragut, *Signore*," replied Luca striving to give no offense, "the lieutenant of Barbarossa."

"That is how I am called in your language, and yes I fly the flag of *Barbaros Hayreddin*. It is good you have heard of me for I will be known to all Christians – I will strike fear into their infidel hearts and have them kneel before me," he replied, trailing off as he gazed out to sea again, perhaps looking toward his rosy future.

Luca observed that like all the many self-important men he had met in his career, Dragut seemed most to enjoy talking about himself – and a shipload of Turkish riffraff was probably not the ideal audience for a man who planned to acquire such a formidable reputation.

Dragut stroked his magnificent moustache thoughtfully. He did, most assuredly, look fully the part of a Turkish pirate. His red turban was ridiculously large, a prodigious length of crimson cloth swirling up high above his head, enclosing the majority of his graying hair; his face was red and weather-beaten from the constant blast of salt sea air and the relentless sun; and his moustache was huge and dramatic, spanning the entire space from nose to ears, completely eclipsing his neatly trimmed beard.

"I gather you need me to translate something for you," began Luca nervously, after he had judged a sufficiently respectful time had elapsed.

"Yes, yes," answered Dragut disappearing into his quarters over the stern, finally emerging with a thin unbound book, little more than a pamphlet. "This is a navigation chart with directional calculations produced for the Christian merchants to sail their galleys most efficiently – to keep on course and to keep to a schedule. I must know what it says. To know this will help me to understand the minds of these captains and will allow me better to outwit and capture them." He looked at Luca questioningly. "Will you help me with this?"

"And if I refuse?"

"Then you will be tortured and killed," he stared at Luca blandly, "I bear you no ill will you understand, but I must know the details of this document, and sooner or later I will catch another such as yourself who *will* help me," Dragut smiled his sympathy.

"Then I will translate the document, *Signore*," replied Luca.

"Then begin!" shouted Dragut with delight.

And Luca proceeded to translate.

The book, with its seemingly endless tables and charts, was confusing for someone without both a good understanding of mathematics and a basic grounding in navigation, neither of which the Painter of Florence could boast. Yet he endeavored to look busy, temporizing as best he could until his master tired of his tardiness, or he was able to make sense of the document; and there was no telling which would come first.

While he was working on the translation there occurred a strange event. One day during a week of protracted inactivity, while Luca was struggling both with the obscure language of the Latin text, and with his inner misgivings about helping the Turk capture more Christian loot and slaves just to ease his own servitude, Dragut emerged from his small quarters and peered over the Florentine's shoulder. Luca, his mind seized by dread, tried to look as busy and authoritative a translator as he could. But it seemed

Dragut had other matters on his mind.

"Why do you Christians worship three gods, yet claim there is only one? We know from the Holy Quran that there is no other god than Allah, and his earthly prophet was the blessed Mohammed, may peace be upon him," said the pirate spontaneously, raising one bushy eyebrow and cocking his hugely turbaned head to one side. Luca was unsure how to proceed. He could endeavor to explain the subtleties of Christian dogma, but wondered if a trap was being laid for him, intentionally or perhaps quite innocently. He did not want to be accused of attempting to proselytize a *Muselmán*, especially one with more than a hundred men and their razor sharp scimitars at his command.

"Your Lordship," began Luca deferentially, "I can indeed explain the apparent contradictions of Christianity, but do not wish to insult the words of the Prophet for fear of incurring your wrath." Dragut burst out into laughter.

"No young translator, I will not punish you for trying to convert me to your religion. I was born a poor Christian yet have become a wealthy man as a Moslem so I have no desire to return to the error and blasphemy of my youth." The wealthy pirate shook his head in remembrance of his infidel past. "But if you can explain I would hear it."

"Well, your Lordship, do you not believe in the one God?" asked Luca.

"Indeed I do."

"And do you not believe in the Word of God?"

"Most certainly."

"And the Spirit of God, that moves men's hearts?"

"And that too."

"Well, the Father is God, the Son is the Word of God and the Holy Ghost is the Spirit of God that moves men's hearts. They are the three manifestations of the one God. A good Christian understands that those are the three aspects of God, but there is only one God. As Jesus said: 'I and my Father are One.'"

"Very good Translator!" exclaimed Dragut laughing.

"Why do you question me so?" asked Luca nervously.

"To be honest I am fatigued by this inactivity and desire some intellectual stimulation. My men are good enough in a fight but, sadly, do not provide very good conversation."

"Hopefully I have been of some entertainment to you *Signore*," Luca was endeavoring to tread carefully.

"Certainly," exclaimed Dragut, "but tell me, why do you worship a God who is so weak – a God who speaks all the time of loving and helping your fellow man, and about turning the other cheek when attacked? Allah is strong and warlike and commands us to go forth with the sword to spread his word, and to correct the willful errors of the unbelievers. As the Prophet said: 'All men are born with the seeds of Islam in their hearts.'"

After a moment of consideration, Luca replied, "I would suggest that Islam is the weaker, as it must be spread by the sword – by death and conquest – whereas the teachings of Christ were spread by peaceful men, the Disciples of Jesus, who simply through preaching the Word of God spread the freedom of Christianity to every corner of the World. And they accomplished this many, many years before Mohammed was commanded by Allah to slay the unbelievers."

"Another good answer translator," laughed the pirate, "you are fortunate that I have given you leave to speak so, as this blasphemy would lose you your head if a devout *Muselmán* heard it."

With a mumbled, "I am sorry to offend *Signore*," Luca realized he had perhaps gone too far and bent his head once more to the translation. But Dragut clapped him merrily on the back in thanks and returned to his small cabin laughing.

Il Salvataggio

The fog swirled in glowing eddies, concealing the monsters lurking in its clammy grasp. He could hear them cry; dark feral screams that echoed in the mist – a tangible translucence. They approached closer; he could see their shadows moving within the spiraling whiteness. Then without warning they burst from the fog, claw and fang open and outstretched to take him. He screamed a silent scream. His throat was closed and unresponsive – it would not respond as if response was irrelevant and unnecessary. He was done; he was the victim of the marauding creatures.

He was dead.

Luca woke up quickly, sweating profusely. The dreams were still with him, even after the painful shock of that hideous destruction at Rome – the beginning of his end; or was it merely a stop along the road of his downfall?

He sat up. The light was yet dim but the fog swirled around them. Real fog. The galley was drifting slowly, creaking, hardly the smallest gust ruffling the huge mass of brown canvas suspended over his head. The watch was staring over the side – to no avail as the whiteness began and ended at the gunwales. They were fogged in.

He stood up from his place on the deck, where slept all the ordinary seamen, and walked to the ship's rail. Dragut appeared from his quarters at the rear of the command deck and looked blankly at the soft white cloud that enveloped them. "Most uncommon," was all he said to Luca, and then shouted a few questions to his crew. Answers came back, but in spite of his few words of Turkish they meant nothing to Luca.

He wondered why they sat becalmed and did not row. "Nowhere to go," came the unexpected answer to his unasked question.

"What do you mean?" he asked Dragut.

"If we row maybe we hit rocks, maybe we hit another of our ships, maybe we row further into the fog. Best to keep still, and watch and wait – and listen." Luca nodded his understanding of basic galley protocol.

"Shhh!" hissed Dragut unnecessarily to the quiet ship. The silence was oppressive, the fog blanketing everything with its blandness. Timbers creaked, the canvas snapped, water dripped.

"What?" asked Luca, confused. Dragut was pacing up and down. He suddenly ran the length of the deck hopping over sleeping sailors, and looked out over the prow, then promptly ran back again kicking the sailors awake as he came. He knew something.

"Load the guns, battle stations!" he bellowed at the top of his voice as bleary sailors jumped to their feet – that amount of Turkish Luca had learned.

At that precise moment the world exploded in a ball of flame and smoke. The deck that Dragut had run just moments before was sliced by ball and shot, splinters of wood flying all about as speeding lead cut bloody channels through the crew – smoke, black, swirling into the whiteness of the fog, as a moment later the world exploded a second time. The front of the galley was almost completely blown off, shattered timbers and the remains of the forward guns blasted across the sea.

The gun crews ran to the swivel guns mounted on the starboard rail as the rest of the crew prepared to be boarded. Dragut grabbed Luca by the shoulder and threw him to the deck, falling on top of him as the third explosion came, ripping through the starboard rail, slicing the shrouds and cutting the gunners into pieces, to fall dripping red on the rowers below.

How could they see us, thought Luca, how could they know

where we are? The thought was cut short as the long narrow galley was rammed. The hit was at the damaged bow and lifted the whole front of the ship momentarily from the water. He could see them now, the monsters in the mist, a huge dark ship much like their own but considerably bigger was locked nose to nose with them, the two ships almost at right angles. Ropes flew, grappling lines and nets to make fast. They were to be boarded. The monsters from the mist had come. Then Luca realized how foolish he was being, these monsters must be Christians, come to rescue the slaves. His thought was eerily echoed by the slaves themselves as they began loudly rattling their chains.

The magazine at the bow had been lost in the second blast, but a few sailors had loaded arquebuses. Kneeling, they leveled them at the prow whence the boarding party would come. As they shouldered their weapons, with a silence that contrasted sharply with the previous crash of the guns, they were cut down by a precisely aimed volley of arrow and bolt. Dragut leaped to his feet and drew his sabre. He screamed commands to his crew who crouched waiting to be boarded – screaming to cut through ears numbed by the roar of cannon, and minds frozen by shock and fear. Luca lay where he had fallen, his ears ringing, watching and waiting with the rest of the crew – to the continuous rhythmic clanking of chains.

It seemed like an eternity, but was probably just long enough for the sharpshooters to reload, ready to provide covering fire to the boarding party. And there they were. Figures moving on the silhouette ship, still barely visible, jumping onto the mangled prow of Dragut's vessel. Because of the shape of the galley, the deck consisted of only three narrow walkways; so only three men could fight from either side at any one time. The three attackers lined up at the prow of Dragut's ship and dropped, as one man, onto their knees. What were they doing? Luca realized with a rush of excitement – they were praying, their swords held before them, points down, as crosses.

Their prayers done, they rose to their feet and began their attack. Dragut's men ran to engage them, but the defenders were severely overmatched. Luca watched fascinated as the lead attacker on the center deck fought slowly but determinedly through the mist.

He handled his sword like no swordsman Luca had ever seen. The sword must be huge, he calculated, two *braccia* or maybe even bigger, and heavy. But the swordsman swung it two handed as if it were as light as a staff. And he did not strike and parry as Luca had been taught, instead he would turn every blocking movement into a strike. One hand on the grip and one on the blade just below the cross-guard he parried a sword thrust but in the same movement followed through and hit his opponent with the pommel, knocking him from the deck onto the slaves below, who made short work of him with their chains – turned from restraints into weapons.

Then he swung the long sword around his head extending the same smooth movement, bringing the razor sharp edge crashing down onto the next man in line, slicing him from shoulder to waist before he could even present his own blade to the attack. Taking a step back and withdrawing the sword he gripped it with one hand at each end, and pushed forward again, knocking Dragut's man over; then, with one motion, whirled it to a vertical position and drove it downward into his vitals.

One of Dragut's men swung at him with a glistening sharp scimitar and almost scored a hit, but he just stepped swiftly to one side and pushed the sword away with one of his armored hands, as if it were no more than a stick, smashing the Turk's face with a metal fist. It was like a deadly dance with the flashing, whirling sword at its center always cutting, slashing, stabbing, bludgeoning the next defender in line with unpredictable speed and direction.

The armored man continued his steady advance as he hacked his way through any of the corsairs who dared oppose him – the blood of the fallen, gushing in crimson spurts from the deck onto the backs of the slaves below, marking his progress. Luca could see him clearly now. He was dressed in a deep red surcoat emblazoned with a narrow white cross – now spattered with blood – over his chainmail; his head was protected with a helmet, his hands with plate and mail gauntlets, and his arms with articulated steel.

Luca watched his movements, entranced. His feet were unprotected save for high leather boots, and he moved nimbly, jumping to left and right despite the bloody, slippery deck as he swung the heavy sword about him. On the two side decks the fight continued in similar fashion and together the three men fought their way from stem to stern.

As the attackers proved completely untouchable the Turks began to lose courage, and backed away rather than risk dismemberment and death at the hands of these three invincibles. Dragut turned to Luca and shrugged, shouted a sudden farewell and leaped from the rail into the waves below, followed by the remains of his crew – preferring to trust their fate to Allah and the sea than to face certain death at the hands of these remarkable Christians.

Luca rose to his knees and watched, transfixed, as the helmeted man with the huge sword decapitated the last defender with a precisely aimed slice, and strode purposely through dark ripples of blood towards him. Suddenly a terrible fear gripped Luca. He was dressed as a Turk. He would be killed out of hand and thrown into the sea as a Turk, never to be rescued – lost to the world and to God. He pressed his hands together and prayed – a quote from the vulgate sprang to his mind:

"*De cetero fratres confortamini…*" intoned Luca as the swordsman raised the huge blade over his head, "*in Domino et in potentia virtutis eius…*" the swordsman stopped, and his helmeted head tipped a little to one side, as if to listen, then he began to speak – echoing the Latin along with the Painter, "*Induite vos arma Dei ut possitis stare adversus insidias diaboli.*"

The swordsman lowered his weapon and dropped to his knees, his two companions joining him. The men prayed together around the three steel crosses formed by the massive swords that towered above them, dripping yet with Turkish blood.

The fog started to lift. The early sun began to filter through the previously impenetrable mist that now swirled impotently away in the morning light. It gleamed in sparkling stars from the burnished helmets. Luca looked up to Heaven, and catching sight of the white-crossed red banners of the Knights of St. John fluttering in the morning breeze, gave thanks to God.

VILLAFRANCA

Two green arms stretch out across the azure sea, welcoming the traveller into the safety of their emerald embrace. One arm short, powerful, terminating in a massive fist, the other long and low, and tipped with bony fingers. To the left is the mountain known as Borone, rolling slopes rich with olive groves, topped with a huge citadel, its powerful guns ranged to cover the entire bay. To the right a headland, a hilly, wooded peninsula called Capo Ferrato, its rocky hand reaching far out into the sea. Between the two arms and into their shelter, into the deep bowl of Villafranca harbor, glided the three galleys. Sails furled and sliding smoothly across the still water to the rhythmic pulling of the rowers, they steered towards the stony beach.

Luca stood at the rail of the first galley and looked at the beautiful scene laid out before him. Beautiful not just in the vision of cultivated hills, the terracotta roofs of the small stucco village under the deep blue arch of the sky, guarded from on high by powerful artillery; but beautiful too in his miraculous return from the hopeless dark depths of Barbary to something so familiar, so warm, so civilized – so Christian.

"It is beautiful, is it not?" asked the dark voice beside him, echoing his own sentiments. He looked up at Henrique, resplendent still in nothing but his pale, rough, linen slave's trousers, contrasting deeply with his ebony skin and displaying his powerful build. Luca smiled his agreement.

Sir Richard, their savior, considered the two men to be his honored guests. The rest of the slaves on Dragut's galley were a collection of captives from the many villages and the various shipping that had been plundered by the pirate and his crew. The slaves labored still at the oars of their galley, but no longer in chains – happy to be rowing this one last time toward freedom and dry land.

Luca and Henrique, on the other hand, had been brought on board Sir Richard's galley as a mark of honor for their status as Painter and Bishop respectively. In truth the accommodations on Sir Richard's galley were hardly superior to those aboard Dragut's. Fighting galleys being slender and delicate affairs, every possible excess weight was stripped from the ship to maximize speed and firepower – to include both food and protection from the elements. But the accommodations differed in these most important respects – they were freely offered and freely taken.

After his bloody and spectacular rescue Luca had been brought directly back with the boarding party to the Knights' galley. The circumstances of his rescue had thrown some suspicion upon him, despite his apparent knowledge of the Bible, dressed as he was in the garb of a Turkish sailor. The three helmeted men had stood sternly about him and, with the crew looking on, questioned him thoroughly.

This had been more complicated than it should have been. The Knights had seemed to Luca to be speaking English, a language he was not familiar with, and after a few moments confusion they had realized that he was speaking the Florentine dialect and had summoned a crossbowman named Jonson who was competent in Italian.

Slowly, in Italian and Latin, the interrogation had proceeded. As Luca had slowly answered their enquiries, explaining who he was and how he came to be there, along with a catalog of the terrible events to which he had borne witness, his mind had begun to wander. And while they had examined him he, in return, had examined his inquisitors; with the keenness of an artist's eye.

They all wore the red and white-crossed surcoat of the Knights of St. John, which hung to mid thigh and was loosely girt at the waist with a black, leather belt. Beneath the surcoat they were each protected by a long, mail shirt with sleeves that terminated in jointed, metal gauntlets; the shoulders and elbows being additionally reinforced by shaped, articulated plates. Their breeches, such as showed, were of some dark, woolen fabric and were covered to the knee by heavy black leather boots.

For knights they appeared very lightly armored – Luca presuming that they used armor sufficient to their immediate protection, but not so heavy as to slow them down in a skirmish on a narrow galley deck slippery with blood. Their swords were all the same pattern he had observed; two handed in use and formed of a simple cross that when held with the point to the ground reached all the way to the chest.

Where their appearances differed was in their choice of helmet. The man to the left wore a rounded helm with a hinged wire visor, and he on the right a teardrop-shaped *bascinet* with no visor; but the Knight in the center, the one who had fought his way to rescue Luca, was the one that most drew his attention.

His helmet was one piece of rounded, formed steel with large, projecting cheek pieces and a horizontal slit opening for the eyes such that the vertical and horizontal openings joined to create a T shape – a *barbute* Luca believed it to be called. It brought to mind the shape of a hoplite's helm that he had observed upon a Greek vase, but without the separate nose protection. Cunningly, in the construction of the helmet the top of the T shape had been extended upward by a riveted inlay of blackened metal so that the helmet gave the appearance of a black cross on a burnished, silver ground.

As his mind had wandered in such observations, Luca had begun to sketch. He had still been clutching the navigation manual that he had been attempting to translate the night before, plus one or two sheets of paper filled with his scribbled notes and a sharpened stick of charcoal in a silver holder.

He had turned one of the pages of notes over and started to draw the Knight – two dark eyes gleaming from the outstretched arms of a black cross, and two gauntleted hands grasping the hilt of a massive sword.

The drawing and the interrogation had both concluded at the same time – the Knights had satisfied themselves that Luca was indeed a painter of Florence who had suffered many tribulations and had finally been redeemed at the cost of much Turkish blood.

As a counterpoint to their decision Luca had presented his sketch to its subject. Again the helmet had tipped slightly to the side as the Knight gazed upon Luca's handiwork. He had passed his sword to an attendant followed by the gauntlets, then finally he had lifted the helmet from his head. Reaching out he had taken the sketch, turning the delicate paper gently in his hands and smiling.

He was an older man than Luca had expected, maybe forty or even fifty years of age. His shoulder-length, red hair was streaked with grey; his moustache and the close-cropped beard that followed his high cheekbones were likewise grizzled. Light grey eyes, although still piercing, were softer once the helmet was removed.

He had run his hand through his hair pushing it back from his face and spoken in Latin so Luca would understand him, "I am Sir Richard Weston of the Order of Knights of St. John. It is my pleasure to make the acquaintance of a painter of Florence. This is superb handiwork Painter, I have hopes that you will be able to grace us with more of your talent before you return home."

However neither man quite understood how long it would be before Luca might be in a position to return home.

Burgos

A small group of riders neared the walled city of Burgos, once the proud capital of Castile, now merely a provincial city. Their black cloaks billowed behind them and a white-crossed red pennant fluttered from the point of a pike.

Hooves clattered across the wooden bridge as they approached the *Arco de Santa Maria*, the main gate of the city, made especially glorious with magnificent statues newly installed in honor of his Excellency the Emperor. The guards raised their pikes in salute as the riders passed hastily through the gate.

They were expected, recognized; they were honored visitors. The Emperor was in residence and was receiving. Emissaries had come from around the world to pay their respects at the birth of his son, or to chide him for his destruction of Rome and the confining of the Pontiff – or possibly both.

Passing more slowly through the crowded, morning streets, the riders pressed on to the cathedral, Our Lady of Burgos, whose massive, crusted towers rose high above the city. At the cathedral they tarried a while in prayer, prostrate before the high altar. Then, with barely a word, they continued on their way up the hill to the castle. It was a gloomy pile of stones, rambling across a hill that rose behind the city, giving commanding views over the lush valley below. Again the guards recognized their black cloaks crossed in angular white, waving them inside, and they rode through the main gate into the courtyard.

They were six in number and had ridden hard through the night from Valladolid in search of the Emperor, leaving the majority of their group behind in the capital. Four knights were deemed sufficient bodyguard for their Grand Master and his standard bearer, and none who saw them would have dared impede their haste for even a moment. Men of God they were, but very dangerous men nevertheless.

As they dismounted, the Grand Master, Philippe Villiers de l'Isle Adam, winced in pain. His standard bearer Louis rushed to his side giving his arm in support. "I grow too old and weary to be chasing this boy king around Castile," he muttered, stiff after hours in the saddle.

"He must needs go who the devil drives, my Lord," replied Louis, adding a nervous, "If I may speak so."

"You may speak so," said the Grand Master, adding grimly, "and the devil is a stern driver indeed."

Their horses were led away to the stables, and a servant dressed in the livery of the Royal House of Castile escorted them into the castle. After passing through seemingly endless echoing stone passageways, they were at last installed in a crowded antechamber that was decorated with a sumptuousness that belied the grim exterior of the citadel. The smooth stone walls were hung with finely detailed Flemish tapestries, and the floors thickly laid with deep red rugs from the Levant, patterned in complex blue arabesques.

The Grand Master sat himself down in a heavy carved chair on a soft velvet bolster, flanked by his stern bodyguard – an island of black in a colorful sea – while Louis paced nervously, or paced as much as the throng would permit. In looking about him at the various courtiers and ambassadors he guessed that the worth of the clothing and jewelry on display in this one room could support the Order for an entire year.

From time to time various of the throng would catch the eye of the Grand Master and smile a greeting, receiving a grim nod in return – he would politick when needed for the good of the Order, but unlike these soft and pampered courtiers he was a knight; a warrior who had leaped into the breach at Rhodes, full armored, cutting down hundreds of Janissaries with his own sword.

Time passed. It could take days – weeks even – to get the attention of the ruler, to obtain those precious few seconds that could lead to preferment. The Grand Master had done this before, too many times in his view, and he had thought a mere five years ago that he might live out his term on Rhodes, and finish his days on his estate without ever again travelling around the courts of Europe begging.

More time passed. The doors at the end of the room opened and closed repeatedly, expelling and admitting colorful clouds of sumptuously dressed courtiers, while the Grand Master and his knights waited in black and white.

When finally his name was called there was a moment of silence amongst the courtiers as the old man lifted himself from his chair, and every eye was on him as he slowly walked the length of the room. Even though he was there with them he was not *of* them, and his existence unnerved them. He adjusted the fall of his cloak and stepped through the carved doorway into the presence of the Emperor.

The furnishings of this *ad hoc* throne room, although magnificent in themselves, were rather austere. The throne was merely a beautifully figured and padded chair, and large expanses of stone wall and floor showed through the tapestries and carpets. The Grand Master walked to the center of the room, politely to await the Emperor's pleasure, while Louis, now acting as his secretary, trailed behind him.

The Emperor, dressed in a heavily embroidered gold suit in the Castilian style, with matching gold hose and oddly pointed shoes, stood with his back to the door, in deep conversation with several dour looking men in black robes. Finally, their conversation complete and the men dismissed, he turned to greet the old man. The Grand Master concealed his surprise at being alone with the Emperor. There were normally several people present to record the event, and to protect Caesar's royal body.

"Brother Philippe!" exclaimed the Emperor with honest-sounding mock joy, "it is such a delight to meet with you again."

And he strode over to the Grand Master to embrace him.

"Your Highness," replied the Grand Master trying to drop to one knee in respect but unable to do so, gripped as he was in the Emperor's manly hug.

"None of that," ordered the Emperor, "that is for occasions of state, we are just two old friends talking about the world." The Emperor's Spanish was shaky and recently learned, with a heavy Flemish accent; but learning the language of his people had been one of the conditions of taking control of the country from his mother.

The Grand Master eyed him suspiciously, barely betraying his concern with a raised eyebrow, and wondered how many others had been swayed by the Emperor's good-humored but insincere chatter.

"Philippe – again let me tell you how much it pains me that Rhodes has been lost to you," continued the Emperor. The Grand Master noted the passive voice in his language, tastefully distancing the Emperor from any culpability in Suleiman's success – or perhaps it was simply his lack of familiarity with the language of his subjects.

"Your Highness, I am pained less by the loss of my home than I am by my loss of faith in the word of Princes," was Brother Philippe's tart rejoinder. There was an awkward silence as the young Caesar looked anew at the old man.

"So how goes the Maltese project?" asked the Emperor by way of a change of subject.

"My men have made an inventory of the islands."

"And Tripoli too."

"Yes," sighed the Grand Master, "and Tripoli too. Although it will spread us thin across the sea in the face of Barbarossa and his pirates."

"Don Pedro suffered much to capture Tripoli as our outpost in Barbary, and we would have it maintained," declared the Emperor sternly. "Although he now suffers more in a Naples prison as a traitor," he muttered to himself as an afterthought. "How are the mighty fallen."

"Indeed we will garrison the fortress at Tripoli your Highness," assured the old man with a final sigh.

"Splendid!" exclaimed the Emperor. "And you must call me Charles – at least when we are alone together."

"The cost is as we discussed in our last meeting?" asked the Grand Master in a tired effort to finalize the arrangements.

"Yes, indeed; a falcon, presented once a year. You understand I make you this loan of Malta as King of Naples, so must ask for some tribute to be paid; otherwise none of my subjects would respect me." He laughed at the ridiculous idea. "Nevertheless, your tireless work against the corsairs of Barbary will be payment enough to all of Christendom. They grow ever more bold in their attacks."

"They do Your High… Charles. If we are finished in our business I will have my secretary…" he indicated Louis standing deferentially at a distance, "finish the documents for your Imperial seal – tomorrow perhaps."

There was a moment of silence. "This town of Burgos, it pleases me, despite that my father died here; poisoned, no doubt, by my grandfather," mused the Emperor, thoughtfully gazing out of the window that gave onto the town and the river below. "Is this aspect not most delightful?" The Grand Master looked at the Emperor, confused. "Come Brother Philippe, join me here at the window." The Grand Master waved at Louis to stay where he was and walked alone to the Emperor's side.

"Charles?"

"There is one other thing," croaked the Emperor in a kind of whisper. He had also changed back to his native Flemish. "This is something that must not go beyond the two of us, you understand?" he croaked again.

"I am a Christian Brother, anything you may confide in me is between us and the Lord."

"Perfect! Now, Let me lay out some history so you may understand why I need to have done what it is I need to have done," began the Emperor obliquely, pausing for a moment to think.

"You know, of course, that I am not King of Castile – as such?" he began, and Brother Philippe nodded, "I am, in a legal sense, Regent. And that is where I have a problem – it puts me in an awkward position. You know my mother, Queen Joanna, is of imperfect mental state?" Philippe nodded again, "Well, in spite of that she is still Queen to the people, even if they do call her *Juana la loca*, and they see me as a foreigner, a usurper if you will. And I in return have little regard for the Spanish. Their manners are harsh and their means are brutal. I hate this place," he hissed. "So much so that I itch while I am here, can you believe that? It is an affliction that only passes when I leave. With all honesty, the only use to me of this benighted land is gold and fighting men." He paused a moment. "The irony is that I used Spanish gold for bribes to ensure my election as Emperor, just so I would be able to leave Spain." He laughed at the memory and the Grand Master sighed, wishing this venal and hypocritical young man would state his price so these negotiations might be concluded, and the Order once again have a home.

"Well, it was not to be. I cannot leave this accursed country. I tried Brother Philippe, oh how I tried. Yet every time I depart this land these miserable peasants conspire against me. They even enlisted my poor mother's help. Well, that was too much; I put them down, quite harshly, and placed all my own people in control – good, trustworthy people; northern people – and life has returned somewhat to the normal." The Emperor turned to gaze out of the window as he paused in his lengthy confession, and the Grand Master shifted his weight from one leg to the other as it began to cramp.

"They have no leader, you see," began the Emperor again suddenly, which surprised Brother Philippe whose mind had begun to wander. "That is what makes them so perfectly controllable, but only while I am here to lead them, the rest is anarchy. They simply fight amongst themselves. However, once in a while a man will appear with the possibility, the potential of leadership – a man of the people, yet accepted by the nobility, and who is able to unite both. A man who might be tempted to plot against me"

"And has such a man emerged?" asked the Grand Master, attempting to speed the negotiations.

"Indeed. This man is a *Hidalgo*, but newly minted; honored for his service slaughtering savages in the New World. And provided with lands in the south of Spain for his service slaughtering Moors in Granada. He is a Grand Slaughterer," exclaimed the Emperor, suddenly realizing his voice had risen from its whisper and quickly modulating his tone while looking over his shoulder. "You know, it is said they kill Monarchs they dislike in this land," he added, explaining his furtive manner.

"This man, this warrior of the people, who has raised his status by the edge of his sword, keeps about him a band of cutthroats and ruffians that he hires out as mercenaries – I have myself made use of his services from time to time. My spies declare him returned from slaughtering Christians in Rome – having, no doubt, run out of heathens to dispatch – and reinstalled in his fortress. His abode is a town a day's ride from Granada on the edge of the desert – a dry and formidable place I am led to believe." He paused again, staring once more out of the window at the lush green landscape as he contemplated this dark fortress in the hills of a barren land.

"That was a bad thing, what you wrought upon Rome," said the Grand Master sadly.

"It was not my fault," exclaimed the Emperor. "As the Lord is my witness, my orders were to force the Pope to submit, not burn Rome to the ground."

"I do not think the Lord's work was done that day."

"Less of this!" shouted the Emperor. "You may not judge me! I am the King, I am your Lord, I am Caesar! I own the very air that you breathe! Do not question my actions nor my motives, what I do I do for the good of the Empire, not to flatter some aged priest's notion of good and bad."

The two men looked at each other – a little differently now. The younger man was flushed slightly, his athletic figure taught with anger. His large chin was thrust forward arrogantly, its neatly trimmed beard pointing like a threatening finger at the Grand Master's heart. The older man, he who had faced Suleiman the Law Giver and sixty thousand Turks, realized, for the moment, that he had met his match in the Emperor. His shoulders drooped slightly and he took a step backward. "I am sorry your Majesty," he said.

"And for the good of the Empire," continued the angry Emperor, "this man must go." There it was. He had finally stated his price.

"We are knights not assassins, Charles," sighed the Grand

Master, knowing, as he had known at Rhodes, that he had already lost the struggle, but was obliged to fight to the end.

"Surely you have annihilated tens of thousands during your tenure."

"We are warriors. We are at war. As warrior priests we have dispensation from the Pope to kill Moslems for the good of Christendom. We are not murderers, to be used to remove the inconvenient and the poorly bred, so that your tax revenues may not be interrupted." It was the Grand Master's turn to grow flushed.

"He consorts with Moors," added the Emperor. "He takes Christian prisoners and sells them to the corsairs and allows their galleys to resupply along his coast. He protects the Moslem bandits in the hills that prey on the local villages. He really is a bad man. Honestly Philippe, if there were any other way…" his voice trailed off.

"What of the Holy Brotherhood? Can their men not deal with him?"

"Hah! He *is* the Brotherhood! His men are the militia and the judges in his lands, and they collect the Papal tax which pays for the Brotherhood."

"And the Inquisition neither I suppose?"

"Those old ladies are scared of their own shadows. They would not dare confront such a man. They are happy to exercise their superior piety in the torment of those who have no power and no protection – an *auto de fe* once in a while to cow the populace and impress the *Cortes* is the limit of their interests. Philippe, you are the only person who can accomplish this deed. You have the strength and the subtlety – and men fit for the task." Brother Philippe nodded in acquiescence.

As the Grand Master was about to pass through the door, back into the colorful swirl of courtiers and sycophants, the Emperor grasped his shoulder and with the other hand pressed a slip of paper into his palm. "Your knights have leave to travel safely anywhere in the world. But Philippe," he paused and whispered close to the Grand Master's ear, "make it seem like an accident." The old man nodded his assent and shuddered a little as he left.

LA RICERCA

Luca was ushered into a large, echoing room in the massive rambling stone citadel that perched at the crest of Monte Borone. He was doing his utmost to appear stylish and artistic, but dressed in borrowed clothes, and sporting a black eye, he had his work cut out for him.

His time in Villafranca, for the most part, had been comfortable, and the Knights' hospitality was generous, but the more he grew at ease with his return to civilization the more his thoughts turned to Virginia. At night when he could not sleep he would go over their capture again; and again wonder if he could have done anything differently – if he could have managed to escape the Spanish and hidden with Virginia, safe in the ruins of old St Peter's while the destruction of Rome roared and thundered about them.

But it was not to be. He recalled that precise moment when the Spaniard had arrived on his huge horse – *Don Cristobal de Guadix*, that name echoed in his mind – and Virginia, so lately at his side, had been torn from him again. Despite his physical comfort these thoughts haunted him, and had been the subject of much prayer and contemplation the last few days. Bishop Henrique had heard his confession.

One evening Sir Richard had visited him at his lodgings in the town, where he shared a room with Henrique, and informed him that Brother Philippe Villiers de L'Isle Adam, the Grand Master of the Order of Saint John of Jerusalem, had arrived at the citadel, and that Luca and Henrique had been summoned to an audience the next morning. Sir Richard had then invited them out for the evening – an innocent-seeming request designed to raise Luca's spirits – to a particular local tavern frequented by many of the knights and men-at-arms.

The evening had begun well. Luca and Henrique had accompanied Richard and his friend Guillaume, along with Richard's young nephew Edmund, and a rude yet charming Welshman by the name of Edryd – a tall, blond knight about ten or fifteen years younger than Sir Richard.

The newcomers had been introduced by the Knights to a strong and pungent locally brewed ale, which to Luca, accustomed as he was to wine, often diluted with water, had been especially intoxicating. Many stories had been told, as the evening progressed, and Luca and Sir Richard had begun to understand each other's languages. But, as the evening progressed further, the events had become more and more blurred in Luca's mind.

In his dim recollection he vaguely remembered a nearby table of young knights becoming embroiled in an altercation with a group of local worthies. It had seemed – and this could have been the ale speaking – that the locals were unhappy with the knights for having taken over their town, along with their imperious and arrogant ways. Further, these young men had been in a mood to take the knights vigorously to task about it.

The arguments and insults had begun to fly back and forth between the two tables, with plenty of creativity shown on both sides, much to the amusement of Sir Richard and his group. But the initial humor of the argument had descended into anger as the level and intensity of the insults had increased, and it had become obvious that a fight was brewing.

Now it may be judged the height of folly to engage in a brawl with a man whose entire life is spent learning and perfecting the martial arts, however the local men were not without some skill of their own, and the close quarters of the tavern, along with the fact that every townsman present joined to their side, had somewhat evened the odds.

As Luca's recollection was impaired by the quantity of ale he had consumed, he was not a reliable witness to the event; and the amount of furniture and crockery flying to and fro had obscured the fine details of the fight. However, he did remember striking a man with his fist as he had leaped with his tablemates into the fray, in protection of the honor of the Knights of Saint John – drunk or not. After the first punch there had been some wrestling and thrashing between the two sides, and out of nowhere a fist had struck him in the eye. In falling he had grasped a large pewter plate, and swinging it like a weapon had struggled to his feet, the edge of the plate causing several nasty wounds upon his opponents.

It had seemed like a long time they were fighting, but in reality it was just a few minutes before a group of militiamen had appeared – their leader discharging his pistol to bring the brawl to an abrupt end. Since off duty knights were not permitted to carry weapons while drinking in the town, the militia, with their arquebuses, swords and armor, had taken the upper hand, and soon the two sides had calmed down.

By the end of the evening the knights had been buying drinks for the townsfolk, all laughing together sharing remembrances of the fight, their animosity disappeared – along with a half dozen injured that had been carried off to the hospital.

This was how Luca had received the black eye he now wore before the Grand Master – an obvious sign of his involvement in the brawl of the previous evening. He struck a stance, and pulled his hat down as far as possible on one side to shadow his damaged eye.

As the Grand Master swung into the audience room with his retinue in train, the entire company dropped to one knee in deference, and he slowly walked the length of the room, mounting a raised platform at the farther end. He wore a low, diamond-shaped hat, formed similarly to a cardinal's biretta, yet black not red. His entire dress, in fact, was black; a black fur-trimmed cloak lined in red silk, and beneath that a black cassock belted with a red cord. The sign of the Order – the branched, white cross – shone from his left breast, ruffles of white shirt from collar and cuffs.

He slid the cloak from his shoulders and passed it to an acolyte, settling gingerly into a large chair centered in the platform. This was the first audience the Grand Master had called since his return from Spain, and the room was filled with suppliants desiring a moment of the great man's time.

After about an hour of standing, feeling progressively queasier, Luca and Henrique were finally called forward, escorted by Sir Richard. The Grand Master looked them over, noting Luca's black eye and Henrique's arm in a sling. "Did the Turk do this to you?" he asked, already knowing the answer.

"No My Lord, there was an altercation in the town last night," answered Sir Richard for the two of them.

"This misbecomes you Sir Richard," admonished the Grand Master, "you know my opinions on scuffling with the townsfolk. I will speak with you on this matter in due course."

"Yes My Lord," replied Sir Richard, suitably chastened.

"And to you, our honored guests, my apologies for having done more damage to you in a week than the Turk did in a month." Sir Richard winced at the Grand Master's words.

"But to the point," he continued. "You sir," he turned to Henrique, "are a bishop?"

"Yes my Lord," replied Henrique bowing.

"Splendid! You must lead us in one of our services. However, I was unaware of a blackamoor bishop."

"I was ordained by my Portuguese sponsors after studying in Lisbon, My Lord."

That seemed to satisfy the Grand Master who replied with a nod and turned to Luca.

"And you are a painter," came the statement.

"Luca, the Painter of Florence, my Lord," declared Luca with his usual flourish, bending deeply from the waist and brandishing his borrowed hat, with as much style as he could muster with a throbbing headache.

"Not just a painter, a Florentine painter no less," said the Grand Master, "we are doubly honored." Luca bowed again. "Perhaps we could induce you to paint something for us before you return home."

"Perhaps, my Lord, but I do not intend to return home," answered Luca, and the Grand Master arched his brow questioningly. "The woman I love was carried off by a Spaniard during the recent destruction of Rome – the very same Spaniard who sold me into barbarian slavery. It is my plan; no it is my Christian duty, to find her and release her from bondage." The Grand Master seemed intrigued, so Luca pressed on, "Once I have finished my time here, and done sufficient honor to the Order for my rescue, I will make my way to Spain and find this man. Then I will release my love from captivity and kill all who oppose me."

This was the first time Luca had expressed his intention in so many words, and the naked truth of the venture, along with its obviously poor chance of success, both surprised and somehow comforted him – he had a quest, he had a plan, and none should stay him. His life, recently so aimless, had taken on a meaning once more. The Grand Master, being the man he was, immediately pointed out the flaw in the plan, "So you, a painter, will challenge a vicious mercenary captain, no doubt protected by his soldiers, for the woman you love – and you expect to prevail against such odds?"

"No my Lord, I expect to die. But I must die in the attempt or live forever as a coward in the knowledge that an honorable woman was dishonored due to my inaction." The Grand Master nodded in understanding of this simply articulated statement.

"But, my Lord," continued Luca, "my chances of prevailing in the endeavor would be increased many fold if I were permitted to…" Luca paused, seeking the right words, as this might be his only chance to put his case before Brother Philippe, "borrow one or two of your knights to escort me on my quest. In return for which," he quickly added as the Grand Master furrowed his brow in astonishment, "I would be delighted to paint a portrait of your good self from life, which would grace your new abode in Malta."

The two men stood a moment regarding each other thoughtfully. Sir Richard had only partially understood the conversation as the two had been speaking in Florentine, but Henrique displayed by his expression that he was fully aware of just what the Painter had asked, and what impudence he had committed.

"Painter," began the Grand Master, "I am not in the habit of lending my brothers to any unlikely quest that washes up on our shores. We have much work to do here in policing the sea, rebuilding our fleet and preparing for our move to Malta. I am surprised you ask such of me."

"Your Lordship, I would not presume upon your hospitality and good nature except that an honest Christian woman was ripped from her home and carried off as chattel by this man, and that he has sold many other Christians into slavery, doing bad business with the Turkish corsairs."

Brother Philippe stared thoughtfully at Luca as a recent conversation came back to him. "And who is this man you seek?" he asked.

"Don Cristobal de Guadix, my Lord, or so-called," came the reply. There was a moment's pause as the Grand Master developed the beginnings of a stratagem.

"Painter, you make a good argument," began the Grand Master as Henrique's jaw dropped in astonishment. "Perhaps a small force could be assembled to aid you on your quest. And believe me, what my knights seek to do, they accomplish."

"I am your servant my Lord," exclaimed Luca bowing again. Sir Richard whispered questioningly into Henrique's ear and received a reply, his eyes growing round with astonishment.

"We will talk later Painter, for now you have your quest," finished the Grand Master with a smile. Promptly rising to his feet and walking out, he donned his black cloak with a flourish in mid stride, flashing brilliant crimson with every step.

LA SANZIONE

Sir Richard found Brother Philippe in his cell. It was a small monk's room, simply furnished, but with the addition of writing materials on a desk, and a short row of books on a single shelf. The Grand Master was at his desk deep in one of his books when the Knight rapped on the half open door, and he peered over the top of his reading glasses at the figure framed in the doorway.

"Richard, a pleasure to see you my friend, come in," he said, and Sir Richard walked tentatively into the narrow room. He had never before been summoned to the Grand Master's personal cell, and he was sure that the recent uproar at the tavern in Villafranca was the reason. He could only imagine the punishment that was presaged by a personal audience with the Grand Master in his own room. He had blithely faced a shipload of Turkish corsairs, but was reduced to a quivering schoolboy by this single old man.

"Sit, sit," insisted the Grand Master, indicating a small chair by the narrow bed. Once Sir Richard had made himself as comfortable as possible the Grand Master began, "You must know my displeasure at your most recent tavern quarrel." Sir Richard bowed his head in contrition. "This seems to be a too frequent occurrence for you while on land, and it is my most urgent desire that you save your fighting for your enemies rather than your confreres."

"I am most sorry my Lord..." began Sir Richard, but Brother Philippe waved him to silence.

"That is not my main thrust Richard, but it does have a bearing on my plans for you," continued the Grand Master. "You know that we are resident in Villafranca and Nizza with the permission of the Duke of Savoy, at the personal behest of the Emperor." Sir Richard nodded. "Well, fighting with his subjects is not an activity assured to endear us to the Duke's heart. In addition, we are in a sensitive area of negotiations with the Emperor to move to Malta as a base for our retaking of Rhodes. So it would be best if we tried not to antagonize our friends against us, and confined our militancy to battling the Turk who grows ever more brazen in his depredations." Sir Richard looked downcast.

"I was able to clear up matters with the Mayor of the town who blames his people for antagonizing our knights as much as he blames us. Also, the fact that we are building a fleet in his shipyards helped the Mayor toward his forgiveness of our transgressions. Nevertheless, as you were the most senior knight at the tavern there must be some punishment, or at least seeming punishment, for your sins."

"Indeed my Lord…" began Sir Richard again, but once more he was silenced by a wave of the old man's hand.

"Richard. I wish you to accompany the Painter of Florence on his quest."

"My Lord!" exclaimed Sir Richard, beginning to explain how his most urgent need was to be here in command of his galley fighting the Moslem corsairs that plagued the coast, but for a third time he was silenced.

"Richard, I really care not if you brawl in the taverns as long as you do your duty at sea, which you do more and better than any other of my knights. You are my best captain, and you are as brave and useful to us here as your Uncle William is to us in London. This is not a punishment, although conveniently most will see it as such." Sir Richard regarded the Grand Master quizzically, confused by his words.

"So I am to be punished by having to act as escort to the Painter on his futile quest, but in actuality my demotion from galley captain is somehow to be seen as an endorsement of my skill?" asked Sir Richard, perplexed.

"Rather it is the opposite," explained the Grand Master, adding further to the confusion. "That is," he continued in the face of Sir Richard's bemused expression, "the duty of escort is the endorsement, and the removal as captain will be seen as the punishment."

That did not help the Knight's confusion much, so the Grand Master drove to the heart of the matter. "The Painter is on a quest as much for me as for himself. The man he seeks, this Don Cristobal, is an enemy of Christendom well known to myself; and the Painter's quest must succeed. To that end I am sending my best knight with a small force to protect the Painter and assure the successful outcome of this endeavor. Does that make more sense?"

"It does, my Lord, but raises more questions that it answers. Most importantly, how does a painter of Florence know a man that you also know, such that you both desire the same outcome for him?"

"There are areas surrounding this business that I cannot or will not explain to you. I only ask that you trust me that I would not put my knights in mortal peril lightly, nor without absolute necessity."

"I understand my Lord, but what should happen when we find this Don Cristobal and the young lady of the Painter's quest?"

"Then you should rescue the lady."

"And if the Don refuses to release her?"

"Then no doubt the Painter will attempt to forcibly remove her."

"And we should protect the Painter in his endeavor?"

"Indeed. It is imperative that the Painter be successful."

"But the Don will try to kill him."

"Most likely."

"And we should kill the Don?"

"Let me just say that you should use your best judgment. However, it would be a thing of great..." he searched carefully for the right word, "expediency. Yes, a thing of *greatest* expediency if the Don met his death at the hands of the Painter over the possession of the young woman."

"Then we are to assassinate the Don?"

"My heavens no!" exclaimed the Grand Master with much hand

waving. "The Painter," he spoke slowly and deliberately, "must kill the Don."

Sir Richard sat back on the stool thoroughly confused. "So let me just rehearse this plan: I am to escort the Painter on his quest and protect him until he finds the woman and the Don. Then I am somehow to supply him, a painter of Florence, the means to fight the Don, a mercenary soldier, and prevail. Not just prevail, but to end the life of the Don."

"Indeed, that is the task I am requesting of my best knight. You must see how this entire plan rests on the subtlety and shrewdness of your approach," replied Brother Philippe.

"But if this Don is selling Christians to the Moslems, then is this not a job for the Holy Brotherhood? Do they not police the lands of Aragon and Castile?"

"It is true that the Brotherhood serves in that capacity, but they are invested at the local level by the noble rulers of the locality. The Don controls the Brotherhood, so no justice will be had at their hand."

"But why us, and why the pretext of the Painter and his quest?"

"Because we are here, and because the Painter will be our weapon, and will be exonerated because he kills to save the woman he loves from slavery, with you to bear witness."

The Grand Master gazed thoughtfully at the book before him, and finally spoke from a different point of view, "Tell me Sir Richard, why do the rulers of the world, both our friends and our enemies, respect us?"

"Because they fear us?"

"Exactly! They know that we are peaceful Christian Brothers, but if you strike one of us then you strike us all. And Suleiman, the Grand Turk himself, knows full well how expensive in men and gold that blow does cost.

"All the Princes of Christendom are happy to fight amongst themselves up and down the Italian peninsula – spending endless sums on their rag tag armies, and destroying people and property for the momentary gain of a few leagues of land. But we, the Holy Religion, are the only force protecting Christendom from the Moslem horde. We are the last of the Warriors of the Cross. We are the Church Militant. We are the point of the lance.

"The irony is, of course, that we make it possible for the Christian Princes to fight each other, without having to concern themselves with fighting the Turk. But they respect us because they are frightened of us, and they are frightened of us because we do not politick and play the game of allegiance and enmity – my enemy is now my friend, and my friend is now my enemy.

"No, we are made up of knights from all the lands of Christendom who work together to achieve a common goal. We are outside their philosophy. We are unique. That is the reason the Emperor dispatches us so easily to Malta, to rid Europe of such a dangerous martial group so eminently skilled in the arts of war; a group both physically powerful, and beyond his ability to safely control; a group that, if motivated, could take his crown and his lands, and make both him and his Pope our vassals."

Sir Richard was astounded at the old man's words. The beginnings of such thoughts had occasionally passed through his head, but he had never heard such seditious and even heretical ideas presented so baldly. "My Lord," he asked, "I understand your meaning, but how does this bear on the matter?"

"In this way Sir Richard: I met with the boy Caesar – he so accidentally become ruler of the world – and he demanded of me this one commission in return for the gift of Malta. Since I am sending you into harms way I owe you the truth of the deal. This Don must die, by the Emperor's orders. But because Caesar is unloved by his people – and his Mother, whom he has imprisoned, is the true Queen and much beloved – he must avoid any connection with the assassination for fear the people will rise against him, as already once they have. Because of our strength we are the only ones capable of achieving such a consummation."

Brother Philippe paused and sighed, "I am sorry to say Richard that we are indeed to be assassins. We are to kill this Don and put him in the ground and salt his grave. But we must endeavor to have the Painter somehow be involved in the picture so that the whole affair has the appearance of misfortune rather than plot. Does that make sense?"

"At last," smiled Sir Richard, relieved at his understanding, "the quest is explained. As knights we will have leave to pass, armed, through all the Christian lands, and none will dare ask our reasons. We will present ourselves at the castle of this Don and demand the Painter's woman be released, in the name of God. And when the Don refuses, as refuse he must, we will kill him and any who come against us. But the Painter will be our motive and our reason, and he will gain the credit or the infamy for this bold act."

"Now do you understand why I must send you, my best man, to perform this sad but important task?"

Sir Richard slowly nodded.

Part Three

EL DESIERTO

A vast, tormented landscape tumbled out to the horizon before them like a stormy sea frozen in the midst of its fury. The horsemen picked their way carefully amongst the rocks and gravel that did poor service as a road through this arid wasteland. Low hills around them were cut by deep and narrow fissures, from a rush of water long since past, and worn into twisted shapes by the constant wind that whipped fine dust in every direction.

It appeared as if giants had done mighty battle here, and their fallen remained behind – as if time and weather had worn away flesh from bone leaving only jagged skeletal shapes; rugged forms half buried in sand, with angular, broken fingers pointing to the heavens.

It was hot and dry, and the wind blew insidious powder into the eyes and mouths of the riders, despite their hoods pulled low and scarves wrapped heavily about them. They were five, and a sixth who wrangled the pair of horses that pulled a canvas covered wagon behind them, its wheels bumping and bouncing from rock to rock, the animals shaking and stumbling in the traces.

Progress was slow; but steadily the small group picked its way along the length of a wide valley. They had passed a sturdy castle a few leagues back, perched on a small hill, and had eyed its Moorish battlements nervously. But as they had come into its range they could clearly see that despite an imposing appearance it had fallen into a decrepit state, and no longer stood guard over the road from the now-ruined city of Almería to Guadix. It was merely a hollowed out reminder of the power of the Caliphate, gone now – for the most part.

They followed the same road that itself followed a small river, crisscrossing the dried up stream's bed. When the rains came the whole road would, for a short time, become impassible, but this was the dry season and it would not rain for another two, maybe three months. So although uncomfortable, at least the way was open.

Despite the early hour the heat was becoming steadily more unbearable. They had been travelling in the mornings and afternoons, trying to rest the horses from the blaze of midday, but the way was too treacherous to travel once the sun went down, so the journey had been taking a lot longer than they had planned. By contrast, as they moved steadily westward through the heat of the desert, away to the south could be seen a purple ridge of snow-capped mountains rising cold and inviting from the shimmering yellow rock; sparkling crisply in the morning sun and taunting the travellers, its icy coolness just out of reach.

They were being secretly observed on their steady progress, from a low hill that dominated a turn in the road. A small, rotund man, resting his arms uncomfortably on the baking rocks, held two glass lenses up, one in front of the other, and squinted through them, better to make clear the details of the approaching group. At their present distance though it was impossible to make out anything more than silhouettes, even with the use of the lenses, especially with the sun directly behind them. The man pulled his cloak over him and slid into a small depression in the rock to avoid as best he could the direct sun, and waited until the riders had come a little closer and the sun risen a little higher.

After a while he lifted his head over the top of the rock once more and stared down the length of the valley. The riders had disappeared. He stood up looking nervously about him, trying to spot the dust cloud kicked up by the horses. Still nothing. He ran down from his perch to the roadway, passing the dead body of his mule along the way, and rounding the corner of a large boulder almost ran headlong into a row of horsemen blocking his route.

He cried out and jumped back in surprise. The men looked down at him. He squinted back up at them, trying to make out the identity of these anonymous riders.

They were four and were dressed in a mixed garb: Berber robes and scarves on top of Castilian boots and gauntlets. They looked ready for trouble, or ready to become trouble – four pairs of dark eyes staring down at him. One of the riders pulled the scarf from his face and spoke. The language, like their attire, was an odd mix of Arabic and Castilian and the small man staring up at them could not understand a word. He asked them what they meant in his own heavily accented version of Castilian, and after a little misunderstanding the men made clear their intention, confirmed by exposing the hilts of their scimitars.

The leader of the group jumped from his horse and with one swift blow smacked the small man across the face with his open hand, sending him spinning to the ground. He pulled the leather satchel from the man's shoulder and emptied its contents, pushing the objects around with the toe of his boot. The small man grabbed nervously at a bundle of papers that fell from the bag, and had his fingers nonchalantly kicked away by the horseman. Finally seeing what he was looking for the horseman bent forward and raised a small purse in the air, displaying it for the approval of his companions. With the forbidding sound of metal on metal he drew his large and razor sharp scimitar, and prepared to end the life of the small, cowering man nursing his bruised knuckles.

The small man stared up at the raised sword held aloft by the robed silhouette as it flashed in the morning sunlight, and prepared to die. It was a foolish death in this barren wasteland, he thought, so to rob the world of his genius – a ridiculous death at the hand of this barbarian whose intelligence could barely be a fraction of his own. Even cowering in fearful anticipation of death, it seemed the small man could not suppress his arrogance.

While he was caught up in the contemplation of his unique version of disdainful dread, something unusual happened. With a swish the swordsman was gone. The small man looked around for him, squinting in the sunlight, and finally found him pinned to a rock by a large arrow, a blank expression on his face.

The three surviving horsemen, their scimitars drawn, looked quickly to left and right, trying to locate the source of the arrow; their horses shied nervously, sensing fear. Then a voice came out from the wilderness, a large booming voice speaking Castilian. The voice offered the horsemen a simple but ominous choice: to lay down their weapons or die.

One of the three, spontaneously defying the imperative, leaped from his horse and grabbed the small man, who squealed in fear and anger. He held the man before him, a dagger at his throat and cursed the unseen voice; cursed him by the Prophet in Arabic. But the curses had barely issued from his lips when a crossbow bolt transfixed his forehead and he fell – dead before his limp body struck the ground. The two remaining horsemen hastily turned their horses, and galloped back the way they had come.

The small man stood perfectly still, stunned by the speed and ferocity of the attack and its equally fast and ferocious outcome, as the cloud of dust kicked up by the departing horses swirled around him like a fog. He stood there with nowhere to run and nowhere to hide, just waiting, his eyes burning from the blowing sand. As he watched, the dust clouds parted and through the receding fog rode five men. Mounted on huge black horses with long curling black manes, they were dressed as Knights of Saint John, their black cloaks billowing behind them – parting to show white-crossed blood red surcoats beneath. All were dressed so, except one, a burly blackamoor who wore black leather armor beneath his cloak.

They drew rein and stood their horses in a semicircle around the small man. He looked up at them, staring into the glaring sun for the second time that morning, and began to speak. Addressing the elder knight in the center, he elaborated his speech with dramatic flourishes and rhetorical subtleties, made somewhat ridiculous by the high-pitched almost feminine tone of his voice. Unfortunately he was speaking German so nobody could understand him.

Sir Richard raised his hand to stop the man, and told him in Castilian that he was poorly understood. The small man paused, a little crestfallen that his dramatic peroration had been for naught; but undaunted he began again in Castilian, "Thank you, My Lords, for your great efforts to save my miserable life, and protect me from these barbarians. My name is Theophrastus Bombast von Hohenheim, but I am known as Paracelsus, and I am at your service." At which point he bowed awkwardly. Sir Richard was about to reply when Paracelsus, as apparently the small, rotund man was known, continued, "I am a philosopher, a doctor of the natural sciences, an alchemist and an astrologer. I am also a physician, skilled in both surgery, and the cure or mediation of those endless ailments with which the Good Lord, in His wisdom, torments us."

Luca leaned over in his saddle and whispered to Henrique, "If his stature were as great as his accomplishments he could have vanquished those thieves with one blow." Henrique smiled his agreement.

"Well then Doctor Paracelsus," began Sir Richard, jumping in before the small man could speak again, "it was our Christian duty and our singular pleasure to rescue you from those thieving *Mudéjar*, but we should move on before it gets too hot, and the bandits return with their friends. I have never ridden with a philosopher before; perhaps some of your great learning will rub off onto an old knight. Mount up."

"But Sir," replied Paracelsus, "I have no mount, I was pursued by those thieves and in my haste I overtaxed my mule." He pointed to the dead animal.

Sir Richard whistled and a moment later came a whistle in return. After another few seconds the wagon pulled into view, a horse, once owned by one of the dead *Mudéjar,* walking calmly beside it. "Good shooting Jonson!" shouted Sir Richard to the driver, whose crossbow was reloaded and ready at his side. He waved in return.

"And my shooting was nothing I suppose?" asked Edryd the Welshman as he stowed his long bow in the sling that hung from his saddle.

"A knight needs no encouragement for his skill and his deeds," was Sir Richard's terse reply, "his sword and his arrows are guided by the hand of the Almighty, his purpose is as the instrument of God's will on this earth." The Welshman laughed at Sir Richard's trenchant words, and shook his head.

"Still, a little practice once in a while does not go amiss," Edryd replied.

Paracelsus, meanwhile, had gathered his scattered belongings, and with a little help retrieved his saddlebags from beneath the mule. They dragged the carcasses of both men and beast to the side of the road and Paracelsus mounted the Moor's horse, the smell of leather and sweat reminding him uncomfortably of being held captive by its previous owner.

The horse shied a little at the unfamiliar and unskilled rider, almost depositing the rotund philosopher onto the ground – to much laughter. But the small man, determined that the next time he lay down that day would be under his own power, hung on grimly – stirrups swinging empty below his feet – until the beast quietened down. And the train, now seven men strong, continued its journey across the desert.

El Pueblo

Although they travelled the length of a long and wide arid valley flanked by distant mountains and their attendant grey scrubby foothills, their way was not smooth.

Indeed, the dried stream whose bed they rode upon twisted through many different landscapes – now rocky, now hilly, now cut by deep ravines. Likewise, late that afternoon they picked their way gingerly down a stony slope with a sandy plain at its foot, and there before them was a small village.

As so many broken teeth jutting from the monotonous landscape, the low, whitewashed buildings clustered on a small flat hill that rose from the center of the plain. Some poor souls, it seemed, were able not only to tease the necessities of life from this wilderness but also to thrive, as evidenced by a well-built adobe church and small monastery that lay adjacent to the town square. As they grew closer they could make out the terraced groves of trees and vines on the low hills to either side of the village, and the shapes of fields laid out on the shallow slopes.

The village was too small to enjoy the protection of a well-built wall, although at some point in its history a bank and ditch had been dug around the perimeter, and the bank piled loosely with fieldstone. Long since fallen into disrepair though, the wooden gate was a mere skeleton – plundered for firewood, no doubt, many years ago.

They rode slowly past the remnants of the gate into the small town, not wishing the appearance of their group of heavily armed men to cause any alarm. They continued along a narrow street of low buildings that emerged into the town square, and tied up their mounts at the well, drawing fresh water and filling the trough for the horses.

The entire place seemed empty, void of activity. It was late enough that the sun was growing red over the western hills, their shadows reaching out long, dark fingers, harbingers of approaching night. Yet there were no women at the well, no children playing, no old men sitting in the evening shade.

With the horses watered, and leaving Jonson to look after them, they walked over to the monastery that stood by the church in the far corner of the square. Sir Richard rang the brass bell hanging beside a small wooden door let into a long adobe wall, and they waited. And they continued to wait. He was about to ring again when the door squeaked open a few inches, and the newcomers were quickly scanned by a pair of eyes, the face remaining mostly hidden in the darkness beyond the door. Then just as quickly the door was slammed shut again.

The group exchanged confused glances, and Sir Richard was in the process of reaching for the bell when they heard voices raised in argument from within. They paused, trying to catch the words, but before they could discern any meaning the door flew open and a robed monk waved them quickly through. "Hurry, hurry!" he hissed as if their innocent arrival were part of some great conspiracy, and he did not relax his agitated demeanor until the last man was inside the cool half-light, and the door shut behind them.

Breathing an audible sigh the monk leaned back against the bolted door. "I am so sorry for the rudeness of Brother Carlos," he began after a moment.

"We are all doomed!" came a cry, echoing from deeper within the monastery, presumably from Brother Carlos.

"Pay him no mind," urged the monk, "he is of a naturally fretful nature."

"You have brought ruin upon us," came another cry.

"Be silent Carlos, you are worrying our guests!"

"Do not concern yourself Brother," began Sir Richard, smiling, "the disquiet of a nervous monk is not sufficient to cause *us* worry." He considered a moment and continued, "We tend more to induce worry in others."

"Indeed Sirs, I believe it was the sight of your blackamoor that most bothered Carlos," explained the monk. Henrique bowed politely. "I imagine he thought him a *Muselmán*."

"Monk, fear not I am a good and baptized Christian like yourself," said Dom Henrique pleasantly.

"He does look rather formidable though," mused Edryd looking the large black man up and down, "for a bishop, leastways."

"A bishop!" exclaimed the monk. "We are most honored to have a bishop in the midst of our humble community. But surely you must be tired from your journey, follow me." And with that he led the party into the depths of the monastery.

They had entered a dimly lit vestibule with narrow corridors that led in two directions. The monk opened another door and they passed into a cloister that ran around three sides of a small courtyard, the church forming the fourth side. "We do not have much room here, but there are only a few of us so your night should pass comfortably enough," he explained. They followed him into a refectory at the far end of the cloister where two more brothers could be seen laying out wooden trenchers on a long table, as for a meal. Seeing this their guide clapped his hands loudly and exclaimed, "The pewter, the pewter Brothers! We are visited by a Bishop accompanied by his bodyguard of Hospitaller Knights! We must use the pewter!"

Sir Richard and Edryd exchanged amused glances at the monk's characterization of them, but neither felt the need to correct him.

As evening drew on, and the horses and wagon were stabled, the weary travellers said a short prayer, and sat down to their meal with the monks. The brothers were six in number, all equally attired in rough brown habit tied loosely with a cord. Even the wayward Brother Carlos joined them, looking singularly unhappy. Their host, Brother Miguel, acquitted himself of his host duties as well as the monks' self-imposed poverty would permit, and as they ate he asked after the names of his guests.

"I am Sir Richard Weston, Knight of England, may the Lord bless his Highness King Henry; and this young man is my nephew Edmund. He is a novice knight and is serving his probation under my tutelage." The young knight, barely more than a boy – for all practical purposes a much younger version of Sir Richard – stood briefly and bowed. "On my other side is Edryd the Archer of Wales," he continued, and Edryd nodded casually. "He is a Knight of Grace, that is…"

"That is," interrupted Edryd, "I earned my knighthood the hard way. Not by the courting of some perfumed prince or cardinal, rather by the counting of Turkish dead at my feet."

"As you can see, Edryd has been with us long enough to have fought many campaigns against the Turk, most recently at Rhodes where he did great service helping us fight the mighty Suleiman himself to a standstill," explained Sir Richard, always amused by Edryd's relentless truculence. "Finally, Jonson is our man-at-arms and teamster." The dark, stocky Jonson stood and smiled his crooked smile, made more so by a long, deep scar that started to the side of his eye and progressed diagonally downward, traversing his mouth and ending at the point of his chin. He was of an age with Sir Richard, and like Edryd they had fought together for many a year.

"We are Knights of St. John – late of Rhodes," explained Sir Richard redundantly.

"And soon to be again once we are grown strong," insisted Edryd.

"Our travelling companions who sit across the table from us are Luca the Painter of Florence." He indicated Luca who nodded. "He wears the colors of a man-at-arms by the special grace of our Grand Master, bestowed upon him for the painting of a most lifelike portrait. Next to him sits Dom Henrique, the most Holy Bishop of Utica, and a Prince of the Kongo." Henrique smiled his big, toothy smile, and waved his spoon between mouthfuls. "And finally, next to the Bishop is our personal philosopher from the German Cantons; Para…" he paused, "Para…"

"…celsus – Paracelsus," finished the philosopher a little testily, in his squeaky voice.

"Yes, Paracelsus. We saved him from some vagabonds on the road who would rob and kill him."

"Did you do them harm – the vagabonds?" asked Brother Carlos, suddenly interrupting nervously.

"Two of them, aye – we killed them," answered Edryd. "They were Moors. They were thieves and murderers. They died. And did you not hear him say they would rob and kill the small philosopher? We would not let that happen."

"We are doomed!" cried Brother Carlos.

"What is it that makes this man so fearful?" asked Sir Richard, rising angrily to his feet as Edryd shook his head in astonishment.

"We are not a free people here," answered one of the monks. All eyes turned towards him and he stood, pushing back the hood that covered his head. He was an old man with a white beard, his pate completely bald, lacking even the circular fringe of the monks' tonsure. He stood a little unsteadily, fixed the travellers with his tired, rheumy eyes, and began to speak.

"What Brother Miguel is not telling you about, and what makes Brother Carlos so fearful, is what you might call the ecumenical problem in this valley." He paused as the visitors looked from one to the other, confused. After a breath he continued, "As our most Holy Catholic Monarchs pushed the Moors southwards they took refuge in this valley, living in caves in the desert hills. Now behind every *Moriscoe* who has converted to Christianity there are hiding a hundred *Mudéjars* – Moors who will never bow to the will of the Inquisition.

"And here they live as vagabonds and thieves, and help the corsairs along the coast when they need food and water. We live an uneasy existence here amongst them. They demand a tribute from us, the *jizyah*, as we used to pay under the Caliphs, and now we pay this to the bandits rather than try to fight them. There are no fighting men here, only farmers and monks, men of peace and hard work, not men of war. Brother Carlos believes that now that you have killed two of their number they will have seen you come here, and will follow you to exact their revenge on the village."

The monk finished his story and stood quietly, his head bowed a little, swaying unsteadily on thin legs. Sir Richard's eyes narrowed as he stared at him. Finally he spoke, "What about the Holy Brotherhood?" he asked, "Do they not police this area?"

"We believe them to be in league with the Moors. That evil bastard that rules from Guadix gives us only words. His Brotherhood soldiers ride through and see nothing, and once they are gone back come the Moors."

Sir Richard thought again a moment. "Would they still come here despite the presence of a group of Hospitaller Knights?"

"They fear nothing these ragamuffins. A half dozen men wearing the cross would most likely just encourage them."

"When will they come?" asked Sir Richard.

"Richard…" said Edryd standing up and putting his hand on the Knight's arm, "Richard, we have a job of work to do." Sir Richard shook the hand away. "We cannot tarry here fighting pirates when we are already late to Guadix."

"They are due to come in two days to collect the tax," answered the monk.

Sir Richard turned on the Welshman, "Were you not listening? These Moors resupply the corsairs with what they steal from these good Christians. The very same corsairs we must fight on the sea."

"But Richard…"

"Surely you are not afeard of a ragged bunch of Moslems, Edryd?"

"Killing them would warm my heart old friend, but do we not have a job to do? Perhaps on the way back."

"Too late then and you know it," replied Sir Richard, and Edryd sighed.

"So," interjected Jonson through his scarred smile, his eyes twinkling, "time to unload the wagon – looks like we have some Moors to kill, eh?"

LA EMBOSCADA

Luca wiped the sweat from his eyes for the hundredth time as he stared down at the bleached white dust of the town square below. Lined up next to him were eight arquebuses and six villagers. He had spent the last three days teaching the villagers to reload an arquebus swiftly enough to allow him to maintain a continuous rate of fire; and with six of them, reasonably well trained, and eight weapons, he was sure he could perform his task.

He wondered if these Moors that inspired so much fear would ever show up. They were already a day late, and this was his second stint sweating on the roof of the church, hidden in the shadow of the bell tower. His consolation was in knowing that the rest of his band were equally uncomfortable, tucked away in various places around the square. He had been selected for duty on the arquebus after telling his story of killing the Constable on the walls of Rome, and admitting he had no skill with bow or crossbow. So here he sat sweating with his nervous assistants, armed with an arquebus, not knowing if it was meant as praise or punishment.

Edryd was sleeping in a hammock in a house across the square from Luca. Three bows and a hundred arrows were arrayed on a shaded area of the roof above him, but for the time being he was enjoying this new import from the New World. The hammock affair was very comfortable and Edryd saw no need to sweat on a rooftop when he had villagers to keep watch for him, and some sleep to catch up on.

Once in a while he would awaken, push the blond hair from his eyes and squint out of a small square window in the adobe wall. Then, seeing nothing of note, he would take a sip from a cup of a delicious spiced fruit juice and wine concoction that had been mixed by their personal philosopher, who had called it *hypokras* in his native tongue. Then Edryd would fall back to sleep.

The Philosopher himself was sweltering in a small wooden hut near the low wall at the back of the village, well away from the town square, and cursing the day he became part of this insane plan to challenge the local power structure in this hellish valley. Of course he could not have refused, and of course he had no love for the Moorish thieves that had almost dispatched him on the road. On the other hand, he would rather have put as much distance as possible between himself and those dangerous Moslems as quickly as possible, not challenge them to armed combat.

He was a philosopher, an alchemist, not a fighter, despite a brief assignment as an army surgeon a few years before. That had been merely to supply his bodily needs while on his travels, his real purpose on this earth was to ponder the weighty problems of the universe, plot astrological charts, mix medicines and concoctions to heal the sick and infirm and, when necessary, set bones and cauterize wounds.

He had made this clear to the Knights, but they had laughed at him and, in no uncertain terms, commanded him to help. He had travelled a long way from the university at Basel on his most recent journey of discovery, and needed their assistance to extricate himself from his currently dire situation, so he had reluctantly agreed to help; although, once committed to the task, he threw himself into it with the dedication of a true philosopher.

Among his many occupations had been a job in the lead mines of the Fuggers back in Villach, the land of his youth, so he had gained much experience with explosives and fire, and had begun to enjoy bringing that experience to bear on the plan Sir Richard had laid out.

Edmund was pacing nervously inside the church and Sir Richard called out to him, "Sit down boy, you are annoying me."

"I am sorry Sir, but the impending battle disquiets me. Are you not troubled?"

"Edmund, this is your first real fight, I understand, but fear has a way of eating at your guts. It lives in your belly, coiled like a snake, feeding on your worries. Of course I am troubled. Every time I face an enemy I am troubled – no I am afraid. But you must kill that snake or it will consume you. If you do not feel afraid you are not a man, but if you do not conquer that fear then you are not a warrior."

"Yes sir," replied Edmund uncertainly.

"Look Edmund," continued the older man, trying a different tack, "there will only be ten, perhaps twenty of these Moors. I could dispatch them all myself. But we have a plan that simply requires we keep the Moors in one place, and they are doomed." Edmund looked hopefully at his mentor. "My boy this will be a good fight for you," he assured the young man. "Your skill with a sword is most excellent, so you have nothing to fear from this rabble."

"Yes sir," replied Edmund with a little more certainty.

The village slumbered in the afternoon sun and waited. From a hill a league or two away Izdârasen Andalousi stared down into the village square and stroked his beard thoughtfully. "Usem!" he called out to his lieutenant, and returned to his contemplation of the village. Usem urged his horse forward until he was next to his commander.

"Sir?" he answered.

"The *kuffār* that killed our brothers are still in the town."

"Yes sir."

"But the question is…"

"Sir?"

Izdârasen stared at the whitewashed buildings below him as if he could glean some particular intelligence by the intensity of his gaze. "The question is," he repeated, "what are they doing down there?"

"Sir?"

"The *kuffār*, Usem," answered Izdârasen, "the knights wearing their infidel crosses. What is their purpose in this scrubby little town?"

"I know not," answered Usem.

"Of course you know not," replied Izdârasen testily, "but do they lie in wait for us? Or are they preparing to leave?" He stroked his beard again for a few minutes and then continued – not really to Usem but more to himself to better clarify his thoughts, "If they would leave we could catch them on the road and kill them all. But if they would stay we shall have to go in and kill them. If they know we are coming for the monthly tribute they may have laid a trap for us." He and Usem sat there in thought for a while longer – two horsemen watching motionless from the hilltop.

"We have to go in," was Izdârasen's decision. "But we will split our forces. Half will go in the main gate and the rest will go over the wall from behind. We will draw them out then flank them and kill the *kuffār*. We will kill all who stand against us. We will show them no mercy."

Usem nodded enthusiastically.

"*Bismillah ir-Rahman ir-Rahim.*"

✠

The afternoon wore on – time hanging heavy in the thick, dusty air. The town was silent and still, the only movements were the small eddies of sand whipped up by the hot wind that swirled sporadically through the narrow streets. Time takes the edge off the sharpest weapon, and the worst part of the battle is the wait for the fighting to begin. Steady hands begin to shake and calm men begin to sweat. An army can be defeated in its own mind before the first blow is struck.

Even Sir Richard, as stoic a warrior as ever drew a sword, was beginning to rethink his idea of facing a numerically superior force with an untested crew. If only one of his group failed then the fight, rather than be the straightforward affair he had planned, could become a hard and bloody slog through dusty streets. Ironically, it was his nephew about whom he was the most concerned. The Painter, he knew, had fought hand to hand and been captured at the siege of Rome; even the blackamoor Bishop had shown that blood lust in his eyes when he had taken the heavy mace in hand and swung it with a practiced arm, nodding and smiling his wide, toothy grin. No, it was Edmund who could be the weak link. What had he been thinking bringing the lad on this quest? He had imagined it would make a man of the youngster, but the deeper he travelled into enemy territory the worse he thought his decision had been. Sir Richard sat there sweating into his armor, and worried.

A shout came from one of the villagers posted on the low wall. The enemy was approaching. Earlier, Sir Richard had gathered the villagers together to explain to them what was to happen. Some had been happy at the thought of being free from the Moslem yoke, others, less sanguine about the inevitable battle, despite the fearsome reputation borne by the Knights of Saint John, had not been confident that seven men could sufficiently defeat the Moors that menaced them. Still, as mere pawns in this chess game of giants, they obediently set about their appointed tasks in the execution of Sir Richard's plan.

From the remains of the village gate, in the low dirt and fieldstone wall, there led a narrow street faced with single storey adobe houses for about fifty yards until it joined the town square; the same street the Knights and their companions had travelled upon their arrival a few days earlier. In the center of the square, which was about forty yards on each side, stood a large stone well surrounded by a circular trough for the animals. In the top right corner of the square was the church and the monastery, the rest of the square was faced with single and double storey adobe houses and shops, loosely connected by a more or less continuous covered wooden walkway – what the Portuguese call a *varanda*. Beyond the square, several streets of low wood and adobe houses led further into the village, ending at the rear wall.

Sir Richard stood and adjusted the fall of his crimson surcoat. He and his nephew were wearing more armor than they usually wore aboard the galleys. They had added a breastplate and jointed steel arm and leg protection, but had kept the leather boots for ease of movement in the coming fight. They looked at each other and nodded. They were ready. The two men pulled on their helmets and walked from the church along the *varanda*, stopping side by side to stare down the street to the village gate, awaiting their foe.

The Moors were a while coming, but finally they rode through the gate and up the long street towards the square. The two Knights watched them approach, their huge swords clasped in both hands before them. The horsemen spread out when they reached the square and lined up facing the Knights. Edmund counted about thirty men, swathed in white and armed to the teeth, mounted on the light, fast Arab horses that lived comfortably in the desert.

One man rode forward from the front rank up to the *varanda* where stood Sir Richard. They stared at each other for a minute or two in silence, broken only by the occasional nervous snorting from the horses, who seemed keenly aware that terrible things were soon to happen. The rider was wearing a dark, indigo *tagelmust*, a long scarf that wrapped his entire head, indicating his rank.

"My name is Izdârasen Andalousi and this is my village," he declared in heavily accented Castilian, indicating his possession with an imperious wave of his hand. "These Christians are my responsibility and they pay me the *jizyah* in honor of my position in this valley. In return I protect them from harm and hold their persons and their property sacred. What do you here?"

"My name is Sir Richard Weston," began the Knight in reply, "and I am a Christian warrior. This village is now under the protection of the Knights of St. John of Jerusalem. These are Christian people and have no need of Moors. For a Christian to pay tax to a *Muselmán* is an insult to the Mother Church and to God himself." He stared into the Moor's eyes that gleamed coldly from behind their deep blue swathe.

"Jerusalem?" jeered the Moor, joined by his fellows, "It has been many a year since a *kafir* knight has been seen alive in *al-Quds*."

The two warriors glared at each other for a few more minutes. Faces obscured, two sets of eyes separated by a mere few feet, yet minds as far apart as the ends of the earth.

"Can you make out what they are saying?" asked Luca of one of the villagers.

"They are measuring the length of their swords," replied the villager, only half in jest.

Luca laughed grimly to himself. He was resting the arquebus on the edge of the church roof and had it lined up on the indigo head of the lead horseman. There was to be a signal and he was waiting nervously for it, keenly aware that any mistake on his part could be disastrous for the entire enterprise.

Across the square Edryd squatted on another roof, peering carefully over the parapet so as not to be seen. He too was awaiting his signal to let loose on the enemy below, and held his best longbow at the ready.

Paracelsus was still sweating profusely, the more so now that action seemed imminent. He peered from his hiding place in the hut that gave onto the low wall behind the village. The villagers with him were chattering nervously, something he did not understand, and he hissed at them to be quiet. He used what little Castilian he had to command them, but he recognized none of the words in their excited chatter. "*¿Qué?*" he asked and they ignored him, "*¿Qué?*" he hissed as loudly as he dare and they stopped and stared at him.

"*¡Enemigo!*" said one of the villagers his eyes wide. This he recognized. He stared out through the narrow window of the hut but could see nothing but scrub and rocks. "*Allí,*" whispered the villager pointing. And then Paracelsus saw it; just a small movement, then it stopped, and then it moved again. The Moors were creeping slowly toward the back wall of the village, just as Sir Richard had predicted, being the least defensible position in the village.

Paracelsus calmed his villagers, and with a few words of advice sent them scurrying off to their stations. With two men he crept out of the hut and climbed up a waiting ladder to lie down on the gently sloping roof, trying not to touch his bare flesh on the sun-baked wood.

From this viewpoint he could clearly see the Moors creeping forward. There were at least twenty of them, and they were spread out across the rough ground. He waited, looking to left and right, but could not see any of his villagers. He was pleased they had concealed themselves so well, but an uneasy thought struck him: perhaps they had simply run off.

He waited, baking gently in the hot afternoon sun. Finally the Moors reached the ditch in front of the wall and slid down into the depression, regrouping before they began their assault. It was time. The small rotund philosopher snapped his fat fingers, and one of his villagers passed him a slow match – a length of cord treated with saltpeter to burn slowly and never go out.

In front of him were three fuses – more cord, this time coated with black powder – that led down from the top of the hut, and with a flourish he applied the glowing tip of the slow match to each one in turn. They hissed and sputtered, and burned off the edge of the hut out of sight. He whistled, a low repeating whistle, and prayed that his villagers were lighting their fuses too.

"The Holy Quran commands us to strike terror into the hearts of the *kuffār*, to wage endless war upon them, to kill them, destroy them and flay the skin from their miserable bodies for eternity," declared Izdârasen, and his men murmured:

"*Allahu Akbar.*"

"But the Prophet was also merciful. He declared that we must try to convert the *kuffār* from their error and their confusion, and if we could not, to live in peace with the People of the Book – but only if they pay the *jizyah*. All people who do not follow the path of Mohammed, may peace be upon him – they must be taxed." Izdârasen's eyes stared malevolently from within their indigo swaddling. "Are you prepared to convert or be taxed Christian Knight?" he asked, already sure of the response.

"Let me explain this to you Moslem. Your holy book is a heresy and a lie. Your prophet was an Arab bandit who spread his evil by the sword. You are Berber, Andalousi; your people were not always ruled by the wickedness of Islam. It is time to free yourself from this Arab heresy and embrace the truth of Our Lord Jesus Christ."

"Amen," said Edmund.

The two continued to glare at each other as Izdârasen's men reached for their swords and put arrow to bow.

"So are you ready to pay the tax, Christian?'

"No. How do you propose to extract it from me Moslem?"

"You are but two men," declared Izdârasen, laughing, "I am sure you are very brave and strong warriors, and that you will slay many of my men, but we will prevail. You will die; we will burn this village and torture all its occupants to death. In the meanwhile my fallen men will be in paradise with Allah."

"I believe you overestimate the strength of your position," replied Sir Richard, "with a wave of my hand I can kill any one of you." The Berbers muttered amongst themselves. "I shall demonstrate!" he declared, and promptly pointed his right hand at a horseman in the front rank. An arrow whistled through the warm air and sliced through the man's throat, exiting the back of his neck and lodging in the thigh of another horseman in the second rank.

The first Moslem fell dead on the spot, dropping to the feet of his horse in a crumpled pile of cloth, while the second screamed in agony. Izdârasen waved the man quiet, and he reduced his screams to whimpers. The two warriors glared at each other for a while.

"I believe you overestimate the strength of *your* position!" declared the Moslem, his eyes twinkling. "Your men may have prepared an ambush, but we have prepared one of our own," he announced.

"Oh," said Sir Richard, in an off-hand manner, "you mean the men who are, at this moment, attempting to enter the village from behind us?" Izdârasen eyes showed surprised. "They are already dead my Moslem friend," continued Sir Richard in a decidedly unfriendly way.

As if to accent his declaration, multiple huge explosions rocked the village sending several balls of orange fire high into the deep blue sky. The horses cried out and shuffled in fear, their riders struggling to control them, as the balls of fire merged into a single crimson cloud swirled in black smoke, rising from behind the village.

"Andalousi," shouted Sir Richard over the noise, "I am fortunate to have a Christian Philosopher with me; behold his work." Without looking back he waved his armored hand above his head as flames leaped high into the air over the buildings behind him.

Paracelsus had been quite taken aback at the violence of the explosion. In truth more than just taken aback, he had been deposited violently onto the rough ground as the hut he was using as a command post had disintegrated beneath him.

Fortunately so, as a roaring cloud of flame filled the air where once the hut had stood. He lay there, his ears ringing, hotter than he had been all day, and waited until the fire swirling above subsided. He had prepared a series of mines in the ditch behind the wall. They had been composed of black powder, turpentine and pitch, as he had wanted an initial blast along with a ball of flame. The pitch had been added to spray sticky, black fire over any who survived the explosion.

Wide eyed, the small philosopher, flanked by his two soot-stained villagers, slowly stood up and surveyed the destruction. His explosives had been more successful than even he could have imagined – indeed, a little too successful as several buildings near the wall were broken and smouldering. He gazed out to where the Moors had been and all he could see, squinting through the eye-watering smoke of burning pitch, were one or two figures, engulfed in flame, who staggered a moment before they fell. The screams subsided until there was just the ringing in his ears, and of course his lack of eyebrows, to remind him of the explosion.

Sir Richard raised his left hand and Luca opened fire. His shots, one after the other as the villagers reloaded, cut through the ranks of Moors as their horses struggled in panic to break free and escape, throwing several of their riders to the ground – trampling, dragging. The front two ranks dismounted in much disarray, and drew their swords as their horses pushed past the third rank of horsemen, finally to make their escape.

The square was now much clearer of horses, but the dust was rising rapidly to obscure the men. Luca and Edryd were shooting at Moorish shapes in the swirling sand, cutting them down one after another as they pushed forward to join battle with Sir Richard.

Clearly, the third rank of Moors was losing heart in the fight seeing their brothers in arms blown up and burned, and brought down by arrow and shot. Being still mounted they made use of the confusion to escape. Wheeling their horses in a collective panic they rode hard for the narrow street that led to the gate and safety.

Once all of the fleeing Moors were out of the square and into the street, a rope powered by falling weights sprang up, spanning their escape route just on a level with the riders. The rope lifted the first horsemen clean from their saddles and threw them backwards into those following. Horses stumbled and men fell.

The Moors, unhorsed, struggled to protect themselves from the flashing hooves as their mounts, regaining their balance, brushed the men aside and cantered riderless through the village gate. The ten were now eight as two of the Moors never again rose from the dust of the street, then another four fell as Jonson and three villagers fired a crossbow volley from the roofs on either side.

Henrique, with a blood-curdling scream, leaped from the rooftop into the struggling mass of Moors, swinging his heavy, studded mace about him, swiftly and cruelly dispatching the survivors before they could even draw a sword.

Sir Richard stepped from the *varanda* into the square and knelt a moment in prayer in the midst of the swirling dust, the yelling men and the screaming horses – *Blessed be the Lord my strength, which teacheth my hands to war, and my fingers to fight.*

Then, his huge sword whirling around him in a flashing circular rhythm, the Knight walked out into the square to meet Izdârasen and his men in combat. The remaining Moors surrounded Sir Richard and leaped to the attack. To the Englishman the Moors' fighting was very sloppy and undisciplined. Their sword work was flashy, but their tactics were poor, and he had no problem keeping them at bay until he could land a blow.

As he turned about and about, he looked over quickly to his nephew, worried momentarily. The boy was simply standing there, in the dirt at the edge of the square, frozen – immobile. His sword trailed on the ground behind him and his left arm hung at his side. "Edmund!" shouted Sir Richard trying vainly to bring the boy out of his reverie. He understood that the only way not to be killed in a battle was to keep moving, Edmund was presenting an undefended target.

Sir Richard began to fight his way towards the boy who continued to stand, motionless yet miraculously untouched, at the edge of the battle, blood and dust roiling around him. Edryd, from his rooftop, had also noticed Edmund's stupefaction, and changed the focus of his arrows to the boy's protection. Every time a Moor came within striking distance of the boy, Edryd would cut him down with a well-placed arrow. Shooting towards his compatriot was not something Edryd would normally contemplate, but the alternative was to see the boy butchered before his eyes.

This situation could only last for a short time, and after a few moments a Moorish archer, from his refuge behind the body of his fallen horse, sent an arrow straight at Edmund which struck him a glancing blow on the breastplate, tearing a jagged hole in his surcoat. The shock of being hit seemed to awaken him somewhat, and he began to raise his sword as if to fight. Again the Moor fired at the boy, looking to find that cleft, that chink that separated the pieces of armor. The arrow was aimed to strike the boy's faceplate and penetrate an eye, but a second time it was deflected, this time off the curve of his helmet.

Through the swirling dust Edryd could just make out the archer who was targeting Edmund and sent an arrow his way that stuck, quivering, in the side of the fallen horse, missing the man by a few inches. For a third time the Moor drew his bow, this time from a standing position, carefully aimed, and loosed his arrow. This was his last shot, as a ball from Luca's arquebus found him and brought him down, falling dead across his horse. But his arrow was released; flying, unrelenting, towards its target.

Edmund was in the motion of raising his sword above his head, at last to enter the fray, when the arrow caught him under the arm. It slipped past the edge of his breastplate and found a small opening, not quite protected by a fold of chainmail. The arrow, although slowed by contact with armor, pierced the flesh, slicing deep into his vitals. He cried out and stumbled, tormented with pain, just as his uncle reached him. Sir Richard could see immediately that the boy was badly injured, and placed himself between the Moors and his nephew.

It was at that moment that Jonson and Henrique entered the square from the opposite side. Having dispatched the Moors that had come their way, they drove into the enemy's flank. Jonson wielded a pair of short and brutally sharp axes, Henrique, the powerfully built blackamoor, was swinging his cudgel about him in a most un-bishop-like manner; and the Moors fell before them.

After that it was over in a few seconds, as Jonson and Henrique hacked and bludgeoned their way towards Sir Richard. The three met surrounding Izdârasen and his last two warriors. Izdârasen cried out, "Wait!" and the six stopped, weapons poised, the fight frozen in a single moment. "We concede!" he added as the Moors threw down their weapons and dropped to their knees.

The dust began to settle as all the horses that could leave had left. Edryd and Luca stood up at their posts, their weapons aimed at the last of the Moors, and Edryd waved cheerily across the square to the Painter. "We surrender!" exclaimed Izdârasen.

Sir Richard ran over to his stricken nephew. "Uncle," began the boy.

"Say nothing, the Philosopher will have some alchemy to put you right," replied the Knight.

"I think not Uncle. I believe I am done in this world," the boy sighed, "and in my first battle."

"No!" insisted Sir Richard, then jumping to his feet he shouted for Paracelsus. The Philosopher, a little smoke-blackened, came running into the square and hurried over to the injured boy. Sir Richard stood back and turned to the three Moors.

"What leads you to believe that we permit your surrender?" he asked, his voice breaking with anger and pain.

"You are Christians, you are merciful, just as Suleiman was merciful to you at Rhodes."

Sir Richard snorted at Izdârasen's impudence and turned his back on the Moors to watch Paracelsus tend to his nephew.

"The mercy of Suleiman was bought with the lives of fifty thousand of his Janissaries, and the option of losing thirty thousand more," he threw over his shoulder. "You are beaten and your men are in hell, you have no bargain to strike."

"Does not your God command you to be merciful?" asked Izdârasen desperately. The Knight ignored his pleas.

Paracelsus turned to Sir Richard and shook his head.

The Knight turned back to Izdârasen and grabbed his throat tight in a steel hand. Staring him in the eyes Sir Richard answered the Moor's question, "Indeed He does. However, if I leave you alive you will simply gather fresh forces and take this village again. And my nephew is struck down. Do his wounds not require justice – by the shedding of your blood?"

The two men glared at each other for a moment.

"Bind him – tight," shouted Sir Richard, throwing the Moslem to the ground, "and kill the other two. I have a plan for this one." Then he turned towards Edmund again. "Bishop, I need you to confess my nephew – quickly." His deep voice quavered as he spoke.

EL ENTIERRO

The smoke from distant funeral pyres stained the morning sky black.

It was a sad procession that wound its short way from the church to the small cemetery yard that lay close by. Dom Henrique, as Bishop clad in crimson robes, led the service of lauds, and thereupon the Hospitallers and their philosopher shouldered the remains of the young Knight. Laid on a wooden board in dress uniform and draped in a blood red cloth, he was carried slowly from the church as the monks gave voice to their gloomy requiem. Sir Richard slipped a small gold coin under Edmund's tongue, and placed the young man's sword, so little used, upon his chest. They lowered him gently to his last resting place.

The entire village turned out to pay their respects to a fallen warrior, dressed to a man in mourning white. The women cried, and the children, wide-eyed, laid flowers around the grave. They said many prayers amongst themselves for this brave man who had given his life that they should be spared the depredations of the Moorish horde. Sir Richard knelt by his fallen nephew and prayed. He did not claim to understand God's reason for taking this young man. He had seen enough killing in his lifetime to know how far beyond the understanding of man was the seeming randomness of death. His concern was only with the young man's soul and its journey to Paradise. And retribution.

After the battle, as the boy had lain dying, Sir Richard had cradled Edmund's head and calmed him. Edmund had no longer been in pain but he had been distressed. He had seemed most concerned that he should not be remembered as a coward. "I am sorry Uncle," he had repeated as Sir Richard had tenderly removed his helmet, letting his soft, amber curls spill out.

"Nonsense boy," his uncle had replied, through teeth clenched tight from sorrow.

"Please do not tell my father that I was a coward," Edmund had continued, a sob catching in his throat.

"Nonsense boy. You stood bravely before the Moors."

"But I did not fight," he had sobbed.

"You had not time. You were caught by a Moorish arrow and taken before you had the chance to cross swords."

"I did?" It was a question and Sir Richard had nodded in answer. "You did."

And Edmund was gone.

After the service, later in the afternoon, Luca tracked down Sir Richard as he lay prostrate before the altar in silent prayer. The older man sensed the Painter's presence and slowly stood. They faced one another, alone in the cool half-light of the simple church, and Luca remarked how tall and powerfully built was the Knight, despite his years.

"What brings you here Painter, as I mourn the loss of my nephew?"

"I am deeply sorry that my quest caused his death," blurted Luca.

"Frankly his lack of fight brought about his death," replied Sir Richard tersely.

"But had it not been…" began Luca and Sir Richard cut him off.

"Painter, you misunderstand our vocations. You paint for the Glory of God, we fight for the Glory of God. To be honest, your quest was the easiest way to test his mettle – much easier than a battle at sea would have been, with less at stake. Indeed, all he needed to do was stand behind me and present his sword."

"Then I am deeply sorry he was unable to do that."

"He was a man, though he may have looked like a boy – a noble man. And he died a noble death, far from home fighting the Moor for the sake of Christendom – wherever it may be. He has found his place in Paradise. That is all there is."

"Thank you Sir Richard, then I will go and leave you in peace." And with that Luca turned to leave.

"There will be no peace for me until your woman is rescued, the Don is punished, the Moors are driven from this accursed valley – and my nephew's soul is avenged."

EL VALLE

"Do you see them?" asked Edryd.

"Aye, I see them," grunted Sir Richard.

"I count thirty."

"Thirty five."

"Thirty five?"

"On top of that hill."

"Oh. Indeed. Should we tell the others?" asked Edryd.

"Those that will be of use have already seen them, those that have not yet seen them will be of no use," was Sir Richard's laconic reply.

"Then we ignore them?"

"Well, we are out of range of arrow or arquebus; if they approach too close then we will warn them off, or if necessary kill them. If we push on we can make Guadix before nightfall."

"Let us pray," Edryd frowned at his companion's terse replies. The Knight had been a different man since the death of his nephew. A slow, simmering anger was beginning to displace his normally even demeanor, and seemed ready to boil over at any minute.

A band of Moors had been following and observing them for the last two or three leagues, riding atop the rocky *mesetas* that rose steep and dusty orange from the edges of the flat valley. The way ahead was open scrubland with no clear place for an ambush; their hope was that this should stay so. At least the quality of the road was improving the closer they got to Guadix. They were, thereby, in a lot less danger of losing a wheel or having a horse go lame.

"If they choose to attack us you know there is little we can do out here in the open," continued Edryd, "and dragging this Moor behind us is like dragging red meat past a pack of wolves." He indicated Izdârasen, the only survivor of the ambush, who was now tethered by his hands to the wagon, and stumbled along in the dust behind them.

"He serves a purpose. He will pay for the death of my nephew by his use to us," Sir Richard growled.

"I saw a fortress a league back down the road, we should seek shelter for the night," Edryd shouted back, but was forced to return his concentration to his horse as Sir Richard, by way of answer, urged his mount faster.

Paracelsus was having the most trouble with his horse, which, although nimble, threatened to throw him at every turn. The small man clung on for dear life, swaying and sliding in the unfamiliar Moorish saddle, and prayed for a safe resolution to this dreadful pass. He had just finished another repetition of his prayer when the pass became yet more dreadful.

As the Christians cantered over a small rise in the road, their way was blocked by a line of Moors on horseback, faces swathed in cloth and blades drawn. It took all of Jonson's skill to slow his wagon sufficiently to avoid a collision.

The two groups sat there for a short while staring at each other, when at last Sir Richard broke the silence. "Step aside and we shall spare your lives. We are Christian Knights and have lawful business in Guadix," he bellowed. The Moors sat motionless. "If you attempt to do us harm you will bring down upon your heads a destruction of prodigious proportions. A destruction we have meted out to countless of your kind. We will find you wherever you hide. You will all be put to the sword, down to the last occupant of the last village, and your villages will be burned to the ground to serve as a memorial to your foolishness and your heresy. I will not leave this hellish valley until you all are dead!" he screamed in fury. Still the Moors sat motionless.

"Helmets!" shouted Sir Richard and the Christians all donned their helmets; except Paracelsus who cried out in a pitch higher even than usual, "I do not have a helmet!"

"Then duck," shouted Jonson, as he feverishly worked the cocking lever of his crossbow. The Christians armed themselves and the two sides faced off not ten yards apart. After a few tense seconds one of the Moors slowly unwound the scarf from his face and spoke:

"You *ferenghi* ride through our valley wearing the cross as an insult to Allah and the Prophet, may peace be upon him. This we might permit except that you also drag one of our brethren with you."

"He is a criminal and we bring him to Guadix for judgment," replied Sir Richard.

"You do not understand the way things work in this valley," answered the Moor obscurely.

"And you, Sir, do not understand the way things work for the Knights of Saint John. We kill Moslems. That is our entire purpose. You may thank your Prophet, and whatever false and heathen god you worship, that your brother is still alive to stand trial as a thief, and not simply burned in a pyre with the fifty or so of his band that we most recently killed." Sir Richard glared at the Moors and Jonson took careful aim at the Moorish spokesman. He had seen too many times in the past how these situations tended to play out.

"You see there is no escape from here Christian Knight?" asked the Moor after another minute or two of silence.

"You misjudge me Moor, I have no need of escape," replied the Knight, "my sole purpose is to kill and die in the service of the One True God."

"Then we well understand each other." The Moor's mouth twisted into a grim smile. "Look around you. We are abandoned here in the land of our grandfathers. We are driven by war and persecution into this dusty corner of our once great empire, and it is demanded of us to give up our ancient ways – under threat of death – and become Christians. The Holy Quran commands death to the apostate, and yet we are to renounce the Prophet and embrace your Jesus at the expense of our immortal souls. Why should we do this? Who dare commands us to abandon our faith and take up another, as a man changes his shirt?' The Moslem's voice echoed off the hillside.

"No, son of *Sheitan*," he continued, "if you think you can kill us, have at it. Here we are. But we will not permit you pass without you do battle. We are the last of our kind and we have no escape from this world except through merciful death in *jihad* against the Christian infidel."

"Then we have much in common Moslem," muttered Sir Richard sadly.

The silence of the light wind that blew nervously around the yellow rocks was broken by the resounding scream of a coal black crow as it wheeled overhead. Sir Richard sat back in his saddle, thoughtful at the Moors words, then after a moment lifted his helmet and spat copiously on the ground. "So be it."

Spurring on his horse he charged directly towards the group of Moors, his huge sword whirling about him in a flashing arc, Edryd at his side. Chaos. The Moors could not control their horses, crying and squirming as the Knights' huge mounts bore down on them. At that moment Jonson loosed a crossbow bolt and felled the Moor before Sir Richard could even reach him.

The Knights' burly horses, well trained in combat, ploughed straight into the Moors and brushed them aside as if they were nothing. The two-handed Hospitaller swords swung to left and right, cutting the Moors in pieces to fall dead from their saddles, and then they were through. Immediately their horses whirled about and started back, ready to finish the job.

From the rocks above, Moorish archers appeared, showering the Christians with arrows. They were lightly fired from small bows, and shot from a distance against armor, but several found a target. Jonson had three arrows in him but was still struggling to reload his crossbow, and Luca's horse was mortally wounded, stumbling badly, such that the Painter was thrown headlong into the dust. He scrambled under the wagon as a second barrage of arrows clattered about him. Izdârasen was felled as he stood tethered in line, and two arrows lodged in Henrique's leather armor.

"The castle!" shouted Edryd as arrows glanced off his helmet. The Christians wheeled around, and following Sir Richard headed back the way they had come in a frantic attempt to reach the castle most recently passed. Luca almost lost a hand while heaving the dead Moor into the back of the wagon and dragging himself aboard as Jonson brought it about.

They had galloped barely a hundred yards when a second group of Moors appeared riding straight for them. The way was blocked as another flight of arrows whistled in from above. Their fate was sealed, or so it seemed. They might be able to kill a great number of Moors in the mêlée, but ultimately they would fall.

The Moorish horse finally threw the philosopher and he fell heavily, lying on his face, immobile in the dirt as his comrades galloped on. It was a moment or two before the Bishop cried out, realizing that they had lost Paracelsus. The wagon stopped and Henrique rode back to pick him up. It now looked as if their final stand would be made around the wagon, as the second band of Moors galloped toward them.

The Knights were about to dismount for the fight when shots rang out. From across the shallow river bed soldiers were firing at the Moors, the first rank of riders falling as the bullets struck home. "Drive the wagon!" shouted Jonson to Luca, throwing him the reins and grabbing his crossbow; and the crew set off again.

A third wave of Moors appeared riding down the slope ahead as they rounded a bend in the road, but before the Moors could reach them a group of soldiers rode directly in front and engaged the Moors, driving them off. Then suddenly they were clear of the ambush, riding out from under the shower of arrows.

Once they were sure they were not pursued, they slowed their pace to save the horses, and the two columns of soldiers rode up alongside them as an escort. There were about twenty of them wearing breastplates and helmets in the Spanish style, and liveried in a yellow, green and red scheme that Sir Richard did not recognize.

One thing he did notice was that the commander of the troopers seemed to be a young man who sat very slight in the saddle, but was also very much in command, as he shouted his orders to the men in a boyish voice.

The castle was built upon a domed, barren tor that rose from the flat valley and dominated the surrounding countryside. They approached through a small village at the foot of the hill, and then upwards by a winding road that forced anyone taking it under the full view of the castle battlements, and into firing range.

It was a formidable structure that, Luca noticed with a shudder, had a passing resemblance to both *Le Stinche* and the fortress of *Capo Passero* – he hoped it would not be his fate also to be incarcerated in *this* stronghold.

The simple building looked as if it were formed from the dirt of the hill, red and dusty, with a few small, barred windows high in its otherwise blank walls, and four round Moorish towers, one at each corner.

The train reached the crest of the hill, and the way led behind a high wall separate from the castle, cut with deep crenels and fitted with a firing step, that protected the single entry point to this gloomy edifice: a huge and heavy door set into the thick stone. The crew dismounted and helped their wounded brethren towards the open door as the soldiers led the horses away to the stables. Two servants assisted them through the doorway, and they stumbled, tired, dusty and bloodied, into this Moorish castle in the middle of the desert.

"Welcome to *El Marquesado!*" exclaimed their host, followed quickly by: "Oh my! You are wounded, come inside my friends and we will dress your wounds." He was a tall, angular, elderly man with a distinctly wizardly comportment; from his long white hair, beard and moustache, to his small, round, brimless hat, and floor length grey velvet robes.

They emerged from the narrow vestibule into the interior of the castle, and in a flash Luca had been transported back to Florence. While the exterior of the castle was of the same rough red stone as the hill – well-worn, and caked in the dust of the valley – the interior was pristine and shining new, entirely fabricated of gleaming white limestone and creamy brown marble, carved and figured by Italian artists. The central courtyard was open to the air with two floors of colonnaded galleries surrounding all four sides, and finished off with a Latin inscription on a frieze that ran around the top. It was like the *loggia* of some Florentine *palazzo*.

To Luca it was as if he could just step outside and be back in the *via dei Servi* – if only. For some reason, somebody had recreated a Florentine villa in the middle of the desert.

"Theophrastus!" cried the wizard, astonished, "Can this truly be you?" Paracelsus, bruised and dusty, looked up from the polished limestone floor where he had collapsed in the paralyzing exhaustion of fear. Slowly his expression changed from one of confusion at hearing his name to one of recognition, as he squinted up at the tall figure, arms spread wide in greeting.

"Melchiorre!" he cried out in return, jumping to his feet and running into the arms of the Wizard. The others looked at each other in confusion. Not only were they the guests of a wizard in a Florentine villa inside a Moorish castle in the middle of the Spanish desert, but also, it seemed, the Wizard was an old friend of their Philosopher. Strange times indeed.

El Castillo

The Wizard Melchiorre made a dramatic entrance, gliding gracefully down the ornate stone staircase his arms held wide, and out into the courtyard where stood the table laid for a feast. His hands barely showed, engulfed as they were in full, wide, purple brocade sleeves that trailed almost to the floor. The Knights, along with Luca and Jonson, had exchanged their dirt and blood stained surcoats for dress uniforms, and Henrique was decked in the magnificent crimson robes he had worn for the funeral. Melchiorre had loaned Paracelsus a suit of clothes, as elegant as it was ill fitting.

Jonson had shrugged off his three arrow wounds as if they were nothing more than pinpricks, and the others' wounds were minor cuts and scuffs by comparison – except that is for Izdârasen, whose remains were stored in a wooden box in the stable.

As darkness fell they had all assembled in the courtyard, at Melchiorre's request, around a long table fitted with benches and chairs, and lit by a king's ransom in fat yellow candles that set the place dancing and sparkling by the flickering of the multitude of their flames. As the travellers had awaited their host, they had amused themselves by eating from the mounds of sweet oranges, which overflowed from square wooden trenchers at either end of the table.

"Welcome to my castle O brave Paladins," cried out Melchiorre as he entered, "and Bishop too." He bowed in Henrique's direction.

"It is a great pleasure for me to entertain brave knights on a noble quest. We are much in need of good company out here on the frontier," he continued with a flourish, "but before we eat let me introduce your savior, without whose timely intercession I fear my brave Paladins would have fallen 'neath a hail of Saracen arrows."

"We had them at our mercy," muttered Sir Richard glumly.

"Nevertheless, let me introduce my ward Bradamante," declared Melchiorre with another dramatic flourish towards the stairway.

The crew gave out a communal gasp of astonishment as a strikingly beautiful young woman descended the stairs to the courtyard. She moved as if she were floating, her pale beauty made all the more stunning by her dark velvet dress – the color of dried blood – that trailed the ground behind her.

The bodice was tight and high to the neck where her translucent white chemise spilled out in a cascade of lace. The skirt was full, and flared from a waist that dropped in the shape of a V from her hips, accentuated by an embroidered girdle terminating in a gold cross that swung, sparkling, a few inches from the floor. The sleeves were heavily sewn with gold thread and encrusted with seed pearls the tone of her flawless, white skin. Her eyes were dark, and her hair, of darkest brown, fell in a long cascading wave over her shoulders. She was a tall woman, taller than the stocky Jonson, and the cut of her dress conspired to make her seem taller still, towering in elegance over the dinner guests.

The men all stood and bowed to the remarkable creature who appeared before them, none of them truly believing that she had led the forces that had most recently saved them from the Moors; yet not prepared to call so fine a warrior liar. She smiled demurely at the group and took her place next to her uncle while the dinner guests looked on in mute admiration.

"Come, eat!" declared Melchiorre and with that they put aside their fascination in the young woman and set to satisfying their hunger. The meal was delicious and expansive, especially considering the remote location of the castle. Several different kinds of meat and fowl were served, along with delicious freshly baked bread, and plenty of the fruit juice and wine concoction that Edryd had so enjoyed during their recent sojourn in the village.

But by far the most striking part of the meal was its location. Beneath heaven's firmament spread out above them, and lit by the multitude of candles below, it was as if they floated in their own small, twinkling, illuminated world through the vast glittering dome of infinite space; unfixed, and for a time at least, divorced from the weight of their temporal existence.

Once the eating was done, Melchiorre rose to speak to the assembly, "Brave Paladins, Sir Bishop, and my old friend Paracelsus, I welcome you most humbly to my home. The which, although not mine by ownership, has become mine for the time being by possession, as you will see." Jonson shifted on the bench and gazed up at the sky, already growing bored with the old man's wordy narrative.

"The story of this fortress, the *Castillo de la Calahorra*, was forged in war, yet tempered by love." Melchiorre waved his hands in a broad gesture indicating the blackness surrounding their table where the castle loomed over them as nothing more than a void in the stars.

"This fortress, or at least the shell that forms its defenses, was built many years ago by a family of *Moriscoes* – Christian converts – as protection from the Moslems that menaced them in those days. Then, as Ferdinand and Isabella, our most Holy Catholic Monarchs pursued their course of conquest, returning these lands, at least nominally, to the Christian fold, the castle came at last into the hands of the crown.

"As was much of *Al Andalus*, these lands were ceded to a noble family for their deeds in ridding Castile of the Moorish threat. But as this is a wild and inhospitable place, not easily tamed, so here the castle sat, unmanned, gazing sightless at the village below. Now, one of the Queen's most trusted advisors, a Cardinal, no less, of the noble house of Mendoza, had a natural son by a companion to the Queen of Portugal."

"It means he was a bastard," whispered Luca to Jonson, who looked confused at Melchiorre's term.

"Rodrigo Diaz de Vivar y Mendoza was this son's name and he became a great warrior, distinguishing himself both in battle and in politics. He married well, and was a close advisor to Queen

Isabella herself.

"Then sadness befell him. His child died, followed by his wife. Tortured by grief he travelled far and wide in the hope of forgetting his past, spending much time in Florence and Genoa learning the new ways of those wonderful places. His travels served him well, as upon his return he fell in love with a very beautiful and very young woman – she was more than twenty years his junior – and wished to be married again. The Queen forbade this, as Maria, his intended, had been promised by her father to another. So, smitten with love on both sides, the couple ran away and were secretly married, with her mother's help." Luca sighed as he recalled a different young woman who had been promised to another and had run away for love's sake.

"Queen Isabella was furious that her mandate had been flaunted so, and she had Rodrigo thrown into prison, and there he languished until the Queen's death a few years later. As soon as he was released he abducted Maria from her convent and married her all over again, as their first marriage had been annulled. Thereupon they travelled to this castle to live far away from the court that had almost destroyed their love.

"To make the fortress more appealing to a young woman, he had the interior remade in the most modern Florentine style by a Genoese architect, and it became what you see today. The pair lived here for several years and produced two children, but Rodrigo's value to the Crown was too great, and he was called back to court and made Governor of Valencia. And there it was that he crossed over these five years past."

"He died," whispered Luca to Jonson, and Jonson nodded.

"After his death the castle became the property of his wife Maria and her family, the de Fonseca clan. However, I remain here indefinitely as a housekeeper."

"And how do you know this history so intimately?" asked Henrique.

"I was, to the *Marqés* Rodrigo Diaz de Vivar y Mendoza, a sort of amanuensis."

"Secretary," whispered Luca to Jonson.

"The *Marqés* discovered me during his sojourn in Italy. I was involved with the *Fedeli d'Amore* which appealed to the *Marqés* in its admiration of *fin amour*, and the poetic traditions of literature."

"Secret society for old intellectuals," muttered Luca in Jonson's ear.

"I was in Ferrara working for Alfonso d'Este at the time, in his library, and that is where I met Theophrastus here." He waved a slender, elegant hand at Paracelsus who smiled.

"I was studying anatomy at the university," added Paracelsus in passing.

"We all became good friends and spent much time together at the meetings of the *Fedeli d'Amore*, and that is how I came to be here. I thought it would be exciting to bring the new learning to Spain, and I helped his Lordship build this beautiful castle in the desert..." his voice trailed off in nostalgia.

"And it was. Look at this wonderful place! There are hundreds of books here, and the climate is most invigorating. And then there is my ward." Bradamante smiled in acknowledgment.

"A most fascinating history Melchiorre," declared Sir Richard, "and may I add that your hospitality knows no equal. But tell me, what is the story of your ward, the charming Bradamante? And was she truly responsible for the... er... rescue today?"

"The mighty Orlando speaks!" exclaimed Melchiorre in mock delight and the assembly laughed.

"I think you confuse me with a character in a popular work of fiction," replied Sir Richard.

"But are you not a brave warrior knight?" asked Melchiorre, and the Knight nodded his agreement, "And are you not Christian warriors fighting for the Holy Roman Emperor against the heathen Saracen?"

"To be strictly accurate, we are not Caesar's army, yet anyway, but indeed we do fight the heathen Saracen – whether Moor or Turk." Sir Richard thought a moment. "And yes, we are those same knights you read of in the stories of Charlemagne; and we are the descendents of Orlando and the Paladins." Sir Richard had never previously thought in quite such a way, although he had certainly considered that they might be the last of the noble knights to fight the Saracen – especially after the failure of Rhodes. He saw the future already handed over to the mediocrity of the citizen soldier, the gentleman adventurer and the mercenary man-at-arms.

"And is this your boon companion, Rinaldo?" asked Melchiorre of Edryd, warming to his bookish theme.

"I am Edryd, an archer of Wales," replied the Welshman before Sir Richard could say anything.

"And Orlando, do you seek the fair maiden Angelica?" continued the old man, enjoying his literary parallels.

"In fact we do, although her name is Virginia, and she belongs neither to me nor Edryd; we have taken an oath of office to the church and must, perforce, remain celibate," said Sir Richard.

"I always considered that to be more a recommendation than a mandate," muttered Edryd.

"The lady in question," continued Sir Richard after a disapproving glance in Edryd's direction, "belongs to Luca, the Painter of Florence." Luca stood briefly and bowed to the old man. "He wears the uniform of the Order by permission of the Grand Master, to do him honor as a master of his craft."

"So, we have Paladins, a Bishop – Archbishop Turpin no doubt – a Philosopher and now a Painter in our midst," exclaimed Melchiorre with delight, "a veritable cornucopia of talent and intellect dropped like manna into our little society, starving for stimulation here in the wilderness. And on a knightly quest to do honor to a beautiful woman. Ahhh!" Melchiorre, transported, was overcome with excitement at the thought of one of his books coming to life and appearing before him in the very flesh and blood.

He sat there a moment while he regained his composure, and looked around the table at the assembly smiling, as if to himself. "You, you noble warriors, you artists, you philosophers, you must have the best histories. Such histories worthy of entertaining an old man, far from home, and destined to end his days in a foreign land beset by heathens. Stories of battle and chivalry and courtly love, stories of adventure and daring, exciting stories of far-off lands," mused the old man stroking his white beard in thought, "You must tell me your stories gentlemen!" he exclaimed with finality. "Call it your gift, to requite me for your lives and this meal."

"Although I would debate that we were, truthfully, in such

mortal danger as you imply, however we will entertain you with our stories. Your meal was delicious, and your hospitality a welcome respite from the rigors of travel. You have been such a charming host we would do you much ill by not complying with your request," declared Sir Richard.

"Oh you flatter me!" complained the old man, flattered nevertheless.

"No Sir," insisted the Knight, "but there is one request I would ask of you before we start."

"And what is that?" asked Melchiorre.

"I would request, both for myself and no doubt for my companions, that you should tell us the story of your delightful ward Bradamante. Of she who sits so quiet and demure at your side, yet, as we know, fought the Saracen horde with at least as much vigor and enthusiasm as did we."

"Very well," laughed the old man, "I shall honor your request, but first I beg that you will honor mine."

LAS HISTORIAS

"So who will be the first?" asked Melchiorre, and the travellers looked one to the other in thought.

"Surely our Painter should tell his story first as it is his quest that brings us to this forlorn land," suggested Sir Richard, "It has much to recommend it both in terms of drama and of love."

"Then so be it!" shouted Melchiorre. "Pray Master Luca, proceed with your harrowing tale."

Luca's story ~

With a flourish Luca jumped to his feet and began his long and tortuous history; along the way making more villainous Vincenzo Cavalcanti, and more tragic his love affair with Virginia.

The fall of Rome and his blessedly brief life as a slave he had no need to embellish. The raw horror was sufficient to provoke gasps of astonishment from his audience. "And that is why we head to Guadix," he finished, and the table burst out in applause.

Edryd's story ~

"So who will be next?" asked Melchiorre, now more enthused than ever.

"Edryd tells a fine story, perhaps he might be able to tell a story of battle and chivalry," suggested Sir Richard, "he has had much experience of both."

"If you wish it, then so it will be," declared Edryd standing up, the better to address his audience. "I will not tell the story of Rhodes and how she was lost to us just recently, I will leave that for Richard to tell as he was more heavily involved in the fighting in the English breach. Nor will I bother you with the many attacks we have launched on the Turkish pirates through the years, which, although of momentary excitement, do not measure up to the telling before such an exalted congregation."

He paused and stroked his beard in thought. "Let me tell you a story that I was told by my grandfather, that he was told by his father. It is the story of the great battle of Agincourt and the triumph of King Henry, made so by the skill and bravery of Welsh bowmen, my great-grandfather, although not much more than a boy, numbered among them." The assembly applauded in anticipation and Edryd struck a pose, beginning thus:

"Picture, if you will, eight thousand fighting men; some riding, most walking, trudging along a rough, narrow road through the sodden French countryside, their baggage train bringing up the rear. They are cold, tired and hungry, and many are sick with the dysentery, which had befallen them after the siege of Harfleur. They are poorly shod, some even barefoot, as they drag themselves painfully through this cold, wet land.

"Their king – Henry, the fifth of that name – had made the choice to march from Harfleur to Calais, rather than travel by ship, in order to taunt the French, to show them the impunity with which he crossed their land – his land by inheritance. But this forced his men to walk for two weeks through the rains that fall almost continuously during October in that northern clime, and he was beginning to regret his decision.

"Henry's plan was to ford the River Somme that lay across his path, but the crossings were heavily fortified all the away to the coast, so he had no choice but to march his men upstream, deeper into French territory. There was some skirmishing along the way; soldiers and armed peasants attacked the column – as flies swarm around oxen – but they were easily swatted away, and the army marched on. But the men became steadily more dismayed and disheartened the further they marched away from the sea and home.

"Finally Henry's army reached an unguarded ford in the river and with relief they crossed to the other bank. The pain of their hunger was growing worse; they had brought only food for one week, and it was now near two since they had left Harfleur. They returned to their march north toward Calais and the sea, while the Constable of France who commanded the French army marched southwards to meet them.

"The English had just forded another small river that crossed their path – the River of Swords, as it is known – when cresting a hill they beheld the huge French army barely a mile distant, swarming like locusts. Rallying in columns under their noble banners the French blocked the road, and the way home, and filled the countryside for miles in every direction. There was no choice but to do battle.

"Henry's soldiers spent their time that evening preparing their arms and their souls; the armorers and the priests plying their trades the night long. The demeanor of the camp was quiet and contemplative as under orders of the King they were to keep their peace and sleep; for the morrow was to be hard fought. The French, on the other hand, spent their night carousing and drinking, as is their wont, so much so that the King's men could hear their wild debauch echoing all the way across the valley. Next day, after the King had rebuffed some French attempts at parley, the lines formed for battle."

Edryd grabbed some dishes and utensils from the past meal and began to sketch out the battlefield to ease explanation of the conflict. "Now, perhaps because they were unfamiliar with the terrain, or maybe from conviction of their own invincibility, the French commanders did not notice how the woods on either side of the valley, through which passed the road to Calais, were formed like a funnel, narrowing from the open French position towards the English position, where the width of the field was barely a half mile." Edryd moved two of the square trenchers of fruit into position and angled them appropriately. "This was to be their undoing.

"Henry arranged his meager forces in three ranks of men-at-arms led by their knights and retinues." He laid out three spoons in a row, "And between each group were archers who wielded the mighty Welsh longbow." He then added wedges of orange between the spoons. "But the bold stroke that won the battle was placing two groups of archers inside the woods on either side, forward of the main army." He added several orange slices to his plan and pushed them up against the trenchers. "Then they waited.

"It was a cold day and the rain had fallen long and hard through the night, leaving the field, tilled as it was for planting, more akin to a swamp than to dry land. Henry's knights lined up on foot, forgoing their horses, the more easily to maneuver in the mud. Then again they waited, until almost noon, but the French would not attack. So, with great reluctance, Henry ordered his army forward.

"The men flung themselves to the ground and kissed it, each taking some earth into his mouth to remind him of the cold embrace of death before they marched toward the enemy in formation. The archers on the flanks moved forward to within three hundred yards of the French front line, concealed within the woods, waiting for the signal to hammer their stakes in and attack. These stakes were a new invention at that time, wooden poles pointed with metal at the tips, like a short pike. As it was thought that horses would not ride against anything sharp, they believed these would serve to protect them from a cavalry attack, exposed in their forward position.

"The French, who outnumbered King Henry's forces perhaps four to one, lined up in similar fashion, yet because of their numbers were set much deeper, as the width of the front rank could not be very much more than that of the English due to the narrow field. This, and the disposition of the archers along the woods prevented the French, with their superior numbers from flanking the small force of their opponents." Edryd laid out three spoons in width opposing the English spoons, and then laid several more behind them. "Before the French army were archers and crossbowmen, but they were of poor quality, I was told they had allowed their bowstrings to become wet during the night, but perhaps that was just an excuse for their incompetence.

"Then came the order, and with a mighty cry that startled the

French with its ferocity, the bowmen ran from the woods and hammered in their stakes. Seeing this happen the French sent cavalry to ride upon the archers but before they could cross the muddy field the archers drew their bows and sent a volley soaring into the air. Imagine, if you will, six thousand arrows loosed at the same time, a black cloud against the white, rain-flecked sky, then crashing back to earth to impale any unprotected thing. The crossbowmen in the French front lines were cut down immediately and those few that lived retired from the field.

"As the French cavalry tried to gallop towards the Welsh archers, they fired another volley directly at them cutting the horses from under the men who were thrown into the mud right and left. The enraged horses, stuck with arrows, wounded and screaming, ran away from their tormentors back through the French lines, doing much damage by their violent passage." Edryd used a scrap of bread to indicate the horsemen, and popped it into his mouth to indicate their fate.

"The bowmen continued their volleys, and the rain of arrows was relentless and destructive, many men and horses falling before the battle lines had even clashed. The French had no option but to march forward or be impaled where they stood, so, dismounted, they trudged to meet the English knights in battle. The first rank bowed their heads against the rain of Welsh steel rattling against their helmets and strode, shoulder to shoulder, through the soft mud of the field.

"It was a sad thing to see, as it was relayed to me, these noble knights trudging through the slough at the pace of a snail, while volley after volley of steel-pointed arrows hammered on their heads, needing only the narrowest opening in their armor to pierce them and bring them down. Many brave men of France died in that slow and painful march, their comrades stumbling over the corpses of their fallen as they tried to reach the English line." Edryd slid the front rank of French spoons to meet the English spoons in battle.

"Despite this slow march these proud men of France still had strength enough to push back the English line, with many casualties on the King's side, but as the field filled with knights felled by stroke or by simply stumbling and being unable to regain their footing, the French progress was arrested. To make matters worse for the French they were forced closer and closer together as the field grew narrower, and then to pass under the arrows of the bowmen firing directly upon them from their flanks. The second rank of Frenchmen had begun their march, and when they reached the battle the press of bodies was so great that they could not swing a sword.

"It was at this point that the shower of arrows was mercifully stopped as the archers had used all they had brought. Thereupon the Welshmen each took up their best weapon and, dropping their bows, leaped into the fray. They carried short swords, daggers, axes, mallets, anything that could cause a wound, and threw themselves against the flanks of the French; commoners raining blows down on the French noblemen – bare-headed, shoeless and half-naked yeomen in a frenzy, killing any French knight that stood before them.

"The remains of the French force that were bringing up the rear, seeing how their countrymen were thus butchered, ran, or at least stumbled through the mud away from the fight. For a quarter of a mile across a muddy field the bodies were piled higher than a man's head as the fight raged around them. Many noble Frenchmen died that day, and many more were captured to be ransomed.

"And that, good friends, is how Henry and his men won the Battle at Agincourt." Edryd bowed deeply and resumed his seat to great applause.

"Splendid!" exclaimed Melchiorre, clapping his hands in glee. "Many thanks to you Sir Knight. Now who is to be next?"

Jonson was asleep, his head on the edge of the table, attention lost a long time ago. As Edryd took his seat he nudged him awake. "Your turn," he said as Jonson scowled at him through bleary eyes.

"Yes!" declared the exuberant Melchiorre. "Let our man-at-arms tell us a story."

Jonson glared at Edryd again and stood up on unsteady feet. He had no idea what he was going to say that would impress the assembly, and stared up at the glittering night sky for inspiration. Then a thought struck him and a smile spread across his uneven features. He began.

Jonson's story ~

"I was a young boy when my father brought me to Rhodes. He was a soldier in the Holy Religion as I have now become. Rhodes was a meeting place of East and West, so many Moslems and Jews and other traders from the Orient passed through her galley port. As a child I heard many stories from the East that I have never heard anywhere else in Christian lands. And it is one of those stories I tell tonight. A story that I venture none of you who were not at Rhodes will have heard."

Melchiorre clapped his hands in anticipation as Jonson continued, "There was, many a year ago, in the land of Iraq a goddess whose name was Inana. She was known as the Queen of Heaven and Earth because she had delivered the necessities of life from Heaven to her people on Earth. The inhabitants of that land worshipped her as a goddess of plenty and of victory in battle.

"After many years of bringing fertility and victory to the people of Iraq she took it upon herself to visit her sister Eresh, who was Queen of the Underworld. Inana prepared for her journey in the following way: she travelled to the priests of the seven cities and said her farewells, and then removing her earthly clothing she dressed herself in the seven garments of her divine power.

"To her priestess Ninshubur, who was called the Queen of the East, she said, 'If I do not return in three days you must mourn my passing; wearing sackcloth you must mourn me in the public square and in the temple.' To this Ninshubur agreed and accompanied her mistress to the gates of the underworld. Once there Inana announced herself to the gatekeeper of the underworld."

"What was his name, this gatekeeper?" asked Melchiorre who was writing in silverpoint in a small notebook.

"Ummm," said Jonson trying to remember, then finally, "Neti! That was his name, Neti."

"Excellent," said Melchiorre, "please continue."

"So… Neti asked of Inana who she was, and she replied: 'I am Inana, Queen of Heaven, on my way to the East.' Then he asked, 'If you are truly the Queen of Heaven why are you on the road from which no traveller returns?' Inana replied, 'For my own sister Eresh.

Her husband Gugalanna, the Bull of Heaven, has died, and I have come to pay my respects at the funeral.'"

Jonson, now feeling less awkward, walked out in front of the table better to address his audience, who were all paying rapt attention to this strange, unheard tale.

"Neti went straightaway to the palace of Eresh and spoke with the Queen of the Underworld. 'My Lady,' he said, 'your sister Inana has arrived at the gates to the underworld. She wears the seven garments of divine power to protect her.' Eresh, who envied her sister for being Queen of Heaven while she was to rule forever in the underworld, thought for a while. Then she spoke to Neti and said, 'Close and bolt the seven gates to the underworld. When my sister approaches, you should tell her that to gain entrance she must shed one of her garments. If she questions you, tell her it is the way of the underworld and she must comply. You must do this at each of the seven gates and bring Inana to me naked and bowed low.'"

"What was the nature of these garments?" asked Melchiorre suddenly, looking up from his notes.

"I do not recall my Lord," answered Jonson, momentarily chastened.

"No matter," said Melchiorre with an easy smile, "please continue with your fascinating story."

"Yes my Lord," replied Jonson. "True to the Queen's instructions Neti bolted the seven gates to the underworld and shouted to Inana that she must shed one of her garments. When she asked why, he declared it to be the way of the underworld. So earnest was her desire to enter the underworld that she complied at each of the seven gates, and was finally brought naked and bowed low before Eresh. She approached her sister's throne but was immediately surrounded by the judges of the underworld. They were called the Annuna." He spoke this last to Melchiorre who smiled and continued his scribbling.

"The Annuna passed judgment against Inana. Eresh cursed her sister and struck her dead on the spot. Inana was turned instantly into a rotting corpse and hung by a hook on the wall of the palace.

"Three days later, when Inana had not returned, Ninshubur put on sackcloth and mourned her mistress in the public places and in the temples. She then decided to visit Enlil, Inana's grandfather, to plead with him for help to bring her back from the underworld. But Enlil refused to help, saying, 'Inana had all the powers of the heavens but craved the powers of the underworld as well. Foolishly she went there, to a place from which no person may return.' Then Ninshubur went to Nanna, Inana's father, asking him to help save her. But he replied in the same manner as Enlil, that she was foolish to enter the underworld, knowing that none may return.

"At last she went to Enki, Inana's mother's father. He grieved for his granddaughter and decided to do something to help her. He created two magical creatures, Kurgarra and Galatur, and instructed them in how secretly to enter the underworld. To Kurgarra he gave the plant of life and to Galatur he gave the water of life. He told them that Eresh would be complaining, as was her way, and that they should flatter her so that she would offer them a gift.

"After their instruction they set off for the underworld, changing into the shape of flies to creep through the gates. They approached the throne of Eresh, and she was complaining of the pain and discomfort she must endure in the realm of the dead. They flattered her by echoing her pain and crying with her, and after some time she turned to ask them who they were that felt her pain so, offering them the gift of water as a reward. They refused the gift. Then she offered them the gift of a full harvest, and again they refused.

"Finally she asked them what they would want as a gift and they replied that they would like the corpse of Inana. So the corpse was taken down and presented to them. Thereupon they sprinkled the plant of life and the water of life upon it, and Inana arose.

"But as they were trying to leave the underworld they were seized by the Annuna. The judges said, 'Nobody may return from the underworld. If Inana wishes to leave she must provide another to take her place.' Inana accepted their terms and they sent the Galla, the demons of the underworld, to ensure that the laws were followed.

"As they passed through the gates of the underworld, Ninshubur, dressed in sackcloth, fell at Inana's feet. 'You may proceed,' said the Galla, 'we will take this woman in your place.' But Inana replied, 'No. Ninshubur is my support and my advisor, she followed my instructions and mourned me, and without her I should not be here now.'

"So they travelled on to Umma, to the holy shrine, and there they found Shara the son of Inana. He was dressed in sackcloth and was mourning his mother, and when he saw her he threw himself at her feet. 'We will take this man in place of you then,' said the Galla. 'No!' replied Inana, 'not my son who mourns his mother.'

"So they travelled on to Badtibira, to the holy shrine in that city. There they found Lulal the other son of Inana. He too was dressed in sackcloth in mourning for his mother, and when he saw her he threw himself at her feet, 'Very well,' said the Galla, 'we will take this man in your place.' 'No!' replied Inana, 'not my other son who mourns his mother.'

"So they travelled on to Kulaba where lived Dumuzi, the husband of Inana. They found him seated on his throne dressed in all his finery, and as they arrived he did not move to greet his wife. Inana was furious at the insult. She cried out, 'Take my husband! Take Dumuzi!' The Galla moved to seize him but he escaped, and they pursued him for many days before capturing him.

"Once he was gone Inana mourned the loss of her husband and cursed her foolishness for consigning him to the underworld. While she was thus lamenting, the sister of Dumuzi came to Inana and begged to share her brother's fate to lessen the burden upon him. Seeing the depth of her grief, Inana told her that she would bring her to the Galla. A magical fly directed Inana's steps, and she beseeched the Galla to take pity on Dumuzi.

"They agreed to take Dumuzi for half the year and his sister, whose name I forget, for the other half. And that is the story." Jonson nodded his head with finality.

"You are correct in your supposal that I had never before this day heard that story, and I thank you most deeply for your telling of it," asserted Melchiorre with delight, and Jonson bowed deeply, a broad smile creasing his well-worn face.

"My Lord Bishop," said Melchiorre turning to Henrique, "perhaps we may learn what events led you to become a man of the church."

Dom Henrique's story ~

"Certainly you may, and I will tell you," replied the Bishop in his warm, dark voice, standing to begin his story.

"I was born into the ruling clan of my country – the *Kilukeni* – indeed, my father is *Mani Kongo*: King of Kongo Nation.

"Kongo is very rich and our goods are traded all across Africa. It has been this way for many, many years and we have traded with Portugal as long as I can remember.

"With the Portuguese traders came missionaries preaching the Holy Gospel and they converted my grandfather from his heresy. He was king when he became Christian and took the name John. He commanded us to become Christian and most of us complied without understanding the meaning of such a thing – I was a mere baby at the time.

"When my grandfather died my father *Nzinga a Mbemba*, who was baptized Alfonso, went to war for the crown against my uncle who would not renounce his heresy. The night before the great battle the Virgin Mary visited my father in a dream and promised her help in the coming struggle. And behold, my father overcame my uncle in battle with the help of a winged Angel of the Lord and a knight who wore a red cross. Sadly I was only ten years old – too young to fight alongside my father and witness these miracles.

"After that victory my father became king and renamed our capital city to *São Salvador*, and built many churches. He read the bible and the teachings of the saints, and desired that I should be educated as a priest. When I reached twelve years of age the monks who lived with us and taught the Holy Gospel, sent me to university in Lisbon to learn Latin and to study the Bible. While I was there I had the honor to be sent to visit the Pope by the King of Portugal, as an emissary of the Kongo church. I was not yet twenty years and needed a dispensation from the Pope to become ordained a bishop.

"When we finally arrived in Rome, Pope Julius was dead, but we were able to secure an audience with the new Pope, Leo, and I obtained my dispensation. The Pope was very charming and declared himself surprised and happy to meet a black man so devout a Christian.

"I returned to Portugal to complete my studies, and I was ordained Bishop of Utica – an honorary title, as Utica is currently overrun by Moors. Nevertheless, I returned to my people about seven years ago to create a priesthood among them, and was travelling back to Lisbon to report on the success of my endeavors when our ship was overcome by pirates. The rest of the story you know. And here I am today aiding Luca, my companion in bondage, in his quest – as much as I am able – and thereby returning to Portugal so I may once again sail for my homeland to spread the Gospel to my people."

The bishop bowed and the guests clapped enthusiastically as he retook his seat.

Paracelsus's Story ~

"And now we must hear from Theophrastus," decided Melchiorre excitedly, "pray tell us what story you will regale us with." Paracelsus looked up from the table at which he had been staring for the last hour or so, and tried to focus. He had been drinking more wine than his dinner companions, and he seemed particularly to be enjoying it. "Tell me Theo, are you *in ipsis tuis*?" asked Melchiorre with a laugh.

"Indeed I do seem to be in my cups, old friend," replied Paracelsus in his squeaky voice, blurred now with a drunken ebullience, as he squinted at the confused group assembled about him, trying to bring them into view. "But imbibing that sweet, Dionysian nectar does not dull my wits; no, to the contrary, drinking that precious elixir expands my mind and gives me... *ideas*."

Paracelsus staggered to his feet waving his hands, and surveyed his audience, glaring at them and raising one singed eyebrow, "I see things!" he hissed in a loud whisper, and proceeded to stalk up and down as he spoke. This was decidedly the most energy they had yet seen from their philosopher.

"My friends," he began expansively, his arms wide in embrace, "I could tell you stories." He shook his head in apparent astonishment at the stories he could tell, but was not going to do so. "Oh what stories I could tell! The alchemists in their battalions slaving over blazing furnaces in their vain efforts to transform base metal into gold – poor fools – and the armies, thousands deep, marching up and down." He waved his hands to left and right.

"The wounds I have dressed, the limbs I have severed; sometimes saving men, and sometimes feeling men die beneath my surgeon's knife – their souls slipping away into the ether above as their blood soaked into the ground at my feet. To the northlands I have travelled, where the rain never ceases."

"He must be talking about England," whispered Edryd to Sir Richard who nodded his agreement.

"I have traversed the deserts of the Levant, penetrated deep into the dark forests of the Seven Fortresses, scaled the mountains and ranged the valleys of Anatolia; and at every turn, at every stop I learned the secrets of that land." Paracelsus's little hands busily emphasized each direction of his travels.

"As every person has his own ways, so every country. I learned cures and methods unknown to most men and un-guessed-at in the philosophy of the academics; for how may a man learn but by travel and experience?" He looked around him for an answer. "Upon my return from the Orient I studied at the academy – in Florence, in Ferrara, in Padua, in Valladolid and Seville, Paris and Oxford I gained my qualifications as a doctor. Yet was I merely a surgeon, and I received the disparagement of the physicians. But what use is a physician without the knowledge of how and where to apply the cure? So I became a physician, but that was no use, I was still driven out because I could cure when they could not – envious incompetents! That good fellow Erasmus appointed me Professor of Medicine at the University of Basel, but again I was chased from my post by the contumely of dullards and halfwits who could not hear me, and by mediocre minds that would not listen; but most of all by mercenary hypocrites who hated me for my efficacy, for my ability to cure the afflictions that confounded them." He paused in his mumbled, vainglorious monologue and drew breath, regarding his audience again.

"The truth is hidden. Hidden to those who cannot see." Paracelsus glared at the diners, the remains of an eyebrow raised, testing the impact this minor revelation had created on his audience.

"Just as the gold and iron and lead are hidden in the earth beneath us by God," he waved his arms and wiggled his fat fingers, "hidden so that we mere men must not simply dig for it at random, but must learn the secrets of where to dig, lest we waste too much energy in fruitless mining. In just such a way the truth is hidden above us by the Almighty, secreted in the fiery firmament that arches over us." He waved his hands above him and stared dramatically up at the night sky framed by the courtyard. All his listeners obediently looked upward at the glittering stars.

"Like the Holy Trinity, where three are one, so the passage of time is a trinity where three are one." Paracelsus paused again to gauge the reaction of his listeners – some were intrigued, some confused, Jonson was asleep, face down in his dish – he pressed on.

"The past, the present and the future. These are the three that are one. As the present is born of the past so the future is the spirit of them both, at the same time aspirational yet hidden – at least to all but those who know where to look."

Paracelsus stumbled a little over a flagstone. Quickly recovering his balance he fixed his audience once more with his intense and expressive stare. "The Father and the Son are manifest in the very fabric of the physical world that surrounds us; they exist and have existed. But the Holy Spirit must be sought – must be sensed through prayer and meditation. Thus the past and the present are part of the physical world – indeed, the echoes of the past can be seen everywhere about us – but the future must be known by the seer as the Holy Spirit is known by the priest, by joining with the infinite mind of the creator. If he can do that the seer can read the future as easily as the past." He paused.

"I see things." He pointed at his eyes. "By the application of astrological principles I can scry some of what may happen." He resumed his pacing.

"You!" Exclaimed Paracelsus turning on Luca with an outstretched finger. "I see death. Your love is surrounded by death. But only through death may your love come alive. Death will release your love from confinement and by your efforts will your love be released from her own death." He whirled again pointing at Edryd. "You! You will fight for the one you love, and yet you will love the one you fight."

"What is this gibberish?" muttered Edryd, "He prates like the Witch of Endor."

"Is this some kind of blasphemy?" asked Luca of their host in a whisper.

"Well, the Inquisition would probably torture him to death, but fortunately he is among friends here. You should understand, when one is a philosopher one must often be circumspect around the devoutly powerful – and the powerfully devout," answered Melchiorre with a grim yet sparkling smile.

"But is he really a seer? Can he really see the future or is this just some drunken prattling?"

"In Ferrara he was often able to give readings by astrology, and, most surprisingly, the better so when intoxicated," insisted the wizard. Luca remained unconvinced.

"But I think," declared Melchiorre, loudly interrupting and changing the subject from Paracelsus's wine-fueled rant, "Sir Richard should now tell us his story, so the first among us shall be last." He looked questioningly at the Knight, as Paracelsus collapsed into a heap on the floor and fell immediately asleep in the cool glow of his eloquent stars.

"For many be called, but few chosen?" asked Sir Richard with a questioning look, and Melchiorre nodded. "Did not my nephew learn the truth of that a few days back as he fell to a Saracen's arrow?" continued Sir Richard with a wry smile distinctly lacking in humor.

"We all mourn the loss of a young man whom we know only by the bravery of his deeds," said Melchiorre with a sigh.

"Perhaps," replied Sir Richard, "but my story concerns the loss of something far greater than the life of a single knight – even one so close to my heart." He paused a moment and crossed himself, then took a deep breath and continued, "I will tell of the loss of a way of life, the end of an age – the fall of the last of the Knights of the Cross."

Sir Richard's story ~

"Rhodes is a most delightful place," began Sir Richard, and a shadow passed across his face as he remembered a life he had forced himself to forget – people and places now gone, and lost to most.

"That is, it was. Under two centuries of rule by the Holy Religion it was as a paradise on earth; a Garden of Eden where our stewardship provided a bounty, a gift from God. But Suleiman, Emperor to the Turkish nation and Caliph of the Moslem Faith, just like the serpent of Eden, was jealous and wished only to pry us from our paradise and cast us abroad.

"First though, I must show you why Suleiman looked upon us with such fear, envy and hatred." With this Sir Richard sprinkled a thin layer of salt onto the table and began to draw a map with the tip of his finger. He first drew a squared-off S shape and in the top opening of the S he drew a Moslem crescent. "This is Anatolia, home to the Turk." He then drew a few squiggles in the lower opening of the S. "This is the eastern end of the Midland Sea – *Mediterraneum* as it is known in the Latin. The land to the east is Syria and to the south Egypt. Both are the fiefdoms of Suleiman, won by his father Selim. As you can see, Suleiman possesses the entire eastern end of the sea."

He then drew a small dot in the sea just off the bottom left corner of Anatolia. "This is Rhodes. Barely eight leagues from the mainland, yet in the possession of Christian knights, it was a constant aggravation to Suleiman and he swore to have it no matter the cost." Sir Richard drew two bigger dots in the sea.

"This is Cyprus and this is Candia, both under the protection of Venice. But due to the faithless and untrustworthy nature of all Venetians, brought about by their unhealthy lust for money, they prefer to remain neutral in any struggle between Christian and Moslem – indeed, *Prima Veneziano e poi Cristiano*, first the Venetian and then the Christian, that is their maxim, damn them to hell. Well, they will get their due reward when they are conquered by the Grand Turk in their turn."

Sir Richard looked at the table for a moment. "You understand, we are in a war for civilization against the demonic forces of Islam?" he asked with a look of profound sadness. "With the passing of each year those forces grow ever bolder and ever closer to the center of Christendom. True, the Christian Monarchs have driven the rule of the Moor from Castile and Aragon – although many still remain to practice their evil and warlike religion against peaceful Christians. But for every Moslem that leaves Spain a thousand more lay siege to the borders of Europe.

"Since the fall of Constantinople and the wicked, heretical abasement of the Eastern church – welcoming the Moslems as their rulers – the Turk has been pushing westward again along the Danube, driving a poisonous, satanic arrow into our very heartland. And now, under this Suleiman, the boy king, they become even more daring. Belgrade is lost these seven years and Vienna will be next, mark my words.

"But I see no concern from the rulers of Christendom. The Emperor, who is pledged to defend the Christian Empire of Rome, pays no attention to the Turkish threat, but sacks Rome instead and chases the Pope from his palace. What gross foolishness and irresponsibility!

"My nephew," Sir Richard paused a second as his voice broke. "My nephew, I say, died fighting a foreign foe in a foreign land, and the great and glorious rulers of our world care naught for that sacrifice. Wherefore did he die, ignored and inconsequent, at the hand of some haphazard Moor, while a hundred thousand of that evil religion lay siege to Europe unopposed?"

"Dear Sir Knight," interrupted Melchiorre, "we who labor unacclaimed and unapplauded here in the wilderness, we who live in this mortal adjoin 'twixt Moor and Christian, we understand your plight. We fight the Saracen horde daily to keep this valley safe from evil – safe for good Christian souls. But the rulers of our world, they are more concerned with the land they may take today than the empire they might lose tomorrow.

"I honor your concern for Christendom, but fear not. Your work will continue and our faith will be defended. I am sure that once the Turk makes war on Vienna then all the powers of Europe will be focused at his destruction. And do not weep for your nephew. His death in the defense of the One True God assures his place in Paradise – better, surely, than here amongst the living."

"Thank you Melchiorre for your good words, and well spoken. But your assurances, although heartfelt, are meaningless. We were just as sure the Princes would come to the aid of Rhodes. Not for our sakes alone, but to blunt the ambition of Suleiman, to blood his nose and cure him of his desire for *jihad*. But we were lost and no lesson was taken from that loss. We are treated as the orphans of Europe, driven from pillar to post at the whim of the Emperor, and now to be marooned on a barren rock for all our trouble."

Sir Richard paused again, bent forward, his head hanging, hands resting on the table. With a slow deliberate strength he raised his eyes to the assembly. "But tonight is a festival. We celebrate our victories. So let me tell my tale, for although we lost something irreplaceable, in the losing we won our immortality – the only army to fight the numberless Turk to a standstill. So rejoice in that loss and hear my story.

"The city of Rhodes, like a beautiful but dangerous creature, crouches at the tip of a lush island, mouth open and its barbed tongue pointing across the sea towards the mainland. We knew they were coming, our spies were of one mind, so the cellars and granaries were stocked, and the armories were filled with ample supplies of powder, and shot of every possible size.

"The defenses were massive – fifty feet high and three twenty foot walls deep in the English sector, a huge tower at each end providing fire the entire length of the moat. The sectors were divided between the different languages, as is everything amongst the Holy Religion, and to our left were the Knights of Provence, to our right those of Aragon, facing southward towards our enemy. The farms and villas of the island, all were razed to provide no comfort to the Turk – and there we waited.

"It was not long coming. Suleiman himself commanded his troops and had his armada of four hundred ships sail past our port, intending to affright us by its size no doubt. A week went by as they landed and pitched camp, bringing their huge bronze cannon as close as they dare to our walls. Finally the bombardment began but we matched them cannonball for cannonball, silencing half their batteries almost immediately. They wasted much of their shot by firing over the walls into the city, causing terror amongst the townsfolk but little damage.

"We settled down to an uneasy state of affairs. We would ride out daily to harry them – their cavalry was weak and poorly armed, and we cut them down and destroyed the batteries where we could – returning with many a Turkish head on our lances. They would bombard us and our gunners would fire back – by the end of a month they were forced constantly to move their guns for fear we would find them and destroy them all.

"The bombardment made little way against the walls due to their multiple layers and thickness, yet the Turk attacked, trying to scale the walls. Suleiman first sent the *Azabs* against us to test our defenses – poor fighters, but expendable, we cut them down like sheaves of wheat at the harvest.

"There was no weakness in our defense but one. Beneath the ground the Mohammedan engineers toiled relentlessly, digging their tunnels under our walls. We, in our turn, dug beneath them and with our own bombs blew many of them to hell.

"After five weeks of this, one of their infernal explosions demolished a section of the English wall, leaving a breach some twelve yards in width. The Janissaries were waiting – slave soldiers in their foolish uniforms, yet brave enough fighters – and they stormed the breach, dying in their hundreds as they clambered over the massive piles of rubble. By simple force of numbers we were overwhelmed, but with the help of reinforcements and the command of the Grand Master himself, we were able to drive them back out of the city.

"After the damage caused by the mine, the battle concentrated more and more on the English sector of the wall. Each day the cannon hammered a hole in the rebuilt defenses and the Janissaries stormed the breach while their engineers continued to work below ground, mining into the city. Our chief engineer was wounded, shot in the eye and out through the back of his head. And while he recovered from this fearsome wound, the Turkish miners dug further and blew more sections of wall.

"Each attack was the same. The Turkish artillery would cease its bombardment and we would gird for the fight. The dry moat was now filled with huge blocks of stone, and out from their trenches dug in behind the rubble came the Janissaries. As they attacked their musicians would play an infernal screeching din – clashing cymbals and pounding drums, with shrieking wind instruments they call *zurna*, like to a shawm, but blown more vigorously and with a martial anger. As they approached us our archers and gunners would start their work, chopping them down in scores before they even made the breach. We would pour Greek fire upon their heads and scatter them, burning and screaming.

"Inevitably, despite the massive slaughter, some would make the breach, and we knights would line up, one sword swing apart – invincible in our faith – and cut them in pieces. Our swords, honed razor-sharp, relieved them of their heads and limbs in a steady rhythm of blood and death, until we were waist deep in Moslem dead and drenched in Moslem blood. The Turks wore only light armor so were no match for a full-armored knight – they died in the hundreds, day after day.

"The miners blew up more sections of our line and we were forced to move back, working ceaselessly to build a mound from earth and rubble thirty yards back from the ruins of the city walls. We mounted small artillery on top and raked the ever-widening breach with a murderous fire.

"It grew cold and winter approached. We had thought the Turk not strong enough to winter in the field. Living in tents, sick and poorly fed, and continuously harried by our cavalry, we had assumed they would leave when the cold rains came. But Suleiman was determined.

"Storms had washed away most of our earthen wall, and in the frigid weather the Janissaries attacked again. Every man that could wield a sword or a pike or an axe rushed up the mountain of rubble from our side to meet them at the top in a final clash of steel. The fight ebbed and flowed for a day in the rain and wind, until the moat was full of bodies, and stank with the reek of blood and death.

"We were all wounded, many such that they would never rise again. My Uncle William lost a finger on his sword hand yet fought on using his left. I was stabbed in the vitals with a pike. After slicing the head from the pike I sliced the head from the pikeman, fighting on, transfixed with Turkish steel." Sir Richard's hand moved reflexively to rub a spot on his left side.

"This was the last battle we fought. We won the battle and yet we lost the city. The Janissaries would no longer dare to approach us; no amount of payment or punishment was sufficient to persuade them to die by our hands, and we stood triumphant on the ruins of our walls. Yet we finally understood, the Turk would never leave and we would soon run short of food and wine, powder and shot. The townsfolk were becoming more and more alarmed that they would be put to the sword if Suleiman broke through, and determined as we were to save the city it became more important to save the Holy Religion – to preserve the Order and not to have it wiped out by the heathen horde; to die alone on Rhodes.

"After some days of negotiation the Grand Turk gave us free passage out of the city in honor of our skill as warriors. Many of us feared some trickery, but he was true enough to his word.

"We marched out of the city on the first day of January. In the lead went the standard bearers followed by the Grand Master and his retinue. Then came the drummers beating a slow march, and the wounded, so many of them, carried in litters. Then came the knights divided by their languages. There were very few of the English language remaining, almost all had been killed, but I stood tall despite my wounds and followed my Uncle, beneath the fearsome glare of the Janissaries that lined our route. Of course Edryd and Jonson who sit here with you this evening were there." He smiled grimly at his companions.

"We left – knights, men and townsfolk, jammed into a half dozen ships to be scattered by the winter storms across the sea. Wandering like cruel Odysseus returning to his beloved Penelope, we struggled back to Christendom. And that is the story of the fall of the most beautiful city that ever was. A story I have never told and shall never again, painful as it was to recount."

Sir Richard resumed his seat after his succinct yet moving history, and there was a moment's silence in honor of the fallen.

"Thank you proud Orlando for favoring us with this most harrowing tale. We will live always with the memory of this night and the story of your brave struggle," said Melchiorre quietly.

"But now gentle host, have we not fulfilled the terms of our arrangement? Have we not regaled you with our tales?" asked Sir Richard, his spirits returning somewhat.

"Indeed you have Orlando! That and more!" exclaimed Melchiorre with enthusiasm.

"Then it is your ward's turn to tell us her story, is it not?"

"And she shall do so forthwith," declared Melchiorre and all eyes turned to Bradamante.

Bradamante's story ~

"Uncle," began Bradamante in a respectful and modulated tone that grew more confident as her speech progressed, "although I am unused to speaking before a group, I am happy to tell my story if it interests our visitors."

"The mighty Orlando himself requested it," replied her uncle, and Bradamante nodded towards Sir Richard as she began her tale. Luca nudged Jonson awake.

"Although my Uncle calls me Bradamante after a noble and knightly lady from one of his books, such that I now answer to it as if it were my own, my given name is Catherine. I was named for the daughter of our most venerable Majesty Queen Isabella; now, as consort to King Henry, the Queen of England.

"My father was a captain of the Holy Brotherhood and my mother was from a noble Old Christian family. He came to this land to fight the Moor and drive them hence, and for a time that war was successful. Then, when the fighting ended, this became the new frontier, and my father was charged with keeping the peace while the Moors departed or converted to Christianity. After some skirmishing it came about that some of the towns were Christian and some were Mohammedan. The Mohammedan towns harbored the bandits who lived in the hills while the Christian towns had to rely on the Holy Brotherhood to protect them.

"I was born in Guadix where my father was based, but we moved further down the valley when I was still quite young to be closer to the fighting. One night, when I was twelve, our town was attacked by a great number of Moors, and my father and his men were all killed, my mother and many of the people of the town were taken as slaves and the entire place was burned to the ground. By the Grace of God, I was hidden well enough that the Moors could not find me, and I was able to save some of my father's belongings, including a short sword and a shirt of mail.

"I lived for many weeks in the wilderness and practiced with my father's sword. I was determined to avenge my parents and prepared an ambush for the Moors. I was in the process of springing my trap when the troops of the *Marqés*, on a routine patrol, came upon me. I had blocked the Moors in a narrow pass and was throwing rocks at them to unhorse them. When the *Marqés'* men rode up I left my position and joined the fight, killing two of the accursed Moslems with my own sword.

"The *Marqés'* men thought I was a boy and brought me back to Calahorra and it was here that the *Marqés* himself discovered that I was indeed a girl. He was so impressed with my living and fighting out in the wilderness that he asked Uncle here to take me into the *castillo* and educate me.

"Uncle loved the idea of a female knight, and his favorite conceit was to see me become the incarnation of a figure from one of his historical stories, thus he named me Bradamante and oversaw my training in arms. That was fifteen years ago, and now I command the castle Militia. We ride out on patrol every day except Sunday, and we are the law from Huéneja to Albuñán. We help maintain the fragile hold that Christianity has on this valley in the absence of the Holy Brotherhood, who will no longer travel much outside of Guadix, and seem to have more in common with the Moslems of Exfiliana than the Christians who labor under the ravages of the Moor.

"One other thing to know about me," added Catherine, "it is said that I will marry the man who can beat me in single, armed combat. Whether this is so or not I cannot say, but many have tried their hand, and here I sit before you still a maid. Perhaps tomorrow will be different. If you so desire you may watch me fight, as I have received a challenge and the match is tomorrow at daybreak."

"Now that," declared Edryd, "would be worth awakening for."

Catherine dipped her head and smiled her demure smile.

EL PRETENDIENTE

The suitor was a large man and burly, and his armor was beautifully chased with intricate gold inlay. The early sun sparkled from the highly polished steel as he strode purposefully to the center of a ring of large fieldstones set out behind the castle. He looked the perfect image of a *conquistador*, broad of shoulder and the high comb of his *morion* helmet giving him the appearance of a giant. He was not a handsome man, but of noble bearing, with a strong nose, short curly hair and perfectly trimmed beard and moustache. And he stood a head or more taller than Catherine.

"This should be interesting," remarked Edryd with an enthusiastic smile, sitting back in his chair. A tented cloth canopy had been set up next to the ring, and chairs placed beneath it for the comfort of the viewers. "She looks like a boy up against that man. He is a big one." Seeing her opponent for the first time he was becoming more interested in the approaching fight.

"Hmmm," grunted Sir Richard noncommittally. Edryd had been the only one to arise at dawn in order to see the duel between Catherine and her latest suitor, but he had dragged Sir Richard with him for the company.

"Well I believe it to be a barbaric method of selection," declared Sir Richard.

"Nonsense!" argued Edryd. "Why would Catherine wish to be married to a man who is not her equal?"

"In your enthusiasm for this unholy duel you have missed the point."

"And that is?"

"That is: she is a beautiful woman of good birth who should be married to a man of equal status, not hauled off by some random ruffian who accidentally wields a better sword. No, she is badly served by her uncle, who seems to be amusing himself with this literary conceit at his ward's expense," insisted Sir Richard.

"Perhaps, but the fight ought to be well worth the price of admission," said Edryd with a delighted smile.

At that point Catherine appeared, dressed in an older style of armor made perfectly to fit her slight build and woman's figure, sheathing her body from head to foot in burnished, articulated steel. A skirt of silver silk brocade hung in folds from her waist and ended at about mid-thigh. She looked a perfect Bradamante; a Knight of Charlemagne, just smaller. She carried a long two-handed sword similar to the Hospitallers' swords, but shorter to fit her stature. She wore no shield or buckler, and carried a simple helmet under her arm. Her hair was tied in a dark swirl on top of her head.

The ruffian, or *conquistador* depending on your position, marched stiffly up to Bradamante – for Catherine had fully occupied that fictional character – and dropped to one knee, kissing her metal hand in formal greeting. She nodded an acknowledgment, and donned her helmet as they parted, readying for the fight. Edryd leaned forward in his chair, fascinated, distractedly munching on his breakfast – a thick piece of bread spread liberally with preserved fruit.

The arbiter who was to judge the duel stepped to the center of the ring and spoke a few words to each of the participants in turn, then walked back to the edge and shouted, "Fight!"

Melchiorre dropped into the chair next to Edryd, breathing heavily. "I almost missed it," he exclaimed in mock horror.

"You know this big fool could carry off your ward to who-knows-what fate? I cannot believe you treat this so casually," chided Sir Richard.

"Not to worry," said Melchiorre with a reassuring smile, "this happens a lot and she is still with me." Sir Richard turned back to the duel with a disapproving snort.

The duelists were circling each other warily. The ruffian carried a shorter sword and buckler, but he had a longer reach than Bradamante. She carried her sword held horizontally across her body, her right hand on the hilt and the left mid way along the blade. The ruffian was the first to strike, whirling his sword in a slash across Bradamante's body. She stepped backwards, nimbly avoiding the strike and not changing her grip on the sword. The ruffian gave the appearance of bemusement and struck again. Again the girl just stepped out of the way.

"See how she simply avoids him?" asked Edryd. "Perhaps she plans to tire him first then attack."

"She is nimble," agreed Sir Richard grudgingly, "but that lout's technique is very poor," he added after a moment's consideration.

"Wait and see gentle Knights," said Melchiorre, laughing.

The same actions repeated themselves several more times – the ruffian would slash or stab and the girl would dance nimbly out of the way. So far she had not even presented her sword, but held it still horizontally as if using it as a balance. The ruffian was becoming noticeably angry – not so much at his inability to land a blow, but more at the girl's indifference to his efforts – and he advanced on her, slashing about him vigorously. "That is not going to help him," muttered Sir Richard becoming drawn, despite himself, into the duel unfolding before them.

Indeed, the ruffian's wild sword work did nothing to advance his cause. As one particularly violent sword slash whizzed past her nose the girl did a curious thing. In one quick movement she dropped to a crouch, one leg extended for balance, at the same time switching her grip to have both hands on the blade of her sword. Then she swung the sword like a club, in an arc, so that the heavy pommel struck the ruffian on the inside of his leg just below the knee. There was a clash of steel and he cried out in pain, stumbling slightly. "I taught her that," remarked Melchiorre with pride.

The ruffian was limping now and ran at Bradamante as fast as he was able in a vain attempt to intimidate her. She stepped aside and struck him on the back of his helmet with a swing of her sword blade, sending him sprawling onto his knees. She quickly followed up with an armored boot to the ruffian's rump leaving him face down in the dirt, and brought the point of her sword against the back of his neck just underneath the bottom edge of his helmet. She held back so as not to kill the man but pushed just hard enough to draw blood, and paused in a classic pose, her knee in his back and the sword in his neck.

"Enough!" cried the arbiter. "The Lady Bradamante is victorious – the duel is done."

"Well done!" shouted Edryd, entranced.

"That was a very skillful display," muttered Sir Richard with grudging admiration. Bradamante stood up and, removing her helmet with a flourish, bowed deeply towards the two Knights and her Uncle, in a cloud of raven hair. They walked over to Catherine as the ruffian limped from the field of battle.

"Well done!" repeated Edryd.

"Thank you Sir Knight," said Catherine demurely.

"That was a very clever strike," opined Sir Richard.

"My Uncle taught me," said Catherine, "he declared that if a man cannot stand then a man cannot fight."

"There is much truth in that. And your Uncle is a very accomplished man who turns his hand easily to many and various tasks."

"What if *I* were to offer a challenge of single combat?" asked Edryd, stroking his beard thoughtfully.

"Of me?" asked Catherine, momentarily both astonished and intrigued. Edryd nodded. "Then I should best you Sir Knight."

"But I am a Knight of St. John, the last of the true Knights of the Cross – bred to combat. Our prowess in battle is unmatched."

"Perhaps, but you are an archer, of Wales, as you declared last night, not a swordsman."

"You are mistaken My Lady, I am an archer *and* a swordsman." The two stared at each other, getting the measure.

"He has a vocation, he is not available for marriage, thus his skill in single combat is moot," interrupted Sir Richard grumpily, and the moment passed.

"Just so," replied Catherine. And with a bob of her head she turned and stalked away.

Edryd turned to Sir Richard and frowned.

EL VIAJE

"My Lord, I have news."

"Why are you bothering me?" asked Don Cristobal testily, "Can you not see I am reading?"

"Yes my Lord, but events are conspiring…" his voice trailed off as the Don glared at him.

"For what do I pay you Faustino?"

"You pay me to order your affairs My Lord," replied Faustino.

"Then pray, hence and order!" demanded the Don, waving his fingers with finality.

"They have killed forty or more of our *Mudéjar* fighters My Lord," blurted Faustino in despair.

"Who?" asked Don Cristobal slowly, "And how?" he added with surprise.

"The survivors say it was a small group of Hospitaller Knights and that bitch from La Calahorra."

"Hospitallers?" asked the Don, confused. "By the devil's name, what are *they* doing here? Have they not enough of their own Moslems to kill that they come here to kill mine?"

"Now, my Lord, you understand why I thought you should know what was happening."

"No Faustino, I understand that you are an idiot and I should consider paying you even less than I pay you now."

"My Lord?"

Don Cristobal sighed. "Where are they now, these knights?"

"My men say they are at La Calahorra."

"And where are they going?"

"I believe that they are coming here, to Guadix, to you, Sir."

"To me? What could a group of armored fools left over from another century possibly want with me?"

"They said it was about a woman."

The Don's face, swarthy as it was, drained of color and he leaped to his feet, grabbing Faustino by the ruffles of his shirt. "How many are there that come here?"

"My Lord," gasped Faustino in surprise, "they are six or seven in number, I believe."

"Then stop them – send my best men, send everyone, and stop them before they get to Guadix."

"You want me to kill the knights?" asked Faustino in shock.

"Yes, kill them!" shouted the Don, "And bury them in the desert where nobody will ever find them," he added. "Once they get to Guadix and everyone has seen them I cannot kill them, so stop them before they get here!"

"My Lord," Faustino bowed as the Don released his grip and, adjusting the fall of his ruffles, backed obediently out the door.

✠

The departure of the travellers from La Calahorra had been a bittersweet affair. There was not a man amongst them, except perhaps Jonson, that would not have happily stayed on at that oasis of culture in the barren void of the Castilian desert.

On the other hand, riding along with the six was a seventh man-at-arms, or rather woman-at-arms. This cheered the crew, both in having along another sword, and that sword's belonging to the delightful Catherine. She had, quite willingly, been loaned to them by Melchiorre as a guide to bring them safely to Guadix, and took the lead, the rest of the group dropping in behind her – Jonson in the wagon as usual bringing up the rear.

La Calahorra perches on a domed hill rising unexpectedly from

the floor of the valley as a kind of geographical precursor to the
Sierra Nevada – those jagged, snow-touched peaks that had
followed the Knights, silver blue in the southern sky, on their
journey through the dry heat of the desert. Between the castle and
the mountains are the foothills – rough, uneven and deeply scored
slopes that ramble and roll higher and higher, all the way to the
hard rock of the Sierra. Catherine turned south following a narrow
track that led upward into the foothills. At Sir Richard's urging,
Edryd rode up alongside her. "We are heading away from Guadix?"
he asked.

"The road through the valley that you were travelling is patrolled
by the *Mudéjar* from Exfiliana and the Holy Brotherhood, best to
avoid them both as they all take their orders from the Bastard of
Guadix. This road takes us through the hills. There are only a few
empty villages and some silver mines up there since most of the
Moors were expelled. We will approach the city from the south. It
is a hard way but we will be in sight of Guadix before anyone there
knows where we are," came her reply. Edryd nodded his
understanding but continued to ride beside her.

It was indeed a difficult route. At one point they were forced
to disassemble the wagon and load the pieces and cargo onto the
horses and two mules. The latter they had borrowed along with the
beautiful Catherine. Taking three trips to convey everything to the
next path, they reassembled and repacked the wagon to continue
on their way through the hills. But she was right; there was nobody
up there, just a few old, abandoned villages – except for one silver
mine that was still operational.

As they passed through the mining camp they could feel the
miners observing them, following their every movement as they
rode past; black eyes set in swarthy faces, mouths in sneers, hard
and pitiless. Edryd, sensing trouble, instinctively reached for his
sword but Catherine touched his arm and shook her head. She
leaned over in the saddle.

"These are *Moriscoes*, they are Moorish Christians who
converted in order to stay here and work the mine. They have no
love for Old Christians like ourselves – especially wearing the cross
so boldly as you do – but they will not cause you any strife and thus

risk losing everything they have." Edryd nodded to her in understanding. "If you were here alone it might be a different story," she added.

After a couple of hot, dusty days and cold nights under the stars, the Knights and their crew began the descent from the hills. At one point Catherine held up her hand to stop, and pointed downward where the rocks parted to allow a view of the distant valley. Along the road moved a small cloud of dust. At its head could just be made out a group of horsemen, and Paracelsus squinted through his lenses in an effort to identify them.

"Holy Brotherhood looking for you," asserted Catherine flatly. How she knew the identity of the riders and the purpose of their journey, and whether her estimation was accurate was neither asked nor questioned.

As they rode downhill, down towards Guadix, the rocky terrain gave way to savannah, which in turn gave way to a dense forest that was much appreciated in its cool verdure, but seemed an ideal place for an ambush. Their fears were groundless however. The Holy Brotherhood was searching for them elsewhere thanks to Catherine's circuitous route.

The travellers emerged from the forest at the crest of a ridge from which the ground fell away in cultivated fields to the city of Guadix.

"That's what they call a city out here?" asked Luca disparagingly.

"It is really not what I expected," agreed Sir Richard.

The city of Guadix was, indeed, not a very impressive sight. True, the fields were well tended, tilled and otherwise disposed, but the buildings were few and squat adobe structures surrounded by a mud brick wall, the whole of which clung to the base of an ugly citadel that rose in a series of orange rectangular blocks stacked one on top of the other, finished off with simple rectangular battlements.

Laughing at their urbanity, Catherine spurred on her horse and led the way down the narrow track between the fields.

✠

"My Lord."

"Faustino, can you not see I am writing?"

"My Lord, it is about the knights."

"They are dead then, never to trouble us again?"

"No my Lord," Faustino mumbled nervously.

"Speak up Faustino!"

"No my Lord. The patrols could not locate them."

"How can I concentrate on my poetry with these interruptions?" Don Cristobal put down his pen and walked over to the window that gave a stunning vista of orchards and fields arrayed below an emerald forest, the whole crowned with purple mountains. Staring out of the window he stroked his beard thoughtfully.

"Perhaps they have decided not to come to the city," ventured Faustino, "perhaps they were driven off by our patrols."

"I do not think so Faustino," mused the Don, "in fact I am sure of it."

"My Lord?"

With a crooked finger Don Cristobal called Faustino over to the window and waved his arm towards the view of the distant peaks. There, making their way through the fields towards the city, like a dagger aimed straight at the heart of Guadix, was a column of horsemen; four of them wore the colors of the Knights of St. John.

"The Hospitallers!" gasped Faustino in horror.

GUADIX

As the Palladins drew closer to Guadix they beheld a group of riders departing the citadel and heading towards them at some speed. Taking advantage of an open area in the road, between the fields and the first of the peasant dwellings, they spread out in a line to await the arrival of the approaching horsemen. They armed themselves, even Paracelsus drew his small sword, and Sir Richard and Edryd rode a few paces in front.

A few minutes later a dozen men drew rein about twenty yards away, and as the swirling dust of their hooves subsided they could be seen arranged across the rocky ground opposite the Knights, blocking their way. The dozen were dressed in the uniform of the *Santa Hermandad* – the Holy Brotherhood. In a reversal of the Hospitaller colors they wore white hooded tunics crossed in blood red and rode upon white horses. With their white hoods raised against the dust and sun, their faces were hidden in impenetrable shadow, and they sat still in their saddles. For a few minutes there was no movement except the flick of a tail and the twitch of a horse's head.

"We are all men of the Cross," began Sir Richard in an attempt to find common ground, as it was obvious at this point that the Brotherhood was not there to escort the Knights to Guadix. "We are here to meet with Don Cristobal on Hospitaller business."

The Brotherhood did not reply. There was a nervous silence

broken only by the sputtering wings of a flock of white doves that launched asudden from the grape vines behind them; swirling, jagged, chalky shapes scrawled across the arch of a flawless blue sky.

"We will meet with Don Cristobal, and if you attempt to stop us we will kill you all," the Knight continued, and the Brotherhood drew their swords.

"Well that shook them up," declared Edryd with a smile.

"Oh these asinine encounters are becoming just too tiresome," muttered Sir Richard with fury as he raised his hand in command.

The travellers raised their weapons and lined up their horses in skirmishing order, Jonson standing on the wagon with his crossbow. "Confess your sins Christians, and pray to God, as I shall take your lives and should not damn your souls into the bargain!" shouted Sir Richard as he wearily drew his own massive sword out of the sling that hung from his saddle.

He was about to order the charge when Jonson, from his elevated position, spied a lone rider galloping towards them from the citadel. "Chief!" he shouted to Sir Richard and pointed out the approaching horseman with the tip of his bow.

"One dead Spaniard more or less should make no difference in the world," opined Sir Richard casually, and slowly lowered his hand, holding off on the attack for the new arrival.

They sat in their saddles glaring at each other across the patch of open ground. Leastwise the Knights and their companions were glaring; the facial expressions of the Holy Brotherhood could not be discerned beneath the deep shadow of their white hoods, glowing in the midday sunlight.

After what seemed an eternity the lone rider drew up to the group, and the Brotherhood parted to allow him through. He held out his hand and cried: "Put up your weapons! The Knights of St. John are welcome in all the lands of Christendom, without let or hindrance.

"Please my Lords, forgive my impetuous brethren," he continued, "these are dangerous times and many bad people are abroad."

"Indeed, but none of those bad people wear the red and white cross of Rhodes," replied Sir Richard.

"I understand My Lord, I will punish the men soundly for their bad judgment."

"A few minutes later and they would all have been dead Sir; punishment would be of no consequence."

"My name is Faustino, I am castellan to Don Cristobal," declared Faustino, changing the subject to something less awkward. "He has entrusted me with your safe conduct into the city, and provisioning you with rooms and refreshments after your long ride."

"Is that so Faustino?" asked Edryd with a smile. "Let us ride then, I am in sore need of refreshment."

With that they formed up in a double column and followed Faustino towards the city. Passing the Holy Brotherhood, who grudgingly made way for them, Edryd flicked a piece of orange peel in their general direction. Silently the Brotherhood fell in behind them. From time to time Jonson peered cautiously over his shoulder, unnerved at a dozen foreign men-at-arms riding so close behind his wagon.

The squirrelly-looking Faustino appeared to have run directly from his office and leaped upon a horse; he was wearing no riding gear – no boots, no tunic – indeed, he was still wearing his soft hose and delicate shoes, all hastily wrapped in a dark wool cloak, as if he were still about his official business as castellan. He did not seem to be much of a horseman; his speedy ride from the citadel had no doubt been one of last minute desperation to avoid a bloody and public battle that might bring unwanted attention to Guadix and his master the Don.

Although sanguine about the confrontation with the Holy Brotherhood, Sir Richard was relieved that Faustino had intervened before the killing had begun. This whole country, with its ambiguous allegiances and shifting loyalties, was assuredly tasking him. He much preferred the simpler job of patrolling the shipping routes and protecting Christian merchants from the piratical Turk. He considered himself too old and too simple a man to get involved so deeply in affairs of state.

Nevertheless here he was, riding willingly into a viper's nest of castle politics, a realm where the dagger and the vial were the order of the day, and he was the only one among his crew who knew the true and deadly reason for their quest. And it must remain that way until the deed was accomplished – one way or another.

As they rode through the ornate southern gate into the city proper, Luca observed that Guadix gave the impression of a city in the midst of a transformation. There seemed to be too few people for a city of even that modest size, yet there was a great deal of building activity – most notable being a cathedral that was going up, converted from a partially demolished mosque.

To Luca's intense discomfiture the city seemed populated primarily with Moors dressed in scarves and robes, *hijab* and *fez*. They were giving him the same angry glances he had received from the inhabitants of Tunis during his slow march to the slave market. And his hand did not, for one second, leave the hilt of his sword as the Christian caravan picked its way through the narrow streets of the *medina* towards the *alcazaba* of orange mud bricks that loomed massively over the entire city.

The enormous iron-studded wooden gates were open and guarded by two liveried pikemen. With the castellan at their head the procession clattered through the gateway and up a stone ramp into the lower courtyard of the castle.

The citadel compound made up about a third of the area of the city; a huge, sprawling structure, surmounted by a tower made up of two tiers that rose above a central keep. What could not easily be seen from without was the way the walls and towers of the keep interlocked, to produce small colonnades and courtyards at different levels that cascaded, in a shower of lush foliage, downwards from the highest tower to the large, open orchards that ran around the lowest part of the citadel.

They dismounted as the Holy Brotherhood turned about and cantered back down the ramp and away. Edryd gazed upward at the lush greenery draped from the terraces hanging above them. "They live well out here in the middle of nothing," he mused.

"Aye," replied Sir Richard, distractedly adjusting the hang of his dress sword, and not particularly interested in the decorations of the citadel.

Luca eased himself stiffly from the saddle. His patience and nerve for all this riding and fighting was running out. He was glad to be here at last, and keen to find Virginia and get away, although as he looked around him at the number of heavily armed men guarding the castle he began to think that might not be such an easy task to accomplish.

At the direction of one of the many attendants that hurried to their assistance, Jonson drove the wagon under an archway and out of sight toward the stables. Other servants helped the riders dismount and led their horses away in the same direction. The castellan, Faustino, turned to Catherine, "You are the commander of the guard at La Calahorra?" he asked politely.

"Indeed I am, Sir," she replied, "and you are Faustino, the castellan to the Bastard of Guadix, no?

"As you wish My Lady," he smiled his most courtier-like smile, "I am castellan to Don Cristobal, and after you are refreshed His Lordship will grant you an audience."

"I can hardly contain my excitement," she answered.

Henrique slapped Luca on the shoulder. "Pray as I did, I never believed we would reach this place my friend," he admitted with astonishment, "now we can find your woman and be gone."

"Your confidence inspires my quest," replied Luca, smiling, "but I am afraid that might be harder than I had expected." He regarded the formidable size of the castle with a deep concern.

"I think not," countered the Bishop with an odd smile, "these Knights can be very resourceful." Luca looked at him, puzzled. But no meaning was to be easily teased from his big, toothy grin, so, together with their companions, they followed Faustino up an ornate set of steps into the citadel.

LA REUNIÓN

The appointments of the castle were quite luxurious. There was a bathhouse, and a barber on duty, and servants to bring the trunks up from the wagon. So the weary travellers were able to bathe and change their clothes, attired once more as they had been for the meal at La Calahorra. Catherine, however, preferred to wear her uniform as Captain of the Guard rather than a gown, as she wished not to be at a disadvantage before the Don.

So it was that a much-refreshed group descended the wide stairs into the great hall, with hair washed and beards trimmed, or in the case of Luca once more cleanly shaven – the shadow born of days of travel pared away by the barber's blade. Paracelsus, with no facial hair to speak of, had soaked himself pink and wrinkled in a huge wooden tub, the bruises and ignominies of his hazardous journey soothed at last by the hot soapy water.

The hall they entered did double duty as a throne room for audiences and as a banquet hall for the feast, and they were, in due course, to enjoy both its faces. From the stairs they could see a large carved chair set on a dais at the far end of the spacious room, decorated with the arms of the Don and adorned with swags of fabric in his colors – turquoise and brown, ornamented with silver.

The rest of the hall, like much of the citadel, was embellished in the Moorish style. Tall narrow columns supported encrusted arches, and arabesques in ceramic and stone graced the walls, floor and ceiling.

As they reached the bottom of the stairs doors swung open and a throng of people entered the room – loud, chattering people, dressed in all the styles and colors of Castile, swelling and breaking around the travellers like a flowing tide. After some minutes the crowd was called to order by a herald who announced the arrival of the Don. And a moment later the man himself burst through a side door and mounted the dais with a careless wave of his gloved and bejeweled hand, as of a mountebank taking the stage.

Luca's blood froze as he recognized the man who had stolen his love and sold him into slavery. He moved forward a pace as if to draw his sword. Sir Richard grasped his arm in a steely grip, pulling him back into the group. "Not yet boy," he whispered, "everything in its time; it must be done right or we shall all die this day." Luca turned to glare at the Knight but his anger melted as he stared into those piercing, weary eyes. He knew Sir Richard spoke the truth, and reluctantly settled back into his place, his fury reduced to a rhythmic clenching of his fist.

"I wonder what medicine he is selling," asked Edryd to nobody in particular, and the travellers laughed, the tension momentarily broken.

Indeed, the Don was dressed in a most extravagant way. His clothing was all shades of brown; his brown brocade *farsetto* was cinched tight at the waist, and overly padded at the chest; similarly his sleeves were large and padded at the shoulders tapering to tight wrists, and slashed the entire length to show puffs of his dazzling white shirt; voluminous lace cuffs almost completely covered his gloved hands. His hose were of brown wool worn very tight, and surmounted by a prominent burnished brown codpiece fashioned from tooled leather.

His boots and gloves were of soft brown leather lined in silk, and were folded down just above the knee and wrist to show the lining. Finally, over the whole went a sleeveless brown surcoat trimmed in marten fur, and on top of his head was a tight fitting hat with a huge brim. But in all this drama of ornament, the most dramatic aspect of his attire was the turquoise. Turquoise beads studded the sleeves and body of his doublet; turquoise silk lined his surcoat, boots and gloves; turquoise jewels set in silver mounts were draped around his neck and adorned the fingers of his hands; topping it all off was a curved turquoise feather in his hat.

The Don bowed to the assembly and settled into his throne. One by one the courtiers and townsfolk knelt on the turquoise carpet in front of the throne, and pled their case or asked for an indulgence, and one by one Don Cristobal disposed of them – an aye or a nay, an indulgent wave of the hand or a dismissive flick of the wrist indicating the outcome of that disposition. Those who enjoyed an audience with the Don were dressed in a variety of styles – noblemen and burghers, tradesmen and workmen, Christian and Moor. As they watched the audience it was quite clear to the Knights that the Don was the law in this city and that they had best tread cautiously with this ostentatious man.

At a certain point during the audience Faustino pointed out the visitors to Don Cristobal, and he leaped nimbly to his feet, pronouncing in his locally accented Castilian, "Ladies and Gentlemen of Guadix I am proud to announce that we have a deputation of knights in our humble city on business with your Lord." With that he gestured towards Sir Richard, and the audience clapped their hands enthusiastically.

"And," he continued, "regard who has brought them into our midst – the bold *Señorita* from La Calahorra." The crowd cheered in a mocking tone and Catherine bowed with an ironic flourish. "A woman dressed as a man – she dishonors her own sex while insulting mine," declared the Don. "Neither man nor woman; she apes the one as she fails most illustriously to be the other." The crowd laughed and clapped.

"Well I may ape a man, but I fear that you, Sir, are more ape than man," replied Catherine, and the audience gasped.

The Don turned and glared at Catherine who proudly stood her ground, walking forward to the edge of the dais better to confront him. "Careful my dear," he warned, "or perhaps we shall cut you open and discovery precisely what you are." With that he flourished a small dagger. It was a beautiful thing; slender, gleaming steel blade mounted with an ebony hilt set with turquoise jewels and decorated with a turquoise tassel. As he spoke he punctuated his words with dagger thrusts and the tassel swung back and forth.

"Remember you are in my house now and you will abide by my rules. Mocking your Lord is not to be recommended; unless your desire is for a disposition most final." He arched a dark bushy eyebrow to emphasize his meaning, but did not smile. The audience laughed nervously and backed away from the seven who now stood isolated in a group before the dais.

"You, Sir, are not my Lord. You are as common as the dirt under my feet and were only made Lord of Guadix for your skill at butchering savages. You are to me as the earth is to the stars. You have no jurisdiction over me – the Mendoza are my Lords. Your threats mean nothing," replied Catherine, spitting on the floor.

"You speak of dirt, girl. Well, you will have much time to become acquainted with it when you are beneath it." Don Cristobal walked to the edge of the dais and stood, legs apart and waist thrust forward, the jut of his codpiece standing proxy for the power of his words with the gleam of burnished leather. He pointed his beautiful dagger straight at Catherine's heart. "Mendoza is dead and you are alone in *my* world."

Sir Richard stepped forward and put his arm in front of Catherine whose hand had moved to her sword. "Less of this talk of finality My Lord, I pray you," he began, trying to assuage the Don's anger. "We are here on a mission from the Grand Master himself who wishes me to counsel with you in matters as delicate as they are private." Don Cristobal glared at the Knight.

"And if you were to…" the Don paused in thought, "disappear while on this delicate mission?" He cocked his head to one side.

"My Lord, I am most sure you do not intend to threaten a Knight of Rhodes," replied Sir Richard with an edge to his voice, "for if you were to harm us in any way – or harm any one of our companions for that matter – then the entire might of the Order would descend upon you and raze this beautiful Moorish castle of yours to the ground while killing all who would oppose them."

There followed a profound silence. Not a person moved, nor dared to move, nor even breathe, as the Don twirled the twinkling dagger in his strong fingers. Suddenly he smiled broadly, and with a flick of his wrist shot the dagger at the floor. The point hit the edge of the dais right between Catherine's legs, and it lodged there quivering in the dark wood. "Now Sir Richard, let me kill him now," whispered Luca in the Knight's ear but he waved Luca away.

"I should never dream of threatening a Knight of Rhodes – or perhaps I might say a Knight *late* of Rhodes since I hear tell that you lost your home to the Turk," replied the Don after a moment.

"We made the Turk pay dearly for that land."

"No doubt you did. But as I say, I would not think to threaten you. I merely point out that these are uncertain times and this is a dangerous land, full of perils and pitfalls set to ensnare the unwary."

"Then we will conclude our business and be on our wary way."

"Just so," smiled the Don.

"My Lord, we have brought something for you; more than a favor but less than a gift," said Sir Richard, changing the subject. He waved his hand, and Jonson and Edryd carried a large chest forward to the edge of the dais.

"I believe we have something that belongs to you. Unfortunately it has suffered somewhat by the journey," continued the Knight. And with that the two opened the chest and deposited the remains of the Moor Izdârasen, already rank from decay, at the Don's feet. He stepped back, his lip curled in disgust.

"What is this insolence?" gasped Don Cristobal in horror.

"We found this along the way. I believe it is one of your Moors. Of course it still drew breath and smelled decidedly better when first we encountered it," said Sir Richard.

"What are you suggesting?"

"Nothing beyond the obvious. But I present it to you as an example – a warning – of what may happen when you threaten the Knights of St. John."

The Don turned on his heel. "The audience is done," he declared abruptly as he strutted from the dais. "You will join me tonight and we will feast," he shouted back over his shoulder, and in a flourish of fur and fabric was gone.

✠

"What are you, a lunatic?" Edryd asked Catherine holding her by the shoulders. He had wanted to shake her into the bargain, but had thought better of it.

"Unhand me Welshman," she snapped back angrily, "unless you wish to challenge me." The thought had crossed his mind several times, but he continued with his theme undaunted.

"You cannot threaten the Don, we are few and he has an army at his disposal."

"Should I threaten *you* then?" she glared up at Edryd, and, appreciating her meaning, he released his grip on her.

Edryd had dragged Catherine to one of the many balconies that formed the hanging gardens of the citadel in order to speak with her in private. Through a hazy curtain, fashioned of a delicate and translucent silk that fluttered gently in the soft, warm breeze, the balcony opened off a wide corridor on an upper level, where the seven had been accommodated.

"Catherine," he began in a more conciliatory fashion, "we are here to rescue the Painter's woman, not to start a war or settle old scores."

"You are here for your reasons, I am here for mine. And the scores are only as old as the last man I lost, killed by a Moor."

Edryd was momentarily nonplussed – an unusual predicament for him. "Nevertheless," he whispered after gathering his wits, "if you are committed to throwing yourself away in killing this arrogant nonentity then I shall not stand in your way, but please wait until we have the lady in question secure before you start a skirmish – we are not here to assassinate the Don, merely to find and remove the lady."

"Actually we are," came a voice from the farther side of the translucent curtain and the two jumped in surprise. Sir Richard pushed through the curtain and joined them on the balcony. "Actually we are," he repeated quietly, "we *are* here to assassinate the Don."

"Do you speak in earnest?" asked Edryd after understanding dawned.

"I should have told you earlier, but I did not want the true purpose of our quest to become common knowledge."

"Is that to say that I am an old gossip given to idle tattle?" Edryd asked, taking mock offense.

"Not at all," said Sir Richard, "but I wanted us to get here safely before anyone should discover our real commission."

"Very well then," exclaimed Catherine with enthusiasm, "when do we kill him?"

"It is not that simple, I have been commanded to dispose of the Don in a way that seems, shall we say, unanticipated," explained Sir Richard.

"And how is that to be accomplished? An arrow in the heart or a dagger in the neck, both are rather anticipated, particularly for a man in his line of work," said Edryd thoughtfully.

"I would be happy to finish him for you," offered Catherine with an enthusiastic grin.

"Yes you could do that and then his men would haul you away and cut you up, and there would be little or nothing we could do," answered Edryd.

"This is how it is supposed to happen," said Sir Richard, "we find the Painter's woman, we insist on returning her to Florence, and when the Don refuses, the Painter challenges him and kills him – or something approaching that sequence of events. I have endeavored to put the Don on the defensive in confronting him with his crimes, by way of the dead Moor. And when the Painter insists on reclaiming his woman the Don will be forced, by a combination of fear and overweening pride, to make the decision we need him to make."

"But the Don is a mercenary soldier," observed Edryd.

"And the Painter is... well, a painter," added Catherine.

"And that is the problem I have been wrestling with all the way from Villafranca – how to put the Don to death and keep the Painter alive."

"Why cannot one of us stand as the Painter's champion, or whatever it is called?" asked Edryd.

"Simply because the Don's death must be unanticipated. There is no possibility that the Don would challenge one of us, and if perchance he did – and of course we should kill him – then the Order would be blamed by the Emperor for interfering in Spanish politics." Sir Richard looked at the two of them. "It is a very sensitive matter, and the Painter has no political connection to the Don, and moreover has been doubly wronged by him. He must be the one that does the dispatching. It is natural."

✠

"Let me present my betrothed," declared Don Cristobal to the assembled company.

Luca dropped his spoon in shock. He had prepared himself for this day in his mind, and rehearsed his reaction many times during the long and arduous quest through the desert, but the reality of it was still deeply unsettling. And the most unsettling part was the way she seemed to be so at her ease in the Don's court.

Happy and smiling, she was dressed in an astonishing turquoise gown that offset her pale red hair exquisitely, and swooped very low to reveal much of the flawless alabaster skin of her perfect breasts through the translucent chemise. Twinkling in the last remnants of daylight – giving way to the flickering of a thousand candles – she floated from person to person in practiced and accomplished style, down the long tables that ran perpendicular to the Don's.

It seemed to all the world that she had been born to this, born to be the Don's hostess and wife, not that she had been ripped from Luca's embrace by force of arms, in a ruined church in Rome – before St. Peter's tomb no less – and transported thence against her will. In fact, her will appeared very much aligned with the Don's at this point: that she should be his consort.

In pursuit of her hostess duties, by greeting the many guests, Virginia worked her way along the table to where the Knights and their companions sat. Sir Richard was first; he bowed and murmured a few words, and then, suddenly, after all those months of separation, she was face to face with Luca as he stood to receive her.

Her mouth fell open in astonishment but she said nothing at the sight of him; tall and handsome as ever, standing before her and dressed as a Hospitaller to boot. They remained there, frozen, as the busy sounds of the room receded into the background, until all they could hear was the beating of their hearts. For a long time – too long – they stood face to face, gazing into each other's eyes, and finally Luca realized he was holding his breath.

He sighed and took her soft, delicate, bejeweled hands in his. "Good evening Virginia. It is so wonderful to see you again." It sounded so trivial.

Her mouth closed with a click and she pulled her hands away from his. "By the Evangelist, what are *you* doing here?" she snapped angrily. "Be gone at once."

LA CITA

"Luca suffered mightily at the hand of your betrothed. He crossed the desert and risked death fighting Moors to rescue you from your captor."

"That is charming and very nice, but perhaps he should have asked me first whether I required rescuing before he put himself to so much trouble to so little end."

"You were kidnapped, right before his eyes in the midst of a war – how could he be expected to ask your permission to launch a rescue?"

"It is not a matter of permission, it is a matter of necessity. Why on earth did he consider it necessary to rescue me?"

"Heavens above, you are an ungrateful, worthless little harlot!"

"Hold your tongue wench or I will have my betrothed cut it from your head."

"Your betrothed indeed! You are nothing more nor less than Don Cristobal's doxy."

"You presume too much!" Thereupon Virginia turned on her heel and with a turquoise flounce stormed out.

Catherine turned to Edryd. "I tried to convince her," she said plaintively.

"Not exactly what I had in mind," he replied, stroking his beard.

"I do not see the need."

"But he has doubly wronged you. He stole your freedom and he stole your woman. Surely he needs be punished."

"Perhaps, but I no longer have the will to be the means and matter of that punishment."

"But that will leave him free to continue spreading suffering and death, to consort with Moors and to betray his country and his religion."

"Those are most important circumstances, both political and ecumenical, but certainly no concern of mine. I shall return to Florence, forget what I have seen and done, and continue my work – to paint for the glory of God."

"But do you not understand? You are the conduit of God's retribution; you are the manifestation of His will. By your hand will His desires become flesh. Surely this man must be punished. The Lord has protected you through all your tribulations to bring you here, now. Now is your time."

"By that argument, Sir Knight, should you not kill him yourself? Heaven knows you are far better equipped than I, and have suffered many more tribulations in your journey." And thereupon Luca turned on his heel and walked sadly away.

"That did not go quite as I had planned," said Sir Richard to Henrique.

The Bishop nodded.

"Perhaps we need to approach this from a different angle."

"Virginia, Virginia," Edryd called out as he ran along the corridor behind the rapidly disappearing, rustling cloud of aquamarine.

"What?" asked Virginia testily, turning to face the pursuing Knight.

"My Lady," began Edryd, bending one knee respectfully, "I cannot believe you no longer feel anything for this man. You were truly in love with him. You followed him from Florence to Rome in wartime, and braved fire and sword to find him. My Lady, I cannot believe you do not love him even more now that he is here to rescue you."

"Well believe," answered Virginia. "And less of this talk. If the Don knew you were saying these seditious things to the woman he is plighted to..." And with that threatening thought left unfinished she took off again, disappearing around a corner. Edryd cursed under his breath and trotted around the corner after her – only to be grabbed and dragged through a doorway. Virginia swung the door closed behind them and pushed Edryd against the wall with the tips of her delicate fingers.

They were inside a darkened bedchamber, and alone. "Of course I still love Luca you idiot. What kind of disgusting person do you take me for?" she hissed. Edryd opened his mouth to reply but Virginia put her finger over his lips. "Never mind that; I think I know the answer." They stood there a moment in the half-light and Virginia removed her hand from Edryd's chest.

She stared thoughtfully at the Knight, then spoke: "You must understand my predicament. When first I was taken I was surely to be ravished and killed, like so many others. The Don, for some inexplicable reason, found me appealing and protected me from his soldiers. From Rome he brought me here, and after some one-sided negotiations I agreed to marry him. The alternatives were not to be contemplated, and I thanked the Lord for my good fortune.

"A deal has been struck; I am to marry the Don." She sighed heavily. "Life here is not bad, I have clothes and food and servants, and from time to time I travel to Granada for some social interaction."

"But you do not love him you love the Painter," insisted Edryd.

"Oh you poor Knight," she shook her head, "were it only so simple. If Luca tries to take me away from here in a misguided attempt at rescue, then the Don will kill him; and you too, and all your crew if you abet this folly. I shall not have the responsibility for so much death on my head. I shall not allow this to happen, because the outcome will be the same, except Luca and all of you will be dead. How is that worthy? How is that Christian, to cause all that death for my own conceit?"

"Luca, Luca!" called out Henrique as he stepped onto the balcony.

"I have made my decision, Henrique, Virginia has made it for me."

"Now listen to me," began Henrique sternly, "she is just a girl, she knows not what she wants, and like all women she changes her mind with the wind. The simple truth is this: she has been stolen away from her family, and whether she thinks she wants to stay here or not, the Don has no right to keep her."

He paused for a moment as Luca considered this new argument, then continued, developing his theme, "It is not about whether she loves you or whether she does not, it is about what is right. If not you then her father has jurisdiction over her person, certainly not the Don. He stole her. If a man steals a horse should not that horse be returned to its rightful owner, no matter how well the horse may enjoy its new surroundings?"

Luca was starting to appreciate this point of view as the Bishop pressed on. "We owe it to her, her father and Florence to remove Virginia from the malign influence of this evil man, and to show this criminal that he cannot escape his crime."

"I do respect your argument Henrique. We have come all this way for one purpose, it would be cowardly and insulting to renege our quest and slink away like beaten dogs," mused Luca. "Let me consider it."

"Virginia, listen to me," whispered Edryd, "this is not about you and Luca; about young lovers at the whim of the fates. No! This is about a cruel and evil man, a man who overreaches and must be stopped."

"But..." began Virginia, and it was Edryd's turn to put a finger across her lips.

"We are here for more than just true love. We are here for the Don. Tell me, do you love the man?"

"Heavens no!" exclaimed Virginia shaking her head and turning down the corners of her pretty mouth. "Our arrangement is one of mere utility. He smells, and his back is hairy like a hog." She paused for a few seconds in thought, then, "Do you really think you can rescue me from this place?"

"Yes I do. But you should make your peace with Luca. To have this plan work we will need you both to play your parts. What we do not need is confusion and misunderstanding."

"There is a place."

"A place?"

"Where Luca and I might meet – tonight – without the Don being any the wiser."

✠

Like a precious jewel hidden inside a box of rude and simple construction, so the glory of the citadel was concealed within its russet crust of baked mud. The exquisite inward beauty of its arches and pillars, its soaring, figured ceilings and mosaic walls – all atwinkle with turquoise and gold – was not even hinted at by the massively sullen pile of bricks that merely described its outward form.

The beauty was of a kind both familiar and foreign – gardens and ramparts, orchards and towers were common enough things, but these particular were conceived of a Moorish mind. These colonnades and cloisters were not of Florence and Rome, nor the Athens of the Ancients, nor even of nearby Calahorra. They were the immediate physical manifestation of the faith that had driven the Christians from Jerusalem, and then from the entire Levant, and to this day pillaged their way the length of the sea. This was what the enemy looked at. This was how they lived.

To Luca the architecture was a constant, uncomfortable reminder of his time in the slave market, and it was no surprise to him that Don Cristobal chose to live this way. His ease with Moors and the world they inhabited spoke loudly of his faithlessness, his criminality and his evil. Luca now understood why Mendoza had chosen to bring a small slice of Florentine civilization to this lawless Moorish valley – to remind himself he was a man of the occident, a man of learning and refinement, a Christian.

On the other hand, Luca spent many hours marveling at the fine complexity of the craftsmanship and the cunning of the design that had gone into the decorations of the citadel. The way the rooms were laid out showed a keen understanding of the desert climate with the constant need to keep cool. The use of translucent fabric allowed light and the arid breeze to penetrate deep into the building's interior while keeping out the direct heat of the incessant sun.

In his current position Luca had even more opportunity to appreciate the architecture as he swung precariously, clinging to the end of a rope. Some way above him Jonson and Henrique strained on the other end to effect his descent in relative comfort, while the two Knights peered down at him from the edge of the balcony, directing their efforts. It was dark, and the moon was hidden by the tower that rose behind them. The flickering of torch and candle was insufficient to illuminate this corner beneath the balcony, and Luca, suspended like a pendulum, descended unseen in a series of uncomfortable jerks as Jonson and Henrique labored to pay out the rope smoothly.

He dropped the last section, about the height of a man, as the rope momentarily slipped the grasp of his accomplices, and Luca was deposited in a heap onto the ground. He jumped quickly to his feet, adjusting his clothes and hair, and looked around him, squinting against the impenetrable darkness.

He was in a moderately sized rectangular walled garden that fit into an angle in the structure of the citadel, which towered darkly over him. He had landed about midway along its length, and he could see at one end, to his left, a magnificent old plane tree that twisted outward and upward, its boughs trained to provide shade from the noon sun. At the other end was a small pavilion in the Moorish style, with pierced screens and thin columns, outfitted with cushioned benches and delicate fabric screens that moved slightly in the night air.

From the base of the plane tree a small fountain bubbled and trickled, feeding four rectangular pools divided by white stone pathways that filled the center of the garden. Around the edge, partly sheltered by the garden walls, were a series of small, neatly trimmed fruit trees – pomegranate Luca thought as he struggled with the darkness. The outer walls were formed from the thick adobe bricks of the rest of the construction, but here inside the garden that rude surface was covered with beautiful tile work and mosaic. His finger traced the swooping calligraphy written in the impenetrable language of *outremer* and wondered at its meaning.

Luca was suddenly aware that he was not alone. There was a movement behind the fruit trees across the garden from him. A figure, almost supernatural in appearance, could be seen floating and glowing blue-white in a beam of moonlight that slipped past the tower behind him. He tried to make out features, but all he could see was the glow that flashed rhythmically as it passed behind the row of trees.

He began to follow the figure along the length of the garden, staying behind the fruit trees on his side until he passed the final tree; at last they faced each other. He could see her now, bathed in blue moonlight, her slight figure dressed in gleaming white; illuminating the garden around her as if she herself glowed with a magical radiance. They walked nervously toward each other and met in front of the pavilion; she lifted the translucent white veil from her face and their hands touched. "Come inside, we can be seen here from the walls," she whispered, and holding his hand led him beneath the canopy, shielded from all eyes by the interlocking arabesques.

They sat in awkward silence a moment. Then both began speaking at the same time, and immediately stopped. "No, please continue," insisted Luca.

"The Moors call this a Paradise Garden," Virginia began, "a tiny sliver of fertile paradise in a barren and dusty purgatory," she mused. "I come here often to think and read. To think of you," she admitted sadly. "It is such a beautiful place and my quarters open directly onto the garden. I can always hear the fountain from my bedchamber. It is a natural spring that feeds the cisterns beneath the citadel." They sat in silence another moment.

"*A garden inclosed is my sister, my spouse; a spring shut up, a fountain sealed,*" quoted Luca from a memory gained long ago and far away, as he gazed at the moonlit garden.

"*Thy plants are an orchard of pomegranates, with pleasant fruits; camphire, with spikenard,*" replied Virginia continuing the quote.

"A fountain of gardens, a well of living waters, and streams from Lebanon. Awake, O north wind; and come, thou south; blow upon my garden, that the spices thereof may flow out."

"Let my beloved come into his garden, and eat his pleasant fruits," finished Virginia smiling coyly up at Luca and they shared a kiss – long and passionate.

"My sweet, we have more important matters to discuss than our love," said Luca, "regardless of how nicely dressed in biblical vestments." Virginia smiled – eloquent yet demure. "Our intent is to rescue you and bring you back to Florence," continued Luca, turning to the business at hand.

"Were I with you, I could be anywhere in the world," interrupted Virginia with a lovesick sigh.

"Nevertheless, our first imperative is to escape the citadel, and do so without fear of reprisal from the Don."

"This is a prison most tightly locked, soft as it may be, and I am only permitted to leave it in the company of a duenna and a detachment of Holy Brotherhood who dog my every footstep."

"Indeed, and we are strong but few in number, so we must do this with stealth rather than force. Our plan is to have you leave the citadel and to separate you from your escort, then escape back to Calahorra by a roundabout route. To that end you must plan a trip to Granada at the earliest convenience and let me know the details so that we may organize our ambush."

As he finished speaking, Virginia pulled something from around her slender neck. It was a chain with a small gold object that twinkled in the moonlight. "Keep this for good fortune," she said, pressing it into Luca's palm. He recognized it immediately. It was the walnut shell he had been given by Sister Emma on the road to Rome. He began to refuse but she hushed him. "You can return it to me when we are away from here and safe," she assured.

"Can you hear anything?" asked Edryd.

"I hear voices but cannot discern the words," replied Sir Richard as they both leaned over the edge of the balcony straining to catch a sound of the two lovers over the trickling of water. For a long while there was silence and the two Knights looked at each other thoughtfully. "He should be back by now," opined Sir Richard, "I hope the passion of his love does not compromise our stratagem."

"The plans of men are no match for the allure of a beautiful woman," muttered Edryd.

"And this you would know?"

Edryd shrugged, "I was not always a holy brother." The conversation was ended abruptly by a sudden tug on the rope, and the four men strained to haul Luca back up to the balcony.

✠

"My Lord."

"Faustino, why do you always trouble me when I am busy?"

"You asked to be informed."

"I did?"

"Yes My Lord, you instructed that I should inform you if the Knights did anything of note."

"Then I imagine they did."

"Indeed My Lord, they visited with your Lady – or rather the Painter visited, with the aid of the Knights."

"It is as I suspected," mused the Don, "do they know that they were observed?"

"No My Lord, I believe they do not."

"You believe?" The Don turned slowly to his castellan. "You understand, Faustino, that these men are not normal, they are not just soldiers, they are knights. They are a force of nature, and the whole world still lives in awe of them and their legacy. We cannot have a misstep. If they are driven into a corner they will fight; and believe me we will be sore pressed to stop them despite our numbers."

"My Lord."

"What I am saying, Faustino," the Don paused and sighed. "What I am saying is we must play them carefully. They are here for the girl, of that there is no doubt, and we must give them no excuse to start a war. We do not need the scrutiny from Granada, or worse still from Valladolid."

"I understand My Lord."

"We may need to let them take the girl and be on their way, but I think I have a stratagem whereby we can make them pay, and perhaps even keep the girl."

El Desafío

"Welcome Knights to Guadix. First let me offer you my deepest apologies for forcing you to wait – this was necessitated by some important business that could not be deferred, and not meant in any way as disrespectful," began Don Cristobal. Edryd rolled his eyes. "Now has come the time for us to discuss the important affair that has brought you so far across the desert to our humble city," he continued. Edryd shook his head and smiled to himself. "Sir Richard, now that we are gathered in more intimate surroundings, perhaps you would care to explain the nature of your visit. Please trust that our affairs here are private."

"Thank you Don Cristobal," Sir Richard stood to address the gathering. They were in a small anteroom within the Don's personal quarters. The two Knights and Luca were there, attired in their dress uniforms, and at the other end of a silver edged table sat the Don and Faustino.

"What I am about to say is not uttered in judgment, nor as a true depiction of the facts of the case, it is simply the information we have been given and which we are currently investigating," said Sir Richard by way of preamble, and the Don nodded his assent to the terms. "It has come to our attention through a member of our Order that a certain young woman, daughter to a well-respected gentleman of Florence, became embroiled, through no fault of her own, in the recent... unpleasantness in Rome. In which unpleasantness I believe you, Don Cristobal, had some part."

"I was employed by the Emperor to bring my small army to his assistance in his quarrel with the Pope," agreed the Don.

"Very well, to continue. During the attack on Rome many depredations were perpetrated on the unfortunate inhabitants of that poor city, but only one of those assaults brings us here. The previously mentioned young woman was kidnapped during the fighting and spirited away to who knows where."

"But you say you do know where," interrupted the Don growing impatient.

"Our intelligence on the matter has led us unerringly to your doorstep Don Cristobal."

"And you are saying?"

"Your betrothed is that girl, the young woman of Florence who was stolen away while in Rome."

There was a pause as Don Cristobal pursed his lips and stared at the encrusted ceiling as if for inspiration. Finally he spoke in an even tone, yet forced, "That is a most pregnant argument Sir Knight and well-reasoned, yet you have not presented me with any evidence of the particulars of this case. No witness has been produced and no sequence of events has been described – you have simply stated your one-sided argument."

He paused and drew a deep breath. "I deny your accusation. Yes, many unfortunate events occurred in Rome, and yes, my men took part in some of those events until I was able to bring them under my discipline, and remove them and myself from Rome as quickly as possible. But as to kidnapping, I deny it." He stood quickly from his seat and slapped the table with the flat of his hand, all pretense at decorum discarded. " I deny it!" He surveyed the small group through narrow eyes, his moustache bristling with manufactured anger. "Bring me a witness, damn you, and have him accuse me to my face or get you hence!"

"I saw you!" shouted Luca, standing to face the Don across the small table, "I saw you take her." And he pointed an accusing finger at the Don's face. "In St. Peter's church, before the tomb of the Apostle himself you stole her; across your saddle like the merest chattel." The two men glared at each other, and recognition spread across the Don's face. Remembrance dawned of a moment in a ruinous church before an ancient tomb – a trigger was pulled and a pistol misfired.

"Remove your finger from my face boy before I break it, and you along with it."

"No Sir I will not. You have doubly wronged me and I will press my accusation."

"Be careful boy you are a long way from home – and this time my pistol will fire," stated the Don in an ominous whisper.

"Perhaps," interposed Sir Richard, "we could enjoy an audience with the young lady – your betrothed – and ask her whether or not she is here under duress?"

"Perhaps," answered the Don, "but unfortunately she is not in Guadix. She departed this morning for Granada, and will be there for several weeks visiting with members of my family."

"This is intolerable!" shouted Luca, and the Don shrugged, an ironic smile creasing his swarthy face.

"I am so sorry young man, it seems your trip here was for naught."

"Then I will kill you now," shouted Luca and leaped across the table a dagger in his hand.

Confusion ensued, but when quiet was returned to the gathering Sir Richard and Edryd had Luca each by an arm, and the Don was examining a long cut in his doublet. "You are a very emotional young man. You should learn to control that anger and direct it to more productive endeavors," he said.

"My anger is what keeps me alive and what brought me here. You Sir stole my beloved and stole me," declared Luca, and the Don seemed confused. "You brought my beloved here for your own vile purposes and sold me to the Moors as a slave." Understanding again spread across the Don's face and he nodded.

"Well boy, I admit to none of your foul calumny but I will offer you a solution that may mitigate your fury," he smiled.

"I can think of nothing but your death that would give me satisfaction!" shouted Luca.

"Then I offer you the opportunity to effect that very end." It was Luca's turn to look confused.

"I will fight you for her," declared the Don baldly. He raised his eyebrows and looked from one to another. "No substitutes, no champions, no war, just you and me. You and I fight to the death. If I win I keep the girl, if you win…" He left that eventuality dangling between them.

"This is most irregular," declared Sir Richard, "the life of a Hospitaller and the person of a young woman are not to be the prizes in what amounts to a game of dice."

"Perhaps not in your world but you are now in mine, and that is the only offer I make. I have fifty men-at-arms in the citadel and another five hundred in the surrounding country. You are but three – plus your absent companions – hardly a tangible threat." The Don arched his magnificent eyebrows inquiringly.

"You knights, you who are so proud and haughty, you are from another age – an age many years past. The war is no longer won by the might of single combat on the field of battle by men of noble birth." The Don laughed bitterly. "War is now a mechanical process, won by a struggling mass of journeyman rogues and *campesinos* swinging at each other in the mud. Your day is over." His lip twisted into a sneer. "You stroke your nobility by wrestling with Turks over a handful of merchant ships, but that is not where the real war takes place. The modern war is for land and gold. That is where I fight, and why I fight. Moors? Yes I treat with them and trade with them. But it is merely a business – I care not what they do as long as they do not dare to threaten me."

"We will send our decision to you anon," said Sir Richard, after allowing the Don to finish his contemptuous rant. "We must discuss this matter amongst ourselves."

"Take your time gentlemen," replied Don Cristobal, "you may enjoy my hospitality as long as you see fit." And he turned to go, suddenly swinging back to face the three. "But this is as much as I will allow, not a whit more. So take it or leave it, the choice is yours, but the disposition will be mine." And with that he was gone, Faustino following obediently in his footsteps.

When he was sure they were alone Sir Richard turned to Luca, "Brave words my boy, well said." Luca nodded, hands still shaking from his altercation with the Don. "By now Jonson and the others will have taken Virginia on the road to Granada, just as we planned, so she will no longer be a pawn in this dangerous game. Now, we must needs train you to fight the Don. Are you up for it?" Luca nodded silently, his jaw clenched in determination.

"That Don, he holds a deal of rancor in his bosom," observed Edryd.

EL RODELERO

The citadel rose like so many randomly stacked wooden boxes from the center of a huge walled enclosure. In the Moorish *alcazaba* it was common to reserve space within the outer walls for orchards and fields to feed the inhabitants in time of siege, and it was to these orchards that the Knights brought the Painter for his training. The setting was as pastoral as the intent militant – frosted mountains rising pale in the purple distance as the Knights laid out the weapons of war in the shade of neatly trimmed fruit trees.

"Now," began Sir Richard, "the Don is a *Rodelero* – a sword and buckler man – so I surmise he will fight that way. You fight in the Italian manner with sword and dagger. This will be insufficient to defeat him." Luca began to defend his sword work but Sir Richard held up his hand for silence.

"Which of us is the knight, ured in feats of arms?" he asked, and Luca fell silent again. "As I was saying, sword work of the Italian style may impress the ladies at a tournament in the *piazza* but it will not defeat a determined adversary – one, I might add, that has successfully fought his way across two worlds with barely a scratch to show for it." Luca nodded, chastened.

"This is first position." Sir Richard indicated how Edryd was standing, buckler in his left hand, sword in his right, with the sword's tip tucked underneath his left arm and the buckler held forward to protect him. "See how he uses the buckler defensively to protect his sword hand without presenting the blade yet. He holds his strike in check to assess his adversary." Luca tried to copy Edryd's stance. "Then when the opponent moves to strike he reacts by swinging the sword out from under the arm and wards the blow." He simulated a slow strike to Edryd's head from above and Edryd parried.

"Always keep the sword and buckler hands together unless you are executing a specific maneuver," insisted Sir Richard. "The bucker is not a shield for the body and should not be used as such – it is not even two feet across – it is intended to protect the sword hand and work with the sword in wards and binds." Luca looked at him blankly. Sir Richard smiled. "Do not distress yourself, you will learn this in no time at all," he declared, as much to encourage himself as Luca.

The teaching of sword and buckler technique lasted, with more or less success, the rest of the day in the green shade of the orchard, and Luca made some progress, although whether that progress was enough to defeat the Don – a man who earned his very good living with his sword – was seriously in doubt.

They finished as the sun was dropping over the mountains, bathing them in a ruddy glow, and the Knights were packing their gear when a commotion began at the edge of the field. They heard it before they saw anything – an antic squeaking interspersed with wheezing that approached invisible through the trees – much like the sound of an asthmatic badger.

"Sir Richard, Sir Richard!" wheezed the voice, and suddenly Paracelsus appeared between the trees struggling to run but obviously worn to the point of collapse. The small man fell exhausted at the feet of the Knights.

"Philosopher," said Sir Richard, "why are you here? Was not the plan executed?"

"No," gasped Paracelsus, "not." He was so short of breath he could not speak.

"Where is the young lady?"

"The Don has her."

"Where are Jonson and Catherine and the Bishop?"

"The Don has them."

The Knights looked at each other in dismay. Their careful plan was unraveling before their very eyes. By now Virginia should be on her way to Calahorra, leaving Luca and the Knights to deal with the Don without Virginia in the line of fire.

"They were waiting for us, they knew we were coming," puffed the philosopher as he regained his composure and his breath, "the woman was not with them, and they took Jonson and Catherine and Bishop Henrique. I was able to slip away and I ran all the way back."

"They let you through the gates into the citadel?"

"They did not seem to care. They mocked me as I ran."

The Knights finished packing, and Luca and Edryd took one handle each to carry the equipment back to the citadel. As they approached the buildings they espied a group of people heading in their direction. Drawing closer they could see that it was Don Cristobal and his retinue of brightly colored courtiers. "Come hither to gloat no doubt," said Edryd.

"Knights and Philosopher," exclaimed the Don with a large smile and a dramatic bow, which featured prominent use of his plumed hat, "how goes the battle on this wonderful evening?"

"It goes well. Luca will be a formidable opponent," replied Sir Richard with much false confidence, "and if you will step aside we should refresh ourselves."

"Of course, of course," said the Don and he and his courtiers formed two lines on either side of the path. The Knights continued between the courtiers, and as Sir Richard passed him the Don added, "Oh yes, I think I have something that belongs to you; a little the worse for wear but still breathing."

"You vex me Don Cristobal," growled Sir Richard bringing his face up close to the Don's and staring him in the eyes, "I would have you return my property and in the condition you found it."

"Of course Sir Richard, they are already in your chambers licking their wounds and feeling very sorry for themselves. Run along now." The Don laughed and his retinue giggled as the four trudged on to the citadel.

"He galls me, this inconsequent upstart who minces and swaggers in front of his gang of sycophants and fawners; he who has the brass to command me, *me*, as were I the meanest churl! I swear I shall bring this preening peacock to his knees," muttered Sir Richard.

✠

"I'm sorry Chief," sighed Jonson. He was sitting on the floor leaning against the wall, his head wrapped in a blood-soaked bandage, and looking most forlorn.

"They must have known our plans," mused Sir Richard, "perhaps the girl…"

"No!" cried Luca. "She would not betray us like that. We must have been overheard in the garden. It was dark and there are many places to hide."

"Nevertheless," continued the Knight, "this complicates our situation considerably."

"Not really," interrupted Catherine, "we are together and we are strong. Luca fights the Don and kills him, and we fight our way out of this heathen hell." She looked from face to face for approval of her bold but unlikely course of events.

"I see flaws in both your assertions but I think I may have a plan whereby we can achieve all our aims and exit this castle in one piece." Sir Richard turned to Paracelsus, "Philosopher I have some work for you to do – some more of your alchemy."

EL DUELO

"So you are Luca, the Painter of Florence?"

"Aye Sir, and you are Don Cristobal the Bastard of Guadix."

The Don laughed at the insult.

"I have killed a thousand men; a thousand times a thousand. I have killed so many men that I can no longer remember their deaths. They are simply one single endless scream in my memory. How many men have you killed Painter?"

"I killed the Constable de Bourbon on the walls of Rome," replied Luca, as calmly as his churning stomach and thundering heart would allow. The Don stopped for a moment, briefly lost for words at the mention of his former commander.

"Huzzah Painter; well said."

They circled each other waiting for an opening. Luca was determined not to strike first, as he had been so warned by Sir Richard, no matter what this chattering fool should say.

"I rode with Cortés across the New World. I was there when he burned the fleet so we might not return without success. I fought to subdue the Mexicas and claim the mighty floating city of Tenochtitlan for Spain. What have you done Painter?"

"I have devoted my life to the Glory of God not the pursuit of riches and land through ravening and destruction."

"Did we not bring the salvation of Christ to those savages?"

"And what did you bring to those Christians you tortured and killed at Rome?"

"Hah!" replied the Don in disgust, and they continued their dance. "I will kill you slowly. No, I will not honor you by killing you, I will humiliate you before your woman – she who now belongs to me – and have her watch as you lose your water. I will slice you in pieces, I will ugly that pretty face and cut your womanly hair. I will leave you alive, disfigured and dishonored, to suffer your life in the knowledge of what you have lost."

"Prate on old man and waste your fight in idle conversation."

"I waste nothing when I waste your life before the woman who sold your secrets for nothing but my favor."

Luca's temper got the better of him and he swung. It was a strong and well-directed blow but the Don parried it with an almost casual efficiency, locking Luca's blade firmly between sword and buckler, the edge of his own blade an inch from Luca's throat. They stood there, frozen, until Luca wriggled free and stumbled back. "I will give you the first strike boy. You could have died right there, but where would be the sport in that?"

Luca gasped for air, hot bile burning in his throat. His sword dragged on the ground and the buckler had become an intolerable weight in his hand. The sudden realization that he was about to die, or worse, to be cut and carved like a game bird for the pleasure of this evil man, was sickening. All the preparation, all the bravado was for naught. He was, compared to this mercenary soldier, nothing but an incompetent – a callow and immature boy who had made a terrible, final mistake.

"Were I you, I would have killed my rival in his sleep. A razor to his throat or a draught in his wine would have done the deed, and simply. There is too much uncertainty in the duel – the only certain thing is death." The Don did not seem to tire from his constant chatter; contrarily, it seemed to make him stronger.

"You are right, I should have slit your throat; driven a bodkin through that black heart. But I am an honorable man, the duel is the honorable way." Luca was not sure whom he was trying to convince.

"As you say boy, have it your way. Die honorably or die a coward – you are still dead."

"The Painter is lost," said Edryd, shaking his head sadly.

"Maybe not," replied Sir Richard with more confidence. Edryd looked at him as if he were mad.

✠

"Do you have what I need?" asked Catherine in a whisper. Paracelsus held a finger to his lips and beckoned Catherine to follow him. In a corner behind a screen he opened his bag and produced a small glass vial sealed with a wax stopper.

"Put this in his food before the duel and it will slow him down enough for the Painter to prevail, but without his appearing intoxicated."

"Thank you Philosopher," said Catherine and turned to go. He reached out to hold her arm and she looked back questioningly.

"The science is not assured," said Paracelsus, twitching nervously.

"What mean you by that?"

"I mean that the effects can be different on different people – it depends on the humors and the stars."

"Well let us all hope the stars know what they are doing," replied Catherine, and left.

It took her almost an hour, carefully negotiating the passages of the citadel, to come unnoticed to Virginia's chamber. Wearing a long gown and a hood over her face had helped her avoid scrutiny, and finally there she stood. Catherine took a deep breath and slipped inside the doorway, carefully shutting the door behind her.

The room was dark except for intermittent slashes of light that slipped past the closed shutters. She stood there a moment waiting for her eyes to become accustomed. The room was empty, but from beyond an archway at the far end she could hear a quiet murmuring. In her delicate, embroidered slippers Catherine trotted silently across the room and peered beyond the archway.

Virginia was inside an alcove kneeling before a small altar set with a cross and two candles whose flickering light danced off the gold frame of a diminutive Madonna that hung on the wall behind. She was muttering in prayer, paternoster beads in her hands, repeating the Latin over and over as if it were a charm to ward off the evils of the world.

Catherine watched her sadly. She remembered quite clearly being young, and how innocence could be casually brushed aside by life – so confounding and cruel – and how the world became even more cruel as the years passed.

"You told the Don did you not?" asked Catherine simply and without malice, and Virginia, surprised, turned swiftly towards her. "Did you not?" repeated Catherine.

"How...?" began Virginia, confused and ashamed.

"I am a woman. And there was no other way for him to know."

"I had to tell him."

"We were almost killed you know? It was only because the Don wanted to avoid a scandal outside of Guadix that he did not simply murder us."

"The Don made it clear that he would kill you all, starting with Luca, if I did not reveal every detail of the plan."

"It may end that way all the same after tomorrow. Luca is bound and determined to fight the Don."

There was a shocked silence as Virginia tried to understand what had happened. "But he is a painter and the Don is a warrior. Surely they will not fight. I cannot believe it!"

"They will fight whether you believe they can or not," replied Catherine bluntly, "but that is what brings me here."

"Are you not here simply to upbraid me then?" mumbled Virginia.

"I have not interest enough in you one way or another. No, I am here for Luca and against the Don, and you will help me."

"Yes of course, if I can help I will."

"You will empty the contents of this vial into the Don's meal an hour before the duel."

"I am not always with him."

"Then make sure you are with him this time, you foolish girl. Use the dissembling, cloying sweetness of your abominable girlish nature to ensnare this puffed up lout. Tell him stories. Lie to him. Dance for him. Seduce him with all your obvious charms. But whatever you do, make sure you give him this draught. If you do not, I swear I shall find you and punish you myself."

✠

The duelists circled and circled. Don Cristobal quickly banged his buckler against Luca's and the Painter jumped back. He barely saw the strike that followed, and barely blocked it in a slipshod way – the Don smiled as Luca backed away. "Do I scare you Painter?" Luca did not answer, "It will be over soon boy."

The Don laughed and for hardly a second his eyes closed. Luca struck. He swung his sword downward and under the Don's buckler then upward, stabbing at his face. The Don saw it coming just in time to parry and sidestep, but Luca's sword screeched across the edge of his opponent's helmet. It was a close call and he staggered backward. Furious at his mistake the Don swung into the attack, three, four, five fast thrusts and slashes, but Luca parried them all, locking the Don's sword at the last one and pulling him in tight.

Face to face their helmets hit with a crash, and Luca could feel the Don's fetid breath on his face. Remembering something Benvenuto had taught him in Rome he brought his knee up hard into the Don's groin. The blow was absorbed by the Don's bulky codpiece; nevertheless it left him breathing heavily as the two pushed apart. "You fight well for a famous painter," panted the Don through clenched teeth as blood from a long cut on his face soaked his beard and dripped from his chin.

"You fight poorly for a notorious warrior." It was Luca's turn to taunt the Don. They began circling again.

✠

"Do you have what you need?" asked Sir Richard in a whisper.

"I was able to get everything from the wagon. It is stored in the stable. Several trips were required though," replied Paracelsus after a furtive look to left and right.

"And nobody questioned you while you were dragging boxes up

the stairs?"

"I seem to be invisible to the Don's men. If they notice me at all they merely mock me for my appearance – or my stature, or my voice. In fact, there is very little about me that does not inspire their mockery. They certainly do not consider me any kind of threat," replied Paracelsus with a sigh.

"But thereby will their downfall be assured, my friend. You are perhaps the most dangerous of us all."

"Indeed my Lord, indeed!" giggled Paracelsus.

"Will you have everything in place in time for the duel?"

"I will my Lord, God willing."

"Worry not about God, I will treat with Him, just be certain you are ready to play *your* part."

✠

The Painter and the Warrior traded blows and parries. The Don had recovered his composure, and with a renewed respect for Luca's swordsmanship had begun a careful war of attrition against him. Luca, on his side, was not making much headway against the Don. He was parrying well but not scoring any hits since the Don's close call with the edge of his sword. The Don was wearing him down. At first imperceptibly, but slowly becoming more apparent to the onlookers, Luca's weakening was betrayed by his missteps, the slowing of his strikes and the desperation creeping into his parries.

"He cannot last much longer," fretted Edryd, "he has done well to last this long."

"I know," agreed Sir Richard, "I trust the philosopher mixed the potion right or we are all lost."

The Knights, wrapped in their voluminous black cloaks, which concealed their weapons and armor, studied the crowd that watched the duel. It was taking place on the site of a chapel that the Don was building, as a Christian appendix to the Moorish citadel. Low walls rose a couple of yards tall from the red dirt, sketching out the shape of the cross, pointing like a finger to the rising sun. And the pair of duelists struggled in the center of the cross, in the center of a translucent cloud of golden dust, sparkling in the morning light.

The Don had called all his courtiers and soldiers to witness the humiliation of the Painter of Florence by the strength of his sword, and they dutifully filled the cruciform arena, sitting on random blocks and scaffold, and standing in the shadows of the half-built walls. Everyone was there; not a single face of the hundred-odd onlookers escaped Sir Richard's piercing gaze. Except one – Paracelsus was missing. "All too much of this plan rests on the shoulders of our philosopher, alchemist, or however he styles himself today," muttered the Knight. He turned to Edryd, "Are you ready to bring the Don's world down on his head?" he asked. Edryd nodded slowly and smiled.

"Aye, and I will relish in the slaughter."

✠

Paracelsus was hiding behind a curtain. Although everyone was intended to be at the duel, there was still a handful of guards wandering the citadel. And, as bad luck would have it, his way was blocked by a small group who watched the duel from a balcony that overlooked the combat below. He cursed under his breath. If he walked past them they would certainly stop him – everyone was to be at the duel. If he stayed put then the plan would not work. His mind struggled feverishly to reconcile his problem. Then it occurred to him – if the circumstances preclude the plan, then change the plan to match the circumstances.

He reached under his cloak where hung concealed several round earthenware pots, and carefully lifted one of them out. In his right hand was hidden a slow match that wrapped around his wrist. He carefully applied the glowing tip of the match to the fuse that hung from the pot, and rolled it, hissing and sputtering, under the curtain towards the group on the balcony. It fetched up against the foot of one of the guards, and he turned back to see what had touched him. It took a moment for him to realize what it was but when he did so his eyes opened wide in horror. He began to shout the warning but it was much too late. The fuse reached the powder inside the jar and the whole exploded with a roar and a flash of flame and smoke. The nails and caltrops that were mixed with the powder ripped through the soldiers, and they were thrown, in a gout of flame, bleeding and screaming from the balcony.

✠

The duel was going poorly for Luca. The swirling red dust was stinging his eyes, and was caked, thick on the sweat of his face. Worse, the Don had landed a couple of good hits – a stab that had barely been stopped by his mail shirt, and a slashing cut that had opened a deep wound in his arm.

He could feel the heat of the dark blood welling from his wound and sprinkling the dry earth about him as he moved – his life slowly ebbing away. Despite his injury Luca noticed that the Don had lost some of his vigor. His blows fell lighter on the Painter's buckler and his footwork seemed less sure. Luca pressed his attack, forcing the Don backwards as he struggled to block and parry. In desperation the Don locked Luca's blade between his forearm and buckler, and suffered a bad slash to his arm as Luca pulled free. The Don staggered slightly as they broke from each other, and Luca could see a new expression in the older man's eyes – fear.

In an attack born more of despair than of stratagem, the Don plunged back into the fight. His blows fell heavy again and Luca was driven backwards, hard put to keep the Don's sword from finding its target. But eventually the Don slowed once more, and began to stumble. "Seems that the alchemist's draught is beginning to take effect," muttered Edryd as he gripped the hilt of the huge sword hidden in his cloak.

"Not a moment too soon," replied Sir Richard.

Luca, seeing his opportunity, pushed the attack. The Don redirected the thrust downward in a desperate attempt to avoid the inevitable and the Painter's blade cut a long, deep furrow in his leg. He cried out in pain, pushing Luca back. The Painter was about to thrust again when a loud report sounded high above their heads.

All eyes turned upward, and the Don used the distraction to retreat outside Luca's immediate reach.

"I was expecting something more… impressive," mused Edryd.

"That cannot be it," declared Sir Richard, angrily rising to his feet. Everyone watched nonplussed as a cloud of white smoke rose lazily from the balcony above them, and four of the Don's soldiers fell screaming in the opposite direction. The broken bodies crashed into the far end of the chapel, raising their own cloud of dust, and the onlookers froze in shock.

✠

The corridor filled with thick sulfurous fumes and Paracelsus stumbled, coughing, through them. A few yards further on he reached his destination, and pulled a length of fuse from where it was hidden in an arabesque screen.

Carefully, his hands shaking, he applied the match to the fuse and ran. He was not quite fast enough and had barely rounded the corner when an earth-shaking explosion and a wall of flame chased him down. He dropped to the ground, his hood covering his head as the roar and the flames flowed over him – gone as quickly as they came. He struggled to his feet, singed but whole, gasping for air in the dense, pungent smoke. He blindly reached a stairway and ran down a level, stopping by another arabesque, retrieving another fuse, and reapplying the match. He took off again as fast as his short legs would carry him, and a moment later another fiery explosion ripped through the citadel.

Still choking, struggling to drag air into his lungs, Paracelsus ran through an archway into the great hall, the site of Don Cristobal's swaggering and prancing in unabashed vainglory. He stood there a moment in recollection, gazing at the huge room and all its complex Moorish majesty. After a few seconds thought he spat copiously and pitched one of his flaming, earthenware pomegranates at the huge coat of arms hanging from the wall behind the dais, watching with a sneer on his lips as it exploded and hurled burning powder onto the dry fabric. Smiling grimly to himself he turned his back, muttering, "Babylon the great is fallen," as he walked slowly away from the surge of dancing flames that filled the great hall.

Like an insatiable monster the fire ate through silk and wood, gold and silver. It consumed the great hall in its flaming maw, rendering all that finery and decoration to so much blackened ash. It marched, unrelenting, from room to room until the entire citadel was aflame; a heavy black pall boldly marking the destruction in the deep azure sky. The sword of Nemesis bringing retribution from the heavens.

✠

"Fight Painter," shouted the Don, "damn you fight." Luca was frozen, confused by the paucity of the explosion; the Don's blood dripped from his blade. Don Cristobal banged his sword against his buckler and growled in pain and anger.

The plan was falling apart and Luca was unsure how to proceed, but there was really only one way to go, and that was forward. With a yell he launched back into the attack. The duelists were slower yet bolder now as they circled each other, hacking and swinging, eager to end the fight. The Don made a strike, Luca parried, and with a move that the Knights had shown him he continued the swing, changing his grip to the blade and striking the Don on the side of his helmet with the sword's pommel.

At that exact moment the first major explosion rocked the citadel, and the Don staggered back in shock and pain. Luca spun the sword around again, and with one hand on the hilt and the other on the blade he rammed it into the Don's midriff.

Don Cristobal collapsed to his knees as the Painter's sword pierced his vitals, sliding beneath the chainmail and below his breastplate, cutting into his belly.

His swarthy face, now ashen, tipped upwards to the citadel as it exploded again and again above him, engulfed in flame. The minor satrapy of his existence was crashing all about him as his life ebbed away. He turned slowly to Luca and smiled painfully, "Well, it seems you have prevailed Painter; against all the odds. I wish you the best of luck collecting your prize." And with that he fell forward into the red dirt, his blood puddling into a black mud beneath him.

Luca stumbled back from the remains of the Don, so recently his enemy, now prostrate before him in the dust. He had dreamt of this day but now that it was come he felt vaguely sick as the world swam. Strong arms grabbed him, one on either side under the shoulders, and dragged him from the field of battle, chaos thundering about him.

La Salida

Kick over an anthill and those tiny creatures will run about, hither and thither. Some run in panic, trying to escape the destruction of their world, and others run with a purpose, to defend their home against the attack.

So it was with the mêlée that followed the exploding of the citadel. The palace guards ran to their rallying points to formulate a plan to save the building; but confusing the matter was the incoherent scrambling of courtiers and members of the Don's retinue whose sole intent was to save their expensively dressed hides.

The Knights and their crew used the confusion to implement the third part of their plan. Jonson, Catherine and Henrique headed toward the stables to obtain mounts for the escape, while the Knights and Luca set out to retrieve Virginia. The last time they had seen her was on the far side of the chapel, her hand held to her mouth throughout the duel.

The Knights ran towards that spot, pushing through the panicked crowd, a bleeding Luca having recovered himself enough to bring up the rear. Virginia was gone, but a flash of turquoise taffeta disappearing around a corner gave a hint as to her direction. The three ran towards the corner but their way was blocked by a group of the Don's militia. With a clang of steel, and the flash of whirling blades the Knights chopped down their half dozen opponents with barely a break in stride. Rounding the corner they came to a small postern that lead back into the citadel just as it slammed in their faces.

With much kicking and cursing the door was forced open and they continued their pursuit. The fire had not reached the lower corridors of the castle, but the way was thick with smoke. They struggled through the heavy atmosphere along a low passageway, then, arriving at an intersection, they came face to face with Virginia. She was being held fast by one of the Don's men brandishing a dagger. "Stay yourselves or I will kill the girl!" he shouted.

The Knights stopped short and Luca pushed between them. "I beg you, do not kill her. What is it you want?" he asked.

"This woman is the property of Don Cristobal. You will not have her," the soldier declared, waving the dagger menacingly.

"The Don is dead and I killed him. The girl is my property by the terms of my agreement with Don Cristobal. Hand her over!"

"The Don ordered me to hide her away or kill her if you should win," insisted the soldier.

"So this is it? I am to be cheated by the Don in life *and* in death? This is intolerable!" screamed Luca, approaching with his bloodied sword.

The soldier backed away, reaching behind him to open a small door that led further into the citadel, "I would not go that way," said Edryd, "the castle is in flames there is no retreat to be had."

"Either she comes with me or she dies, my life means nothing," declared the solider, ignoring the warning. His last word was drowned by a loud shot that echoed down the passageway, and a neat, round hole appeared in the man's forehead. He slowly released his grip on Virginia and slid lifeless to the ground at her feet. She ran crying into Luca's arms.

Luca held Virginia tight, as her legs seemed ready to give out, and the two Knights whirled around, looking for the source of the shot. Through the swirling smoke they beheld Faustino, the Don's castellan, and a soldier next to him with an arquebus, recently fired. The Knights readied for the fight, but Faustino waved to them anxiously, shouting, "Come hither, we must escape before the castle is destroyed upon us."

Without another thought they all set off to follow the castellan and his men, as he led the way along twisting, smoky passageways, through doorways and up and down steps. It seemed they were getting closer to the fire, and at one point they could see flames chewing through the finery of the palace. But after a while the smoke thinned and they emerged on the far side of the citadel. They ran across an open square, narrowly missed by falling timbers as the palace began to collapse upon itself, then finally through a door, and they were far enough away from the fire to stop, gasping for breath.

"So you slew the dragon Sir Luca, bravo!" declared Faustino.

"I did, it would seem, although are you not his man?"

"I have not been his man for several years. My personal guard and I have been informing to the Emperor on his activities in an effort to have him removed. Then I received notice that you were here to dispose of him, and I have been doing my utmost to protect you ever since. He was an evil man, you know."

"We know," smiled Edryd.

"Thank you for your help Sir, it was well given, since we have prevailed," said Sir Richard with a bow.

"Prevailed so far, but you must escape beyond the castle walls before the Don's men find you and kill you for spite and revenge," urged Faustino. Then turning to Virginia, "I am sorry *Señorita* that I was not able to rescue you myself."

"There is nothing to be sorry for Faustino," she replied, "I ought be thanking you for administering the draught to the Don."

"You did it?" asked Edryd in surprise.

"I caught Virginia trying to poison the Don and stopped her, as her actions were sure to be noticed. I took it upon myself to drug him. I trust it worked to your satisfaction."

"Your timely intercession is much appreciated Faustino," declared Sir Richard.

"The Don was drugged?" asked Luca in surprise and just a little shame.

"Yes, heavily. If he had not been he would have killed you in a minute or less, boy," laughed Faustino. Luca shook his head in astonishment, as one of Faustino's men bound his deepest wound to staunch the bleeding.

"I fear I am too old and infirm to fight, but take my men, they are loyal to me," said Faustino, "they will get you to the gates."

"The rest of our crew is to meet us with horses in the square," replied Sir Richard.

"Perfect! Then make your escape brave Knights, and the whole of Granada thanks you for your help in ridding us of that preening parasite," Faustino bowed low as he spoke. "You too Painter," he added as an afterthought. Luca nodded and smiled sheepishly.

The quickest way to the main gate in the curtain wall lay across the orchard where Luca had practiced just a few days before. The whole group, Knights, Luca, Virginia and about twenty of Faustino's men-at-arms, set off at a run through the evenly planted trees, as the castellan watched them go.

After less than a minute, a shouting and hallooing echoed through the orchard coming roughly from their intended direction, followed shortly by a cry of, "There they are, kill them all!" A volley of gunfire and crossbow bolts crashed about them, bringing down two of the men, but otherwise absorbed into the rhythmic planting of the trees.

They could see the Don's soldiers now, running between the trunks, their weapons discharged, swords held aloft. Faustino's men dropped to one knee along a pathway and aimed carefully, firing a volley on command as the attackers appeared through the trees. The shot and bolts were well aimed, and dropped the front rank in its tracks. Then with a feral cry they threw down their crossbows and firearms, and ran at the Don's men, their fury at last set loose. The Knights raised their weapons as if to help, but the commander of Faustino's men shouted to them to keep moving. "We can finish these miscreants, make good your escape." And then he was swallowed up by the trees.

Sir Richard and Edryd looked at each other. It was not in their nature to run from a fight, and these soldiers were willing to give their lives to protect them. It seemed churlish to creep away unscathed while men were dying.

"Surely it will not take much of an effort," insisted Edryd, smiling.

"No indeed, just an incidental problem easily solved," replied Sir Richard. "Luca remain here and guard the girl," he ordered, and with that they plunged through the trees into the fray.

✠

The stables for the citadel were located beyond the square that lay at the top of the ramp within the main gate. Jonson had been there with the wagon and horses when the travellers had first arrived at the castle, so he now lead the way through the storm of shock and dread that swirled about them after the citadel had burst spectacularly into flame.

They directed their steps around the base of the buildings towards the main gate, using the wall to protect their flank, and fending off the occasional attack from members of the Don's militia. The fighting was not sufficient to slow their progress – Jonson, wearing the crossbow on his back swung his two axes most effectively, blocking with one while hacking with the other. Catherine made good use of her sword, and Henrique followed up wielding a spiked mace. By the time they reached the square all their weapons were dripping with blood.

"This way," shouted Jonson as the burning citadel exploded above them in a shower of sparks and debris. They ran across the empty square to the stable buildings beyond. The stables were long wooden buildings set apart from the citadel, with stalls for horses and bays for wagons. Jonson stowed the axes in leather loops hanging from his belt, and busied himself with horse collars and harness, while Catherine opened the stalls to their horses. Henrique stood guard outside the door while the other two worked. Tacking up a group of horses is not swiftly accomplished, especially when the horses are nervous from a fire raging not fifty yards away, but finally the wagon was hitched, and Catherine was wrangling their six restive mounts.

"Some assistance would be welcome!" came a cry from beyond the heavy stable doors, and Jonson and Catherine ran outside to witness a group of twenty or so of the Don's soldiers surrounding

Henrique, who was swinging his massive mace to left and right, barely sufficient to keep his enemies at bay. His two companions drew their weapons and were about to join the fight when a discorporate voice from above demanded they take refuge inside the stable. With barely a glance between them, the three backed into the stable and barred themselves in.

Almost immediately a large explosion shook the massive wooden doors, causing panicked crying from the horses. Then there was silence. They unbarred the doors and peered out. Their opponents, moments before so fierce and determined, lay scattered about the square, smoking and bloody, one or two attempting to crawl away. The voice came again and they looked up. Perched at the ridge of the stable roof was Paracelsus, his face sooty and clothing singed, flashing a big smile. "Help me?" he squeaked. Henrique reached up and the alchemist jumped into his arms and so to the ground.

"I think you have dispatched more of the enemy than any of us, with your bombs of brimstone," declared the Bishop with undisguised enthusiasm.

"They should be here by now," muttered Catherine, concerned.

"They're coming," answered Jonson with a sly wink, "they've come through much worse than this." And, as if on cue, the Knights appeared with Virginia between them approaching the stable at a trot, and Luca, exhausted and bleeding, struggling behind them. Virginia had hitched her gown up so she could move faster, and her dainty slippered feet picked their way carefully between the blackened remnants of the Don's militia.

"Open the gates," shouted Sir Richard, and the Philosopher headed off at a run across the square and down the ramp. The rest of them mounted up and followed him, the wheels of the wagon bouncing across the bodies of the fallen. They started over the top of the ramp and immediately stopped. Paracelsus was struggling with the two guards that still remained at the gate, which had been shut and barred after the explosion of the citadel. The alchemist was running around trying to avoid them but could not light his fuses to bring down the massive wooden gates.

"Edryd, Jonson," shouted Sir Richard, but they were already

armed and shooting. An arrow pinned one guard to the gate, a crossbow bolt knocked the other off his feet, and Paracelsus waved his thanks. He promptly applied his match to the hidden fuses and ran.

The explosion was not huge, but situated to destroy the hinges, and with a creaking roar the huge gates crashed outwards in a thick cloud of white smoke. They started down the stone ramp, the Knights and Catherine to the left, Luca, Virginia and Henrique to the right. With Jonson's help Paracelsus struggled into the wagon. The horses clattered over the fallen gates and through the cloud of smoke, which parted around them in misty swirls.

Again they stopped. Facing them in a semicircle outside the gates, blocking their escape, pikes and halberds lowered in a bristling line of sharpened steel, was the Holy Brotherhood – mounted on their white horses, white habits gleaming in the morning sunlight, their hoods raised in shadowy anonymity, crosses on their chests blood red.

"How many more of these fools must we kill?" asked Edryd in resigned astonishment.

"We are few and they are many," muttered Sir Richard.

"Do you fear death at the hands of this rabble?" asked Edryd.

"Of course not, but it is our obligation to protect Virginia. I am not sure how we can do that."

El Final

"Lay down your weapons. You are prisoners of the Holy Brotherhood of Guadix. Our sanction comes from Don Cristobal of Guadix; the *Cortes* of Granada; Charles, King of Castile and Holy Roman Emperor; and the Pope himself."

"Now *there's* an unholy gang of thieves and reprobates," muttered Luca with a sneer.

Here we go again, said Sir Richard to himself. Then he shouted back to the Holy Brotherhood: "The Don is dead, and the Pope is in hiding, fearing for his life." There was muttering in the ranks of the Brotherhood and he continued. "We are here on the orders of the Emperor himself, and I give not a whit for the *Cortes* of Granada whoever they may be. You have no authority over us. We are Knights of St. John of Jerusalem, the only sanction we need comes from God himself, and..." he paused for effect, "the strength of our arms."

"Lay down your weapons," came the implacable reply.

Sir Richard sighed heavily, and once more longed for his galley and a shipload of Turkish corsairs to butcher. Being forced to kill Christians was starting to rankle.

"Paracelsus," shouted Sir Richard, no longer having a problem remembering the philosopher's name.

"Sir Knight," came the reply.

"Do you have any of your pomegranates left?"

"Just two my Lord."

"Then two it is. And how is your throwing arm?"

"Better for the practice."

"Will you throw them into the center when I signal?"

"Indeed I will."

"Jonson."

"Chief."

"After the explosion, drive the wagon through the gap in the center and down the street beyond. Stop for nothing."

"Chief."

"Luca."

"Richard."

"You and the Bishop will take Virginia and follow the wagon. Ride as fast as you can."

"And you?"

"We will defend your retreat."

And so it went. Paracelsus launched his fiery projectiles directly at the center of the line of horsemen. Men and horses disappeared in twin flashes of flame and smoke, slashed and torn by sharpened metal shards. Jonson promptly drove his team straight at the billowing cloud, depositing the philosopher onto his back in the wagon. He was closely followed by Virginia and her escort, the Knights and Catherine bringing up the rear. The heavy, charging horses brushed aside what was left of the Holy Brotherhood and they galloped down the sloping street away from the blazing citadel. Townsfolk and market traders gaping at the flames leapt from their path as they thundered past.

About a hundred yards from the explosion the Knights drew rein and dismounted. Catherine whirled her horse around shouting to them, "Come we must escape."

"It is not in our nature to run *Señorita*, ride on and protect our charges," replied Sir Richard, "avaunt woman!"

"But you will be destroyed. This Holy Brotherhood keeps its own motives. They care nothing for your sanction, nor your truth," she screamed.

"Then we will grasp our truth in both hands and beat them about the pate with it until they cry *enough*."

Catherine leapt from the saddle and slapped her horse sending it trotting away. "My fate is one with yours now brave or foolish Knights, I know not which." And so saying, she drew her sword and closed the visor of her helmet.

Edryd pulled an arrow from his quiver and drew his bow, sending the arrow slicing the air into the cloud of smoke. They could hear the shouts and screams of riders and horses from beyond the drifting white pall, but otherwise the long street was quiet, empty. The three armored figures stood and awaited their fate, not yet rethinking their impetuous actions.

The Welshman turned to Sir Richard, "Have we met our match?"

"Perhaps. It has been a long time coming."

"Indeed."

"How many of our friends have we seen killed over the years? And still we remained standing – the arrow always struck another, the blow brought down a different man."

"Well my friend, it has been a pleasure and a privilege to serve with you in the Army of the Lord," declared Edryd and the two Knights embraced in a last farewell.

"Do you not think we could win?" asked Catherine optimistically. Sir Richard shook his head.

"I am sad we did not have a chance to cross swords in single combat My Lady," said Edryd to Catherine.

"We are not dead yet," insisted Catherine.

At that moment Luca and Henrique rode up behind them and leaped from their saddles. "Why are you not with the girl?" asked Sir Richard angrily.

"And leave you to face these demons alone?" replied Luca with a grim smile.

"She is safe with Jonson and the philosopher, our place is here," said the Bishop with finality.

"Luca, you will not last two minutes with those wounds," insisted Edryd, looking the bruised, cut and bleeding Painter up and down.

"Then they will be the most glorious two minutes of my life," replied Luca through clenched teeth, "when I stood against the hordes of hell with the Knights of Saint John."

The five dropped to their knees in the middle of the empty, dusty street and Sir Richard led them in prayer:

"*O remember not against us former iniquities: let thy tender mercies speedily prevent us; for we are brought very low. Help us, O God of our salvation, for the glory of thy name: and deliver us, and purge away our sins, for thy name's sake.*"

And then they were come. Bursting through the swirling smoke, screaming horses spurred on by furious riders hurtled, clattering on the cobblestones, towards them. Edryd loosed an arrow, the first man fell, another and another fell, but still the thunder came onward. He threw the bow to one side and took up his massive blade. The two Knights ran a few paces forward and dropped to one knee, ready to cut the legs of the lead horses from under their riders, while the other three spread out across the street, weapons at the ready.

Then a different noise assailed them, the hammering of iron wheels on stone that burst from a side street just a few yards ahead. In a moment their view was blocked by a wagon, a laughing driver waving to them.

This was all they had time to see as the first of the Holy Brotherhood struck the wagon. Their horses tried to jump, but it was too close and too high, and they tumbled, crashing, smashing through canvas and wood, splinters, riders and horses flying to left and right.

The five separated, Edryd dragging Catherine with him, running from the street to press themselves against the houses on either side, avoiding the flying bodies and kicking hooves. They looked up to the torn and shattered wagon, and there, astride its jagged bones was Jonson, loading and firing his crossbow repeatedly into the mêlée.

Luca climbed onto the remains of the wagon and the sight he beheld was a terrible one. Men, thirty, forty maybe, and their mounts, were jammed into the narrow street. The horses, not trained for war, were screaming and kicking in their fear and pain, riders falling beneath trampling hooves as they tried to escape. Luca looked back at the Knights.

"You have done your duty Sir Richard, let us be gone and shake off the dust of our feet. These heathens are not worthy of your steel."

With a shrug Sir Richard retrieved his horse, and within moments they were gone, leaving Guadix smoking behind them in remembrance, as they spurred their mounts up into the hills and safety.

El Nuevo Jefe

"I am Don Diego Hurtado de Mendoza y Lemus. What terrible things have happened here?"

"I am Faustino, castellan to the late Don Cristobal. By the orders of Charles, King of Castile and Holy Roman Emperor my men have relieved the Don of his property and his life – may it please your Lordship."

"The King dispatched me hither from Granada to confirm what has been done and to restore order in whatever fashion may be required – as I did most recently in Valencia." Don Diego waved his hand to indicate the long line of heavily armed mounted troops that followed him.

"Your Lordship, the twenty soldiers under my command have the situation most eminently in hand within the castle. But your men would be a great help in subduing the town and surrounding villages."

Don Diego rode through the smashed gates and up the ramp, accompanied by Faustino. A line of men was laboriously piling corpses to one side of the square, the ruins of the citadel looming dark and smoking over their work.

"You achieved such destruction with twenty soldiers?" asked Don Diego, astonished.

"I had some help from a gentleman; he was most angry. The Don had stolen from him his freedom and his woman, and thereby he wreaked a dreadful revenge," smiled Faustino, "he was a Painter of Florence."

Don Diego turned to the castellan in disbelief.

THE END

Il Poscritto

A fine mist clung low to the ground, moistening the delicate green fronds that dripped in the still morning air. Two figures appeared in the faint distance walking stiffly towards a small rise that appeared from out of the haze, as an island in a sea of swirling white. The tendrils of fog clung to their heels as they climbed from the mist onto the mound; two dark figures alone, floating in the early morning shade.

At that moment the sun broke the horizon, the first fiery fingers of dawn reaching out to the two figures, inciting bright stars to sparkle from their polished armor. The two figures bowed one to the other, and walked to either side of the mound. As they stood facing each other, across some twenty feet of open ground, more figures appeared. They climbed out of the mist and stood in a rough circle around the two, lining the edges of the mound.

There was a man with a woman, both wrapped in cloaks against the morning, she holding his arm and leaning on his shoulder for support, he with one arm bandaged, yet standing tall – wounded but not weakened. Next were two men; one short and stocky the other tall and elegant, the crosses on their black cloaks glowing white in the morning light.

A few feet further on stood a tall blackamoor and a small round pink man; the black man stoic, arms folded, the small man fidgeting with his hat. Finally, a little apart from the others, was a wizardly figure who seemed simply to grow from the mist as it eddied around obscured feet.

The wizard raised his hand, holding it a moment above his head. His long sleeve fluttered slightly, as a flag in the slight breeze. Then his arm dropped, the flag signaling a beginning. The two armored figures presented their swords and closed for the duel. The swords swirled and sparked in the sharp, morning light as they swung again and again, the screech of steel on steel echoing through the still.

The fight wore on, observed in silence by the small crowd – a dance that whirled about in flashing arcs of light, as the sun rose slowly in the eastern sky. Many blows were aimed but none was landed, such was the skill of the combatants, and the sun rose high in the sky as the battle raged on.

It seemed that there could be no winner to this clash of equals until a most singular event took place. With a flourish the smaller of the two stepped back from the fight and, placing a much-used sword on the ground between them, knelt as if to receive the final blow – resigned to fate and the mercy of an opponent. The larger swordsman stood a moment, weapon raised high, lost in thought.

Then, throwing his sword to the side, he bade his opponent stand, and the two embraced.

newprestonhill.com

www.ingramcontent.com/pod-product-compliance
Lightning Source LLC
Chambersburg PA
CBHW022207010726
47493CB00002B/458